"What are you doing here?" she c

"Oh, we're hunting," one of the r voice. He gestured to his rifle. He vest, and, when he turned to look around, she saw that it had his hunting tag on the back.

"We have children here, and the land is posted. No hunting or trespassing!" she barked. The children froze at Taylor's tone. She glanced back at them and ordered, "Get back to the house, now!" The now was added to avoid argument, but she needn't have worried. The kids took one look at the hunters and scurried off towards the house. Taylor turned back to the men with guns, glaring holes through them.

"Oh, we didn't know. We've been hunting these woods for years," he said, continuing in his same tone.

"You walked by at least a couple of the signs to get into these woods." She kept a secure hold on Staffy's leash. He had already tested her a couple of times, ready to lunge at the trespassers.

"Well, we had permission of the owner ..." he began, seemingly hurt by her own stiff tone and eyeing the cropped-eared dog warily. He exchanged a look with the man beside him.

"No, you don't have that permission anymore," she said, sounding ominous. Her ears pricked up at the sound of her children going into the house. All her own protective instincts were aroused. "My wife and I bought this property last summer. We've been building ever since, and one of the first things we did was put up the signs that you walked by. Get off our land, and don't come back. Tell all your friends."

"Look, this is simply a misunderstanding ..." he began, trying to reason with the angry woman.

"No, you walked by several signs telling you clearly you weren't welcome, and now I suspect your lying to save face. Get off my land before I let my dog loose on you!"

Both men looked alarmed at the dog whining and tugging at the end of the leash. One of them shifted his gun, almost protectively.

"If you use that gun on my dog, I'm going to shoot you," Taylor bluffed.

"What's going on here?!" Bree called from the back door, where she had just come outside onto the deck.

"These *gentlemen* are just leaving!" Taylor called back without turning away from them.

"You're *hunting*?! On *our* land?!" Bree asked, alarmed. All her initial fears which had led to them posting the land returned in an instant.

"Apparently, they can't read, and the owner gave them permission!" Taylor mocked as she held a menacing stare. She addressed the two hunters, who were looking decidedly uncomfortable. "Get off our land!" Then she called up to Bree, still not taking her eyes off the two. "Go get my gun, now!" She didn't see the startled look Bree gave her, but she heard the back door close, and the two men turned as one and hotfooted it back through the woods.

A K'Anne Meinel novel

Also by K'Anne Meinel:

Novels in Paperback:

SHIPS *CompanionSHIP, FriendSHIP, RelationSHIP*
Long Distance Romance
Children of Another Mother
Erotica
The Claim
Bikini's Are Dangerous
The Complete Series
Germanic
Malice Masterpieces 1
The First Five Books
Represented
Timed Romance
Malice Masterpieces 2
Books Six through Ten
The Journey Home
Out at the Inn
Shorts
Anthology Volume 1
Lawyered
Malice Masterpieces 3
Books Eleven through Fifteen
Blown Away
Blown Away
The Alternate Cover
Small Town Angel

Pirated Love
Doctored
Veil of Silence
Malice Masterpieces 4
Books Sixteen through Twenty
The Outsider
Pirated Heart
Recombinant Love
Survivors
Inn the Dog House
Flight
An Island Between Us
Malice Masterpieces 5
Books Twenty-One through Twenty-Five
Malice Masterpieces 6
Books Twenty-Six through Thirty
Beauty and the Beast
Home ~ The First Nillionaires Club

Vetted Series:
Vetted
Cavalcade (Prequel)
Pioneering (Prequel)
Vetted Further
Vetted Again

Novellas in Paperback:

Sapphic Surfer
Sapphic Cowgirl
Sapphic Cowboi
Sayyida
The Northwood Lodge

The Malice Series:
Mysterious Malice (Book 1)
Meticulous Malice (Book 2)
Mistaken Malice (Book 3)
Malicious Malice (Book 4)
Masterful Malice (Book 5)
Matrimonial Malice (Book 6)
Mourning Malice (Book 7)
Murderous Malice (Book 8)
Mental Malice (Book 9)
Menacing Malice (Book 10)
Minor Malice (Book 11)
Morally Malice (Book 12)
Morose Malice (Book 13)

Melancholy Malice (Book 14)
Mad Malice (Book 15)
Macabre Malice (Book 16)
Marinating Malice (Book 17)
Macerating Malice (Book 18)
Minacious Malice (Book 19)
Meddlesome Malice (Book 20)
Meandering Malice (Book 21)
Maniacal Malice (Book 22)
Monitoring Malice (Book 23)
Marked Malice (Book 24)
Mandating Malice (Book 25)
Methodical Malice (Book 26)
Malevolent Malice (Book 27)
Militarial Malice (Book 28)
Machiavellian Malice (Book 29)
Malefic Malice (Book 30)
Religious Experience
Lied

All Novels and Novellas in paperback are also available as e-books.

Novellas in Paperback Continued:

A Woman Down Under Series:
Shanghaied (Prequel)
Outback Born
Outback Bred
Outback Heritage
Outback Native
Outback Splendor
Outback Yearnings (Prequel)
Outback Escape
Outback Future

Pocket Paperbacks:

Mysterious Malice (Book 1)
Sapphic Surfer
Sapphic Cowgirl
Meticulous Malice (Book 2)
Mistaken Malice (Book 3)
Malicious Malice (Book 4)
Masterful Malice (Book 5)
Matrimonial Malice (Book 6)
Mourning Malice (Book 7)
Murderous Malice (Book 8)
Mental Malice (Book 9)
Menacing Malice (Book 10)
Minor Malice (Book 11)
Morally Malice (Book 12)
Morose Malice (Book 13)
Melancholy Malice (Book 14)
Mad Malice (Book 15)
Macabre Malice (Book 16)
Marinating Malice (Book 17)

In E-Book Format:
Short Stories

Fantasy
Wet & Wet Again
Family Night
Quickie ~ Against the Car
Quickie ~ Against the Wall
Quickie ~ Over the Couch
Mile High Club
Quickie ~ Under the Pier
Heel or Heal
Kiss
Family Night 2
Beach Dreams
Internet Dreamers
Snoggered
On the Parkway
Stable Affair
Kept
Stolen
Agitated
Love of my LIFE
Quickie in an Elevator,
GOING DOWN?
Into the Garden
The Book Case
The Other Women
Menage a WHAT?
The Wicked Stepdaughter

LARGE Print Novels

SHIPS CompanionSHIP, FriendSHIP, RelationSHIP
Erotica Volume 1
Long Distance Romance
Children of Another Mother
Bikini's Are Dangerous
The Complete Series

Malice Masterpieces
The First Five Books
To Love a Shooting Star
The Claim
Represented
Timed Romance

**Dedicated to anyone who thinks I'm writing about them.
I am.
K'Anne**

K'ANNE MEINEL

HOME

First Nillionaires Club

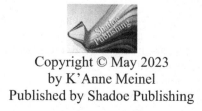

Copyright © May 2023
by K'Anne Meinel
Published by Shadoe Publishing

ISBN-13: 978-1959436157

Copyright © K'Anne Meinel May 2023

All rights reserved. No part of this book may be reproduced, stored in a retrieval system or transmitted in any form or by any means without the prior written permission of K'Anne Meinel, except by a reviewer who may quote brief passages in a review to be printed in a newspaper, magazine, or journal.

K'Anne Meinel is available for comments at KAnneMeinel@aim.com as well as on Facebook, or her blog @ http://kannemeinel.wordpress.com/ or on Twitter @ kannemeinelaim.com, or on her website @ www.kannemeinel.com if you would like to follow her to find out about stories and book's releases.

www.shadoepublishing.com

ShadoePublishing@gmail.com

Shadoe Publishing is a United States of America company

Cover by: K'Anne Meinel

Home

First Nillionaires Club

PUBLISHER'S NOTE

This is a work of fiction. Names, characters, places, and incidents are the product of the author's imagination or are used fictitiously, and any resemblance to actual persons, living or dead, business establishments, events, or locales is entirely coincidental.

The publisher does not have any control over and does not assume any responsibility for author or third-party Web sites or their content.

K'ANNE MEINEL

What does Nillionaire mean? The word nill is an archaic word meaning 'unwilling.' In our case, for the purpose of this series, the characters are 'unwilling' to become millionaires or billionaires because, they are simple, everyday people, just trying to work in common jobs, doing regular things. They are just like you and me.

CHAPTER ONE

"I think I found it," Bree told Taylor with excitement, pulling up the listing she had finally found in an online site. She pushed aside the coupons she had cut from the Sunday paper to make room for her wife.

"I think I've heard this before," Taylor teased as she came to look over Bree's shoulder. They'd been looking for nearly a year for the perfect place to live and planning for it even longer. She glanced around their cramped apartment, a three bedroom, one-and-a-half bath space that housed the two of them and their four children—happily, but definitely overcrowded. They loved it here, but with the children getting older, it was unquestionably time to get a bigger place. They'd scrimped and saved for years, as much as they could with so many children under the age of eight, determined to get their own place. They didn't want to rent anymore; they wanted to own. They wanted something completely theirs.

HOME ~ First Nillionaires Club

"No, this time I'm determined," Bree spoke forcefully, as if stating it aloud would make it happen. She wanted to put it out there into the universe, make it happen by willing it.

"Oh, okay," Taylor responded with a smile, not willing to take the mickey out of Bree's enthusiasm and coming to look at Bree's flickering monitor. They needed a new one to replace this second-hand one, but they were waiting until the desktop needed replacing, one of the many to-dos they were foregoing until after the move.

"Wow, this isn't the picturesque and quiet little home they advertised in the paper," Bree whined. As the pictures slowly came up on the screen, the monitor distorted the colors from blue to purple, and the red showed as a sickening pink shade. The images were turning their dream home into a nightmare.

"Wait!" Taylor squinted at the run-down house, and Bree stopped scrolling. "Does this place have a garage?"

"Yeah—wait, that's not a garage, that looks like ... a barn?"

"Yeah." Taylor frowned as she tried to get a better view, turning her head sideways, but the screen started to flutter uncontrollably, and she sighed as she reached out to smack it.

"Don't do that," her wife warned, afraid she'd knock the monitor off the desk that was barely holding up on its own, already propped up by a book on one leg. The computer was just too old to handle the newer websites, and the desk it was on wasn't in much better shape.

"Maybe we should take a ride?"

Bree sighed, signed out of the website, and turned off the computer before it overheated. "Why bother?" she muttered, now sounding almost defeated. They probably had enough for a down-payment but hadn't found any property that felt right. They would have to sacrifice a few things in order to buy just the right place, a house with a garage and a few acres so the kids could play in a healthy atmosphere. The children had had it rough before coming to live with them, and Taylor and Bree were determined to give them a better life than what they'd experienced in the system.

They'd begun adoption procedures on the first three kids as soon as the option became available, and those were now finalized, Taylor and Bree now their legal parents. They were hoping to adopt the final child they had fostered, Jack, in the next year if or when that option became available. Their caseworker was aware of their commitment and fully supported their efforts.

"I don't know; we have a free afternoon tomorrow with the kids all in school. Let's go check this place out. It's got to be better in person."

"C'mon, you know I like to clean the house when no one's home." Bree gestured to the small space. It was the perfect opportunity. With none of the kids getting in the way of vacuuming, she could get all the toys picked up, and she could finally do ALL the laundry. She'd have time to baby the washing machine that was limping along on its last legs until they bought a new one, another expense delayed until after the move.

"Let it go just this one time," Taylor wheedled. "I'll drive," she offered.

"I think you're going to have to." Bree slapped the newspaper ad which in no way did the listing justice. The pictures online at least hinted at a house that could work for them, and it listed the property address so they could go look at it without calling the real estate agent and getting their hopes up. "It's down a dirt road," Bree explained.

Taylor grinned. She'd like nothing more than taking their Jeep down a dirt road. Having to use the 4-wheel drive would make her ecstatic.

* * * * *

They turned to the kids and began the process of getting them ready for bed, making sure homework was complete and ready for the next day and bathing the youngest who would go to afternoon kindergarten so he could ride home on the bus with his siblings.

"You'll be home when we come home?" Jack fretted as Taylor finished drying him off, rubbing behind his ears and fluffing his hair with the towel.

"Sure will, and I'm sure Bree will have something delicious planned for dinner tomorrow." She knew he had abandonment issues since his birth parents had left him at home alone while they went on a cruise. He was only two years old at the time, but, while he didn't remember a lot from that time, the sense of abandonment and the fear that no one would find him stuck with him. Fortunately, Jack had gone over to the neighbors after a couple of days when he ran out of the food left on a table for him and asked if they had seen his mommy or daddy. The police and child services had made sure to arrest the parents for child endangerment when they returned home, and he'd been taken from their custody, perhaps forever. Taylor and Bree weren't sure, but they'd had him for two years now, and he was going to pre-kindergarten, as they'd discussed, tomorrow. She tried to make it sound easy and normal, knowing why he needed to be reassured they'd be there. The poor guy had bounced around a couple of homes before landing in theirs, and they were doing their best to make sure he didn't bounce from their home, staying in close contact

with his social worker while the case against the parents worked its way slowly through the courts.

Bree entered the bedroom as Taylor tucked Jack into his big-boy bed. He smiled, knowing he was loved by these two women who ensured he was warm and secure. Dutifully, he kissed each of them on the cheek as Taylor raspberried his tummy, eliciting a giggle.

"You good, squirt?" Taylor asked Bryan on the top bunk above the big-boy bed.

"All set, Mom," he assured her, leaning over to give her a hug and a peck on the cheek.

"But, are you *sure*?" Bree asked, getting a hug and a kiss of her own.

"Yep!" he answered with a smile, their routine well established.

Taylor turned off the overhead light, and Bree switched on a blue lava lamp they had bought second-hand at Goodwill that sat atop the dresser. Every night, the boys would watch the lamp, hoping to see it bubble up before they fell asleep. It provided them with enough light, more than a night light would, and offered hopes and dreams if they were lucky enough to see the shapes take place. But they rarely ever saw it bubbling, and one of the moms would come in and turn it off on their way to bed, always finding the boys fast asleep.

Taylor headed into the girls' room, seeing their own pink lava lamp on the dresser. Smiling at the two little girls, she leaned over to check they were tucked in 'correctly' before receiving a hug and a kiss. She tugged the covers snuggly along both sides, almost trapping the girls in their beds, and they both giggled.

"Goodnight," she whispered, first to Melanie on the top bunk, and then to Barbie on the bottom, as she closed their door incompletely behind her. Both children's rooms were left open that final crack in case any of the children had to get up to use the bathroom or to find one of their moms. Bree waved behind her, blowing kisses as she said her goodnights.

Back downstairs, Taylor gestured to the paper they'd left next to the desktop. "So, are we going to look at this place, at least?"

Sighing, Bree shrugged. "I don't know that we should bother. It's a ways out. Wouldn't they be in the next school district?"

"I don't know. We can find out after we go. It wouldn't hurt to take a look, would it?"

"You just don't want to clean tomorrow. Admit it."

"I won't. I'm just concerned about running out of room."

She wasn't wrong. They'd already had to get a storage unit where they kept some of their extra stuff, and they rented a workshop where they both produced pottery to sell at various marketplaces. Space was becoming too

tight, and they knew they needed a central place to work from and maybe—someday—expand.

"Yeah, I know it's time," she admitted, knowing Taylor had worked a second job in order to help them save faster. All her tips had really added up. While the state had paid them to foster children, they had spent very little of that while saving up to buy their own house. They couldn't afford to buy in the area they were in, but maybe they could find something a little further out of town.

That was where they found themselves the next morning. After giving Jack hugs and kisses and watching him take his kindergarten teacher's hand and walk confidently to the classroom, Bree and Taylor headed out to the property.

"I don't know about this, Bree." Taylor frowned as they bounced all over the road leading out to the property. It looked like a back road, but the address said it was part of the property. "Are you sure you got the address right?" The ruts weren't caused by cars but by hundreds of thinner tire tracks, maybe made by ATVs or bicycles. The Jeep was handling it okay, but Taylor had to keep her hands firmly on the wheel so they wouldn't get pulled off the road.

"Yeah," Bree almost yelled. As one particular rut had her bouncing hard, her hand was on the grip above the window, helping to hold her in her seat with seat belt across.

"Is this a road or a driveway?" Taylor asked, worrying as the road got worse. She couldn't see beyond a hill in front of them. On the left were some woods and what looked like a swamp, and on the right, a pasture of some sort.

Near the hill, the ruts seemed worse. Both sides had places where water ran off, causing puddles that teemed with deep, narrow ruts. To get through it, Taylor had to gun the engine, and the Jeep nearly bounced off the drive as they crested the hill. On the other side, the road was mostly level, and the road evened out as they pulled up beside the dilapidated old house.

They peered up at it skeptically, observing that the vegetation had practically taken over.

"I don't know about this ..." Taylor repeated, contemplating how much work it would take to fix it up.

The house was barely visible, and there were bare spots where some boards had fallen in. If they weren't hanging off by one nail, some looked like they had jumped off the studs at some point, or someone had pulled them off. They were all weathered, and then a few patches of insulation

peeked through, revealing that yellow fiberglass type that had both women itching at just the thought of working with it.

"I don't think we should go in there." Taylor eyed the six-foot weedy prickers and grasses that constituted the front yard. There were sapling trees growing all over, Mother Nature trying to take back the open area that had once been a front lawn.

"I don't want to go in there," Bree agreed. "But look," she pointed and got out of the Jeep, "it's all grown up near the house, but it seems clear most of the way to the barn." The path was well worn, the weeds not as high, and it even looked like the grass was cut at some point.

Feeling a bit spooked, Taylor followed, less out of curiosity than her urge to protect her wife.

The path to the barn was hard packed, like some large vehicle had travelled it frequently. The ground seemed harder here and the grooves not as deep, but bicycle and what looked like ATV and maybe motorbike tire ruts lined what they could see. The barn was at least thirty-feet wide with a pointed roof, fifteen feet each way, meeting in the middle, and at least twenty feet high at the peak. Stealing a look through the cracks, they could see hay stacked up inside the metal pull-barn

"What are you doing?" Taylor asked her wife who was reaching for the door.

"I want to see what it looks like in there." She yanked on a door she was convinced was rusted shut, but it opened quite easily. Light from outside spilled into the first ten feet or so, which was clear of hay. Bales had been stacked up to provide a seating area. Bottles and a fire pit revealed this to be a meeting place of sorts.

"Look, it has a concrete floor," Taylor marveled, stomping her feet.

"We could have the ovens over there," Bree added as she waved to the far side of the barn, assessing the building and already making plans.

"We'd have to put up insulation."

"That wouldn't take long with these straight walls."

"We could get a lift and put up racks."

Their enthusiasm went on and on as they looked over the barn that was half-filled with hay. There was packed down hay leading up into the rafters. A large round spot in the middle was fluffed up.

"What do you think they do there?"

"Jump," Taylor answered matter-of-factly.

"What?"

"I bet they climb those bales of hay." She pointed at the stacked piles that were aging, the twine around them slowly pulling apart where it had

slipped off a few of the bales. "Then jump from the rafters," she pointed to where the high bales reached the wood, "into the hay."

"Why would they do that?"

"Because it's fun."

Bree looked at her wife. "Did you do something like that when you were younger?"

"Well, I sure wouldn't do it now, but yes. The rafters in my neighbor's barn were at least thirty feet up, and I could do a complete summersault or flip before landing."

Bree smiled, wishing she had known her as a child. From her stories, she had been the ultimate tomboy. "Why'd you stop?"

"My mother found out what we were doing and didn't want me to break my neck. I didn't tell her about the time we found a pitchfork buried in the hay. The neighbors then started letting their dog use the barn to shit, and it ruined it for all of us because it was all over our cushion of hay."

Bree wrinkled her nose at that part of the story but looked around the barn, wishing they could buy it and outfit it as the pottery barn they had both dreamed of. Right now, they only had one small oven and could only make four large pots or eight small ones at a time ... which reminded her. "We should probably stop at the shop and put in some painting time."

"You mean, I should paint while you spin some pots?" her wife teased, knowing her wife's likes and dislikes.

"You mean throw some pots?" Bree teased back, correcting her wife's deliberate teasing. She knew that throwing a pot would actually confuse those not in the know, but Taylor enjoyed getting it wrong.

"Let's look around some more."

They closed the barn back up and walked around the place, dodging trees and weeds. The large sliding door had probably been used to bring in the hay at one point. It was obvious someone or several someones were using the property to hang out. Some of the graffiti on the back of the barn was obscene. Still, it was well-built, much more so than the house, which they couldn't even see from the jungle growing between the two buildings.

"I don't know," Bree said hesitantly as they bounced their way back down the drive. "It's a lot of work, and there really isn't a house on it. That place was falling down."

"It's pretty cheap, too," Taylor agreed, suspicious as to why it cost so little. Granted, they probably had it marked down because of the house, but she wanted to look into it a bit more before contacting the real-estate agent.

When they reached the end of the driveway, they had to wait for a line of cars to pass before taking the road east around a few curves and back to

town. Beside the property, a large hay field extended slightly into the woods, and at the end of the woods, there was another drive that ended abruptly a little way in.

They made what they hoped would be a quick stop at the town assessor's office to see what they could find out about the property. At first, the clerk had difficulty finding it on the map.

"Oh, I see it's in the Riverview district, that's why," the clerk told them peevishly, as though they had deliberately moved it from his map.

"I didn't say which district," Taylor mouthed to her wife, who nodded, amused.

"Well, taxes haven't been paid on it, and I bet that's why they are selling it. It has over ten acres there on the west side of town," he mused as he looked it up. "Here is a topographical map," he said, showing them but not allowing them to hold the map, almost as though they would take it.

"Can we get a copy of that?" Taylor asked, pointing.

"It's one dollar per copy," he answered automatically.

She smiled and pulled the money out of her pocket, placing a dollar on the counter.

He sighed but made a color copy of the topographical map. It was crisp and larger than a normal piece of paper. It showed the woods, part of a field that had to have been mowed when the picture was taken, and a creek. Quite a bit of the woods on the front of the property looked to be swamp. There were woods behind the house, almost all around the barn, and behind it.

"It includes that natural stream flowing through the property. In fact, I would bet that's the boundary line," the clerk pointed out, showing them the borders of this parcel.

"Thank you," Taylor said sincerely as they took the map with them.

They kept discussing the property as they approached their workspace, pulled up behind the building, and went inside. They followed a long hallway with flickering lights down to their shop, unlocked it, and rolled up the back garage door that led outside in order to bring plenty of natural light inside and to air out the space.

"You start painting those, and I'll try to throw another batch," Bree offered, pulling a smock on.

"You're so bossy," Taylor teased.

"I could paint, and you could work the clay," she offered, knowing that Taylor was just as good and frequently came up with more exotic pots that sold well. But Taylor didn't like getting the clay under her nails, as she needed clean hands for waitressing. Sometimes the clay, depending on

what they were throwing, got into their pores to the point that it changed the color and took days to get off. This was unattractive, and stained fingers didn't look good when she was delivering food. The painting could be worse at staining their hands, but they'd worked out the different colors and pigments they used to make their beautiful pots. Depending on the clay they used, it also dried out their hands, which made it difficult to get out the stains.

As they worked over the next couple of hours, they discussed the property, what they could do with it, and if it would be worth the hassle.

"Why don't we talk to the realtor. Maybe we can get them to come down on the price. And we can talk to the bank about a loan."

Bree hesitated immediately. "I don't want a loan." She had a desperate fear of going into debt, which was why they were saving every dime they could. She was very thrifty, finding coupons for all their food-shopping and cutting corners whenever she could. Her parents had always been in debt, and she had hated the banging on their doors from time to time when collectors came around, and worse, repossessions. Even now, she hated people pounding on doors, or even doorbells. Taylor had told her she probably had PTSD.

"I mean, we obviously can't live in that house. If we owned the place, maybe they would let us borrow, a mortgage against our own land," Taylor pondered as she closed the door on their small oven. She'd put some really pretty lines on the pots, a design she had seen on Celtic sites that she hoped wouldn't conjure up any of the old gods. She grinned at her own whimsy. "We could put a decent house on there."

"We don't know anything about building our own house."

"What about a ready-made house?"

"I don't want a mobile home," she replied, sounding snooty. She hated the ones she'd seen around town. They always seemed run-down and dirty. The poorest of the poor living in them. She had to admit the ones that were for seniors only looked nicer, but she'd never been in one and really didn't like them on principle.

"No, nothing like that. They aren't all like that and the new ones are actually quite nice," Taylor reminded her. She had tried to talk her into buying one once before, but they did seem to attract the wrong element in their area, and she was glad they hadn't bought one in Hilton Head. They'd have lost money on the deal and not been any better off than they were now in their small apartment. "Still, if we paid our rent as a mortgage, how would that be any different?"

"True," Bree agreed reluctantly. Having a mortgage could only improve their credit. "I guess we need to talk to a few people."

That would have to wait, though, as they baked some pottery. Bree made enough pots that could dry and would wait for one of them to paint them. They put separators between the ones they'd thrown the other day and baked and packed them up to take to the next market they attended. They were building up inventory to go in the small trailer they had out back. It was a good way for them to earn extra money, and they both hoped to make enough that Taylor could quit her extra job and work full-time with Bree. They both thought about the place they had looked at as they worked.

They were home in time to greet their kids' bus, embarrassing them with hugs and kisses as they talked over and around them, asking about their school day, and letting them know how happy they were to see them.

"You have some paint there." Melanie pointed to her mom's cheek, laughing and knowing she had been working on pots that day.

"You went without us?" Barbie asked, disappointed. She loved going to the shop.

"Yep, had a lot of work to get done today," Taylor told her. What she didn't say was how it was a lot easier to get work done without the four kids running around the shop. It was what it was; they all knew work had to get done. On most weekends, they loaded up the trailer and pulled it behind either the Jeep or the minivan to go to fairs and festivals all over the state and sell their artwork.

"Maybe you can go next time," Bree promised as they talked to Jack about his first day, making sure he knew how important it was. He was shy at first about it but then enthusiastically told them he had made a best friend and couldn't wait to go again tomorrow.

"I'll drop you off on my way to work," Taylor promised, setting a schedule. She'd make some of the calls in the morning about that property, but now their time was all about the kids.

"I'm going to start dinner," Bree put in as they all piled into the apartment. The kids were thrilled when they saw the boxes of macaroni and cheese she pulled out of the cupboard.

CHAPTER TWO

Taylor knew that calling the realtor probably was a bad idea. Getting the guy's hopes up as he enthusiastically told her about the property he was trying to offload, he repeated some of the things the clerk had already told them. She felt a small bit of guilt as she listened to the guy's sales pitch, where he shared many of the things she'd already heard from the tax assessor.

"Yes, you can enjoy the country living lifestyle in the peace and quiet on your very own ten-point-three acres!"

Taylor wondered if this guy was faking it.

"It's on the west side of town. You can enjoy the wildlife, and it has a natural stream flowing through the property. I don't know if your husband hunts, but it has great hunting!" She immediately resented his assumption she was the *little wife* calling on behalf of her husband. "There is a possible building opportunity, too. It's in the Riverview district, and ..." he went droning on with every potential selling point.

"Yes," Taylor finally interrupted, "my wife and I went and looked at it yesterday and—"

"You went and looked at it already?" His tone came through as disappointed and a little aggrieved as he interrupted.

"Yes, it's pretty overgrown, and there does seem to be a lot of activity on the drive."

"Oh, that's because the local kids use it to race their BMX bikes and motorbikes on it. I'm sure they use their ATVs, too. Still, they don't mean any harm and usually the gate is across," he stated musingly. "I take it the gate wasn't up?"

"Didn't even see one," she admitted. They hadn't either. Didn't even realize there was one.

"Darn, must have come down again," he said jovially, not sounding worried about it in the least.

"The house is almost non-existent ..." she began hesitantly.

"Yes, that's why it says 'building opportunity,'" he said, quoting the ad.

"Is there some agreement with the neighbor regarding the open field they are harvesting?"

"They're cutting?"

"Yes, the map shows an open field that crosses the property line. It's obvious the neighbor is cutting the hay on it."

"I wasn't aware he was doing that." The realtor's tone had switched from sales to conversational. Now, maybe Taylor could get some real information.

"Do you think they'd come down on the price?"

"And why would they do that?"

"Have you seen the place lately?" She was also thinking about the taxes.

"Well, not since we put up our realtor sign," he admitted reluctantly, not willing to tell her how long it had been on the market. Now he wondered if he should have been inspecting his client's property.

"It's so overgrown, and the house is almost completely gone."

"Gone?" he choked out, determining that he must check it out, and soon.

"The only thing of value is the land itself, but it's so overgrown that I really doubt it's usable. The barn is obviously a hangout for who-knows-what." *In for an inch, in for a mile*, Taylor thought. She was exaggerating ... maybe.

"I'll ask," he promised, sounding a little strangled. The owner wasn't going to be happy hearing this. "May I get your information?"

She gave it to him; fully aware she'd be inundated with sales calls or have her information sold to mailing lists. She inwardly sighed as she got ready for work. Today, she would be working at the diner, at least twelve hours on her feet, but the tips were always good since Tweety's was

located right off the interstate. She longed for the day that their pottery business made enough that she could quit. Meanwhile, she'd take her shift and make the most of it.

She mentioned the property to Lenny and Gretchen, a couple of friends who were her regular customers, and they warned her to be careful not to get scammed.

"Yeah, but this could take The Nillionaires Club to a whole new level," she teased them as they raised their water glasses in salute. She joined them in a drink of water before hurrying off to serve other customers.

"Think they'll get the place?" Lenny asked Gretchen after Taylor went back to work.

"I don't know," she began, sounding trepidatious, "Sounds like a lot of work." Taylor had lain things out realistically about the place for them— the weeds, the swamp, the BMX bike tracks, but she sounded enthusiastic about the barn.

They worried about their friends, knowing how hard the family had worked to save their money. They had to do something, and soon. Their apartment was about to burst at the seams with all those children. The common thread, though, was, "They're buying a swamp?"

* * * * *

Bree took the call a few days later.

"May I speak with Taylor Moore?"

"This is *Mrs*. Moore," she answered, wondering if they'd missed paying a bill. She was always on top of those things but constantly worried about falling behind.

"Oh, sorry, Mrs. Moore. When we spoke the other day, I didn't realize ..." he left off. "I'm calling about that property off of Restlawn Highway?"

Bree frowned and then realized he must be the realtor Taylor had called several days ago. "Yes?"

"The owner has generously consented to a discount on the property due to the state it is in, but we must have a formal offer in the next day or two."

"Oh, do you have other interested parties?"

"Well, the owner plans on making improvements, but if he doesn't have to ..." He left the thought hanging for her to make her own conclusions.

"How much of a discount are we talking?"

"Ten percent!" he said triumphantly.

"Oh, no, that place isn't worth that. We'd need at least twenty-five percent off the asking price. Have you seen the state it's in?"

"I haven't," he admitted in a tightly controlled voice. If they discounted the property twenty-five percent, his commission would go down considerably.

"Then you wouldn't know how much work it would take to have a decent house built there. My wife and I are not carpenters, so we certainly aren't going to be building it ourselves."

"Your wife?" he choked out.

"Yes, my wife Taylor and I. You said you spoke to her the other day?"

"Oh, I thought you were the Mrs. Moore I spoke to the other day?"

"No, that would have been my wife," she explained, dismissing what she sensed was a touch of homophobia. She wasn't going to let it bother her. She expected it half the time and ignored it. "We certainly wouldn't pay full price for the amount of work that is going to be required to make it livable. I'll discuss it with Taylor, and, if the owner is willing to come down further, we will make a formal offer."

"I see," he said tightly. He wondered if they really had the money to buy the place or were just making him jump through hoops for fun. It happened all the time in real estate. "Are you aware of the acreage involved? That's a lot of prime hunting land and—"

"It's swamp land, and have you seen all the brush in there? It's probably prime hunting land only because no one can get in there. The only open areas are by the house, which is slowly going to seed, and the field out beyond the woods on the other side of the creek. You certainly can't build anywhere else on the property with all that swampland."

"I see," he repeated. How did these women know more than he did about the property? He had visited the place at a different time of the year than they had, apparently, and that could affect how it was viewed.

"Thank you," she said, her voice dripping with saccharine. She knew that would annoy some people, but they also couldn't accuse her of being rude. "I'll be looking forward to your call." She paused for a second, then hung up. She knew it was unlikely she'd get another call from the man. *Oh, well.* It had been nice to dream, owning their own land. The place had possibilities, but she knew better than to set her hopes on anything. She thought about that barn for a minute, having already pictured how they'd place the oven, maybe get a second, bigger one, and all the different items they could have made in there. She sighed as she let her dream go, and not for the first time. Meanwhile, she had laundry to fold, toys to pick up, and a dinner to plan.

* * * * *

Taylor was home late that night, having worked a twelve-hour shift. She groaned as she sat down in her pink uniform. She despised the color; it was so not her thing. She kicked off her tennis shoe orthotics, and she sighed when Bree sat on the footstool and took her foot into her lap, peeled off her stockings, and started rubbing her foot.

"Better?" she asked, smiling at her spouse lovingly.

"Oh, gawd yes," she groaned, arching her foot into her wife's knowing fingers. "I may need you to walk on my back tonight."

"Rough night?"

"Some motorcyclists came in off the interstate, and there had to be about thirty or forty of them. I lost count."

"Run off your feet?"

"I don't mind that part. It's the 'honey' and the 'baby' I could do without. I wonder if those guys—even some of the women—realize how sexist that sounds."

"Yeah, but you didn't say anything?" she asked cautiously, worrying that Taylor might get fired if she did. Taylor had been warned for that before, and they needed the money her job brought in.

"No way. You know I play that up." She smiled, showing off her even and very white teeth. Her incisors were a little large, a bit vampire-ish, but she liked them, having inherited them from her mother. Her hazel eyes were sparkling as she recalled her night. "Ohhh, that feels good," she whispered as Bree dug a thumb into the arch of her aching foot and rubbed downward.

"On stage, were you?"

"Maybe … Okay, tonight I was Flo; last night I was Alice." She laughed.

"That's good, as long as you weren't grumpy Mel." She laughed in return, referring to the TV show 'Alice' and its characters. She knew Taylor used their personalities to cope with working at the diner. It helped make the job more interesting and got her through the long hours. Some of the regulars had caught on and loved it. "Have you ever played Vera or Jolene?"

"Nope, I refuse to play stupid." She went on to mention Lenny and Gretchen, who had stopped by, wishing that Bree had been there for the water toast. They laughed at what they called the annual meeting of The Nillionaires Club. It wasn't a real club, just whenever three or four of them met up, they called it one. None of them had a lot of money,

probably never would, but it didn't stop them from having hopes and dreams.

Bree switched feet, removed the other stocking, and began rubbing that one. "That realtor called," she mentioned as casually as possible, watching her wife's expression.

"Yeah, what'd he say?" She was going to have to bathe before she got into bed, the smell of sweat and greasy food lingered in her clothes and on her skin, getting into her pores.

"That the owner would reduce the price ten percent."

"Yeah?" She opened one eye to look at her wife. "That sounds pretty good. What'd you tell him?"

"I asked if he had seen the state it was in. He admitted he hadn't. I said that we'd be more interested if he could get his client to take twenty-five percent less because there is no house on the land and it's so overgrown."

"You're going to make us lose this deal!" She opened both eyes and sat up.

"I didn't know we were *that* interested in it," she retorted, letting go of her wife's foot.

"Well, if we could get it for less, it would be good, wouldn't it?"

"But if we buy it, we'd have no place to live on it. What's the point of buying it except for the barn?"

"That's just it, we could put a prefab on it after we knock down that house."

"Just as long as it isn't a mobile home."

"I already said no mobile home," she promised, reminding her wife of their conversation. "Why don't we go by one of those places that put a house on the place for us already built?"

"Because then we would also need to go see our banker and see if they'd give us a mortgage, and I don't think they are going to do that since I don't have a *real* job."

"You have a real job," Taylor insisted.

"Yeah, but they will look at your job, see you're a waitress and judge us. That's after they realize we are a same-sex couple. Then, they see we are also self-employed and foster parents. They may not even care about seeing our tax-returns."

"Look, you're putting obstacles in place before we even know the answers to the basic questions. I have a job, we count our market sales from the pottery as a job, our proceeds, including what we get from the kids and the state—all of that makes for a fairly decent income. Surely, that will be enough to buy a house."

"Well, I guess we could go look at the prefabs. At least we would be getting some ideas," she answered reluctantly, not wanting to fight with Taylor after her long day. She was tired herself after going a few rounds with Melanie over homework she didn't want to do it in the first place. "When is your next day off?"

"I took Friday off for Tomahawk market days. Did you forget?"

The event was Friday afternoon and all-day Saturday and Sunday. They'd be taking their minivan so they could sleep at the fairgrounds and keep a guard over their booth at night.

"Do you know next week's schedule?"

"I could manage Monday morning." She still had to bathe and knew she better hurry up or she'd pass out, smelling like the greasy diner. That smell got on her skin and in her pores, she needed a hot shower or bath to get it off her.

"You are going to want to sleep in Monday from the weekend."

"Yeah, but when else would we get a chance to look?"

CHAPTER THREE

Bree packed up the trailer by herself while the kids were in school on Thursday afternoon. Taylor was already at work at the diner and hoping to be home for dinner. That was good because they could go to bed early and get the van and trailer up to the market. It was a fifty-mile drive, but they expected thousands of people to come out that weekend, and it paid to be ready early. She loaded and secured the tent and its poles on a rack on one side of the trailer and carried in one box at a time, fitting one pot in at time according to their sizes and weight to balance things out, since some of the pots were quite heavy. She packed them well with plenty of cardboard, newspaper, and bubble wrap salvaged from packages they had received over the past years. Some of the plastic was pretty dusty from years of use.

She liked the Aztec lines of some of their pottery but had to admit the Celtic designs Taylor had drawn recently were interesting. Their vivid colors and shiny finish would catch people's eyes and should sell well.

She carefully hooked up the trailer to the van, which desperately needed replacing, and looked around once more before turning out the lights and locking up the shop.

She drove home carefully, the trailer bumping along behind her. She was never completely comfortable with the added weight, but Taylor always looked confident behind the wheel and she hoped she would be up

to the drive tomorrow. She never felt too confident with all that weight behind her vehicle.

She parked in front of their apartment complex, making sure the doors were locked, and double checked the padlocks on the trailer. Once, she'd found the trailer wide-open because someone had cut the lock. Taylor replaced the locks with rounded ones that were so thick it was nearly impossible to get a bolt cutter around them. To break these locks, you'd have to have a drill or a saw of some sort. They hadn't been broken into since then, but they both tried to be conscientious and careful about their merchandise since it was their livelihood.

Glancing at the clock, she saw she had half an hour before the school bus arrived. She hoped their teachers remembered to have their extra school work ready for them. She had called and left notice that they wouldn't be in on Friday. She checked the mail, saw something from the state, and assumed it was about Jack because he was the only one they hadn't adopted yet, and, technically, they were only foster parents. She hoped the letter would announce Jack's birth parents had finally lost custody. They'd been fighting it, probably afraid that they would look bad to everyone they knew, otherwise. The fact that they hadn't seen their son in two years because they had left him alone for several days to go on a cruise didn't seem to faze them. They still saw nothing wrong with their behavior. They had, after all, left him food, and he knew how to use a bathroom himself. Bree and Taylor had dealt with the little boy's issues compassionately since they'd gotten him. The bed wetting, nightmares, and clinginess—the little boy needed to know that his moms not only loved him but would be there for him. He was getting better every month he was with Taylor and Bree. The last sixteen months had been good for the boy, at least in Bree's opinion. She stared at the envelop, unsure if she should open it without Taylor.

The letter could be time sensitive, so Bree took a deep breath and ripped it open. There was going to be yet another court date, and this time they were ordering Jack to appear with them. The social worker would be there, along with a court-appointed lawyer for the boy.

"Damn!"

Bree took a deep breath. This could mean the birth parents wanted to see the boy, which would confuse him further. He barely remembered them, but his psyche was healing and he didn't need flashbacks or nightmares to set back his progress. She put the date on the calendar right away so that Taylor could make sure she had it off and made a note to tell her about it later when the kids were in bed. There was nothing either of the foster moms could do about it, and she wasn't happy.

Bree pulled out a casserole she had made the other night. It always tasted better once everything in it had time to set. She placed it in the oven to warm slowly so it would be ready by dinner time. She set the table so the kids didn't have to and washed some breakfast dishes she had missed, making sure to soak her hands, anything to get some of the paint and dirt out of her pores.

"Mom!" Melanie called as she came through the door with her three siblings trailing behind.

"Not so loud," Bree cautioned the oldest and then quickly added, "Don't slam that door." But it was too late, and Jack let it bang shut behind him. "Damn," she whispered under her breath, knowing one of the neighbors was sure to complain. She put on a happy smile and greeted each of them with a hug and a kiss. They each told her about their day, and she handed them some fruit chews she had made. Even though they tasted horrible to her, the kids seemed to like them, and they were sugar-free, which was probably why they tasted bad to her. "Well, put your school bags in your rooms, and bring me your lunch bags," she told them once they were all caught up. "Change your clothes, and then you can play. I'll let you watch TV for an hour until Mom gets home and we eat dinner."

She had to tell Melanie twice to put her school bag away, but she could tell the eight-year-old was testing her. She could always let it go, but the others were watching to see if they could get away with it, too. If that happened, she'd have a mutiny on her hands. She didn't remind them that they were leaving for the market tomorrow, getting a day off from school. The school was already informed, and she'd picked up their homework for tomorrow, for those who had it, so they could do it while they all worked at the market. She checked that their weekend bags were packed, their sleeping bags all ready, and got out the cooler and left it in the kitchen to pack with ice in the morning. It wouldn't last until Sunday when they packed up, but they could make several sandwiches to avoid buying meals. If she and Taylor watched the kids closely and kept the cooler closed, an almost impossible feat with the kids, the ice might last until Saturday night.

* * * * *

"This is delicious babe," Taylor said as she forked the chunks of chicken into her mouth. "This is what, cream of—"

"So ... the trailer is all packed for tomorrow," Bree interrupted, repeating herself while she pointed her head towards the girls. Both girls

hated the idea of mushrooms, but what they didn't know wouldn't hurt them.

Taylor frowned at being interrupted but then caught on. She nodded. "I'll put the bags in," she promised, glancing down the hall from her seat at the head of the small kitchen table.

"I'll help," Melanie offered.

"Me, too?" Barbie and Bryan said together.

"Me, too?" Jack echoed, although he didn't have any idea what he was asking to do.

"We'll see," Bree said with a smile. "Eat your dinner."

After dinner, Bree had the boys bring the dishes to the counter while the girls helped Taylor take the sleeping bags, extra blankets, and a bag of clothes out to the van and pack them away for the weekend. One of the bags carried toys the children weren't allowed to play with except when they went to these weekends at the market. It kept the kids busy while the two women were selling their pottery and kept them out of the hair of their customers.

After Taylor put the kids to bed and took a shower, she slouched into the bedroom and collapsed on the bed with a groan.

"Tired?" Bree asked Taylor.

"Probably no more than you are." She gave her a warm smile.

"Want me to brush your hair?"

"You don't have to ask twice." Taylor reached for the brush on the dresser and handed it to her wife. She almost purred as Bree slowly pulled the bristles through her hair. It wasn't too long, just below her shoulders, but she wore it up in a bun at the diner, and it only added to her old-time waitress uniform. "I think I might have picked up a job next week with one of my customers. He was looking for someone to cut his lawn, and I asked how much, and we had a conversation."

"What's Vinnie going to say?" Their landscaping friend, one of The Nillionaires Club, had all the tools necessary to take care of the yard.

"She told me to take it since she's too busy. She's looking to get another crew going."

"How much is he going to pay you?" Bree asked, amused. She knew how much Taylor liked being outdoors.

"One hundred bucks," Taylor bragged, smiling at her wife in the mirror as her eyes shut with the relaxing feel of the brush on her scalp.

"Just how big is this yard?"

"He said at least an acre but that his last lawn-cutter went off to college and left him high and dry."

Bree chuckled. "I miss cutting lawns."

"You could call up your parents and ask if you could cut their lawn," Taylor teased.

"Yeah, and have them tell me that I have too many kids and ask if I have come to my senses about you?"

"Well, there is that. Have you?"

"Have I what?"

"Come to your senses about me?"

"Never. You leave me senseless," she said seductively, leaning down to nibble along Taylor's neck. The corresponding goosebumps that went down her wife's arms were satisfying to see. She rubbed them with her hands, warming them. Further caressing ensued, causing other sensations to come up between them.

"I'm tired," Taylor confessed but didn't stop her.

"Me, too," Bree agreed, continuing her lovemaking as the brush fell to the wayside.

Their lips met, which told each of the other's need, despite their fatigue. Both knew the other's pressure points and quickly began their familiar lovemaking.

Taylor had a spot on her neck that if kissed right, tongued, always made her go limp.

Bree couldn't stop when Taylor reached up with her fingertips, despite the shirt she was wearing, and lightly touched her fingertips over her nipples. The warm palms that followed demanded skin on skin, and Bree pulled her shirt over her head and straddled her wife's lap, then continued running her tongue and lips along her wife's neck.

"Mmmmm," Taylor moaned into Bree's ear, leaning her head away so she could access the long neck.

"You taste delicious."

"You taste pretty good yourself," Taylor responded, licking at the pert nipples that were now conveniently in her face, squeezing the corresponding breast as she tongued first one, and then the other. She could feel herself creaming her clean underwear, knowing she'd have to change them but didn't care. She tongued her wife's nipples harder when Bree hit the right spot, wanting her to bite it, and then, when she lightly scored it with her teeth, felt the need to suck hard on her wife's nipple.

"Careful, babe," Bree warned but didn't stop trying to drive her insane.

Taylor's hand began to sneak down inside the shorts her wife was wearing, pleased to find how wet she was for her. "Someone's been thinking naughty things."

"Nuh-uh. Someone inspires me." she responded, enjoying the feel of Taylor's fingers as they played between her legs. She threw her head back when Taylor gathered the hair and tugged, enjoying the pleasured pain that ensued. The fingers that delved into the hidden folds felt wonderful, and then ... she plunged. "So quick," she protested but not in anger. She welcomed first one, and then a second finger as Taylor tongued her nipple at the same time, using her knee to force her fingers in deeper. The angle was difficult, but she was going to make it work.

Taylor smiled around the nipple that she was working, knowing what she was doing to Bree, making her come undone very quickly as she thrust. Every third thrust she curled her fingers slightly so she would hit the front of the passage, and she heard that welcome intake of breath she wanted. She was going to have a hickey on her neck if Bree wasn't careful. "Like it?" she teasingly whispered.

"Right ... there," Bree gasped, trying to grind down on the fingers giving her so much pleasure.

Taylor moved her leg to hold her wife there, the fingers delving deeper as she increased her pace. The squishing noises told her that she was exciting her. In—out and ... in —out.

In no time at all, Bree threw her head back again and nearly shouted out as she came on her wife.

Taylor attempted to reach up and capture her wife's mouth with her own, but the angle forbade it. Instead, she kissed deeply into her neck, nudging aside her hair, as she ground down on her fingers, nearly breaking them. Slowly, she eased back a fraction of an inch.

Bree finally looked down at her wife and halted her kissing long enough to capture Taylor's lips with her own. She rose up slightly, and Taylor's fingers fell out of her with a plop. Clamping her legs on either side of Taylor's hips, she rolled them, nearly falling off the bed as she pinned her wife. Frantically, she thrust her tongue in Taylor's mouth and was rewarded with a hard suck on that appendage. Her hands brushed gently down Taylor's arms as she began to scooch down her body, making sure to rub her own exposed nipples down her wife's body. She pulled the panties off her wife when she got there, smelling how wet she had become from what they had been doing.

"Yummm," she moaned as she nuzzled the slit, and her mouth started lapping its way down and then inside Taylor.

Taylor spread her legs to accommodate her wife, feeling the need badly now.

Gently, Bree's fingertips spread the folds, lifting her wife's legs over her shoulders, allowing her face between them as she plunged her tongue inside her.

"Oh, gawwwwd," she moaned aloud. Her head turned from side to side with pleasure, and she reached down to hold her wife's head between her legs as she arched up.

"Shhh! You'll wake the children." She grinned devilishly, knowing what she was doing to Taylor. Holding her breath, she plunged her tongue in as deep as it would go, waiting for the sensitive skin to feel that warmth so she could lap up the moisture. Her nose was just right to rub the clit with its tip, but she couldn't inhale or the moisture might drown her. Taking a quick breath, she could sense Taylor getting near, so she tried to hold her breath longer and longer before pulling out yet again, and again. She nearly passed out as she held in as long as possible to give her wife those sensations, the grip on the back of her head was pulling the hair out at its roots. And then, finally, Taylor began to tremble

The tease of the tongue stopping nearly drove her insane. The warmth ending, even in the time that Bree took to take another breath was maddening. The touch of her warm, no ... hot tongue on those nerve endings was incredible. Each time it seemed longer, and she kept arching into her wife's face, never realizing she was smothering her with her folds and wetness. As the tingles started she followed them, releasing her body to convulse as she came, and came, and came.

Bree could have sworn that her nose was full of wetness and nearly broken as Taylor's pubic bone came up and hit it, but she never let on. Instead, she tried to use her fingers to continue rubbing the sensitive area, but as Taylor finally began to come down from her high, she slowly backed off to wipe her fingers on their sheets, and discretely rub her already sore nose.

"Ah, baby, that felt gooood," Taylor breathed, pulling her legs from Bree's shoulders.

Bree smiled as she slid up her wife's body to hug her tightly. "That was unexpected."

When Bree gave her a kiss, Taylor could taste herself on her wife's lips but didn't mind. She was still tingling, feeling little pulses of delicious sensations between her legs. She felt around the bed and found Bree's shirt and helped her get it back on. She laughed to herself as she blew her nose into a tissue, thinking she'd probably done that to Bree a few times over the years.

Holding each other close, they were soon asleep.

HOME ~ First Nillionaires Club

CHAPTER FOUR

Early the next morning Bree and Taylor carried the six-year-olds and put them in the minivan car seats.

"Yes, I know sweetie. Shhh," Bree consoled a crabby Bryan as she strapped him into his car seat.

"I don't think she even realizes she left her bed," Taylor whispered. She closed the car door as softly as possible and locked it. They both looked at Barbie, sound asleep in her pajamas, a blanket wrapped around her. She hadn't woken as Taylor strapped her into the car seat.

"Two down, two to go," Bree said quietly, already weary as she thought about all the work they had to do in the day ahead.

Next, Taylor carried Melanie out, the largest of their children, and put her in the back of the van next to Bryan, who stared up at Taylor with bright eyes.

"How are you even awake?" Taylor asked the chipper little boy.

"Going to market," he sing-songed.

"Shhh, you'll wake your brother and sisters." She handed him a homemade breakfast bar which he chewed on happily, dropping crumbs onto the seat.

They locked the kids in the van once more and hurried to get their coffees to go, the cooler, and their cash bag.

"Ready?" Bree saw her and called out to Taylor, who nodded and locked the door behind her.

They were both excited but weary, too, at the early morning start. Driving north towards the market, something they did several times a year for this particular show, they were both quiet. It was going to be a long couple of days, but they needed the extra money. They would enjoy it once they were all set up and the kids settled into the routine.

Taylor parked in their usual spot. They'd sent in their payment well over a month ago, and one of the show coordinators came by to give them their vendor card to put in the van window. Both moms pulled the tent poles from the trailer in a well-rehearsed and familiar habit. They quickly had the poles attached to the corners with the tent corners pulled taut, hooking the edges all around before lifting the tent onto its legs and raising it. They pushed the legs straight, all six of them until the tent was set up. Next, they attached the sides, rolling them up and attaching them to the cross-beams of the tent so everyone could see into their booth. Next, they placed tarps on the ground and over those pieces of cardboard. They left the van door open so they could hear the children, and the back of the vendor tent would eventually hide the van and trailer from view.

"I've got him," Bree said as Bryan squawked at being left in the van. "Shhh, you'll wake your brother and sisters," she repeated. He'd dozed on the drive up, but was now fully awake. She handed him a bag of his toys as he shimmied out of the van, and, as per the routine, she laid out a small tarp in the corner of the tent for him to sit on.

Bree then went to help Taylor unload the many pots they would be selling.

"I've got this; set up the vendor table," Taylor told her as she lifted box after box and then carefully placed the various pots into organized rows inside the tent.

Bree set up the collapsible desk they'd found at a garage sale and added wheels for an easier setup. The drawers were just the right size to store all the things they needed for vending—a small register and till, credit card swipers, signs, business cards, and brochures. Bree pulled these things out and began setting up. Taylor handed her the cash bag, and she counted out a number of ones, fives, and tens as she put them in the till, then put the bag with extras of each in a locked drawer below the cash register. So many people came to these markets and pulled out a fifty or a hundred, not realizing the vendors didn't have the change. They had to be prepared, or they could lose a sale.

"Hi, Margaret," Taylor said kindly as she put some of the larger pots out on their tarp, seeing their usual neighbor setting up next to them. Margaret sold pillows of every design and color.

"Morning," she mumbled sleepily without pausing her work to chat.

There were so many different vendors, it was fascinating to watch, and Jack ignored his toys to watch all the people coming and going. He knew better than to leave the tent, though. He had his protective square of tarp behind the cash register to play on, or, if he got tired, he could tell his moms and go back in the van and sleep in his car seat. Many times, he'd just grab a blanket and sack out on the tarp, oblivious to the hubbub going on around him.

"Good morning, Taylor!"

Taylor looked up from the new larger pots with vibrant colors, where she was placing them along the front side.

"My, aren't these pretty." the woman commented, stopping to admire the patterns.

"Hello, Gretchen. I have your order in the trailer. Did you bring your husband?"

"He isn't up yet," she said grumpily. "I did bring my son to help … and a cart." She pointed to a pre-teen boy standing a few feet away and smiling sheepishly.

"Hey, there, Aaron. Bring it around the tent to the trailer," Taylor said with a smile. She looked for and found the boxes Bree had loaded and labeled for Gretchen. Carefully, she stacked them in the hand cart, knowing it would be heavy to pull. "I'm going to have to carry this one if you'll carry that box?" she asked Gretchen, who nodded. As they followed Aaron to Gretchen's booth, they chatted amiably. She sold flowers and plants, which jived well with Taylor and Bree's pots. "Oh, that's a beauty," Taylor said when she saw the large spider plant hanging down the middle of Gretchen's booth. It was very full, had variegated edges, and was sending out lots of babies.

"Here you go." Gretchen handed Taylor a check to cover the invoice that had been tucked in the box. They'd unloaded the cart at the back of Gretchen's half-displayed booth and put down the boxes on a table. "I want some of those bigger pots if you don't sell them this weekend. If you do, I want to order at least six. I saw that Aztec design and wish you had told me about them before you brought them!" she complained good-naturedly.

"We're trying different patterns and designs. Doing it free-hand, there are so many variations," Taylor complained in return with a smile. "We'll get it automated, someday."

"I don't know; I like knowing everything is hand-made." She stopped to admire the paintings on the pots. "By the way, have you heard from the realtor?"

"He called once, but Bree told him we wanted a big discount since there is no livable house on the property."

"Sounds like you'd have your work cut out for you if it did go through."

Taylor nodded in agreement, happily anticipating said work.

"You sure it's a good idea?" she fretted for her friend, knowing how long they had scrimped and saved.

Taylor shrugged. "We all have to start somewhere."

She nodded. "True. Well, have a good day."

Taylor took her cue, knowing the woman still had to put up the rest of her booth and her husband would be of no help. He was probably sleeping in the small RV they drove on market days. She envied them that, wishing she and Bree had more than their rusted-out van, but, then, they also had four kids to raise and it all cost money. She returned to her booth, waving at several vendors she recognized from past shows along the way.

"Gretchen wants some of the Aztec pots if we have any left at the end of the market," Taylor mentioned to Bree as she handed her the check.

"We have to figure out a way to get pictures and put them online so we're prepared."

They both knew they needed a camera, a decent computer, and a website.

* * * * *

People started showing up before 8 AM, wanting to be the first to see the wares, even though the rules prohibited sales before nine. By ten, the place was packed. They didn't just come for the crafts but the fresh produce and ready-made food. It felt like a holiday, as people talked, shopped, and explored.

Before long, the kids were all awake and playing in and out of their area, on and off the tarp. Between watching the kids and tending to customers, both moms were kept busy. They took turns quieting down the children, who were naturally rambunctious but knew better than to interrupt their mothers when they were helping a customer.

"I have to go to the bathroom," was a familiar refrain, and whenever they had a break from the constant customers, one or the other mother escorted their children in a group to the bathroom. They were slow and

distracted as they looked at the bright colors, the things others offered, and the expensive food they knew better than to ask for.

By noon, the kids were hungry, and the moms opened the cooler and handed out sandwiches. They ate them on the tarp, getting crumbs all over it, but enjoying the juice boxes Bree had put in for them. This necessitated another trip to the bathroom soon after, but the moms took turns as they waited on customers, answered questions, and helped to load pots in people's carts.

"Whew! Thought I wouldn't get a break to come over here. I want that large pot you have out front," a woman gasped, proving she had nearly run to get to their booth.

"Hiya, Lenny," Bree said, seeing her friend, another member of the First Nillionaires Club, and smiling. "How's carts?"

"Yeah, yeah, yeah," the woman said, brushing aside the niceties and pulling out her wallet. It was stuffed with money from her own booth. "How much for that big blue pot with the woman on the front?"

"That's a god," Bree corrected her with a smirk, "and it's twenty-five."

"Is that a friend's discount?"

"Yes, cause that's a $50 pot," Bree answered in a lower voice, feeling a little put-out that Lenny would even have to ask.

"That's half price and not acceptable," Lenny whispered so other shoppers wouldn't over-hear. "I won't let you." She shoved $45 at her friend and turned her back as she went to go take the pot.

"But …" Bree said and then shrugged. Lenny had the vendor spot for all the carts and could well afford a $50 pot. Lenny lifted the heavy thing onto a platform dolly cart, pulled up the sides so it wouldn't rock off, and hurried away. She couldn't afford to be gone from her booth for too long. There were always people coming and going, needing carts or returning them. Since she kept a healthy deposit and their driver's licenses that needed to be returned in exchange for her carts, they weren't always patient.

Taylor finished up with a woman who bought two smaller pots with a moon theme to them, wrapped them in tissue paper, and put them in a box before handing them back to her. The woman handed her $50, and they nodded and smiled as she left.

Bree rang it up, knowing the price to put in the register so with tax it would come out exactly to $50. They did this to avoid dealing with too much coinage, which was a pain, and even numbers worked better for both them and the customers. She glanced as Taylor went by to go under the tent wall and get more stock from the trailer, locking it behind her after she pulled more pots from the door.

By 4 PM, both women were exhausted under the hot sun, even under their shaded tent. The market was slowing down, and some vendors, especially those selling produce, began to pack up for the day. They were allowed to leave and come back the next day with more and fresh produce, while vendors like Bree and Taylor could close up their booth and not tear down until Sunday. Like them, many of the others would be camping out on the grounds to help security ensure their merchandise was safe.

At six, they rolled down the walls of their booth, tying the corners to hide their merchandise from prying eyes. It couldn't stop stealing completely, but security was pretty good at this show, and theft was rare. They took the kids to the park next door to the market to let them run around and play on the swings and other equipment while they discussed how their day had gone. They weren't the only parents who brought their children to work the long hours of the market. In fact, they saw several families they recognized and chatted with a few parents, as they watched the children work off their excess energy. It was a treat at the end of the long day for both parents and children.

They returned to the van to have a small dinner, followed by a bathroom trip not only to wash up from their day but to do their nightly bedtime routines. Together, they put down the seats in the van to create a large platform for their blankets and sleeping bags, and they all piled in for the night. Bree and Taylor could have slept in the trailer or put up their camping tent, but they wanted to be nearby if anyone got scared, and it was too cold this time for the tent. They envied some of their fellow vendors who had a full RV or camper setup as they snuggled in with the four kids. Introducing them to this lifestyle over the years had required a lot of explanations, rules, and learning. Child Protective Services had required explanations, as well, but after three successful adoptions, their case worker knew the couple and their business pretty well. It was only when they had gotten a new case worker that problems arose with a lot of the same questions and explanations.

Predictably, the kids were fairly good that first day, not so good the second day, and absolutely bored by the third and final day. The only saving grace was they would be taking down the booth on the third day and leaving.

At night, they kept the money bag under the folded-down seats where they slept, not making a big deal about it so the kids wouldn't notice. Still, they were a bit paranoid, with all the cash, credit card slips, and checks they had in there.

To entertain the children, they told stories and read from books they only brought out during market or show weekends. It was another way to make the time more special.

By Sunday, they were all grubby and ripe from camping in their van. The family, their merchandise, and the tent were all coated in a fine layer of dust from the park, and taking down the tent made them even dirtier. After they packed and loaded up all the leftover pots, they took Gretchen the ones she wanted so she could pack them with her leftover plants, order some more, and say goodbye.

"Got that," Taylor said as she lifted the tote that held all the corner pieces of the tent. It packed away well in the organized trailer.

The trailer had been one of their better purchases. It was great transporting their pottery to markets, swap-meets, and gift shows, and it held their excess inventory. But the trailer was heavy, despite all they had sold, and they knew the load was wearing on their poor minivan. It was better when they could drive the Jeep, but all four kids barely fit comfortably in that, and they certainly couldn't sleep in it. They always had to set up their camping tent when they used the Jeep.

"Damn," Taylor said when they got back to their apartment to find no spots available on the street out front. "Take the kids in the house, and I'll take this to the shop." She thumb-pointed at the trailer.

"Are you sure?" Bree worried, knowing they were all very tired.

"Got this," she said with a smile. She double-parked and helped get the kids out of their seatbelts and watched as Bree took the cash bag, slipping it unobtrusively under her clothes as she escorted the kids into their apartment. At the shop, Bree unhooked the trailer, chocked its tires, and made sure the tongue had a lock on it so no one could steal it or the merchandise they still had inside it. By the time she got home, the kids were already washed and asleep in their beds.

"Didn't they want any dinner?" she asked, looking in on them.

"They barely got a few mouthfuls of the Ramen I made," Bree told her and then showed her how much they had made at the weekend show. She had showered already and was sitting in lounge pants and a muscle shirt, looking fresh and clean.

"I wish we had—" began Taylor, but Bree rose quickly enough to silence her with a kiss.

"Someday we will have," she assured her. She didn't mind being poor, but they'd made a decent amount that weekend, enough to pay for the shop rental, the storage unit, and for the supplies they had used to make their pots, with a bit left over. She was pleased because that meant more could

go into their savings. It was hard work, and sometimes they wondered why they did it. But there was a goal.

"I better shower," Taylor sighed. She'd have to be back at the diner tomorrow from noon to closing, and she would need her sleep.

"When do you want to go check out those prefabs?" Bree hesitated to ask, knowing they were probably out of their depth.

"Let's take Jack and go in the morning?"

"Really?" she asked, surprised.

"The money is earning interest, but, if we don't move forward with our dreams, what is the point of all this?"

After a weekend at market, Taylor always felt more determined than ever to get out of their tiny apartment. Sleeping together in the van was fine when the kids were little, but Melanie was getting big and the two six-year-olds were restless sleepers. Jack was the only one that seemed to fit in there with the two adults. There were so many things they wanted, and a camper was just one of them.

"I'm scared." The thought of their savings all being used on buying land and a house scared her. Especially that land, which had looked pretty overgrown and swampy, and, then, there was that falling down house. What if something went wrong?

"Me, too, but we gotta try something, right?" Taylor asked as she left to go take her shower.

CHAPTER FIVE

"No, no, scat!" Bree said as she returned from walking the kids to the bus.

"What's going on?" Taylor asked as she came in from the kitchen where she had just cleaned up and was drinking some coffee.

"There's this stray that keeps trying to come in. The kids pet it, so that's why."

Taylor laughed as the orange cat, which was on the skinny side, tried to get past her wife and into their apartment. It nearly succeeded as it rubbed against the woman's legs affectionately. "Awww, how can you resist?" she asked as Bree firmly shut the door in the disappointed cat's face.

"I don't want to steal someone's cat."

"I don't think anyone owns that stray. It looks pretty young."

"Are you almost ready to go?" she asked to change the subject.

"I'll just grab my uniform in case I don't have time to change later."

Taylor had cleaned up Jack who was humming along as he played with a train on the coffee table. "You ready to go, bub?" Bree asked him.

"Going?"

"Yeah, Mom and I have some errands and thought you'd like to go with us before school." He wouldn't need to be at the school until noon so they had a few hours' window to get anything accomplished.

"Sure!" he said amiably.

Bree marveled how quickly the kids bounced back from the weekend at the market. She was dragging and could use a nap. Her body felt worn out, and she knew they both sported some bruises that were inevitable from the work they did. Both she and Taylor did the majority of the work, lifting the heavy pots and packing as well as unpacking and repacking the trailer. The sun sucked the life out of them, too, but that was much better than the weekends when it rained and they lost business. They'd spend the next month or so restocking their shelves, filling orders for a few stores around town, and hoping to find other accounts as well as coming up with new designs.

After they stopped at the bank and deposited the weekends proceeds, they found themselves in Taylor's Jeep, bouncing along to one of three prefab builders in the area, looking at the impressive displays they had and listening to hopeful salesmen and women.

"As I said, we don't know the dimensions and we are just looking," Bree and Taylor both explained time and again as they looked at their options and viewed the house set ups. They even toured a couple of the houses the dealers had on site; the salespeople didn't appreciate the rambunctious four-year old running through the rooms.

"Wow, those sure aren't anything like I expected," Taylor admitted as she drove towards the school to drop off their kindergartener.

"Yeah, I guess I had it in my head that they were only one step up from mobile-homes," Bree agreed.

"Me, too," she smirked as she pulled up, put the emergency brake on, and put the SUV in neutral so she could open the back door and unbuckle Jack. "Ready, bub?" she asked the little boy who was very excited to be going back to school after missing last Friday. He had so much to tell his friends about what he saw and had done over the weekend and couldn't wait to hear what they had done.

Bree watched her wife hold the enthusiastic boy's hand as he skipped into school. She looked over the brochures in her hands, marveling at the full-color images and the information offered to the potential buyer. She knew she and Taylor should really do something like this brochure with their pottery but wasn't comfortable having someone else do all the photos and mock-up despite a well-meaning friend's offer. Elsie had promised to show her how when they got a new computer, but that would have to wait.

"I'm just going to drop you at home and then go to work so I'm not late," Taylor told her as she got back in the Jeep and buckled in.

"I think we should have the realtor go with us to the property," Bree told her.

Taylor stopped from putting the SUV into gear. She exhaled slowly. "That's a lot of money that we can't get back if this goes bad," she cautioned, releasing the brake and putting it into first.

"I thought you wanted this?"

"I do, but I'm also still scared," she admitted. That safety net meant a lot to them. They'd been building it up for years. Still, nothing ventured, nothing gained.

"Do you want me to call the realtor for an appointment?"

After thinking for a moment, Taylor nodded. She'd wanted this as much as Bree and they both had seen that barn which, with a bit of modification, would help their business grow. She'd still have to work at the diner, but now she had more of a purpose. Every tip would have to be put towards the home they wanted so badly.

"We'll have to go talk to the bank. too," she added.

CHAPTER SIX

Your mom called and wants a family dinner on Wednesday, Bree texted Taylor, knowing she might not see it for hours when she took her break.

Gretchen was in and invited us and the kids over for Thursday, was texted back a few minutes later.

Two free meals? she texted with a smiley face emoji and one with a tongue sticking out.

Deal.

They were always surprised anyone in their small group wanted them to come over, knowing all the kids would come, too. Everyone knew how badly the couple had wanted children, and fostering had been a way to help out. They'd had an income with fostering which helped their bank account as they saved toward someday owning their own home. Adoption was a result of falling in love with these children, but, financially, it had hit them hard. They'd have made more over just fostering the kids indefinitely, but they wanted them to know they were with them for always, that they were *their* kids and they weren't going to abandon them, *ever*. Still, it was a lot of work and they were happy with the chaos. None of the kids looked one bit like the two women with their long brown hair, Bree's a shade blonder, but they knew that despite all their differences—that both women encouraged—they were loved.

* * * * *

Taylor's mom had been pleased to finally get some grandchildren out of this strong-willed daughter of hers. She'd been surprised when her daughter had settled down, convinced that the artistic gypsy that was her daughter would never have a husband and children. She'd been even more overjoyed when Taylor brought home Bree and not surprised at all at her interest in a woman. Bree was a settling influence, or so she thought. The girl was even more of a free-spirit than her own wayward daughter.

"You can sit where you want," Ellen assured her grandchildren after welcoming hugs. They knew she wasn't really their grandmother, but she'd accepted them with open arms from day one, and she was probably the only grandmother they would ever have.

"So, you cut some stranger's lawn?" Ellen asked Taylor after she mentioned one of her side projects. "Don't you have a friend who is a landscaper?"

"Yes, that's Vinnie, although she calls herself a 'lawn care specialist.' I don't know how small a job she would take, but I had the time and the opportunity. And it was cash."

"How'd your weekend up at the market go?" Ellen handed a bowl down the line, helping the smaller children put some on their plates.

"It was good," Bree told her, dishing up some food for Jack.

"I don't know why you two bother," Taylor's sister Tia put in. "It's not like you're ever going to make a fortune at those fairs or festivals."

"It helps get our product out to be seen and provides us with some extra money," Taylor patiently explained in a tone that showed she had explained this many times before. She wasn't about to tell Tia how much they actually made from the fairs and festivals because she recognized a fishing expedition when she saw one. Tia wanted to borrow some money from her, money she would never pay back.

"Whatever," the young woman said, dismissing it with a wave of her hand. "It's an awful lot of work for very little return." She had helped out one weekend long ago and had said she would never do *that* again.

Ellen exchanged a look with her older daughter, almost apologetic, but they both broke eye contact and continued with the family dinner.

"No, Blaine," Tia said, slapping at her son's hands when he reached for a bowl of Jell-O. "That's dessert."

He immediately started kicking the leg of the table, disrupting everyone else who was trying to eat.

"Knock it off," Eric, Tia's husband, admonished his son. "And don't cry, or I'll give you something to cry about."

Bree and Taylor exchanged a look, and both could tell what the other mom was thinking on hearing that. But it was Eric's right to discipline his son, and they wouldn't interfere.

"We have a cat," Melanie informed her grandmother.

"You have a cat?" Ellen asked her daughter, glancing at Bree who almost cringed.

"No, we don't have a cat." Taylor shook her head. "We have a stray who is trying to become our cat."

"The dang thing won't go. The kids pet it, but I won't let them feed it," Bree added.

"You shouldn't let them pet it; they'll get germs," Tia put in.

"It's a nice cat." Barbie looked worried, as if she'd done something wrong.

"A real nice cat," Bryan backed her up, hoping they could keep it.

"It's doing its best to ingratiate itself on the team." Taylor laughed, knowing her mother would understand, having raised kids herself as a single mother.

"I could take care of it for you," Eric offered, and both moms immediately said no, knowing what kind of care he implied. Fortunately, the kids didn't realize what he meant.

* * * * *

"Thank you so much for coming," Ellen told them sincerely as she made sure to kiss each of the grandkids, giving each of them a squeeze and then hug both her daughter and Bree. "You all come next week, too, ya hear?"

"We'll try, Mom," Taylor assured her as she helped Bree with the children, and they herded them to the van.

As they headed home Bree murmured to her, "The check engine light came on."

"Just what we need," Taylor mumbled, sighing. Both vehicles needed tune ups, and they'd have to do something about that, this one sooner than later.

"I'll take it in tomorrow."

"See how much a bumper to bumper tune up would cost?"

"You want to do that?" She was surprised if she did, knowing it would be pricey.

"No," Taylor said, shaking her head, "but I want to know how much it would cost instead of just fixing each problem that comes up."

"Ambitious," she teased. The costs never seemed to end.

* * * * *

The meeting with their banker didn't really go well. He was cautious about them buying land, especially out in the area they were contemplating. "That new housing development is going in on the far side of this property," he said musingly after they showed him the map. "While the property will rise in value, I don't think that swamp on it will be to your benefit."

"That wetland empties into the creek and drains the land. There is this area," Taylor indicated a field on the map, "that is all cut, and we can get hay from our section."

"As you said, this section here," Bree put in, pointing to the back of the land beyond part of the woods, "is scheduled for a housing development. It can only increase the value of our land." She hoped by her emphasizing the positive he'd be more willing to give them the loan they might need. She suspected part of his caution was because they were women.

"You haven't bought the land, and I really don't think it's worth the price they are asking. Have you gone and seen it?"

"We have." They both nodded.

"And?"

"The barn will be excellent for our business."

He knew a lot of the funds he saw coming in to the bank were from their pottery business. He didn't think either had any business sense or think much of their so-called business, but it generated a steady income, and they saved a lot of what they made. At least Taylor had a job with a guaranteed income, but she was *only* a waitress. He didn't think much of that, either. "And the house?"

"That will have to be replaced," Taylor confessed. She saw in his eyes he didn't think they should buy the place, and her heart sank.

"I wouldn't, that's too much of a gamble. And neither of you knows how to build?" he fished and not even waiting for their answer, asked, "Can you afford to have it built for you?"

"We were thinking of putting a prefab on the spot," Bree informed him.

He sneered a little as he studied the map. He wouldn't have been surprised if she had said mobile home, but he'd have been able to refuse them a loan quicker then. The county had certain requirements for mobile

homes. "Why don't you move into Happy Acres?" he asked, sitting back and watching the two women.

"Because we don't want to live in a mobile home park, and that place is a dump," Taylor said tightly. She knew what he was doing; he wanted them to know their place in his world. Two moms with adopted children, with a foster child, shouldn't own their own home in the country. They were being too ambitious.

"Still, you could buy a newer mobile home, and it would be in a park," he pointed out, not in the least put out that he had angered the waitress.

"Thank you, no," Taylor answered.

"Well, we thank you for your time. We wanted to know our options," Bree said in a chirpy little voice as she gathered their paperwork. No one who didn't know her well would realize how angry she really was at his *helpful* suggestions, adding insult to shooting down their purchase of the land. He had offered nothing that was helpful at all.

"That's what I'm here for," he said in an ingratiating voice, sure they had averted disaster and the funds would remain in the bank keeping their low-yield account intact. He shook both their hands, never even realizing how annoying he had been to them.

"Well, that was a disaster," Taylor said as soon as they got back to the Jeep. She headed for the mechanic's shop where their van was being fixed. As expected, the bumper to bumper tune up was out of their price range.

"How dare he?" Bree was angry enough to spit feathers.

"He dares because he thinks he is in the power position. We both know he's wrong," she quickly added to keep Bree from exploding.

"Happy Acres! Are you kidding me?!"

They both knew the crime in that overly large mobile-home park was because most of the people who lived there rented out the dilapidated old homes. The owners didn't care if the renters destroyed them; they'd just take their deposits, make them barely livable, and rent them out again. And the renters were already poor and barely able to afford the rent, so they couldn't get out of their situations. That place was a trap.

Even though Taylor and Bree lived in a cramped apartment, the rent was decent and one they could afford. But with the income they had managed to save when foster children came into their home and the business they had started, they were ready to move. They wanted more; they wanted better. Being put in their place by people like that arrogant banker infuriated them.

"I have half a mind to change banks," Bree sputtered.

"We need to keep the money there if we are going to get a loan for the house," Taylor pointed out. "We need the credit history."

"Maybe not ..."

"What's going on in that beautiful mind of yours?" Instead of staying mad and ruining their time together, her partner was thinking, creating, or possibly plotting.

"One of the prefab brochures said financing was available."

"We can't afford—" Taylor quickly began, thinking of the interest rate that private financing usually charged.

"No, we can't, but we can look into it. Meanwhile, I'm going to open us a savings account at the local credit union as a backup, and we are going to see what that realtor has to say."

They hadn't mentioned the property at all at the family dinner on Wednesday. They would wait. They hadn't even talked about it with the children, not wanting to get their hopes up.

"It was just a sensor, probably from pulling that heavy trailer of yours," Sam told them when they went to see how much the van was going to cost. "No charge," he added. "You need to buy a truck," he advised.

"How do we fit four kids in that with the car seats?" Taylor asked her friend; grateful they could trust him to be honest with them.

"King cab," he answered promptly, grinning at her. He'd had a crush on her in high school, but, seeing her with Bree, he understood why that was never to be. She was so cool. With her long flowing hair, she was still attractive to him, but being her friend was better than nothing. "But that van is showing wear and tear from the weight."

"Just what we need: another expense," Taylor griped that evening as they prepared for bed.

"Don't talk finances in front of the appliances," Bree joked.

"How are we going to afford all this?" she asked reasonably. She nodded towards the brochures on the table and got up to follow her wife to bed.

"How about we take it one step at a time and trust in the fates to provide for us?"

"Nuh-uh," she griped as they slid underneath the sheets and snuggled close before going to sleep.

CHAPTER SEVEN

Thursday morning, they spent a couple of hours throwing pots, both painting patterns free-hand and then furnace-firing the finished pots. "We need to learn to screen-print to make the designs all the same." Bree rubbed off some excess paint from something she had drawn.

"I think I've heard that somewhere before." Taylor was drawing a horse, but it lacked the real feel of what she saw in her head. She'd also advocated getting a printing press to get consistent screen-printed pictures on their pots. There were several things they could do if they could find the equipment used and had the space to work. Like their house, this shop was becoming overcrowded, and they'd both been thinking about that huge barn.

They chatted and discussed the land for most of the morning. They were going to see it again after they dropped off Jack. The little boy was playing with his shop toys, staying busy and out of the way in a corner, and oblivious to their conversations. They only had a couple more hours as Taylor's shift started at three that day. She was working only three hours, but it was three hours during the dinner shift. She'd have to meet Bree and the children over at Gretchen's, and they both hoped she wouldn't be asked to stay over the three hours she had agreed to.

The road hadn't improved since the last time they were at the property. In fact, the hill seemed even more rutted, as they bounced over it, carefully picking their way towards the barn.

"Careful there, or we'll go into that swamp," Bree warned, alarmed at how close to the edge of the drive the hill went. "This wasn't well thought out." She grabbed the grip on the door in a way that showed she feared for her life. It had rained since they'd last been here, washing out the last of the snow in the woods and causing the swamp to rise alarmingly close. It edged the driveway in some places.

"I don't think this hill is natural. It isn't that hilly over here. I'm guessing someone put a lot of dirt here, maybe to keep people out, and over time it became part of the driveway."

"Stupid idiots," she murmured under her breath, relieved when they made their way back down the other side and the overgrown yard came into view. A car was sitting in front of the house, waiting for them.

"Mr. Davidson?" Taylor said, holding out her hand to shake the realtor's hand. "I'm Taylor Moore." She turned proudly to Bree and said, "This is my wife, Bree."

"How do you do?" he asked politely. He was certain they couldn't afford the parcel of land he was offering for his client. They'd already indicated they would want to have a percentage off, but now that he had seen the overgrown yard, he understood why. Still, the barn was standing, and he could work that into something positive.

They walked around where they could. The weeds kept them from getting anywhere near the falling down house, front or back. The path to the barn was the same as before.

"A development company has bought the parcel behind you and intends to build very nice homes. That will only improve the value of this parcel," he pointed out.

Bree and Taylor exchanged a look and were hard-put not to laugh. Was this guy related to the banker? He was clearly worried about his commission.

"There is so much work here," Bree said pointedly to Taylor, but so the realtor could hear. "And there is no house." She sounded every inch the aggrieved housewife. "It will take forever to get any of this cleared."

"Yeah—careful there. Isn't that poison ivy?" Taylor asked the realtor, who had walked into a patch of the three-leaved plant.

He nodded and walked along with them, across the little patch of land that was clear. "Looks like kids have made this their own little hideaway," the realtor said prissily when he saw the inside of the barn. He'd seen the

tire tracks deeply imbedded in the hill, both sides. Getting his sedan down the driveway had been a miracle.

"Hope they don't burn it down," Taylor said with concern. It was obvious the intruders were lighting fires on a concrete slab inside the barn. With all that hay, it was a real concern. She wondered how bad the house actually looked that the kids hadn't bothered to dig through the weeds and use that. She supposed the barn was the path of least resistance.

"Maybe I should get the sheriff out here."

"Look, Mr. Davidson, we are interested in the property but not for the asking price—" Bree started.

"He did offer a ten-percent reduction—" the realtor countered.

"Yeah, that's not going to work. It's not enough," Taylor interrupted him now, doing it with relish. She was always amazed how many people showed their manners by interrupting, and she'd not liked that he did that to Bree. "Tell your seller that if he can meet our price, he'll have a quick sale."

"Then you're ready to put in an offer?" he asked eagerly, unconsciously rubbing his hands together greedily.

He wasn't aware they knew what the taxes were on the place, as well as the last evaluation. While his price would have been fair if the house was intact, their twenty-five percent that they were asking off made it a deal for them.

"Yes, we'll put in an offer, and it's not negotiable. If he would give us a further discount for say ... cash?" She left that hanging.

"You have the cash to pay for this property?"

She nodded but didn't elaborate. She and Bree had agreed to use this tactic but only as a bargaining chip.

"And you'll put that in writing?"

"Absolutely. Do you have the paperwork?" She nearly laughed as he raced to his car and pulled out a standard contract for an offer from his satchel in the passenger seat. If the seller agreed to the price, they'd be the owners of 10.3 acres with a stream that bordered it on one side, draining the swamp, woods, and a standing field of hay out across the other creek. Behind their house and barn was another woods and beyond that was a large field, a former pasture, with a future development that would indeed increase their property value once they put a decent house on it.

Taylor and Bree both looked over the contract, adding the conditions of a further percentage off for a cash offer. Once the offer was accepted, they would have the money put in an escrow account while the land was surveyed, buildings inspected, and the property was checked for liens, including for the past due taxes (that Bree and Taylor already knew about)—that everything was in proper order. By the time both women signed and the realtor hurried off, they knew they had to get back to town for Taylor's shift.

"Are we nuts?"

"Yes, we are," Bree agreed, hugging her wife but looking around the weed-covered area with ideas in her head.

* * * * *

"What do two broads know about buying land?" Barry asked as they told Gretchen about the land they were looking to buy. They had been keeping their voices low so the children wouldn't overhear them, but not low enough that he hadn't heard them.

"Barry," Gretchen hissed, embarrassed at her friends being called broads.

"I would appreciate it if you called us women, even females, and if you really can't think of a proper word, girls or even chicks," Taylor put in drolly, looking directly into Barry's eyes. She knew he hated that. And, sure enough, with a scoffing noise of annoyance through his nose, he turned away and fiddled with the TV channel changer, turned up the volume, and snubbed them.

"Well, we don't have an agreement yet, but it would be nice if we got it," Bree said to their friend, ignoring her husband, who they all thought was a jerk. He didn't help out at the market, either, and instead went along to make sure how much Gretchen made, pocketing his *share*.

They chatted a little while until the kid's bedtime approached. Gretchen walked them out, helping to put seat belts on them. "You let me know what happens. That's so exciting," she told them as she watched Bree get behind the wheel of the van and Taylor get into the Jeep. She reluctantly went into her own house, wishing Barry wasn't home as she heard how loud the volume was on the television.

CHAPTER EIGHT

The seller tried to counter their offer that next week, raising their final price to more than they were comfortable with. They reluctantly countered with a slightly higher amount than their previous offer, sure he wouldn't accept. But, after a weekend of thinking it over, he did accept, demanding they put the money in escrow immediately so the process could get started.

"Oh, my God," Bree said, getting off the phone. She'd agreed to writing a check the following day, when the realtor would pick it up and drop off more paperwork at the same time. She had to go to the bank to transfer the amount from their savings to checking.

"I know, right?" Taylor said in awe. She'd sat next to Bree, listening as soon as she realized it was the realtor on the phone. It was late for them, for a week night, and they'd just put the children to bed.

"I can't believe he accepted our offer. That leaves us some wiggle room with the extra money."

"Extra money?" She frowned. "What extra money?"

"We didn't have to spend all our savings. We are going to need a lawn mower and a few other tools."

"Not to mention the new kiln."

"What new kiln?"

"Aren't you going to want a bigger one to fire pots? We'll have room for it in that barn."

"And we'll have to run the electric out there," she reminded her.
"We have so much work to do."
"I don't mind."
"Me, either."

They hugged each other hard, excited and a little bit scared at what they had just agreed to do.

It was late before they went to bed, as they talked over so many ideas and plans, and it kept them awake with their thoughts as they lay there in the dark. They resolved not to share the good news until the sale was finalized and they'd told the kids.

"It's going to be hard not to say anything to anyone."
"We did already tell Gretchen."
"Yeah, but we told her we were just looking. She doesn't know we have anything."
"We are going to have to ask Vinnie for some help to clear that lot."
"Well, escrow is what? A month?"
"At least, although sometimes for cash they can hurry that up, I heard. I do want the property lines marked clearly."

There was just so much to think about and discuss, and, naturally, they were excited. It was a while before either of them dozed off.

* * * * *

Bree transferred the money over into checking first thing the next morning. She went into the bank to do it, in a way wishing they had a computer to do it online but also grateful they didn't. Having never banked online, it just sounded like people had problems with how easy things had become and didn't do things like they used to with all these conveniences. She put a little extra into their checking account for some things they'd like to buy. "I'm going to be writing a large check from this account," she warned the cashier, asking her to note that on their account. "We are buying some land." She knew the teller didn't care, but she didn't want any problems with the check clearing, plus to brag a little to someone. She wanted no issues to arise with the money being put in escrow. She didn't see their banker, glancing towards his closed office door, but, remembering the credit union, she went there next. Jack was on her hip as she opened a joint checking account for her and her wife.

"Your wife can come in any time to give ID and sign the papers." The accounts manager told her helpfully, not turning a hair over a lesbian couple opening an account with them. The woman seemed happy to have them as members, giving Jack a lollipop to entertain him as Bree filled out

the paperwork. Bree loved how they treated her at the credit union, a totally different vibe than the bank. She texted Taylor to stop by and sign her part of the paperwork after work.

The realtor needed their signatures on his paperwork when he picked up the check but would be by well after Taylor got home from work. He had sounded so anxious, almost strangled, when he had called to arrange this, but Bree didn't care. They were going to buy that land. Swamp or not, it was going to be their home, and she was eager to get started, eager to tell their friends and family about it. Keeping it to herself was going to kill her as they waited for it to get through escrow.

* * * * *

The realtor was very nice to them, despite the children chasing around the apartment until Bree finally sent them to their rooms. They'd eaten their dinner and were just running off excess energy.

"I'm sorry. Usually they are better behaved." Taylor glanced up from the paperwork she was reading, signing where needed.

"I'm sure they are." He'd judged them over the small cramped apartment and too many children the moment he'd walked in, but it wasn't any of his business. He just wanted his now tiny commission and to be done with it. "Here ... here ... and here." He pointed out the signature lines.

"There are some weird terms and conditions in this state," Taylor said. She didn't completely trust this guy, and the print was rather small.

He nodded. "The state does try to protect the land owners."

Bree signed, too, and handed him the check made out to the escrow company. She'd put the document number on the check, too. He looked at it almost suspiciously, checking that both their names were on it before putting it in his breast pocket. He just hoped it was legitimate and these two weren't trying something. It didn't look like they could afford the land, much less this overcrowded apartment. Still, he put on a smile and told them to call him if they had any questions.

"Oh, my God," Bree exclaimed as she closed the door on the man.

"Oh, my God is right. What have we done?" Taylor wondered aloud, looking at her wife with wide eyes. That had been a large chunk of their money that constituted years of savings, even before they had started fostering children and making their pots.

"We've taken a helluva chance," Bree told her.

* * * * *

"Let's go out to the property again," Bree suggested a couple of days later, unable to hold the excitement in anymore and feeling like she was going to burst. They'd tried to work hard, making pots and planning shows, signing up for extra ones now, as they knew they needed more money for renovations. But keeping busy for the anticipated shows hadn't stopped either of them from obsessing over the property.

"Need to see that it's real?" Taylor asked knowingly. She too felt antsy and was dying to hear from the realtor. They had been warned escrow could take the full month, but they wanted to know *now*.

"Well, I need to do something."

"Why don't we start designing the house?"

"Because until we know it's our land, I don't want to get my hopes up."

"Yeah, I know how you feel."

Still, they drove the Jeep out to the property, going down Restlawn Highway to the driveway. It looked as overgrown as ever, and, if they didn't know what it contained, they would have assumed, like anyone else who drove past the turn-off, that it was just a drive for some farmer to get to his fields or another backroad in the county. Across the highway was just such a road, and this could have been the continuation of it.

This time, though, they encountered some of the interlopers who had made the ruts. As Taylor stopped to engage her four-wheel drive at the base of the hill, several young men on motorbikes, some teens on BMXs, and even one guy on an ATV came racing over the crest, some of them airborne, before rushing down the hill, straight at the Jeep.

"What the hell!?" Bree yelled.

"Holy crap!" Taylor yelled at the same time and rolled down her window talk to some of the riders.

"This isn't open for four-wheeling," a young men said in a belligerent voice.

"Hey, could you do me a favor?" Taylor asked pleasantly, resisting the urge to smack the mouth behind that snide voice.

"What?"

"Let your friends," she nodded to the ten or so guys and one girl on the various bikes, "know that this place has been sold and it will be off limits soon to this." She gestured at their bikes.

"Yeah? Who says?" another asked, in an equally challenging tone.

"The new owners," she said, gesturing to herself and her wife. She waved and put the Jeep into first gear, driving on as she rolled up the window. The bikes got out of her way.

"Nothing like meeting the neighbors," she said to Bree with a little grin as she concentrated on the road for any stragglers. That blind top was something she would take out as soon as she legally could. She glanced in the rearview mirrors at the kids intently discussing something, glaring, and gesturing towards the Jeep.

"There is so much to do," Bree marveled, wondering how much a weed whacker would cost. Living in an apartment, she'd never had a need of one, but they still hadn't seen the house except to ascertain that it was falling down.

"I can't wait," Taylor answered, rubbing her hands together and then starting to crack her knuckles as she thought about all she wanted to do.

"What first?"

"Oh, we get ..." she began, pointing to things she wanted to take care of and plans she had. "What do you think of ..." They went on for a good hour as they discussed things, looking at the jungle they had just bought. Waiting to do it, though, the patience involved, might just kill them.

* * * * *

Every free moment they had, and a few that weren't quite free, Bree and Taylor talked about the what ifs, the whens, and how much everything would cost. They talked above, around, and without the children. They told no one—not their friends, families, or, in the case of Taylor, her employer, about what they had done. They knew it was a gamble, and they might have just bought a swamp. They were on pins and needles about the whole process when the call from the realtor finally came in one day around mid-morning.

"Um, I have bad news," he told them, swallowing audibly.

Bree, who had recognized the number and was ready to burst with excitement, felt her heart fall. Immediately, she thought something was wrong with the money, the property, or who knew what. "What?"

"Someone burned the house down," he informed her, as though it was the direst of news.

As neither she nor Taylor had actually seen the interior of the house and had planned to tear it down anyway, this wasn't unwelcome news. She held her tongue, though. "And the barn?"

"The fire department arrived and managed to save the barn, but I suppose you are going to want to back out of the deal?" He sounded convinced they had already made up their minds, and he had lost his small commission.

"I'm going to need to discuss this with my wife. Can we get back to you? Wait—was it insured?"

"No, other than property insurance, I don't think he had the structures insured. I'll look into it, of course."

"Thank you. I'll call you back after I've discussed it with my wife."

Bree wondered what that meant for them. They weren't buying the place for that dilapidated old house, anyway. She sighed with relief that the barn was safe, but now what? She looked over at Jack who was playing with the cat they had finally allowed in the apartment on his insistence and only for short periods of time, then glanced up at the clock. It was a little early, but she would have to take Jack to school and get lunch at the diner. Maybe Taylor could talk to her between customers, and she could have a meal she hadn't cooked herself.

"Oh, that's actually good news," Taylor assured her when she heard about the fire. She poured her wife a coffee from the endless coffee pot she carried around the diner.

"How so?"

"We may be able to pay even less." She thought for a moment. "You know, I bet those guys finally broke into the house and did us a favor. Want me to call back, or would you like to?"

"You better, I don't think I could do it with a straight face."

"Honey, you don't do anything straight," she quipped, walking off, leaving her wife blushing and grinning. Bree looked down at the BLT Taylor had brought her and sipped thoughtfully on her root beer as she checked out her wife in her uniform. She glanced at the coffee, wondering if she would float if she drank that, too.

The realtor was not happy to hear they wanted to readjust the agreement with the owner over the loss of the house on the property. The owner wanted to unload this parcel. It was a matter of timing because the taxes were plaguing him, but, at the same time, he didn't want to lose money on the deal. He could try to claim the fire on his insurance, but it wasn't likely to result in any sort of payout. These women were the first and only legitimate offer they had received in a very long time. The developer behind them had considered it a swamp and not entertained it at any price, despite his offers. The realtor tried to entice them with how much the place was going to be valued at with the housing development, but Taylor wasn't falling for that tactic.

"Well, we are still interested in the property, but, without a house, it's not worth nearly as much as we agreed on," Taylor told him, sounding convincing. "I do hope he still wishes to sell. Otherwise, we are going to

have to ask that our money be returned from escrow. We entered into this in good faith."

Neither the realtor nor the owner wanted to lose that money; it represented a nice chunk of change for the relatively useless parcel that had sat empty and unsold for years. The land survey was already in progress, the money paid out by the owner in anticipation of the escrow money he would be receiving. The realtor had counted on his small percentage for a property no one wanted.

Taylor wasn't surprised when an addendum was made to their agreement to compensate for the loss of the house. She would bet the owner hadn't been there in years, and the realtor hadn't told him it was a fallen down corpse of a house. They signed the approval for the addendum, and, two weeks later, they had the paperwork showing they were now the owners of 10.3 acres of land. Now, they could enjoy their country living lifestyle, like the original ad for the place mentioned.

The survey markers went right down the edge of the driveway along the barbed-wire fence between them and the farm next door. They continued into the woods, the pink or orange flags showing the property line across the back and down in a straight line until it crossed the creek and followed along the far side. It clearly showed they owned the creek, and the survey also showed they owned a section of the field their new neighbor had been cutting hay from for years, all the way back to the highway out front. On both sides of the woods, both sides of the field, the person or persons making the survey painted along a tree on each side, the flags running across the field on their stakes. Along with the packet of paperwork, a check was included for the difference in their addendum agreement for the loss of the house.

"We're going to have to walk this someday," Taylor told her wife with glee as she anticipated doing just that. They were looking at all the paperwork together, sitting in the Jeep.

"I can't wait," Bree agreed, excited and afraid all at once. "Now what?"

"Now, we get to work."

It wasn't like they hadn't worked, having done two weekends of smaller shows with their pottery since they'd entered escrow. Taylor's employer hated that she wasn't available on some weekends, but she had explained she had another job and children, and she worked so much during the week he couldn't expect so much from her. Now, she would have even fewer hours to offer him, depending on what she could manage.

CHAPTER NINE

"You bought what?" Vinnie asked, wondering what her friends had gotten themselves into. She paused while eating her lunch at the diner. She'd enjoyed sharing it with Bree before Taylor got a few minutes and joined them.

"We bought a parcel of land and need your advice as to what equipment we should rent to clear it," Taylor told her.

"You want to clear-cut the land?" she asked frostily. She hated when people did that, and her friends knew it.

"No, but we would like to be able to see where our house should go."

"You're going to build a house?" Vinnie wondered where her friends had gotten the money. She'd seen their crowded apartment and knew how thrifty they were. Suddenly, they had money for land and a home?

"We were thinking more along the lines of a prefab," Taylor answered. "We can show you what we're looking at when we have more time. So, we should probably rent a backhoe and get rid of all the brush and undergrowth, right?"

"Ohhh, talk dirty to me." Vinnie smiled. They were talking her language. "You need a brush cutter for that, babes. A backhoe is for digging. Or you can use the front-end loader to move stuff. I suppose you could knock down brush with it, but it's really not the right machine for the job."

"See, that's why we want you to come out and advise us," Bree said. She couldn't wait to get started.

"Okay, okay. When do you want me to come out, and where is this paradise you're telling me you bought?" She returned the grin. She could see how excited her friends were about their purchase, and she wouldn't take that away from them.

They told her where it was, and she narrowed her eyes, trying to remember what was out there. She knew a lot of addresses by heart around town. It was her job to know, but she couldn't recall the exact spot. "Hmm ... wait a minute. Did you buy a swamp?"

They both nodded enthusiastically. "Hey, before you get upset with us ..." Taylor raised her hand to stop her before she could berate them for their purchase, "we have plans. And there is a house—or was—and an excellent barn that we can turn into a pottery studio."

"Okay. Now, the barn makes sense, but what do you mean 'was' on the house?"

"It just burned down, right before we closed." Taylor told her matter-of-factly.

"You didn't have anything to do with that, did you?" Vinnie asked suspiciously, trying to hide her smile that would tell them she was kidding.

"Hell, no." Taylor grinned as she shook her head at her friend. "There are a bunch of kids that hang out there, and we told them we had bought the property. Maybe this was their protest."

"That's the dirt track they use to jump their bikes," Vinnie said musingly, remembering the property.

"You knew of it?" Bree asked, surprised.

"Yeah, but it's pretty sketchy. Don't be surprised if they don't give it up easily."

"Will you come out?"

"Yeah, I'll be there," she promised.

* * * * *

There was an equipment rental in town, and Taylor rented the promised back-hoe. She had an idea, and, while she didn't have the whole day free to work out at the property, she would do what she could. She and Bree had discussed what they wanted in a house but felt they couldn't do anything if the site for it wasn't clear of overgrowth. Whether Vinnie helped or not, they needed to knock down all the stray saplings and tall weeds before anyone from the prefab places could come out to give them a quote for building a house.

"So, you rented one." Vinnie met Taylor on the driveway just below the steep hill. She and Taylor were watching the rental company backing their truck carefully down the long driveway. There was no way they were climbing the hill, and they had left the backhoe after giving Taylor a basic run-down on operating the machine. She was prepped with several gas cans in the back of the Jeep and ready to get started.

Vinnie had brought something she called a brush cutter.

"Yep, didn't know what you were bringing," Taylor said as she gestured to the odd machine on Vinnie's flatbed trailer. She, too, hadn't wanted to attempt the sketchy hill.

"You know, that isn't natural," the dark-haired woman said to her friend. She gestured to the hill they were standing near.

"Yeah, I thought that, too." She looked at the ruts in the road, and, while she'd been over it a couple of times now, she still didn't trust that blind top. She had thought to at least flatten the top edge off with the backhoe. She now saw some deeper ruts that weren't there before. They could only have come from the fire engine that came to put the fire out. That must have been spooky as hell in the dark. She inwardly shuddered at the thought of a fire engine toppling off that hill into the swamp.

"Let's see what you have for me," Vinnie said, climbing the hill on foot with Taylor following. "Where's Bree?"

"She's throwing some pots. I got all those painted that she had thrown the other day. They're in the kiln, and she'll come out when she's fired those and made some more."

"Amazing what you two can make in that small shop." Vinnie grabbed some weeds to pull herself up and nearly fell over when the weeds suddenly pulled out of the ground. "God, what were they thinking, making this a driveway?"

Once at the top, they looked out over the property. To their immediate right was the open field of one of their farming neighbors. The rusting barbed-wire fence held in cows that were placidly chewing their cuds. Two of the cows stopped for a moment at the appearance of humans, watching them warily but returning to their chewing, along with the others. Below and to their left was the swamp. Several trees inside it looked like they were rotting, and all along the edge were tamaracks, their needles waiting to drop into the water. There were all sorts of other trees, as well, many Taylor knew she couldn't name. In front of them were the burned out remains of a small house. It must have been bigger than Taylor had thought it was, but it was still smaller than what they would have needed. To the left of that was the barn, and she could see where the green plants at its edge had burned before the fire engine had arrived and put out the flames. Thank goodness, as that barn was important to their future business. It was still hard to see anything beyond the overgrown foliage.

Vinnie let out a little whistle and gestured with her chin. "You realize that this is a pretty good-sized plot there?"

"I guessed," Taylor agreed, wondering where to start.

"Okay, I'm going to come up here with my brush cutter. I'm so glad I didn't bring the brush hog."

"Isn't a brush hog what we need?" All these names for machines were confusing. She wasn't confident she could run the back-hoe, especially with the small amount of instruction she'd had.

"No, a brush hog is just a fancier term for a large lawn mower. That's why I brought the brush cutter. It will mow down that smaller stuff in no time." She gestured to the weeds and smaller trees that were popping up all over their yard. "I can give you two days, and I'll see what mischief I can come up with for you there."

"We'll pay you—"

"You will not," Vinnie interjected shortly as they walked back down the hill. "That's what friends are for. You can pay for the fuel, but my little cat doesn't drink too badly." She indicated the machine on her trailer. It was a CAT with a large mulcher on the front that spun and could gnaw smaller trees and brush up in no time. Not all of them would be chewed up; some would just be knocked down, but they would rot on the forest floor and clear the way for other growth. She quickly started removing the chains that held the machine to the bed of the trailer with Taylor helping her. Slowly she backed it off the trailer and set the brake, turning it off.

"You good with that?" she indicated the back-hoe as Taylor hesitantly got up on it and sat carefully in the seat.

"Well, I'll just go careful at first," she said.

"Tell you what, I'll clear the way around over there," she indicated the growth around the very edge of the swamp, "and you can start digging that." She pointed to the hill on the driveway. And then start moving it towards there." She pointed towards the swamp, then towards the overgrowth she was going to clear. "We'll see how much of that we can knock down."

Since she had no clue of a better way to attack the problems, Taylor agreed and started up the machine, gingerly sliding it to test the levers as the rental agent had shown her. Confident enough to start, she drove it up and over the hill then down the other side, following Vinnie, who probably should have been driving the machine instead of her. Taylor wished the man had mentioned needing ear covers because the sound of both

machines was deafening. She shrugged and turned the machine back towards the hill. On her first attempt, she got almost nothing in the scooper, as the road was well-packed by time, riders, weather, and gravity. Still, what little she'd removed she dumped to the side nearest the swamp.

Vinnie was making some headway, though. As she dug into the large yard, she turned on the rotating heads and adjusted her ear coverings, which were Bluetooth and noise-cancelling. She could easily hear her favorite songs from her phone above the loud machines. She loved using the brush cutter. It was amazing to watch it grind young trees and brush into mulch, even though it did leave some large sticks behind. Clearing out a path towards the swamp, she continued over to what would become her friends' front yard, making wide swaths and avoiding the larger trees except to lift the teeth up to grind away low-hanging branches or to clear dead branches out. She wasn't sure what her friends would choose to do with their land, but she was amazed at these two. Buying this land had taken grit, and she would bet even they didn't realize its potential ... yet.

Finally figuring out the hill was too compact to try to scoop up, Taylor turned the backhoe around to use the digging tool. She set the legs carefully and hesitantly scraped with the bucket. Getting bolder, she dug a little deeper, a little harder, and moved some of the dirt to the side. Once started, the earth seemed to move effortlessly, as she dug a deeper hole and began to widen the hole to the edge. Before long she had built another hill beside the one that was their driveway, until it was too tall for her put any more on top. The hole in the hill had become a crater, but she didn't stop, caving down more and more of the sides and creating another hill beside the huge one until she was nearly hemmed in. She finally pulled up the legs that made the arm of the hoe so sturdy and turned the backhoe around to push at the edge of the smaller hill she had made. She pushed the loose dirt on top of the mulch Vinnie had created, burying it several inches deep as she pushed it further and further out towards the edge of the swamp. She only went as far as Vinnie had cut, not trusting she wouldn't get the backhoe stuck on the edge of the swamp.

When she finished clearing the first two hillocks, she started more, making a rather significant gouge in the hill, moving forward but not confident to dig higher. She began to dig along the edge, making more hillocks and moving the dirt further into the woods and yard where Vinnie had cleared.

Vinnie cut along the path towards the barn, widening it with every sweep. She exposed what was left of the house, cringing when she hit real boards or concrete. The sound was definitely different from it mulching

weeds or trees. Pulling back, she slowly cleared the brush from in front of the house, then started around it. When that was done, she decided to clear around the barn. There must have been quite a garden there at one time, if the vegetation was anything to go by. There weren't as many stray trees in this section as there were in the front yard. Whoever had built here had really wanted their privacy. She wondered at what they had intended for the land that was now her friend's acreage.

The cut in the hill was becoming dicey to maneuver around, and Taylor desperately wanted to ask Vinnie's advice. But neither Vinnie nor her amazing machine were in sight, and Taylor was afraid to seek her out in the woods. What if she didn't see her and that machine came at her? She shuddered at the thought of what such a machine could do to a human.

Taylor was getting more confident in what she was doing, digging along the side of the hill. She wished she felt she was doing things right. She was afraid someone would try to climb the hill, and here she was digging on the other side, out of sight. She had to stop thinking like that, concentrate on the job at hand, and get it done. They only had this machine for a couple of days. She hadn't wanted to pay too much money out, even if they had gotten some of their payment for the property back because that money could go to other things they needed for their new place.

The side of the cut she was making was getting higher as she dug along the hill. It worried her that it would crumble into the machine she was using to loosen the soil. She kept chickening out, using the arm to dig deeper, making a cave as it crumbled into the hole, time and again, so she could use the front-end loader to clean it out and spread it out over the lawn and towards the swamp. She was pleased to see how much she had done, but this hill was bigger than she had thought. She'd had a distorted view from the Jeep when she drove over it. She was now working on the theory that someone must have dug some dirt out of the swamp, made a couple of dump piles right on the driveway. Then time, the elements, and a lot of people driving over it had compacted it into a part of the environment. But it hadn't belonged here, and, as she kept digging carefully, she marveled at what kind of equipment someone had used to make this large pile of dirt.

As she turned the machine around for the millionth time, she saw Vinnie sitting and watching her from the CAT. She waved and turned off the backhoe, setting the front-end loader down on the ground.

"Hey, what's up?" she asked. Her ears felt odd with the absence of machine noise, and the ringing in her ears made her feel like she was talking inside a tunnel.

"I'm going to have to go for a few hours. My foreman texted me that there is a problem with one of my accounts."

"Oh, that's too bad," she said, walking towards the CAT. She glanced back at the hill. "I don't think I'd drive over that if I were you."

"I don't intend to. You've destabilized it, but if you continue on like that you'll come through the other side," she teased, hinting at a hole dug to China. "Seriously, though, you have to bring down that higher stuff so you don't have it falling in on you."

Taylor looked back at the large hill and appreciated what Vinnie said was true. From this perspective she got a whole different view of what she had accomplished. She wished she'd had Vinnie's great advice before she'd made it look like that. It was very intimidating.

"Why didn't you drive up and dig down?" Vinnie asked, curious, as she got off the CAT.

"I didn't feel confident then," she admitted, walking with her up the hill. The road there was still covered in deep ruts. As they neared the top, Taylor was pleased to see Bree in the van just coming up the drive. It was a relief because her imagination had driven her to thoughts of someone coming up over that hill that didn't have a complete other side, now. She gave her a wave, and it was returned.

"Well, I'll say a quick goodbye to Bree and be back when I can. Don't touch my CAT."

"I won't touch your pussy," Taylor quipped and laughed as Vinnie blushed. Her friend had been looking for a girlfriend for a long time.

"I'll have to get you for that," she promised. "Maybe I'll bury you in your swamp."

"You can try."

Taylor laughed as she watched her hurry to her truck and unhook the trailer in record time. As good as Taylor was with handling her own trailer, Vinnie was better at unhooking the much larger and heavier trailer from her truck.

Bree drove the van up past the truck, and Vinnie pulled forward to get clear of the trailer and then expertly reversed down the entire length of the driveway. Taylor was impressed. She gestured to Bree to back up and park as she walked down to her wife to greet her.

"Hi there, you."

"I thought you might like a sandwich," Bree said, holding up a Subway bag.

"Oh, gawd, yes. Remind me never to come out here without water, too."

"I brought this," she said, holding up a cup of what she hoped was Dr. Pepper.

"Did you eat already?"

"Nope, this is mine," she said, picking up another bag and cup.

"You have clay on your nose," Taylor informed her, leaning in for a peck on the lips.

"Oh, damn. And I went into Subway looking like this." She rubbed her nose with the back of her hand, the one holding the bag so it banged against her chin.

"Missed it." Taylor teased her as they carefully walked up the hill towards the barn.

"Why'd I have to park there?"

"Because I've been digging this hill and getting rid of it."

"Why?"

She explained the hill wasn't natural and getting rid of it would be a good thing, with all the kids that played here. "It will discourage them from coming out here if the hill is gone. It will really upset them." She discussed some other plans she had for their place, hoping Bree would agree with her. She'd had even more thoughts while working on the backhoe.

"How can I get all that hay out of the barn?" Bree wondered, looking towards the barn.

"I bet Vinnie has a tractor we could borrow. Maybe she might be interested in it herself."

"Will we need it?"

"Not right now, I don't think. We can ask her when she comes back."

They discussed some of their plans, and Bree was amazed to see around the house site, see the burn damage and all the terrain Vinnie had exposed.

"Oh, wow, look how much she did!"

The comment, though innocent, stung Taylor a little. "I did a bit myself here, too." She gestured towards the gaping hole that was now lopsided and over towards where she had spread the dirt.

"Oh, wow," Bree said, skirting the hole and walking down the far side.

"I have to get over to the other side and start pushing that towards the swamp to even things out."

"Why did they put this here?" Now she could see the hill for what it was, she could tell it wasn't formed naturally.

Taylor told her what she and Vinnie had talked about, and they went to sit on a downed tree Vinnie had left un-mulched.

"This would be nice with a picnic table and benches," Bree commented, biting into her BLT.

"Ohhh, this is nice." Taylor took a long drink of her soda before biting into her Teriyaki chicken.

They discussed what they could see, amazed how much Vinnie had exposed and how much more there was to do.

"The more she cuts, I bet, the more we find on this place."

"That reminds me ... I should text her about that tractor." Taylor quickly shoved the last of her sandwich in her mouth and started typing on her smart phone. She soon sent a couple of short messages to her friend, asking about the hay in the barn and either borrowing a tractor or renting one.

"What are you going to do now?" Bree asked, watching as her wife stood up and stretched.

"Lunch is over, and, if I'm not mistaken," she said, checking the time on her phone, "I have a couple of hours I can still work. I'd like to get through that hill so no one tries to drive it on the far side."

"Good idea, or we will have to put up barriers."

"What are you going to do?"

"I think I'm going to explore for a while, see what I can find." She kissed Taylor and took their food wrappers with her to do start her exploration.

She had been looking forward to it, although she'd worried somewhat about bugs. Ticks especially grossed her out. Still, she was eager to find out more about this land they had bought. *Oh, my God, we own this!* she thought as she explored, wandering along the clearing Vinnie had cut in the undergrowth, which was now revealed to have once been a fairly large yard.

Taylor pulled herself back up on the backhoe with a groan. Her body really didn't want to keep working, and she knew she was going to pay for it in the morning. Still, her enthusiasm returned as she slowly cut away at the hill, moving forward towards the front where her Jeep and the minivan were parked. It was slow work, and she was surprised at how much she had moved when she finally broke through to the other side of the hill (not China) and piled the dirt into several hillocks to be spread out later. She extended the arm time and time again, scooping up as much dirt as the hoe would allow, until she could clearly see the vehicles on the other side. She actually felt a tinge of sadness when she had to back out of the passage to turn the backhoe around and use the front-end loader to push the hillocks aside. The dirt was really rich, and, if this was from the swamp, she was really sorry she couldn't use it for something.

Then, she thought of their friend Gretchen. This soil was probably like gold to someone who raised plants. She'd be surprised if Gretchen couldn't make use of at least some of it, and it would be great to help out a friend. She resolved to call her on the way home.

Once Taylor had cleared a passage wide enough for the machine to make its way through, she used the bucket to break up a trench all along the front of the hill so no one could drive over it any more. Slowly, she cut the passage wider, eating at the side as she had on the other and pushing the rich dirt farther and farther into the woods and over the lawns. She checked her phone and realized it was nearing 3 PM. They'd have to go home to meet the kids soon, or maybe Bree would and let her continue working on the hill. She'd known she couldn't work all day, but maybe Bree would let her work a bit longer.

She turned off the machine to call Bree when she saw her making her way across the weed-strewn path from the barn. "Hey, there. Are you going to get the kids, or should I?"

"I was just coming to ask you that very thing. Maybe we should talk to the school about letting them come out here on the bus on certain days so we don't have to stop work to go get them."

"Good idea. Explain that we bought a new place, and somedays the kids should ride a different bus."

They'd already determined the children didn't have to change schools, which had delighted them. It was best that they didn't have too many changes in their life, and school was very important to them all. Moving was going to be a big change, but they hoped the excitement of it would make the children enthusiastic.

"Yep." Bree was pleased they were on the same page.

"How long do you think it will take you to go pick them up?"

"Oh, ho. So, I'm the one that has to go pick them up?"

"Was hoping you didn't notice that," she admitted with a sly grin. "I'd go ... but I know how to work this," she gestured at the backhoe.

"I can't believe you did this much. Look at this!" Bree marveled. The passage was narrow, kind of scary, actually, as the mound of dirt could come crumbling down, but she could see that Taylor was breaking down the sides. "You have *got* to teach me how to do this."

"I would, really, but one of us has to go pick up the kids."

"Yeah, yeah, yeah. I'm going."

"Hey, invite Gretchen out. Surely, we could sell her some of this, or she could tell us if there is a market for it." She indicated the mounds of rich dirt she was spreading but still piled thick along the swamp and in the yard. She hadn't figured out how to pack it yet, and the backhoe's wheels went deep into the loose soil.

"That's a great idea!"

"Good. You can tell her it was yours."

While Bree headed off to get the kids, Taylor climbed into the backhoe and got back to work. She started it up and began ripping more of the dirt from the hillside and piling it into hillocks. Once, she scared herself when a small avalanche sent loose dirt down on her and covered part of the backhoe. She managed to back out of the passage, though, with little effort. Then she widened the drive a bit since she was getting so much loose dirt on the lawn, and the tires of the backhoe weren't enough to pack it down. She stopped after a while to take a breather, wishing she had brought a bottle of water. As she stood up, she pulled dirt from inside her shirt and brushed it from her seat. As she sat down, she patted the backhoe and said, "I won't tell Bree or Vinnie if you don't."

CHAPTER TEN

Taylor was relieved to see Bree return but jubilant to find out Vinnie was on the way.

"I got Gretchen on the phone, too, and she's bringing her truck." Bree gave her a sheepish grin as she released the kids from their car seats and they ran over to Taylor.

"Hi, there," Taylor greeted them from the top of the backhoe, turning it off in time to hear Vinnie's truck pulling down the drive. She was towing another trailer, this one with a Kubota tractor, and she was followed by a large truck. She frowned, watching her friend as she greeted the kids who were excited to find out they had bought a place. They were talking animatedly over each other and looking around.

"Where else was I going to take them?" Bree shrugged, and Taylor had to agree. They really didn't have babysitters set up to take over.

"Easy there, easy," Taylor warned them as they tried to climb up on the machine. "Yes, you will have your own bedrooms. A girls' room and a boys' room," she said in answer to one of the questions. She turned to her friend, shushing the children as Vinnie walked up.

"Hey, I brought my Kubota. I'm going to teach you two how to use the tines so you can get that hay out of the barn, into the truck bed, and wherever you want to stack any extra," Vinnie said. "That's Dan. He's going to take a load of hay to one of our properties when we get it full." She pointed to the truck trailing behind her.

They all watched, fascinated, as she unchained the tractor from the trailer and slowly backed it down the ramps. She removed the front-end loader and switched it with an attachment that had two long prongs like a forklift. Heading for the passage Taylor had cut across the much-diminished hill, she carefully drove through it with Bree and the children following along behind on foot.

Taylor got back up on the backhoe. If she was lucky, she could get a couple more hours of work done. It looked like it was going to take several days to move all this dirt with the front-end loader.

"Hey, mind if I give it a try?" a voice yelled at her from below.

Taylor had never met Dan before, but she guessed he probably had experience with machines like this. She nodded, slid out of the cabin, and gestured for him to go ahead. He easily climbed in, started the engine, shifted it into gear, and began to use the front-end loader to smooth out the hillocks she had been making. In no time at all, he was using the same front end to pat down the dirt along the driveway, stomping it down with not only the loader but the tires as he drove carefully. He set the legs down and then, using the arm of the scoop, quickly began to peck away at the hill, bringing down a lot of loose dirt from inside the hill. Taylor could easily see the difference between his confidence and level of expertise and hers. She watched and learned.

Once he was pushing dirt out into the swamp, she went to see what Bree and Vinnie were doing. She joined her kids on a hay bale pushed out of the way as they sat watching Vinnie teach their other mom how to work the tractor. The barn door was wide open, and they were moving the big round bales of hay out of the barn one by one.

"Okay, take it over to my truck, and then we will fill the trailers," Vinnie yelled over the sound of the tractor.

Taylor was envious, wanting to drive the tractor, too, as she watched her wife learn to move the levers and operate the large machine.

"Mom, why is she taking the hay out of the barn?" Melanie asked for them all.

"We want to clean the barn out so we can build a shop for making pots," she explained, not taking her eyes off the tractor.

"You already have a shop for making pots," the child pointed out with perfect logic.

"Yes, we do, but we want one out here."

The children were enthralled, and Taylor had to admit she was, too, as she watched Bree move the tractor carefully, carry one of those heavy

bales, then drive it across the mulched lawn, easily cutting through the deepening dirt and to the driveway again to make her way to the hill they were removing. Vinnie must have been explaining things as they made their way around the hill, along the drive towards the truck, because Bree didn't hesitate before raising the round bale and, with Vinnie giving her instructions, dumping it inside, causing the whole truck to bounce on its springs. Bree backed up the tractor and waited while Vinnie climbed down and opened the tailgate.

"We're going to live out here?" Bryan asked, now that the noise of the two machines was further away.

"Well, eventually," Taylor admitted. She looked around at all they had accomplished so far that day. So many of the weeds had been taken down and the mulcher sat in front of the house waiting for Vinnie. She watched the kids, who were staring wide-eyed at the machines, and saw Bree already heading back with the tractor and bringing Vinnie with her. Dan was removing dirt in record time and spreading it out. Taylor welcomed the break but felt a little left out. Someone had to watch the kids, after all, and she'd been at it all day.

Bree went to get a second round bale, and Vinnie left her to go start up the mulcher and return to the woods in the back of the house. Taylor kept the children from following the loud and dangerous tractor, and they continued to watch Bree and Dan at work.

Once the second bale was loaded, Dan parked the backhoe, tied down the bales to the truck bed, and took those bales to wherever they were going. As he started to back down the drive, he was stopped by another truck that had just arrived. They eased past each other and exchanged a few words before he continued backing out to the highway. Gretchen parked alongside the trailers and the backhoe and followed Bree as she returned to the barn for another load.

Fascinated by the machine that Vinnie was working, Taylor wasn't aware that Gretchen was there as she watched Bree head back to the barn another time.

"Hey, there!" Gretchen called out as she walked around the hill. "What is going on here?"

Taylor whirled around, her heart beating double-time as she acknowledged her friend in surprise. "Holy shit, you scared me!" She clutched her chest with a dirty hand.

"Mom, you said a bad word!" Bryan whined.

She stifled a grin. "You're right, Bryan. I did, and I'm sorry." Gretchen had heard not only what she'd said but Bryan admonishing her. She gave Gretchen a wink, and the woman tried not to laugh aloud.

"Bree's in the barn," she explained, ignoring her.

"Yeah, what is going on here?"

"This is the place we told you about, and we're trying to get it into shape. It's been abandoned a long time," she explained. "Didn't Bree tell you?"

Gretchen shook her head and glanced around, wondering how much had been done since they bought it. The rich dirt from the deconstructed hill looked dark in the afternoon sun. As it dried out completely, it was nearly black underneath, but the sun was turning it gray.

"Want some dirt for your plants?" Taylor asked, seeing her checking out their mess.

"Well, this stuff should go through a furnace before I put plants in it, and it's going to have to be run through a sifter," she explained musingly, talking her thoughts aloud as she looked at it.

"Can you do that, or is it too much?"

"I don't know if I brought enough baskets for that," she admitted, not having understood exactly what Bree wanted.

"Why don't we put the baskets in the seat of your truck and fill the bed with dirt?" Taylor offered.

"How much would that cost?"

"You can decide the first load. I trust you."

"I don't know if I can turn around ..." she began worrying.

"No, the drive isn't wide enough yet." She looked to where she had been spreading the dirt, how deep and loose it was. "You'd probably get caught if you tried. Can you back down it if we fill the back of your truck?"

"I don't know," she admitted, looking at the hill they'd been digging in and worrying her lip.

"All we can do is try."

After helping Taylor put the few baskets she'd brought into the cab of her truck, Gretchen found herself watching the four kids while Taylor used the backhoe to load dirt carefully into her truck bed. She put down the lift gate and watched Taylor start up the backhoe, carefully digging into the dirt and dumping it slowly in the bed of the truck, one bucket load at a time.

Bree waved when she brought another roll of hay around the hill and placed it on Vinnie's trailer.

"Do you need any hay?" Bree yelled over the noise of the two machines.

Gretchen shrugged, not knowing what to do with her friends' generosity. "I don't know how much of this I can afford," she admitted.

"Pay us later," Bree yelled. "I'll go get you some square bales, okay?" Gretchen nodded, stunned, as she watched Bree happily drive off.

"I don't know how I'm going to thank you two ..." she began hesitantly as Taylor turned off the backhoe and jumped down.

"What are friends for? You'll think of something, I'm sure. We have all this dirt that has sat here for years, and you can use it. We are going to need some flowers and such when we get this all taken care of, and I know you'll love to help us plan it."

Gretchen knew Taylor was right; she *would* love to help her friends get the plants situated. She didn't do landscaping, but she did know plants. "Is that Vinnie's?" she asked, pointing to the retreating tractor Bree was driving.

"Yeah, she brought it over. I rented this," she said, patting the backhoe, "but we only have it for a couple of days. Couldn't afford to go too overboard." She was watching the children try to climb up on Gretchen's truck. "Down," she ordered them.

"You two got a nice place here. So many possibilities," she said enviously as she looked around and thought about what she would do with it if she owned it.

"Your place is nice, too. Someday I'm going to want a greenhouse, and you can help us with that, too."

"Oh, yeah. So many possibilities," she repeated. She noted all the undergrowth that had been mulched down and the rich, black earth covering the front yard. "Do you know what you are going to do about the house?"

"We went to a couple of places to look at prefabs. We have sketched out what we want in a house." Taylor watched as the kids ran across the deep, black dirt, not caring in the least about getting their school shoes filthy. They were just so happy and healthy, and that was one of the many reasons Taylor was so happy to own this place.

"What's happened to the old house?"

"Someone burned it down when we were going through escrow. Thankfully, it didn't spread to the barn." She gestured towards the barn, where Bree was getting the hay. "Do you have a tarp?"

"I think I do in the backseat—I'll have to look. Hey, some of those burnt boards from your house might come in handy. People are always looking for things like that if you can see the burnt texture, but not the ash."

"Oh, yeah?" Taylor asked. "We were going to rent a garbage bin and put it all in there."

"Look at the wood first. There are all sorts of stuff on the internet about slightly charring wood, and then you use steel wool on it to make crafts. People buy that stuff up."

"I'll check it out," she promised and then yelled to the kids to watch out for Bree returning. They both turned to watch her carry long rectangle bales of hay on her tines that she placed on top of the dirt in the back of Gretchen's truck. One fell right off, and she backed away.

"Got it!" Taylor waved her wife off and then watched the kids who were still fascinated by the tractor.

"I'll help you," Gretchen said as the two of them lifted the heavy bale of hay onto the truck. "I don't think I can manage any more than this."

"Well, Vinnie is taking the round bales, but if you want more of the square bales, bring your truck by and we'll fill the bed."

"I should really take more of this dirt," she said musingly, running her fingers through the rich soil.

"I'll be sure to save you at least one truckload, but you'd better get a move on. I want this hill gone by tomorrow." She told her about the young guys and girls who had used it for their dirt bikes, BMX, and ATVs. "I don't want any accidents happening back here. One of them probably started the house on fire. Something was going on in the barn, too, and we just don't want them around."

"Funny, when we were kids, we would have done the same thing."

"Yep, we sure would," Taylor agreed, grinning. "And, we wouldn't have understood the adults telling us no, either."

They both laughed. Gretchen dug around in her now crowded back seat, found a tarp, and they spread it over the hay bales which stuck up over the heavy dirt. They finally got it battened down, using bungies, as they closed the tailgate.

"Now, don't move all of this until I make it back," she gestured to the pile of dirt Taylor was digging up.

"Then, you better hurry because I only have this machine one more day. We got a lot done today." She wiped her brow, which was slightly sweaty, and smeared dirt across it. Gretchen refrained from telling her.

"Thanks again. See you tomorrow." Gretchen got in her truck and started to back carefully down the drive. It was hard because she only had her side-view mirrors, the rearview mirror completely blocked by the load. She took it slow and finally made it the length of long drive.

Taylor knew she wouldn't get much more done that evening. She sighed as she resigned herself to leave moving more dirt to the following morning

CHAPTER ELEVEN

The kids were excited and asked Bree a million-and-one questions on the way back to their apartment.

"Do we really get to live there?"

"When are we moving?"

"Are we going to get a swing set?"

"Can I have a dog?"

"Can I have a cat?"

The kids had started as soon as they'd gotten in the car, throwing questions at her faster than she could even start to answer.

"What about the cat we already have?" Bree asked in return, trying to slow them down. She was following Taylor and wished she had thought to split the kids between the two vehicles. At least then she wouldn't feel so inundated.

"Can we have a second cat?"

"Let's just see where this goes," she said. "We'll see," garnered some groans. The kids had so many ideas, and she hoped the better ones would come together for them.

She was tired but triumphant after filling Vinnie's trailers with round bales. With only a few more remaining in the barn, they were left with several rectangular bales, the kind she remembered from when she was a kid that one person could handle.

"Tired?" Bree asked Taylor after they had both parked and were shepherding still-chatting children into the apartment.

"Exhausted." The dust and dirt on her face was in every crease, every laugh line, and in her pores. "I feel a sense of accomplishment, though."

"I feel we both are going to be needing showers. I'll wash up and start dinner if you'll shower, and then we switch off. "

"What about the kids? Do you see how filthy they are?"

"Oh, damn," she answered, having thought she had it figured out. "Well, I will have them wash up and then, after dinner, baths for everyone."

That sounded good to Taylor. She would have loved soaking in a bath but knew there was no time. It was an idea, though, for the house they would have built on their new place. It was still so exciting, and only her fatigue would allow her to sleep. They'd been making plans for weeks but wouldn't make decisions until they knew the land was theirs. Now those plans could become concrete when they talked to the builders.

* * * * *

"Okay, now twist," Taylor told Melanie, holding onto her length of hair. "Keep going ... and going," she encouraged the child until she had spun around at least six times. "Okay, halt." She quickly grabbed a hairband to wrap around the twisted hair, doubling it so it would hold the knot high on her daughter's head. "There you go," she said, giving her a slight swat on the butt. "All set."

Melanie preened in the mirror for a moment and smiled her thanks.

"Me, too!" Barbie demanded. "Me next!"

"Please?" Taylor prompted the enthusiastic little girl.

"Please," she lisped, contrite for not remembering her manners.

Taylor gathered all of Barbie's hair in her hand, pulling it back a couple of times to make sure she had it all. When she did, she said, "Okay, now twist," and watched the six-year-old mimic her sister's twirl, although not as gracefully. The girl nearly fell twice, but she finally got there.

"Okay, halt!" Taylor quickly tied it off and sent her on her way. She noticed Bryan waiting for her attention with a wistful look. "What, you want me to do your hair, too?"

Before she could touch his hair, he said, "Nuh-uh," and ran off.

"Come back here—let me at least comb it!"

"Hey, you kids!" Bree called from the kitchen, then the kids gathered around her. "I have your lunches made. And don't forget them on the bus. Today, you are taking the number twenty-nine bus out to the new

property. I have it all squared away with your school. Can you each remember that?" She looked in particular to Melanie who would make sure that Bryan got on the right bus. The other two nodded their heads solemnly, Barbie making sure that her twisted up hair remained in place. "Don't you two look nice," Bree told the girls. "Did you boys get your hair combed?" She'd heard Taylor and Bryan's interaction.

Bryan turned right around and ran into Taylor, who was approaching with a comb. "Let me get that, sport." She quickly finished, then did Jack's hair, since he was up and ready to start the day.

The two moms and their younger son watched the kids go off on the bus to school, waving until it was out of sight.

"Amazing to realize that someday they'll take the number twenty-nine bus from our new place, too, isn't it?" Bree murmured as Taylor put her arm around her.

Taylor nodded and sighed. "Well, I have the rental this one more day before they pick it up, so I'd better get ready to work."

"How you feeling?"

"A little sore, nothing that a couple of days of regular life won't take care of."

"Let's get breakfast for us and get on our way."

When they opened the apartment door, the orange cat slipped in, ready to be petted by his chosen humans.

"Think he'll like living out at our new place?" Taylor mused.

"Will we be stealing him from anyone?"

"I don't know. It's not wearing a collar, and I bet doesn't have a microchip."

"I don't know that we can afford to take it to the vet," she said as she popped some bread into the toaster. "Jack, honey, do you want cereal or toast and eggs?"

The four-year-old considered before answering, "Toast."

Bree grinned and cracked an extra egg into the scrambled eggs she was already making. Taylor quickly started washing the other kids' dishes and, by the time she was done, Bree had their breakfast on the table.

"We have to make appointments for the prefab people to come out and take measurements," Bree mentioned as she passed the orange juice to Taylor.

"I thought we'd narrowed it down to the one?" she asked as she poured everyone a glass.

"Yeah, but we should find out if the others can't build what we want, shouldn't we? Maybe it just wasn't in their brochures."

"That one I liked was almost exactly what we want."

"The one I liked was less expensive."

They both sighed, knowing they would have to compromise. Still, owning the land had been the first step.

Heading out, they realized they'd have to take two vehicles again. They hadn't yet arranged to have Jack picked up on the school bus for afternoon kindergarten and one of them would have to take him in and make sure it was okay.

When they got to the property, which took a good twenty-minutes from their apartment, the trailers Bree had filled the day before were there and empty again, and Vinnie was already there, hard at work.

"Amazing," Taylor said, admiring how much work her mulcher did. They could now walk from the area that would be their back door and see all the way to the woods, spot any wildlife that would walk under the trees there. Before, there had been no paths and no way to see anything but brush and unwanted trees. The amount of foliage the mulcher had taken down was phenomenal.

"Don't get too excited, there. You have your job to do again." Bree could see her wife liked the idea of using Vinnie's big toy.

"Why don't we switch off, so you learn how to use the backhoe and I learn how to use the Kubota?"

"Because I'm comfortable now with this, and, as much as I'd like to learn the backhoe, I want to get these jobs done."

Taylor agreed with her wife. Now, what to do with Jack ... "Hey, partner, you wanna ride with me?"

"Should you?" Bree fretted.

"It's either that or with you on the tractor."

They couldn't leave a four-year-old alone in the car or playing in the yard. They both knew it could only take a moment for him to disappear.

"Please be careful," Bree admonished her wife, even though she knew she would be.

Jack was really excited and yet scared to get up on the big machine. It was nothing like the little trucks that he loved to play with. Taylor had him sit on her lap as she worked around him. Occasionally, she held him one-handed as she used the bucket to pull down more and more dirt. They only had today to finish tearing down the hill, to get the dirt moved and smooth out the driveway, and she wanted it done. It was expensive to rent equipment like this. Taylor was relieved when, after a couple of hours, Bree had removed all the hay bales from the barn. Vinnie's trailers were full again, but there were several bales stacked over where their front yard would be. They were going to spread it around, after planting some grass, to protect the seeds from birds.

Once Bree had finished, she took Jack, and they sat back and watched as Taylor picked up her pace, more confident now she wasn't tending a small child. After a while, Bree caught Taylor's attention and pointed to her watch. As she watched them drive away, Taylor was secretly glad at not having to quit to take Jack to school. When she glanced at her own phone, she was surprised it was still early in the day. She watched around a load of dirt as Bree drove down the drive. When they had gotten there earlier, they had backed down the driveway, the whole length, so they could just drive out. As Bree was leaving, she waved to Gretchen who had just arrived. They both pulled to the right of the driveway in their respective paths, which was far too narrow to pass comfortably, but they managed.

"Hey, there!" Gretchen yelled over the backhoe's engine when she got to where Taylor was working.

"Hi! Want another load of dirt?"

She nodded rather than yell again.

It only took a few loads from the backhoe to fill it, and Taylor felt a lot more confident than the previous day. She pulled back and shut off the machine. Shaking her head at the sudden silence, she smiled at her friend and hopped down.

"Well, this is coming along nicely." She pointed at the hillside with large chunks taken out of it.

"Yeah, I hope to have it all done today."

"You are going to have a very thick and rich front yard."

"I'm going to put some along the side of the barn now, and maybe some in back of the house."

"What's with those bales?" Gretchen asked. "May I have them?"

"I think those are going to be used on the front lawn when we put some seed down. The hay is Bree's department; you'll have to ask her."

"I did bring a bag of lawn seed, I thought, in partial payment for the dirt, but I wasn't certain what kind of grass you were going to plant."

Taylor shrugged; grass was grass to her. "I have no idea. I am sure Bree and Vinnie will discuss it."

"What are you two going to do about the house?" she asked, pointing to where the burnt-out shell of the house sat above a caved-in basement, very visible now that Vinnie had cut around it. Between the tall weeds, smaller ones still poked up between concrete blocks. Gretchen wondered if most people knew concrete could burn if things got hot enough, but, more likely, it would just burst. She was certain with the two of them making pots, Bree and Taylor knew this.

"We're hoping to find a prefab that they will build for us. We have to get a couple of companies out here for a quote, and, as getting up the driveway was iffy at best, I'm solving that problem," she answered, gesturing at the remains of the hill she had left. She frowned, seeing several motorbikes making their way down the long drive towards them. "What the heck is this?" she asked, not expecting Gretchen to answer, as she walked around her to wait for the bikes to arrive.

"Hey, what'd you do to our hill?" one of the riders asked belligerently.

"I told your friends the other day to spread the word. This place has been sold, and we are going to be living here."

"Not without a house." The other one laughed.

"What do you know of the house?" she demanded, and he suddenly looked uneasy.

"You didn't have to take our hill away," the first one continued peevishly.

"Look, sorry about that, but this is now private property. And I'd appreciate it if you spread the word. I have young kids here, and you can't be riding on our land."

He looked at her angrily and muttered something to himself. They started their bikes back up, turned, and left.

"What was that about?"

"Oh, some of the local kids. Guys really that should know better. They used to ride here with their bikes and ATVs, but I took away the best part of the ride, I guess," she answered, still watching them retreat down the long drive.

"That's an accident waiting to happen," Gretchen murmured.

"I'm wondering how many accidents have happened here that they didn't tell anyone about," Taylor agreed. "And I hope we don't find any evidence of other things they've done here."

"You think drugs?"

Taylor hadn't meant that at all, but it was possible. She was remembering the spot in the barn where they'd found remains of a campfire. She shrugged.

"What is Vinnie doing?"

"She's using this really cool machine called a brush cutter that cuts down trees and grinds them up like a mulcher. It will allow us to get through the woods without all the underbrush and weeds. She's also cutting off the lower limbs of the bigger trees to make the easier to work around."

"That sounds nice," Gretchen told her sincerely, envisioning all kinds of things the couple could do with the property. She was loving her own

small greenhouse and was about to suggest getting one when Vinnie drove her large, intense machine around the barn and down the side of the black lawn, careful to follow in the track marks left by the tractor. She stopped across from the two.

"Hey, there," she called, turning off the machine.

"That looks marvelous." Taylor nodded towards the woods behind the house.

"Yeah, I left a little brush between you and that field back there along your fence line, but you can easily knock it down or cut it if you want. I got the poison ivy." She didn't sound happy about that last part as she used her gloved hand to brush at her clothing. "I'll see how much of that ..." she pointed towards the woods near the swamp, "... I can get to, but I don't think I can do all of your land."

"Oh, hell, Vinnie, I don't expect you to do it all. I'd have been happy with the front and back yard. But it's so cool that you got as much done as you did. I'd not have thought of doing that." Taylor nodded towards the brush cutter. "It'll be nice, when we have the house built and are living here, to be able to walk in the woods under the trees."

"I brought some seed," Gretchen said lamely.

"Grass seed?" Vinnie asked to make sure. Gretchen did grow all sorts of things to sell.

"Yeah, but, as Taylor pointed out, it might not be the kind Bree wants."

"Well, we will have to see," Vinnie admitted. She glanced Gretchen's way but gave most of her attention to Taylor before evaluating Taylor's work on the hill. "Looks like you don't have that much more to do. If you don't mind, I'll have one of my big dump trucks come in for you to fill."

"You bet."

"Let me make a call, then," she said, pulling out her cell and walking away from the two of them.

"Well, that was nice," Gretchen grumbled.

"What?"

"She can't even stand looking at me, anymore."

Taylor blinked and then remembered; her two friends had dated for a while long ago, back before Gretchen married her husband. She didn't know why they had broken up.

"I'm sure she's just concentrating on getting this done so she can get back to her paying jobs. She's doing this for us for free, after all. When she started, this whole front and back yard were deep with brush. You two are still friends, though?"

"I don't know." Gretchen shrugged, and she sounded a little hurt.

Taylor wasn't sure if condolences were in order or what. She wished Bree were here; she was much better at things like this.

"Well, I'm going to take my dirt and pile it next to my greenhouse. I'll leave my bag of seed for you to use or not," she said, back to her normal chirpy self.

"Thank you, Gretchen." Taylor took the bag, wondering if she should have said something more, but she was anxious to finish flattening the hill and still had an area next to the barn she wanted to cover with soil. She watched Gretchen back down the drive. Not everyone could easily reverse for that length of time but, like Vinnie, she did fine.

"I've got to get this hill gone so everyone can turn around," she mumbled as she pulled herself back up into the backhoe's seat and put the bag of seed down next to her. She glanced over to where the driveway ran beside the house site and behind it in an L-shape. She thought a circular drive would look nicer, and she'd have to remember to talk to Bree about it.

By the time Bree returned after stopping to pick up their push broom from the shop, Taylor had dumped many loads of dirt over by the barn and was now smoothing them out. She waved at her wife as she took the broom into the barn to sweep the entire floor. Bree had already used the pitchfork she'd found to get most of the hay out, but now she wanted the smaller bits and pieces and dirt out so they have a clean floor.

* * * * *

Meanwhile, Vinnie had cut several acres of their land, under and around the denser trees. All of the trees behind the house had been trimmed back, and the underbrush was completely gone, except for that one thin layer between the properties. She did the same on the east side behind the barn, right up to the pink and orange flags of their property line, then worked her way north until she met back with where she had worked before. When she realized her machine was almost sinking into the swamp, she stopped and reached out as far as she could with the grinders before pulling back. She couldn't afford to get it stuck in the swamp. She retreated down a pre-existing trail leading into the woods and cleaned that area before bursting through to another field where the pink flags continued right across, clearly outlining her friends' ten acres.

Vinnie's crew arrived with a large dump truck, and Taylor never felt more self-conscious than when she used the bucket to dump load after load of dirt into its large bed. Two men had gotten out and were watching her, and she couldn't help but feel either of them would have done a better job using the machine than she did. Still, slowly and surely, she filled the large truck, and, by the time the guys waved her off and got back in the truck, the hill was almost completely gone. She used the front-end loader to move the last of the dirt, smooth out the driveway, pack down where vehicles would go, and to place the last of the dirt alongside the barn.

"Wow! We probably should have kept more of that dirt," Taylor said to Bree as she finished with the backhoe. She parked it next to the driveway, hoping she'd left it in a good spot for the rental place to pick it up. They could turn around now, at least.

"We'll just have to dig out more from the swamp," Bree teased.

"That swamp bothers me." Taylor looked over to where Vinnie had stopped at the end of their front yard, where the ground became too wet for her wonderful machine to mulch. She could hear her in the woods but couldn't see her or the machine.

"I was wondering how much it overflows the driveway with the winter melt."

"The driveway seems too narrow along where the swamp is. I'd hate to drive off into that." Taylor shuddered slightly at the thought.

"Surely, it can't be too deep?"

"I have no idea, and I don't want to find out. When we can afford it, let's get some gravel in there and widen the drive slightly. Even a foot or more on each side would make me feel better. Maybe even a decorative fence?"

Just then a truck came barreling down their driveway. The driver frowned, seeing the two of them standing there. He stopped and tried to do a U-Turn onto their black lawn.

"There's a perfectly good drive right there!" Taylor yelled. The guy was going to put ruts in their lawn. Sure enough, his tires started sinking into the loose dirt. He spun his tires but kept going until he made a three-point turn and rushed back down the drive.

"What the f—"

"Language."

"The kids aren't here," she shot back, angry at the trespasser. "He came down the driveway like he owned it." She stood with her hands on her hips, glaring at the back of the truck as it sped back down towards the road.

"Maybe he thought it was a back road."

"Let's not excuse the behavior." Taylor looked back at Bree and calmed down. Changing the subject, she asked, "Did you get the barn swept out?"

"Pretty much, but I'm covered in dust now, and I know I didn't get everything out. We need some kind of blower or something."

"Can I get a leaf blower?" Taylor asked eagerly, suddenly excited at the prospect of owning such a tool.

"Why don't you ask Vinnie if you can borrow one of hers?"

Taylor slumped her shoulders. "Okay," she said dejectedly.

"We don't know how much the house is going to cost, and we can't be spending money we don't have. Besides, we don't know what we will need for our shop yet."

"You're right." Taylor was still annoyed but ready to move on. She listened for the mulcher, wondering how far Vinnie had gotten.

Just then they spotted a bright yellow school bus driving along the highway at the end of the next-door neighbor's field and then stopping at the end of their own driveway, the red lights blinking. "Wow, that driveway is long," Bree commented as they both started walking down it towards the oncoming four children. Melanie, the oldest was running, outdistancing Barbie and Bryan easily, with Jack trailing even farther behind. Jack started yelling, and by the time the children met up with their moms, he was crying because they hadn't waited for him. His cries were echoed by crows sitting on the power lines, watching the family.

"Hey, you guys, you can't do that. You have to walk together," Bree admonished the three older children, while looking directly at Melanie.

"He can't keep up," Melanie whined, her head bobbing from side to side to try and see what their moms had accomplished. She was hoping to see a house there. She really wanted a new bedroom, even if she did have to share with her pesky little sister.

"That's no excuse. You're the oldest: you wait for him. And you two …" Bree addressed Barbie and Bryan, "It wouldn't hurt for you to wait for Jack." Taylor was consoling Jack, who was still crying.

"Can I ride on the backhoe, too?" Bryan had apparently heard about Jack getting to ride with Taylor.

"No, you can't," Taylor said as she balanced Jack on her hip. "Put your school things in Mom's car," she nodded towards the van. "I have to leave soon, and someone should be coming to pick up the backhoe."

"Why don't we take a walk and see what Vinnie has done behind the house. We'll have to figure out where some of the things we want can go?" Bree suggested to distract Bryan. She could see an argument starting from the little boy.

Taylor agreed, adjusting Jack as she put him on her back and gave him a piggy-back ride. As she galloped down the driveway, his tears gave way to giggles, and Bryan looked on enviously.

Barbie cried, "Me next, me next!"

The kids' backpacks were soon tossed in the van, and the family walked around the house lot, avoiding the burnt-out mess. The kids were curious, but their moms steered them clear of the burnt timbers that jutted out, the broken glass that was everywhere, and the shingles that had collapsed and melted. There were still a few weeds, and another patch of poison ivy jutted up from the rubble.

The kids loved the size of what would become their backyard. They ran over the mulched ground, tripping a few times on the larger sticks. They were excited as their two moms discussed getting a swing set, maybe even a trampoline at some point. Both moms noticed they were listening more, hoping to get these things as soon as possible and impatient to play on them. They had to be careful what they said around them now.

Taylor started heading for her Jeep, seeing that she had to get home, clean up, and then get back to her job. She only had so much free time and had used it up to move the last of the hill of dirt. Bree followed, encouraging the children to move along. They didn't want to leave, and everyone stopped when they saw Vinnie coming out of the woods with the fascinating mulcher.

"Hey, there!" she greeted them, shouting over the noise of the machine. "Let me get this thing on my trailer!"

Taylor debated waiting for her friend. She wanted to hear what she had to say, but she also needed time to shower and get ready for work.

In relatively short time Vinnie had the mulcher on its trailer, tied down with its chains, and hooked up to her truck. She came over to where the kids were running around, enjoying the sight of their footprints in the deep dirt.

"We can rake that out and plant some grass," Vinnie offered. "In exchange for the dirt and hay," she added after they made to protest. "What kind did Gretchen leave?"

Bree showed her, and she nodded, not commenting on the large bag.

"What are you going to do about the house?"

"We have to get a garbage bin in here and clean out everything. Gretchen mentioned some of the boards may have value for crafts, so I guess we'll sort those out from the rest."

"You are going to need the backhoe again to pull that all out," Vinnie explained. "I'll leave the front-end loader for my Kubota here and you two can use that. Knock down the poison ivy first, though, and stay away from its oils."

"I saw on YouTube where people repurpose the cement blocks," Bree mentioned. "Maybe we can incorporate them into our pottery."

"That's clever," Vinnie said, surprised.

"When'd you see that?" Taylor asked, equally surprised and pleased with her wife.

"You know, in my spare time."

"Do you remember how to change the tines to the front-end loader, or do you want me to?" Vinnie asked.

"I'd rather you did it, and do you have a leaf blower we can borrow? I need to finish cleaning out the barn," Bree asked sweetly as she explained.

"Done," Vinnie said. She went over to the Kubota and easily changed out the front end. Taylor kissed her wife goodbye, waved to the kids, and headed off.

"That's a good idea on repurposing the blocks," Vinnie told Bree when she was done and had parked the Kubota.

"Well, I'm just glad that not everything is going to go to waste." She sighed as she looked around the mess they had to sort through.

"Try not to scratch my Kubota," Vinnie teased, knowing her friends would be very careful with anything she lent them.

Bree laughed, knowing she was being teased. Vinnie had watched her go slow on the tractor until she felt more confident in driving it with the heavy bales on the tines.

As they were chatting and Vinnie was getting ready to go, they both saw some ATV riders heading up the driveway. Bree was exasperated, wondering how often they came when neither she nor Taylor was here. Word apparently hadn't gotten around.

"Who is that?" Vinnie asked, watching them as they stopped, seeing the large trailer with the mulcher chained to it and the truck.

"No idea, but I have a feeling we are going to have to get a gate." They had seen no gate at all, and they had looked for the one the realtor had mentioned.

"You need no trespassing signs."

"Another expense."

"Ask Elsie if she knows a screen printer," Vinnie suggested.

"Good idea," Bree answered, sighing as the ATVs turned around and sped off down the long drive throwing up dust as they drove away.

CHAPTER TWELVE

Over the next week Bree and Taylor cleared out the house site. The blocks were pretty damaged from the fire, and most were unusable. They went through the salvaged wood with an excited Gretchen, who showed them how to burn some of it more, use steel wool on it, and oil it. When they finished, the wood looked pretty cool, and they stacked it in the barn for future sales as shelving.

They cleared the poison ivy well away from the house, digging deep to get the roots, gloves on their hands they put aside to use only on such things as they didn't want the oils getting on anything else. The plants were some of the first things in the garbage bin. The electrical panels and wires, the shingles, and any metal they put in the garbage bin hid the plants that were shriveling in the hot spring sun.

They stacked up the usable concrete in a pile next to the barn, most of it broken up from banging it out with chisels, hammers, and the front-end loader.

"Now, can we call those salesmen and have them come out?" Taylor teased Bree who had been just as anxious as she to have them come out and give them a quote.

"I'll call them when we get home," Bree promised.

They were cleaning up tools they had borrowed from Vinnie, determined to buy their own, now they were homeowners. They were watching Craigslist and the Marketplace for deals.

Today, they had raked the last of the large front yard, getting their footprints filled in with the dirt as they sprinkled grass seed down. With the rich dirt they worried it would burn the seeds, but they'd also sprinkled hay down to protect it from the birds and from sun. Also, it was supposed to rain that night, which would save them watering it.

They'd made the large circular drive, using the front-end loader to clearly define it and, in the island of dirt in the middle, they'd plant flowers when they were ready. Already, some weeds had started to come back, determined to reclaim the spaces they had cut down and covered. On the far side of the circle was the short drive to the barn. They'd blown out the last of that debris from the large barn. The only tell-tale sign of the trespassers using it: a large blackened part of the concrete where they'd had a fire. They were planning on moving their shop to the barn once they ran electricity to the site. It had been a long time since the house was occupied, and the electric company had to come out and assess what was needed before any work could be done.

They watched as a truck attempted to make a three-point turn in their narrow driveway, a common occurrence. The two women were on their property at least once a day and really wanted to be there daily to protect it from trespassers. They didn't always come up the whole drive where they could have used the circular drive they'd made. This repeated incident reminded Taylor. "Did you ask Elsie about a screen printer for the signs?"

"She said we could get by with the purple paint law."

"What's that?"

"In our state, private property can have purple paint on a fence or trees. It's based on a law called "The Purple Paint Law," and, in essence, it tells them to stay away, keep out, keep off, or no trespassing."

"Purple paint has magical properties?" Taylor laughed, and they started walking around the barn.

"Yeah, that was my thought. She also said she could print up the signs on paper, and we could plaster them on trees."

"I'd kind of like aluminum, but I guess it would be cheaper to put on paper. Maybe laminate them?"

"Yeah, aluminum sounds longer-lasting, but her idea isn't too bad, and I told her to go ahead."

"Hey, I thought we were going to discuss things we buy for our place," Taylor gestured towards the land they now owned. They both stopped in

the back of the barn, looking at the graffiti that was spray painted on the metal siding.

"Sorry, I meant to, but I just want something up before someone argues about the hill we took down." They'd had quite a lot of guys, mostly in their teens or early twenties, upset over their hill.

"Yeah, we better get something up."

"I'd love to eventually have concrete posts, maybe with brick, on both sides of the driveway, with lights?"

"That sounds lovely but expensive."

"Maybe after we work with that," she gestured to the concrete pile they were going to work into their pottery, coloring a lot of the smaller chunks to make designs, "we can talk about the pillars?"

"Bet we could use solar for the lights," Taylor mused. "Remind me to pick up some paint to cover the graffiti."

"We'll have to paint the whole barn eventually to combat rust or corrosion." Bree showed her a few panels that were the worse for wear. "Even if this is, what, aluminum? Corrugated steel?"

"One step at a time," her wife promised as they completed their walk-around. "I think we need a door on this end, too, in case of fire."

"Yeah, I don't want to be trapped in there if something goes wrong with the furnace." She was not looking forward to moving their entire operation over here, but they would eventually.

As they were getting in their respective vehicles, Taylor to go home, shower, and hurry off to work, and Bree to go pick up the kids as they hadn't told them to come out to the farm as they were calling their new place instead of the apartment, a truck came up their drive. Sighing, they waited for it, expecting it to turn around when it realized that the hill was gone or that this wasn't a backroad. They were surprised when the driver stopped and got of the truck.

"Hello, there," he called as he shut his door.

The two women exchanged looks and got back out of their vehicles. "Hi, I'm Taylor Moore, and this is my wife, Bree."

"Howdy, I'm Eric Norman. I'm your neighbor." He jerked his head towards the fence, where the cows were chewing their cuds and watching the humans as they grazed the field.

"Hi, Mr. Norman. What can we do for you?" Bree answered.

Bree held out her hand, and Eric Norman shook it .

"I own the field there," he indicated the same one and then jerked his head towards the woods and added, "and I have the field on that side of your property. I saw the pink flags through the field."

"We had the property lines drawn so they were clear," Taylor added, wondering if this was going to turn bad.

"I'd like to continue cutting the whole field as I have in years past. Maybe we can work something out that I give you some of the bales?"

The two wives exchanged looks and nodded. It was Bree who answered. "That sounds reasonable. How many do you think that section would be worth?" She hadn't walked down the trail through the woods to look at it yet.

"Well, those round bales are pretty heavy." He considered for a moment, scratching his chin as he thought. "How about three round bales for that section?"

"Can we get back to you on that?" Taylor asked. She too hadn't explored their whole property.

"Sure can. We need to replace that fence, too, eventually. We both have to maintain it according to the county," he indicated the fence between them and the cows.

"I would think you know a lot more about maintaining a fence for your cows than we would," Taylor said in a teasing voice. "We would like to put up some No Trespassing signs, though."

"On the fence posts?" he asked, surprised. At her nod, he added, "You are going to make a few hunters unhappy with that. They've hunted here for years. There are a lot of deer living in that swamp and bedding down in the woods."

"We have small children, Mr. Norman. We can't have hunters coming through the land anymore," Bree mentioned gently. She could see that his statements had annoyed Taylor.

He nodded agreeably but looked thoughtful as he checked out all the work they'd done on the place.

"Are you the one who sold that land behind us?" Taylor asked, thumb-pointing behind them.

"Yep, some developer paid me a fortune for it. He's considering the hayfield, too, but hasn't gotten back to me on it. I'm patient. Meanwhile, you let me know about that section and the bales?" He waved to where the trail that Vinnie had made through the woods went.

"I think three bales delivered here would be good to start," Bree decided for them both. "I appreciate you being neighborly."

He smiled at her and looked around once more at the improvements they had. He had noticed them taking down the hill from his own cow field. "Going to build a house?"

"That's the plan," Taylor answered.

"That's nice. Well, if you need anything, my farmhouse is over there." He pointed across the field where they could only faintly make out a house inside a grove of trees.

"Thank you," Bree said politely, and they watched him as he put his truck in gear and went around the circular drive, waving and saluting against his hat as he drove away.

"Well, he seemed nice," Bree said as Taylor watched him drive down the drive.

Taylor turned around. "If they build up those houses behind us, imagine how much our ten acres will be worth?" The banker and the realtor both had pointed out that possibility, but nothing had been built.

"Thinking of selling already?" Bree laughed.

"Nope, just pleased we got it before that developer realized how much it is worth." She spread her hands out, gesturing at the land about them.

"They think it's swamp land, baby. But, look, that standing water has cleared up a lot."

"Someday, I want to dig up that swamp and put in a pond."

"Oh, that sounds pretty. Just add it to the list," Bree teased. Their list of things they wanted for the farm was pretty long. "Oh, I forgot to tell you; I found something on Marketplace you need to look at before I call on it."

"What'd you find?"

"It's a tractor."

"A tractor!" Taylor gasped, but she was definitely intrigued. "We don't need a tractor!"

"But it's a good deal, and I was thinking, if we got that attachment with tines like Vinnie has, we could put our pottery on pallets to load in the trailer."

"We probably need a truck to pull that heavy trailer sooner," she said, indicating the well-used vehicles they were driving. "Maybe we should get that first?"

"The tractor won't wait."

They compromised and agreed to discuss it later when they got home. Taylor agreed that good deals on equipment would actually, in the long run, save them money. If it was in good shape when she went to look at it, she should buy it. They could write it off as a business expense.

Bree went with Vinnie to check the tractor out, and Vinnie hauled it to their property for her with one of her trailers. It had been a good deal, the farmer having gotten too old and the relatively new tractor going to waste in his shed.

"I'd have bought this if I had seen it," Vinnie griped good-naturedly.

"I'd lend it to you anytime you wanted it," Bree promised, pleased with her purchase. She would watch the ads for a good used truck, too, the thought of the van being unable to tow their heavy trailer too much longer worrying her. They had shows to go to and pots to sell, and their loads weren't getting any lighter. She mentioned that to Vinnie, telling her of her concerns, and her friend nodded thoughtfully and offered to keep an eye out for a bargain.

CHAPTER THIRTEEN

Taylor spent her next day off walking the entire perimeter of the 10.3 acres, marked by the flags of the assessors. With the kids in tow, she was distracted, and a chore that should have taken a couple of hours was taking most of the day. Bree was with them, of course, helping her staple the laminated No Trespassing paper signs, with the required one-inch lettering, onto fence posts to warn people not to come onto their land. The signs were bright white with red lettering, and their phone number and the name T & B Moore were printed across the bottom. They tried to keep it even, putting them up on trees and posts, when available, every two-hundred feet. Below the signs they even sprayed a swath of purple paint in case the sign came down. They were only required to put them every five-hundred feet, but Bree had been genuinely worried about the hunters their neighbor had mentioned. With four small children, she wasn't taking chances that the hunters would say they hadn't seen them.

"You know someone is going to rip these down," Taylor informed her wife as she put one on each side of the driveway, knowing that people just didn't like posted land or being told what to do. "Careful there Melanie, make sure they don't go too far into the woods," she called, smiling at her daughter encouragingly as the children explored. She appreciated that their oldest daughter had kept the younger ones entertained. Jack had to be carried a few times as they walked around the property. They'd kept the kids on the far side of the fence as they painted and stapled signs up along the cow pasture. She laughed as the kids cawed back at the crows who were curious about what these humans were up to.

"Sure do," Bree responded cheerfully, "but all we can do is try." She glanced across the highway at the other backwoods road. That side was paved, but, since it was directly across from their driveway, it was no wonder people thought their driveway was a continuation of that road. She also watched the busy highway and noticed how it curved right here and that people didn't slow down for it.

They liked the back of their property. Vinnie had left just enough brush that it still looked like an impenetrable wall to their woods. There was a line of old fencing, including rusted barbed wire, holding it all together across the length. They could see stakes in the ground of the field behind their woods where the developer had begun plotting out the housing project.

On the east side, they had to cross the creek to put the signs up on trees. The creek meandered out of their property and into other woods, but their pink flagged stakes were a good way to tell them where to go. When they saw the field where Eric Norman had been cutting hay, they realized that the three bale trade wasn't really much of a deal, considering how big their side of the field was. The pink perimeter stakes had been pulled out and thrown to one side of the field, but they put No Trespassing signs along the woods on the edge and on either side, just in case.

"I'd let the kids carry these back," Taylor began as she collected the stakes, "but those sharp edges …" They'd find a use for them back at the barn.

Bree shook her head, understanding immediately. "Too bad Vinnie broke through there," she indicated where the mulcher had cut from the path through this part of the woods. She'd liked the impenetrable wall at the back of their property, hiding what was in their woods.

"I'd like to cut along our property line all through there. See where the creek lines that Southeast section? We could take walks there."

"Well, let's talk to Vinnie about that someday. She's in her busy season, so we'll have to wait."

"Did you know that it's a misdemeanor to trespass on private property?" Taylor asked as she stapled another sign to a tree. When Bree had brought the large stack of laminated signs, she hadn't thought they would need them all. They were running out now, but they were almost done.

"Isn't there a fine or jail or something?" Bree asked, waiting for Taylor to finish so she could brush a swath of paint underneath the sign. She was

carrying a can of purple paint with a wide brush in it. Taylor had carried the stepladder all around the property, stapling the laminated paper higher up to make it harder for anyone to tear down the signs. They were only required to put them three to five feet off the ground, but Taylor was putting them up over six feet to keep them safer. Or so she hoped.

"Yeah, something like imprisonment for thirty days. I think the fine is around $250."

They chatted as they worked and watched the kids, who were definitely tired from having hiked around the entire ten acres with their moms.

"Hang in there, partner. We're almost done," Taylor cajoled a crabby Jack, who was definitely ready for a nap. Come to think of it, she might be, too.

They came out along the highway and finished, with only a few signs left to spare. Each took turns carrying Jack up the drive and teasing the others to races, as the other carried the staple gun, boxes of extra staples, paint can, and stepladder back to the barn.

"Whew, that was a good day's work!" Taylor exclaimed, putting things away neatly in their tool box they were now keeping in the barn. They were watching the ads for some decent shelving they wanted not only for the pottery but for tools and such. Next, she put the lid back firmly on the can of paint, pouring some thinner into the can to keep it from scabbing over as it dried in the can.

"I got lunch in the cooler," Bree told a delighted crew. She insisted they use wet-wipes before they helped her lay out a blanket under a tree in the front yard.

"We should keep an eye out for a picnic table. Even if it isn't the best, we could fix it up or paint it," Taylor said as she came up.

"Purple?" Bree asked with a grin.

"When do we get a swing set?" Melanie asked, glancing to where the backyard would be and back at her moms.

"We're looking for a good one. We can't have just any old swing set," Taylor promised as she ate her sandwich. She chugged some of her water, using a bottle she loved with the filter in the cap and squeezing the refreshing liquid into her mouth. She'd worked up an appetite as well as being a bit dehydrated.

"When are we getting a dog?" Bryan asked.

"Let's build our house first?" Bree offered, almost as a consolation prize.

"I want my own room!" Melanie insisted.

"And yet, you'll share with Barbie," Taylor said sternly, a warning to the youngster who subsided and ate her own lunch.

They bantered and talked back and forth.

"Hey, I think the grass is coming up," Bree observed, peering around and through the hay they had put down.

"Great, we will need a lawnmower eventually," Taylor pointed out.

"The salespeople are coming out this week. I have four appointments."

"Four?" They'd only gone to see three of the local builders of prefab homes.

"Yes, there was one farther out that I called for a quote. I know we didn't see their lot, but I figured why not, the estimates won't cost us anything."

"What's an estimate?" Melanie asked.

"An estimate is when they figure out how much it will cost to build our house," Bree explained. She knew the others were listening, but how much they would retain was up to them.

They enjoyed their property despite the fact they didn't have a house. The kids ran around in what would be their front and back yards, running on the hay that had grass peeking up through it. The sunshine and fresh air along with the hike around the property and all their hard work, insured that they all slept well at night.

* * * * *

"We need to get a mailbox up and start telling the credit card companies and other bills our new address," Bree told Taylor, thinking practically. She was going through the brochures for the prefab companies they were meeting. They'd allowed an hour for each of them.

"Mailbox," Jack repeated from the backseat. He had a couple of his trucks he wanted play with. Bree knew she was going to have to stop at home on the way back to give him a quick bath. There was no way he could go to school right after playing in the dirt at the property.

"Add it to the Home Depot list," Taylor advised, knowing they would have to shop there eventually, but first they were buying everything they could second hand. They had found a couple of shelving units on Craigslist, which were now in the back of the Jeep with the longer sides strapped to the rack on top.

"That's going to be quite a trip," Bree mumbled, opening her phone to add it to the list. They were keeping several lists.

"And expensive," Taylor agreed. She met two bicycle riders on their driveway and rolled down her window to tell them off. "This is private property. Please stay off." They both looked at Taylor and Bree in disgust and rode away angry. "We better look at getting a gate," she mumbled after rolling up her window.

"I think I might find that on Craigslist or the Marketplace," Bree agreed. They couldn't have strangers coming on their property anytime they wanted to drive down here.

Taylor parked by the barn and helped Jack out of the car seat so he could play. He chose to run around the large, open barn as his moms put up the shelving units.

"How about here by the door?" Taylor asked as she brought the first side in from the Jeep.

"I want the oven over there." Bree pointed out the far corner. "That way we can put a door in over on the far wall. Maybe I'll find one on the Marketplace."

"Just need some electricity," Taylor said as she put the side down where her wife wanted it. "We should wall off the pottery manufacturing from the household things," she added, nodding towards the tractor they now owned that was parked in the barn so it didn't get rained on.

"Good idea," Bree said, pulling out her phone to add that to the never-ending list. "We should leave a passageway for the trailer to be backed in and loaded."

They discussed all their plans, something that was a common conversation piece between the two excited moms. They were putting together the first shelving unit when Jack called out that there was a strange truck coming up the drive. Expecting the first of the salesmen or women, they stopped, wiping their hands on their jeans to greet them.

They discussed what they were looking for and gave him a rough sketch they'd made of the house they wanted. The basement was already dug, and they needed new concrete blocks. The salesman took measurements and listened attentively, always eager to make a sale for his company. He left them more brochures and his business card, promising to get an estimate back to them by the coming week.

All four of the prefabricators had sent men out to the property, and Bree wondered aloud to Taylor after the last one left, "Don't women work in such industries?"

"I bet they do but behind the scenes. Sadly, some people wouldn't have confidence in a woman for these things, but they should. We know what we want."

"We better get home; Jack is filthy from playing in the dirt," Bree said. Taylor had left a pile of dirt next to the barn for their future gardening needs, and Jack's trucks had made a track up and over the mound. "I want

to remind Vinnie we could use some sand, but I keep forgetting. If you see her at the diner, remind her?"

"We have to build that sand box or pick one up," Taylor reminded her, helping to put away the tools they were keeping in the barn and locking it up. With as many people they had caught trespassing already and the BMX bike tracks across their lawn telling of even more, they couldn't chance something getting stolen out of the barn.

CHAPTER FOURTEEN

"Why don't you let me see your list, and I'll see what I come across at my various clients' places?" Vinnie asked while she ate the beef stroganoff Taylor had served her.

"Because Bree doesn't want us to take advantage of your generosity. You've helped us so much," Taylor said. She left to take another order in her section and turned it in to the kitchen, then checked for any ready orders before returning to talk to Vinnie. Picking up where she left off, she said, "Besides, we really do realize how much you did with removing all that brush."

Vinnie waved off the thanks. She loved having the equipment to help them. She'd heard updates as they progressed and was pleased that they had the salesmen out to give them estimates on the house they were so worried about. "Why don't we move your storage unit or the shop on your next days off?" She gestured to the table next to hers that had just been filled. "We'll all help."

"Wait, what are you volunteering us for?" Elsie asked.

"Wait, what?" Lenny asked at the same time, looking around at Taylor and then Vinnie.

Vinnie laughed at her two friends. "I was saying we should help them move their crap from the storage unit out to their barn."

Elsie considered for a moment and nodded. "It would save you rent if you moved that stuff," she pointed out to Taylor, who she could see was about to refuse.

"We aren't ready. We don't have electricity in the barn yet, and the less we move stuff, the better off we'll be so things don't get broken." Still, it did give her an idea, and she quickly texted Bree to suggest she get the electric company out there. "You two want the usual?" she asked her friends who both immediately nodded. The menu at Tweety's never changed, and they ate there often enough that Taylor knew their likes. She went off, writing it up for the cook. She took a couple of plates to another table and asked a couple how they were doing, before seeing that Vinnie's dessert was up and taking it out to her.

"Why not move the stuff out of your storage unit to the barn so you don't have to pay for that anymore?" Vinnie continued as though they hadn't been interrupted.

"I'll mention it to Bree, but I'm sure she doesn't want to chance mice or something getting into our stuff."

"You have mice out there?" Lenny asked, having not seen the place yet.

"Probably," she mumbled as she rushed off to take another order.

Her friends discussed what they could do to help Bree and Taylor without doing too much. They all had their pride and knew Bree and Taylor wouldn't appreciate being made to feel like a charity case.

"We have a picnic table at work that no one uses. Do you have a trailer that we could tie it to and haul it, Vinnie?" Elsie asked her.

Vinnie immediately nodded, and the three of them talked about when she would pick it up and take it out there for them.

"How'd the No Trespassing signs work?" Elsie asked when Taylor delivered their lunches. Her printing shop had made them up and laminated them.

"We put them all up, but what we really need now is a gate of some sort to keep people out. I knew they would ignore the signs, but this is ridiculous." She waited a few moments. "Did you need a refill?" She quickly went to bring them filled glasses of soda, taking their old ones away when she bussed the table across from them. "I can't believe how many people assume it's just a road."

"Once you get a mailbox up, that will give some a clue," Vinnie pointed out.

"Yeah, it will take time for word to get around to those kids," Elsie added.

"It isn't just the kids. There are adults who should know better who use our driveway as a road. Where they think they are going, I have no idea. They seem to appreciate the circular drive if they come all the way up the drive," Taylor added. She quickly went to bus another table and put the tray of dishes into the back kitchen for the dishwasher, before washing her hands, taking another order, filling up a few coffees, and returning to her friends. "It's creepy, these random trucks, usually guys, just coming down the drive as if they own the place."

"I might have a source for a couple of columns," Vinnie mused thoughtfully as she finished her meal.

"We'll pay for ..." Taylor said automatically.

"You aren't made of money, and we'd have to haul them off to the dump or crush them up, anyway."

"We appreciate ..."

Vinnie raised a hand to silence her friend. The thanks were appreciated, but she was just trying to help. She knew they had less money than she did, but they had helped her a few times when she was building up her lawn care business, which had become a landscaping one.

* * * * *

As Taylor walked into the house, she found Bree frowning at the space over the refrigerator. She followed her wife's gaze to see a pair of white feet attached to a fluffy cat with its butt hanging over the edge. Nothing else was visible, and she laughed because the cat was lying on its back, completely relaxed. She reached up to tweak each of the toe beans and then yanked slightly on the now twitching tail. The orange cat twisted around so he could fix an eye on this human who was interrupting his nap. He watched as Taylor leaned in to give Bree a sideways hug and a kiss on the cheek.

"Sorry I'm late. The dinner rush was quite something."

"Well, wash up. You reek of cooking oil," she said distastefully, wrinkling her nose at her wife. She smiled because it was a familiar refrain, and Taylor hated the smell, too.

Taylor headed for the bathroom and changed out of her uniform after a quick shower. She just had to get the smell out of her pores, off her skin, and out of her hair. She enjoyed working at Tweety's, but, at the same time, she detested it. She liked seeing her friends from time to time. They all eventually came in to see her, and they ordered food so that management didn't mind them visiting. But there were some customers

who made her job difficult, who treated her like a dumb waitress, not knowing her circumstances.

Seeing the dessert her wife had scratched together to share in their alone time, her heart melted. Bree had even lit some candles. Sitting down at the kitchen table, she smiled her delight to her wife and reached out to squeeze her hand. "Thank you," she said with a heartfelt sigh as she dug into the ice cream sundae with cashews. She saw her wife had the same dessert but with pistachios on top. "I saw Vinnie at the diner. She might have a line on a couple of columns for at the end of the driveway."

"Columns? For what?" she asked as the strawberries slid easily off her spoon onto her tongue. "Mmmmm. I picked these over at clover field."

"Oh, bet it was a hot one in that field. Vinnie figures if we make the driveway look like a driveway some of our visitors will stop trespassing."

Bree thought for a moment before adding with a tilt of her head back and forth, "Maybe."

"We'll need a gate eventually if we're to keep them out, but that can wait," she quickly added, knowing Bree was going to mention the expense. "Maybe we should move our stuff from the storage unit to the barn. We'll save on the rent, and we'll have our stuff more easily available."

"We'll have to put a better lock on the barn," Bree mused in between spoonsful of ice cream.

Taylor liked that Bree was at least listening, not dismissing it out of hand. "Do you think we'd have to worry about mice? That place isn't exactly mice-proof."

"When I go to the Home Depot, I want to also pick up some of that foam insulation. We'll put it all along the edges where mice can get in under the metal of the barn."

"You're going to have to get more than one can if you want to do the whole barn. Vinnie volunteered Elsie and Lenny to help us move our stuff. They were in the diner tonight." She laughed.

"Did you thank Elsie for the signs? You know she gave us a discount on those."

"I told her we put them all up. We should take our grill out there and have a small gathering of our friends." Their grill barely fit in its space on the patio, but at least they could grill, even though they rarely used it.

"I don't know that we can afford to host all those people. And where would they sit?" Bree fretted.

"We can afford it, but timing it would be a problem," Taylor said as she thought aloud. "If they help us move the storage unit, we could pack a

cooler with things to put on the grill. Paper plates. It wouldn't be an issue."

"Sounds like a plan," Bree agreed, relieved it wouldn't cost them too much. She'd go to Home Depot and pick up some things tomorrow so they could get started insulating against rodents. She looked up at the cat who had lain back, its tail twitching over the edge of the fridge as it slept on its back, still relaxed and at home. She wondered if it was a good mouser. "We are going to have to think up a name for that cat." She stared at the beast.

Taylor turned in her chair so she could look at him. He was a big orange thing, filling out now that he had regular meals. "I'm surprised you haven't named him already."

"I was thinking Marmalade?"

"That's a mouthful."

"You certainly know what marmalade is."

"I was thinking about the kids. Not many know that word." Taylor squinted at the cat, wondering if the name would fit. "How about Garfield?"

"Naw," her wife protested. "He doesn't seem as snarky as that cat. We'll see if the kids have any opinions."

The name did prove to fit, possibly because the M was lengthened and the cat appreciated their attempts to communicate with him. They were pleased to know he was fixed but knew adopting him meant they would have to be responsible for his veterinarian bills.

"I mean, we need to know if he's microchipped and that no one owns him."

"He's looking pretty healthy to me," Taylor pointed out. The orange cat was filling out pretty nicely, keeping himself clean, and generally taking over their apartment. His fur was definitely an issue, and they'd had to buy sticky rollers to keep it off their clothes.

"Yeah, he was pretty scrawny when he arrived," Bree countered. She sounded proud she'd managed to feed the cat, despite their own tight budget. The kids were thrilled to know they'd be keeping the orange tom.

* * * * *

"Is that your cat?" Their landlord happened to catch the cat following them out to their car one morning after they had let him out for the day.

"No, it's a stray," Taylor said automatically, knowing their lease didn't permit animals.

"I thought I saw him come out of your apartment?" he asked, sounding suspicious.

"Oh, it's always hanging about by people's doors." Bree entered into the spirit of Taylor's lie. She knew their landlord could be a jerk. They'd gotten into it a few times about the number of kids they had in the apartment at any given time, and someone—they had never figured out who—had reported them to the landlord a couple of times over the years. She didn't hesitate to lie to this man who hadn't been kind to them or their family. She suspected he was a homophobe, too, from the looks they had received.

"I'm going to have to get animal control to come in and capture it. We can't have strays," he asserted himself, sounding important but only to his ears.

"I'm sure it's just taking care of mice on the property," Taylor mentioned as she swung Jack into the back seat to strap him in. He was still too small to go without a car seat. He was busy playing with a toy Bree had given him, a 'car toy' to keep him busy. It had to stay in the car so he could only play with it there.

"We don't have rodents!" the landlord insisted, insulted.

"Everyone has rodents from time to time. It's nice that the cat might be hunting those you don't see," Bree added, knowing it would needle the man. "Have a nice day!" she called as she went around to get in the driver's seat.

Talking quietly so Jack didn't hear the adults' conversation, they decided to capture Marmalade and take him out to the barn to live as soon as possible.

"We can move him with the stuff we're going to store in the barn," Bree asserted, worrying what the landlord would do to the poor cat. They hadn't bought anything but food for the poor stray.

"I think we better grab him tonight before Bozo, there," she pointed back to their contentious landlord, "has a chance to grab him and give him to animal control."

Bree agreed and put it to the back of her mind. They were going to pick up a mailbox and a few other things from the Home Depot. She would paint the mailbox with paints from their shop before they put it up. She was looking forward to how pretty that would look.

It was hard to shop in Home Depot because they both had so many things they wanted for the new place and they couldn't buy everything. For now, they were only getting what they absolutely needed, but Bree saw Taylor slow down as she walked by the lawnmowers, both riding and the smaller push ones. She pretended to look away, but Bree knew her wife was looking forward to taking care of their place. Already, the spots Vinnie had cut were growing back, the grass lush as the rains came to feed it.

"Let's get a couple bags of Quikrete to put in the hole after the post is in," Taylor reminded her as they put a few things in their cart.

Mailbox, post, hardware, Quikrete, a large tarp, and several spray bottles of foam insulation later, and they were ready to escape before they spent too much.

Taylor had been mostly quiet at the store, too afraid to let on to Bree how much she wanted for their place. It didn't make sense to buy anything until they were ready, but, boy, was it tempting. She appreciated that Bree was keeping an eye out for things on Craigslist and the Marketplace for their future home. That tractor alone had been a good bargain. They'd both practiced using it as a forklift, and they'd picked up a few discarded pallets to use for their pottery.

They used a post hole digger they borrowed from Vinnie to dig the hole, having asked at the local post office about which side of the driveway and which side of the highway the mailbox should go on. It was a good thing they asked because where they had planned to put it didn't match with where the postal service wanted it. They also had to go to the nearest post office to their new place and register that the address was in use again.

Using a tape measure, they made sure to position the mailbox forty-one inches from the road surface. There was some official regulation that said you could only position it forty-one to forty-five inches. There was no curb out here, so that part of the regulations didn't come into play. Now they had their house number, or official address, they'd start having their credit cards and certain bills changed over to this address.

"When I paint this," Bree said almost lovingly as she handled the silver mailbox, "I'll put our address on this side." She was envisioning butterflies and other designs on the box.

"Just not our names," Taylor reminded her as she filled in the hole around the post with Quikrete. They'd had to use soda bottles to get water from the swamp. Not realizing they needed water; they hadn't brought a bucket. Repeated fillings made them realize they needed their stuff out at the new place, even if it was in the barn and under tarps to protect it. With Marmalade out here, he could keep any rodents away from their things, if he would only cooperate with their plan. They'd decided complete strangers didn't need to see their names on the mailbox, and the post office had advised to only have the address, too.

"I think, if our friends don't mind helping, we should move the shop, too. We can give notice at both the storage rental place and the shop, then, and save on rent," Bree said happily.

"Did you forget we don't have electricity out here yet?"

"Oh, I forgot to tell you. They called me back and will run the new lines this week!"

"That's great news, and, yes, you forgot," Taylor answered a little testily. "Did you forget I don't read minds?"

"I'm sorry, babe," Bree responded as she helped to pat down the rise of dirt from around the hole with her foot. "Jack, stay near us here," she called to the little boy who was attracted by a butterfly on the fence. A nearby cow was watching the boy and chewing her cud. The wind blew from the cow's direction to the women tamping down the dirt around the post. "Wow, they stink."

"And there are going to be flies from their plops," Taylor pointed out, the wind also bringing them the scent of fresh cow manure.

"I wonder if ... what's his name?" Bree asked, pointing at the neighboring farm house they could see in the distance.

"Eric or something?" she said as they gathered up the empty bag of Quikrete and tools. She called Jack to follow them back to the barn.

"I wonder if we can get manure from him for the garden?"

"Well, you don't want that stuff fresh," Taylor responded, wrinkling her nose.

"Yeah, the acid is bad for the plants. I remember what Gretchen told us." There had been an incident where they had discussed fresh versus old manure, but that was regarding horses.

They were pleased with how far the few spray cans of insulation went but saw they'd have to buy a few more.

"We can lay out the furnace over there and put up the shelves for our pots all along the back wall," Bree said, imagining it.

"We're going to need lighting in here," Taylor pointed out, but she would agree to whatever made her wife happy. She was pleased they had bought this place with the big barn. "Any word from the salesmen on the house?"

"Nothing has come in the mail, no phone calls." Bree sighed, glancing toward the open door to watch Jack playing with his trucks. "Let's get him cleaned up for school."

"We should have the water hooked up in here, too," Taylor mentioned as they put the kids' toys away in the barn to lock it up. There was a sturdy padlock on both the large sliding barn door and the smaller door, now.

"We should see if Vinnie can also find a door so we could put one on the back of that side wall." Everything Bree had found was outrageously expensive.

They agreed on so many things about this place and were eagerly looking forward to the bids.

HOME ~ First Nillionaires Club

CHAPTER FIFTEEN

The bids came in the following week, and both of them were blown away at how expensive the house was going to be.

"Maybe we should plan on putting a mobile home out there," Taylor tried to compromise.

"Not if you want to remain married to me," Bree contended, angry at the thought. They'd bought the place with the intention of having a home for their family. "Have you done the math with our down payment of what's left after we bought the land? It will be less than our rent here," she pointed out. "With having the storage unit and the shop rent gone, we are coming out ahead."

"No, I didn't realize the down payment made that much of a difference. I was looking at their total numbers for what we want. That guy up north has the best price for what they are offering. He's not the cheapest," she said, forestalling Bree's attempt to interrupt, "but we get an extra bedroom and the walk-out basement."

"True, true," Bree admitted. She was willing to go with one of the other three, one of which was cheaper, but she hadn't liked the salesman's pitch.

"Well, should we call this guy and tell him we'd like to proceed, or do you want to think it over?"

"I think we should call him and then take the trailer out to the barn and unload it completely."

"Why?" Taylor asked, alarmed.

"We need to start moving the delicate things like the pots out there, and then, when our friends help out this weekend, it won't be such a big deal, and we'll have an empty trailer to help us move."

"How goes looking for a new truck?" Taylor asked, knowing Bree was watching the ads for them. She'd already found a few tools they'd acquired that were now stored in the locked barn. They'd also finished using the spray foam along the edges and installed Marmalade in the barn with food, water, and a cat door on the side. The door was operated by a collar that only allowed the cat in and out of the barn. It was an expense they hadn't enjoyed paying, but having a cat safe to hunt mice without other animals getting into the barn made it more than worth the cost.

"All the trucks I've seen are so expensive, and we'd have to pay cash. We can't afford to buy it until after we sign this deal on the house and get the financing."

"Think there will be any trouble getting the financing?"

"No, not now that we own the acreage which we will be using for collateral, along with the house they build for us."

"When they estimate the value, I bet the brush that Vinnie cleared will make it all look nicer and maybe our loan will reflect that?"

They did contact the out-of-town company to build their prefab house. They had to go up to their facility and sign all the paperwork. A bonus of signing with them was that they had their own financing, and the credit union they used was happy to deal with for a home loan. The interest rate was competitive, and Bree had called around to make sure of that. In just under three months, they should have their home delivered and set up for them. They were both excited that it was well and truly beginning. They'd both been surprised how fast it went and that the credit union hadn't sent someone out to the property to appraise it, taking their acreage and recent purchase as collateral and the builder's estimate as proof of value. The loan officer had heard them enthusiastically tell of the improvements they had already made and took them at their word. He could see they were hard-working parents who just wanted to make a better life for their family.

"Here are the final specs on the basement we will need to have in place," the housing agent told the two women after the paperwork was signed and the check written for the down payment. "Now, we can put it in for you, but there would be an additional fee," the woman told them,

showing them the figures. "Please let us know when you decide. We need to know it will fit the house we are building for you."

"Thank you," Taylor said trepidatiously. She knew they'd have to dig out a little more for their house, but she was still kind of shocked how big it seemed.

"Thank you," Bree echoed as she picked up Jack, who had been playing on the floor, and they left the place.

"I don't know where we are going to get the concrete block for this," Taylor worried.

"Relax, we know people, and we have three months before it has to be in place. You can practice digging with the front-end loader on the tractor until then."

"I don't think you realize; it isn't just the block walls but the concrete slab. The one that is there has all those burn marks, and we'll have to go even wider."

"We'll manage," Bree said confidently, but inside she, too, was worried at all the expenses.

That night as they planned for the weekend when their friends would be helping them move, Taylor helped Bree move their barbeque into the trailer so they could take it to the barn. They'd already gotten the gift of the picnic table from Elsie, and Bree had painted it a bright white. It was startling against the green backdrop of their lawn coming in. Not just grass was coming in, though, and they kept gloves nearby to pull up saplings, itch weed, and even some more poison ivy coming through their rich dirt and the seed they had planted.

"Did you know we are poor?" Bree asked Taylor as they put a few other things from their apartment into the trailer just to get them out of their way. Since they had extra space in the trailer, they also took some things that wouldn't be needed, and it helped make the apartment more livable. They would have to move them anyway in three months, and moving them now made them both happy.

Taylor looked at her wife in consternation. "Bryan told me he had a school family planning lesson today," Bree started to explain.

"How'd that go?" Taylor asked, amused.

"He was embarrassed."

"They didn't go into detail about sex, did they? He's only six, after all."

"No, but he told me that he nearly died of shame. One of his friends had argued that the stork brings babies. Then another friend said you can buy babies at an orphanage. They know that Bryan is adopted, so I bet she thought we bought Bryan. But another kid said you can buy babies at the hospital."

Taylor was amused at the story and smiled to encourage her wife to continue.

"I told Bryan that was no reason to be ashamed. He then told me that we were so poor that you and I had to make him ourselves."

Taylor snorted through her nose at that. "Did you explain to him that it wasn't possible for two women to have made him?"

"No, I was just trying not to laugh at his story. He was really upset."

"You didn't let him think that was all true?" Taylor asked, her amusement fading.

"No, nooo," Bree answered, trying not to laugh again. "I explained that he had his birth parents who made him, but that we were lucky to have chosen him to come live with us. And that we loved him very much. That consoled him and his shame."

Taylor put her arm around her wife as they made their way inside from the latest load they'd taken to the trailer. "Atta girl," she complimented her, hugging her close.

"Oh, that isn't the only thing that happened today," Bree continued. "When we had to leave the barn, Jack got upset because I wouldn't let Marmalade drive him to school."

Taylor laughed through her nose again, giving a snort. "That's not too bad. Last week he told me that his bath was too wet."

"Bryan told me he wanted syrup for breakfast ... just syrup. That necessitated a conversation about healthy food habits."

"Did you hear the fight that Bryan and Barbie had in the car because Barbie kept looking at him?"

"I heard that one but pretended I didn't," Taylor admitted, and they had a good laugh over their children's behavior.

"We have to tell Mrs. Henderson that our address will be changing."

"Any news on a court date about his adoption?" Taylor and Bree were attempting to adopt their last foster child, and the social worker had been working with them. She needed to know they would be changing their address in a few months in case that affected any of the paperwork they had filed.

"Excuse me. Have you seen an orange tom cat around here?" a man asked them before they could go into their apartment.

"Do you own him?" Bree asked, worried that they had stolen the cat from someone. They'd forked out the money for the vet, including getting a microchip that he hadn't had, not to mention the special collar and cat door. She wouldn't be happy if it had been wasted.

"No, but animal control is in the courtyard and looking for him."

"No, we haven't seen him in days," Taylor admitted, now knowing that moving him out to the barn so soon had been a good idea.

"Yeah, me neither. Hope he's okay," the man said. "Sorry to bother you. See you around."

The two moms exchanged delighted looks as they unlocked the door and went inside.

* * * * *

That weekend went well. It helped that the two moms spent their mornings moving as much as they could themselves, and then, with their friends' help, they moved the heavier items, like the oven, into their enclosed trailer. Once the old shop was empty, Vinnie used her blower to get rid of the last of the dust that was everywhere. Wearing a ventilator and goggles, she did a very thorough job.

Seeing the cloud of dust coming out of their shop, Bree worried. "She's breathing that stuff; that can't be good."

"She's having the time of her life. She loves dust." Gretchen laughed off Bree's concern. "Besides, she's got a ventilator on her mask."

"I can't believe we're out of here," Taylor said as she watched enviously at what looked like fun with that blower.

"You've been in there a long time," Elsie agreed, standing back to look at the now empty shop. "Did you inform your landlord?"

"Yeah, we gave our notice, and we're paid to the end of the month," Bree told her.

"You were only month to month?" Lenny asked.

"Just the last couple of months. We had a lease before that. I can't wait to move out of the apartment," Bree confided.

"We ready to go?" Vinnie asked, walking up with the blower in one hand and her ventilator and goggles in the other.

"Yep, that's all the shop stuff," Taylor told her with a smile. They'd all carried things out to the trailer, but the heavy stove was what they'd really needed the most help with. The racks had rolled up the ramp with no problem.

"Well, let's get it out there, then," she said in a mock-angry voice. "Then the rest of your stuff from the storage unit?"

They'd gotten some pallets from Gretchen and a few more from Vinnie. Both of them ordered things by the pallet load for their businesses and had extra. They put some of their pots on these but used them mainly for their things from the storage unit. Lamps, extra couches, and

miscellaneous things that hadn't fit in their apartment were brought out and put into and onto the trailers and tied down. It took most of the weekend, but, finally, they were all out at the barn with the last load. When they had an empty storage locker, Bree happily turned the lock and keys over to the site manager.

Once the final load had been stowed inside the barn, everyone gathered around the picnic table where Taylor and Bree had a nice picnic ready for them, as they had the day before. Taylor was frying up hot dogs, hamburgers, and some of the first corn of the season. Bree handed out hard lemonade, beer, and soda to her friends and soda and juice for the kids. They all watched as Bree and Taylor's kids played with Gretchen's son Aaron.

"Barry didn't want to come out?" Bree asked. "He was invited."

"He didn't want to move you. That implied work on his weekend off," Gretchen answered, starting to feel the alcohol she was consuming. She'd volunteered her own trailer and truck to help with the move, and Barry hadn't liked that bit of generosity, although she kept that to herself.

"Well, we appreciate all your help," Taylor said, saluting her friends with the black cherry lemonade she was drinking. It was alcoholic but mild.

"This is going to be a fine place you have here," Vinnie told her friends, and not for the first time. She slapped at a mosquito buzzing about.

Taylor and Bree had made sure to tell everyone about Vinnie's hard work with her fantastic machine. Already some of the foliage was trying to grow back, but everyone could see where she'd cleared through the trees, and it made a nice impression.

"On my first date with Elsie, she walked into the restaurant. I watched her," Lenny was smiling at her tale.

"She let me walk all around the whole place," Elsie added, gesturing with her beer.

"She forgot what I looked like," Lenny added, laughing. "I eventually had to wave her down."

"But not until I'd walked around and looked for about five minutes! I thought I'd been stood up!"

They all shared a laugh.

"I once took a girl to Arizona Pizza Factory for our first date," Vinnie contributed.

"Did she dump you then and there for taking her there?" Taylor teased as she flipped the burgers.

Vinnie and the others laughed, but she proceeded with her story. "She put so much garlic powder on her pizza, and I asked her why? She told me this was in case I was planning on kissing her later." They all laughed at her. "I wonder why that relationship didn't work out?"

Not to be left out, Gretchen had a tale to share. "On our first date, Barry had been diagnosed with an ulcer. They gave him meds to clear his stomach. He farted and burped the entire time. It was so embarrassing, and boy did he stink! I still married him." They all laughed with her, but it wasn't as intense or as funny as the other stories. They all knew that being married to Barry wasn't easy.

Trying to keep the gathering happy, Bree told them a story they had heard before. "I remember, on one date with Taylor, I choked on an omelet and blew onion out of my nose. She still married me!"

Laughing with the rest of them, Taylor asked, "Do you want onions on your hamburger, babe?"

They made sure to feed the kids first. With only the one picnic table it was easier for the adults to eat standing. Once the children were done and had gone off to play again, the adults sat down to finish eating and continue their conversation.

Vinnie had another story. "I met a girl for a blind date once. It was weird because she didn't say anything throughout the dinner, and, believe me, I tried. She walked out after dinner as though she had somewhere to be. I thought perhaps she just wasn't that in to me. Then, I checked my phone, and the blind date girl had texted me that she couldn't make it that night. Who the hell did I eat dinner with? Who the hell does that?"

They were laughing uproariously at their friend's story as they imagined it.

"You should plant some fast-growing trees along the property line if you don't want the flies from your neighbors' cows," Gretchen was telling Bree after dinner while everyone took a walk around the place. They'd been swatting at flies, gnats, and mosquitos all evening.

"I can get you some birch, but you'd do better to get cuttings of willow. That grows like weeds," Vinnie contributed.

"I just want people to stop coming up the drive," Taylor grouched. They all stopped to stare at a truck who was turning around in the driveway at that very minute. The driver just ignored them and kept driving, looking determinedly ahead as if there wasn't a family obviously having a picnic there.

"That's a lovely mailbox you put up, Bree," Elsie contributed. "I especially love the brightness of it. Did you paint it yourself?"

"I did, but Taylor is the one that put the butterflies on it. She draws better than I do. I just painted them in." She was amazed, as homeowners, how much more mail they were getting. So many letters were addressed 'Dear Homeowner,' proving their name and address had been sold once the land sale went through.

"Now that you have the shop, are you going to screen print some of your pots?"

Bree nodded. "We definitely have the room for racks that can hold the screens, and, you know, someone with an exposure unit to burn the designs?"

"Yep, been waiting forever for you to do that," she teased.

The conversations went on for a while until it started to get too dark to see.

"You are going to have a lot of mosquitos out here," Vinnie warned, waving a few away again.

"I'll bring you some citronella plants to plant between those trees," Gretchen promised and then blushed when Vinnie looked at her. "I have several I started for you in my greenhouse when you gave me the dirt."

They all had a lovely time, roasting marshmallows before Taylor turned off the grill flame so it could cool.

"I have a toast I'd like to give to our friends in honor of the home they are building here," Lenny proposed to everyone, holding up the last of her soda. "To Taylor and Bree, many happy years!"

"Here, here!" several people seconded her toast.

They looked in the barn, which now contained their complete shop and held everything from the storage unit. Already, Marmalade had confiscated a chair, lying on the tarp that covered it and enjoying the crinkle of the polyethylene. It gave him a good view of the entire barn where he now lived in. He was happy. He saw his people daily, and they didn't bother his sleep too much. He could get outside through the cat door when he wanted to hunt or to use the woods for his cat pan. He liked his new accommodations.

"Can you work here?" Vinnie asked Bree as they helped to clean everything up. Taylor was wheeling the barbeque back to just inside the barn.

"Well, if I couldn't, we'd be in trouble," she teased. "Look at how much room we have," she gestured to the large barn.

"Does this mean you can make more pots?" Gretchen asked, having discussed designs she wanted exclusively for the pots she purchased.

"Not only that, but we have room to grow and can even make a showroom for our clients," Taylor bragged. She gestured to the garden

that they could have next to the barn, as well as the front of the barn itself, explaining her vision of what it might look like. She looked up at the electric lines that had been piped in, Taylor and Vinnie having put up some lights in the barn, with more planned as they needed them.

All their friends were pleased for them and eagerly anticipated many parties like this one. "One last toast," Vinnie insisted with the last of her soda. "To the First Nillionaires Club." She lifted her drink, and the others followed, laughing at the moniker they had taken on so long ago. "Now, remember, if you become rich and famous for your pots, you might have to change your membership."

"I'm sure we won't be rich or famous for our pots," Taylor quipped, returning the salute to their friends, the only members of this illustrious club. "But I'll always proudly be a Nillionaire as long as I have friends like you people."

"Here, here!" several people agreed, raising their bottles again.

"I have one more story," Vinnie added. "That is if you want to hear it?"

Several people encouraged her to tell.

"I went to a fancy restaurant, trying to impress my date. I thought I was looking quite cute, dapper even. When I introduced myself at the bar, she said, 'I thought you'd be thinner.'" She smiled at her friends' gasps.

Vinnie wasn't thin, by any means, and her work kept her quite fit. But she was solid in the middle.

"I grabbed her drink, poured it over her head and into her lap and said, 'I thought you'd be smarter?' I turned and left the restaurant. Had a great pizza that night."

As they chuckled, heading for their vehicles, Taylor quipped, "Not at Arizona Pizza, I hope?"

"No, you know the only good pizza comes from Chicago?"

"Nuh-uh, New York has the best pizza," Elsie argued.

"You are all wrong, Pizza Hut works for me," Lenny interjected just to get some laughs. She smiled as she saw the light of battle in her friends' eyes.

They all got into their vehicles, watching as Taylor and Bree effortlessly gathered their children, who were dead tired. They'd helped load things in the trailers, but running around all afternoon and evening had really worn them out.

Gretchen had difficulty getting Aaron in their truck. He was just as tired as the other kids but cranky and fighting sleep. She finally muttered threats in his ear, and he sulkily got in the vehicle.

"Everything okay?" Vinnie asked her, concerned.

"Everything is fine," Gretchen replied with a too bright smile as she waved and got in the truck herself.

Everyone drove off one by one as Taylor and Bree watched their friends leave. Then, they got in their van and followed the last car down the driveway. Already, they needed headlights as the evening closed in.

The children settled down right away and dozed off for the short drive back to their apartment.

"That was a lovely day," Taylor said quietly.

"It was. The first of many. I would love to have them over more often. I'm so glad we chose that house. We can picnic on the back deck, eventually."

"Eventually," Taylor agreed. "God, those stories were hilarious." She laughed again, thinking about them.

"I had a friend in college set me up on a blind date," Bree told her. "I wasn't in a great mood because I got stopped by a cop before I got there. He gave me a traffic ticket that I don't think I deserved." She exchanged a look with Taylor over that statement. They both had agreed long ago that Taylor was the better driver, but Bree wasn't as particular about certain rules she followed … or didn't follow. "My day got worse when the blind date showed up and turned out to be the cop who had given me the ticket."

Taylor laughed through her nose, snorting at her wife's blind date adventure. "What did he say?"

"He laughed, but we kept the conversation away from his job."

"Gee, did you have a second date?"

"He asked, but I knew it wasn't going to work out. I was pretty sure I was more attracted to women, and, besides, I met you not long after," Bree said affectionately, reaching out to squeeze her wife's arm.

"I had a date that was trying to parallel park. He suggested that I get out while he, the *manly man*," Taylor mocked, "park the car. He tried three times and failed each time. Once, he was too close and went up over the curb. Another time, he was way the heck out still in traffic and not near enough to the curb. After the third failed attempt, he drove off, embarrassed. I had to walk home!"

Bree laughed, having heard this story from Taylor before. "Remember that time I went on that date with Susie Drinkwater?"

"You went on a date with Susie Drinkwater?" Taylor asked, jokingly, sounding dismayed. "Aren't you two cousins?" She knew this story, and it never failed to make her laugh.

"Well, neither one of us knew that at the time, but, yes, we're third cousins. And the only way we found out was she took me to a family barbeque, and we both knew too many people there and figured it out."

"You never had sex with Susie, did you?" Taylor asked, a grin on her face.

"You know we didn't," Bree hissed low, not sure the children were soundly asleep and couldn't hear.

Taylor snorted. She did know; she'd been Bree's first and only woman. Still, that dating a cousin story was priceless. Bree didn't see her family anymore since her parents objected to her marrying a woman, and it was probably for the best. She knew that Bree would have liked to have shared their children with her parents but didn't want to bring it up. It would only cause her to be sad, and today had been too good a day to ruin it.

HOME ~ First Nillionaires Club

CHAPTER SIXTEEN

"Did you know playing Frisbee with a four-almost-five-year-old child is just like running around after a Frisbee?" Taylor asked Bree when she came out of the barn from having set the oven with their latest batch of handmade pots. Taylor had been planting trees they had gotten from Vinnie and the plants from Gretchen to ward off mosquitos. "I hope the cows don't eat these," Taylor had murmured as she planted the citronella.

"At least you're wearing him out." Bree smiled as she saw her wife looking all sweaty—and hot. She could feel her desire for this woman building.

"Well, he's tiring me out more, but, then, I think of his inspiring words that encouraged me so when he uttered them."

"Oh, what were those?"

"Remember when he puked carrots up all over the living room floor?"

Bree nodded, wrinkling her nose in distaste.

"He said he was going to need more carrots." They both laughed at the incident. "For some reason, when I get discouraged and want to quit something, I remember those inspiring words and laugh."

They were both smiling about it. It had been a worrying incident when he threw up, but it hadn't fazed the little guy in the least.

"Well, you could take heart over Bryan and your fashion attire," Bree teased, reminding her.

"Halloween or the other incident?"

"Halloween," Bree said, a little testily. The first incident was when Bryan saw Bree all dolled up for a fundraising party and asked if she was wearing all that for Halloween. The second one, Bree wasn't as fond of. She'd put on a skirt to look nice for court, and Bryan asked if she'd borrowed it from Taylor's mom because it was the kind of skirt she would wear. Bree hadn't been able to wear that skirt ever again.

"According to Bryan, I should stop being wrong," Taylor added a while later, repeating a conversation she'd had with their son.

"Now why?" Bree was driving the two of them back to the apartment so Taylor could shower and get ready for work.

"We were arguing that a baby on TV wasn't as cute as Jack when he was two. I was saying that Jack was way cuter than the one on TV, and Bryan finally got fed up with me and yelled, 'Stop being WRONG!'" The two moms laughed hard about that one, enjoying their children.

They adored their brood, which were with them all through the summer vacation, playing around the large yard they now had. The children weren't allowed to go into the woods or near the swamp without an adult, but they had fun playing in the yard with the many downed and mulched trees Taylor was piling up. She intended to build a fire pit with the trees, but, in the meantime, the kids were using them for swords and to make forts. The kids look very healthy and tan, and they knew the rules. Taylor used the tractor to place heavy logs on the edges of the lawn, which signaled the out-of-bounds area. She'd seen the kids try to move them, but they were too heavy.

* * * * *

Bree finally found the used door and frame for the barn she'd been looking for online. After they picked it up, Lenny and Vinnie helped install it, and now they finally had a second way in and out of the barn. Bree helped cut the hole in the metal barn, as well as frame and install it, learning a lot in the process about balancing, shimming, and building. They'd lucked out and gotten a really nice door with a paned glass panel in the middle, and Bree found some used blinds to go over it so no one could look in. When they were throwing pots, they opened the blind for natural lighting in an otherwise dark area of the barn. Sometimes, they opened the door to get a cross breeze with the heat of the ovens going.

"What are you doing?" Bree asked, walking out the door and seeing Taylor on a ladder at the back of the barn.

"Painting," she answered blandly, brandishing a roller she then dipped in paint and continued rolling against the wall.

"Why didn't you tell me? I'd have helped."

"I've got my helpers." She pointed to the kids, who were collecting dead twigs and piling them up.

"How is that helping?" Bree frowned. They weren't going into the woods, which was against the rules, but finding firewood on the edge of the lawn and under the hay, which was now raked back to the sides to allow the grass to grow better.

"You need wood for a bonfire and marshmallows," Taylor answered back as though Bree should know this. It sounded perfectly logical.

Bree blinked, watching her wife cover the graffiti, and looked back to the children, who were piling the sticks up closer to the house site. Nodding as though this all made sense now, she went back into the barn and went to paint designs on their pots. They'd gotten a pretty healthy order from one of the nurseries, and she suspected her friends had spread the word they had a larger shop and could supply more. She was hoping to find a used kiln, a larger oven to handle the increase in orders. The money was certainly welcome. She thought about what her wife was doing—finally painting over the graffiti they had noted the first time they'd come here. Then she thought about the way Taylor had cunningly kept the kids out of their hair and cleared the way for the lawnmower at the same time. She glanced to where it sat in front of the barn, keeping grass from growing in that spot. She smiled and shook her head at her wife's cleverness and got back to work.

* * * * *

They eventually put up a wall of plastic sheeting in the barn, one to keep the kiln and their old oven away from the high dust areas. The pottery wheel they had used to play the scene from the movie Ghost to—and more than once—was in action more often than not these days, usually with Bree humming away happily as she worked and created. The second oven was a used one, still in good shape, they'd found on Craigslist, and it was a lucky deal, too. Bree caught it moments after it was listed, and, if she hadn't called on it immediately, it would have been long gone. It was much bigger than the one they had and would help them not only make bigger pots, but it could fire up many more at a time. They'd had to have an electrician come in and change the electric in the barn, upping the power so it could handle the increased volume of usage without triggering

the breaker. Until that happened, Bree and Taylor had to turn everything else off when they used it.

"Happy, babe?" Taylor teased Bree, watching as she whipped out more and even better quality of pots in her pleasure.

"You know it." She smiled up at her wife as she worked the clay, her agile fingers sculpting it into the designs that sold so well for them. Later, she would use the molds to make some cookie cutter and more traditional designs. She found those boring and sold them at a discount, but they were more in line with what people expected.

Taylor was a little more adventurous in her designs, easily adapting to various patterns and methods as she experimented. Using the damaged concrete from the basement, she made large tiles and added glass stones from the dollar store to make interesting pieces. They learned not to turn the heat up as high on the ovens when working with glass. The explosions were rather impressive, but they didn't want anyone to get hurt from the chards that went flying. It also ruined the pot, making them have to start over in another design and recycle what clay pieces that they could. Taylor repeated the various designs over and over again, as she played with the additional substrates to their clay base. She'd learned that doing this could lead to people buying sets, rather than just one pot that caught their attention.

"Delivery for Clay Designs?" a voice called from the front of the barn, where the children had been playing to keep out of the rain while their mothers worked behind the plastic wall.

"Hi, there." Taylor wiped her hands on a rag and came out from behind the plastic curtain to greet the delivery guy. "Whatcha got?"

She directed him to back his truck up to the barn while she used the forklift on the tractor to offload the pallets of supplies Bree had ordered. They had found new suppliers now that they had the room and ordered in bulk, ultimately saving money. The kids watched avidly as she used the tractor to place the pallets carefully near the wall.

"Here's your invoice ... if you'll sign here," he said, handing her the paperwork.

Taylor glanced over it as she confirmed what was on the pallets and signed. Bree came out from where she had been setting up the pots on their racks to go into the kilns. The ovens heated the barn quite nicely on this rainy, cold summer's day.

"Thank you," he said once she had signed. As he closed up the back of his truck, he worried about driving back through the deep water encroaching on the driveway. He shuddered at the thought of going off into that dark swamp in what looked like deep water with his truck.

"Wow, did you over-order?" Taylor murmured to Bree. There had been three pallets full of supplies.

"No, we got that family chain of Spiegels who sampled some of the pots and placed a large order. I'm only about a quarter of the way to finishing the first store, and they have four more!"

"Why didn't you tell me instead of letting me play?"

"We need your designs for the Fourth of July Market up in Twin Rivers." Bree used some shears to cut the shrink wrap around one of the pallets.

"Well, I think the trailer is nearly full for that." She wondered if they were getting too busy to keep up with their orders.

A little while later, another voice called out a hello, and the children recognized her. In walked the social worker, Mrs. Henderson, who was handling Bryan's case. The children ran to give her a hug, very familiar with her after meeting her so many times.

"Hey, there," Bree said brightly, a little forced, but only Taylor realized her chagrin at being caught looking a mess.

"Hi," Taylor answered, smiling sincerely as she scanned the barn for problems the social worker would notice. They'd invited her out several times, explaining they were expanding and would soon have a house for their family on the site. The toys in the barn were well used, many of them bought off Craigslist, the Marketplace, or from second hand shops and kept in the barn rather than on the grass that was growing through the black dirt. The kids enjoyed the clean barn, but it got them dusty-dirty. It was still better than having them out in the rain or outside, where a parent had to be present at all times. They both worried about the swamp.

"My, this is much larger than your last shop," she said admiringly over the heads of the children she was hugging. She had, of course, seen their last set up. Anywhere the children she supervised went, she was required to go and check the place out for their well-being.

"Oh, yes, and we're hoping to expand," Taylor said, parroting Bree, who was so enthusiastic and optimistic about their plans.

"I'm going to have to get copies of the plans for the house so I can sign off on that," she informed her, watching the two adults. She'd known them for years, and, while she knew them to be excellent foster parents and had readily agreed to them adopting their wards, she still had to do her job.

"Well, we don't have them here, but we can get them to you," Taylor said slowly, but then she thought about 'Do Not Copy' being stamped on their blueprints. Apparently, the construction company had proprietary rules about their work. "Better yet, why don't you come by the apartment and see them later?"

"I will if I can." She let the children go back to playing, watching them and determining they were doing well. "Say," she said, lowering her voice, "what is going on with that swamp?"

Thinking she was concerned because of its rising levels, Taylor lowered her own voice and said, "We're working on getting it cleaned up. We want to widen the driveway and fill in some of—"

"No, I mean it's starting to spill over your drive already. That can't be safe for the children ..."

"Yes, we're fixing that," she lied cheerfully. Well, they did have plans to do something about the swamp, just not immediately. She made a mental note to make it a priority now.

Because of the torrential downpour they were now getting, they couldn't do anything but look at the building site and discuss the house, as well as the two women's plans.

"Are you certain you can afford all this?" the social worker worried. It wouldn't do if the two women got in over their heads and couldn't meet the children's basic needs.

"We saved for a long time, Mrs. Henderson," Bree told her quietly, while the playing children's voices echoed in the barn and would have drowned out theirs even if they had been trying to overhear the adults. "We bought the land outright and have plenty left over to expand." Her hands took in the barn where they were standing, the rain beating down on the metal roof.

Mrs. Henderson looked around at the pallets of what were obviously household items, probably tarped to keep out dust. She saw the plastic wall they were using to separate the open area of the barn from their work area. The barn also held a tractor and some more pallets of what looked like product to create their pots. The women certainly were organized.

Bree continued, "We arranged to finance the house, and the payments are even less than our rent at the apartment."

Taylor piped up, annoyed they were having to defend themselves, "You know how small the apartment was getting as the children grew. This way we have enough room for all of us, and the girls can have their own larger room, as well as the boys. And we even have an extra bedroom, should we need it. The pictures the building company gave us makes it look rather attractive."

"I'll be happy to look at the plans," she replied non-committally. It was her job to look after the well-being of her charges. Even though the older three were already adopted by these two, if she felt they were in danger or

neglected, she would have to take action. Her eyes glanced out to the rain to where the swamp was even now filling up with rainwater.

They ended with agreeing to meet later at the apartment so she could look at the house plans, then Bree and Taylor saw her off, watching her run out to her sedan through the rain and get in.

"I better call Vinnie and see if she could recommend where we could get some gravel for that side of the drive," Taylor murmured to Bree.

"How much is that going to cost?" Bree fretted.

"No idea."

HOME ~ First Nillionaires Club

CHAPTER SEVENTEEN

Their day wasn't over, and, with Mrs. Henderson coming over, they hurried back to the apartment to straighten up. Spending so much time out at the property not only for working on the property and making pottery but also to keep the kids entertained, they'd let things go at the apartment. Everyone had something to pick up or clean before the social worker got there. As they were rushing to straighten up everything, the phone rang.

"Hello?" Taylor answered the phone as Bree was cleaning in the girls' room, running the vacuum with the door closed.

"Hey, are you avoiding me?" Taylor's mom started without even a hello. "I haven't heard from you girls much this summer. What's going on? You up to something? You can't possibly be that busy with shows for your pots?"

Taylor laughed at her mother, not letting her get a word in edgewise as she peppered her with questions. "Hello, Mom," she emphasized her manners, the laughter in her voice as she continued, "No, we aren't avoiding you; we've just been really busy. Why don't we come over for dinner sometime and explain what we've been up to?" They had been so busy and hadn't thought of including her mother in their decisions.

"How about Thursday?"

Taylor considered, trying to remember if she was working that night and glancing at the calendar Bree had hung up. There was nothing on it that would prevent them from going, so she agreed and penciled in the dinner.

"Who was that?" Bree asked as she came out of the bedroom, rolling the vacuum cleaner into its closet. She'd heard Taylor say goodbye.

"My mom. We have dinner next Thursday ... if that's okay?" She half hoped there was something written on the calendar so they wouldn't have to go, but, at the same time, she missed seeing her mother.

"Oh, lordy, we forgot to tell her!" Bree exclaimed, slapping her forehead as she realized.

Taylor, still amused at all her mother's questions, laughed again. "Then, I guess we will have to go next Thursday and tell her."

"Do we have to tell Tia, too?" she mumbled so the kids wouldn't hear, and they both shared a laugh at that.

* * * * *

Mrs. Henderson was pleased with the house plans. The two women had chosen a pleasant ranch-style house, and, with its walk-out basement, it was the perfect size for their family. She was certain they wouldn't want to foster any more children and looked forward to finalizing the paperwork on their final adoption. The apartment was a little less crowded because some of the furniture was moved out, she noted, and, while they had obviously cleaned up for her visit, the place was a bit shabby from the previous crowding. There was an obvious need for spackle on the corners and paint on the walls. They clearly needed a larger place, and the children had all that space to run and play out at the new property. She just worried about that swamp. She was in a fairly good mood and understood why they couldn't give her a copy when she saw 'DO NOT COPY' stamped on the blueprints.

* * * * *

"I've got to find a way to expand the driveway. Know of any cheap gravel?" Taylor asked Vinnie as she filled her coffee cup.

"I thought you were looking for gates?" she teased, remembering the last story of someone driving up on them. It happened too often, despite the obvious differences once that hill was gone.

"That, too," she complained good-naturedly as she left to take another order.

Vinnie thought about her friend's dilemma. She had a line on some gates that might do. They might, in fact, be too much, but she wasn't

certain and hadn't mentioned it to either Taylor or Bree yet. Gravel was going to be expensive. Still, they needed a base, and expanding the driveway, especially where it was a bit swampy, would require gravel.

"I'll keep an eye out for some gravel if someone wants to get rid of theirs. But, if you want it right away, I get a contractor's discount over at the quarry." She smiled to herself when Taylor admitted she'd wait for her to find some instead of buying it new. They both knew that it wouldn't be cheap.

* * * * *

"Hey, there," Ellen greeted her daughter and daughter-in-law, bestowing expected kisses on each of their cheeks, pleased to see them. She then promptly ignored them to greet her grandchildren.

"Hey," Tia added upon seeing Taylor and Bree, lifting her chin in her own version of a greeting. Eric glanced up from watching the TV and actually grunted before returning to the show on the screen.

The children were soon playing with Blaine, who, while older than all of them, acted a lot younger than his age, especially when his parents weren't watching closely. Both Bree and Taylor kept an eye on the teen, knowing his parents didn't discipline him the way they would and that he often bullied the younger children.

"Have you had a lot of shows?" Ellen inquired as they settled around the table. "Eric, turn off the TV and come to the table."

He gave Ellen a resentful look, but he turned off the TV, hauled himself out of the easy chair, and came to the table. He affectionately cuffed his son on the back of the head in greeting as he sat down.

"Yes, we're doing more than ever," Bree stated cheerfully as she helped to bring food to the table, passing Tia who had finished laying the place settings.

"More than last year?"

"Well, we're trying to earn as much as possible," Taylor put in, bringing the large casserole her mother made to the table and slapping at both Blaine and Eric's hands as they reached for the spoon to help themselves. She moved it to her mother's side of the table so she could serve. Once they were all around the table, Ellen passed everyone a plate with a helping of casserole for them to add from the vegetables and other dishes she had prepared.

"Money tight?" Tia asked, and both Taylor and Bree could hear the tinge of avarice in the tone of her seemingly innocent inquiry. She seemed to enjoy holding it over them how tight money could be with four children in that small apartment, despite her own situation of living with her mom and frequently having no money of her own.

"No, we're doing okay there," Bree answered sweetly, knowing it would annoy her sister-in-law. But she did not elaborate further.

"What's this?" Eric asked, having overheard the children talking about their new yard. He glanced at Blaine to see if he knew what the others were talking about.

"That's what we were going to tell you about," Taylor put in before someone could make an issue out of it.

"Tell us what, dear?" Ellen asked around a mouthful of food. It was tuna casserole, and the potato chips across the top had made it crunchy.

"We bought some land and are having a house put on it," Taylor blurted out before taking a bite of her own casserole and reaching for the cranberry sauce. The combination sounded odd to most people, but it was really quite delicious.

"You what?" Ellen asked, cheeks bulging from the bite of food. She chewed rapidly to get her mouth empty.

"Yes, we found this beautiful opportunity," Bree stated, again in the chirpy voice. She and Taylor exchanged amused looks and waited for the explosion.

Ellen swallowed hard. The food hadn't been chewed enough, and it hurt going down with the sharp potato chips, but she waited a second to speak. "What do you mean you're putting a house on it? Where's this land?"

"It's out on the Restlawn Highway, and Bree found it for us," Taylor said with a proud smile at her wife as she reached to one of the children to prevent them making a mess across the table.

"How could you afford that?" Eric asked. He could see the resentment on Tia's face and knew he was in for an earful later.

"We've been saving for years." Her tone told him that he should have remembered, but it was really a reminder for the whole table.

"All your savings?" Ellen asked in wonderment and with a touch of worry. "What if it turns out to be a bad investment?" She was trying to remember if she had seen any of the land out by Restlawn Highway.

"Oh, we're being careful, and it actually saves us money on our monthly bills. When the house is on the land, our mortgage will be less than our rent payments."

"How can you afford that and the rent on your other places?" Tia asked, a triumphant note in her voice that hid the jealousy. She just knew they were lying.

"We got rid of our shop and our storage unit months ago. As soon as the house is delivered and hooked up, we'll be moving from our apartment," Taylor answered dryly, knowing more was in that loaded question, even if the others—except for her wife—didn't realize.

Tia had passed by the shop one day on her way to work, and, seeing it shut down, had thought her sister's business had failed. To hear they were still going to shows had only confused her. She still thought they were lying. "How could you get rid of your shop?"

"There's a nice barn on the property," Bree told her, trying to stay calm. She knew from Taylor's tales over the years how deceptive Tia's *innocent* questions could be. "We had to get rid of the house."

"Why was that?" Ellen asked, her meal forgotten as she listened to the women.

Taylor explained about the abandoned property and the house burning. She made the hill removal sound exciting, and it was obvious how much she liked the property.

"Good thing you know that Vinnie chick," Eric put in with a slight sneer. He didn't like the butch-looking woman that was their landscape friend, even if she did sport long hair like a real woman. Over the years, when Taylor had her friend over, Eric had always felt uncomfortable around her.

"Yes, it is a good thing we know Vinnie," Taylor answered, a tone coming into her own voice in defense of their friend. "She has all those wonderful machines for her business, and helping out a friend is more than we could ask. She's been very generous in helping us out."

"You put all your things in this barn?" Ellen fretted, wondering if that was a good idea. She was picturing an old-time farmer's barn, where cattle were below the loft, full of hay.

"It's a metal framed building, Mom," Taylor responded. "We swept it out first," she added with a smile.

"It's a lovely size and much bigger than we need for our business at the moment. So, we put all our things from storage in there." Bree smiled at the knowledge of how much they'd saved on the storage unit and the shop they'd given up at the beginning of the summer.

"A barn? Isn't it full of rats and mice?" Tia sneered.

"No, it's very clean, large, and we have a lot of room to grow," Bree answered, turning her smile on her wife's rude little sister. She knew it would annoy her. "We have a cat now, and he's keeping it rodent free."

"A cat?"

"Remember that cat we told you about last time we were here? He's really settled in quite nicely. Good thing, too, as the landlord was going to catch him and get rid of him."

The children piped up, now that they were talking about the cat they so adored.

"I hope you aren't going to have that cat in your new home." Ellen regained her composure and offered seconds to everyone. Only Eric and Blaine took her up on it.

"We don't know if Marmalade is simply an outdoor cat or an indoor cat, too," Taylor stated matter-of-factly, already tired of her family's negativity. She knew her family could be a bit much, and she wasn't going to let them get ahead of her with their pessimism, especially her sister.

"Isn't it chancy moving out of your shop into this barn?" Ellen worried. Taylor was the only daughter who kept a job long enough to pay her bills. She was doubtful Tia would ever get her life together enough to move out.

"Well, we own the land and the barn, and we didn't see the point of paying rent at the shop or the storage unit anymore."

"So, you're actually saving money by moving out?" she inquired, surprised.

"Actually, yes," Bree spoke up, having to calm down the children and their exuberant stories about the cat. "It makes more sense not to have the overhead of the old shop. Plus, we have more room and have been able to expand."

"Expand?"

"We found another oven online."

"Bree finds the best deals on the Marketplace and Craigslist," Taylor bragged proudly.

"You shouldn't go on those places and meet people," Tia said, the tone of her voice making the fake concern sound disparaging.

"Well, I rarely go alone to buy anything, and, if they are selling something used that is a good deal, why wouldn't I buy it?" Bree knew very well not to engage Tia in an argument. One never won with someone so obviously unhappy with her life.

"When is the house going to be built?" Ellen asked, trying to be happy for her daughter but quite worried she would lose everything she and Bree had been working towards for years. If they lost their shirts, what would happen to the four children they had taken in? She glanced around, wondering where she would put them all. There simply wasn't the room in her place for more with Tia, Eric, and Blaine there.

"We hope by the end of summer," Bree said resignedly. "Any later, and we have to worry about the ground freezing, snow, whatever."

"They can't put in a house in the snow," Eric mansplained, sounding triumphant.

Taylor and Bree ignored him, as they often did. Tia usually encouraged his derision of the two lesbians, having resented their apparent *success* for years. Not only did Taylor and Bree have what appeared to be a good marriage, but their children, who weren't even their blood, seemed normal. Her own son, Blaine, was a constant disappointment.

Bree gave Ellen a rundown of the house's design. "We can add on later if we can afford to, but, for now, it should be good for our needs. We just need to build the basement."

"Oh, I forgot to tell you Vinnie said she had a line on some of the decorative bricks you two were talking about," Taylor put in.

"Decorative bricks?"

"For the basement?" she returned, frowning as though her wife should know.

"That sounds expensive," Ellen put in thoughtfully.

"Oh, Vinnie finds all sorts of deals around town. People hope she can haul it off for them, and she does."

"The junk man cometh," Eric murmured disparagingly.

"For a junk woman, she earns a helluva lot at a business she has built up since she was twelve," Taylor pointed out, offended on her friend's behalf.

"Yeah, yeah. We've all heard about the hero building it up from a push mower her mother had in her garage." He shook his head and ignored them as he tucked into the rest of his meal.

"What is your house going to look like?" Ellen asked. Her food had grown cold, so she picked up the plate to reheat it in the microwave.

They told her about the ranch style house they had picked out.

"And we're going to have rooms of our own!" Melanie added importantly.

"No, that's not quite right," Bree corrected. "You will share with your sister." She pointed at Barbie. She saw that Melanie looked crestfallen and knew the girl was trying to get a promise that wasn't there. They were going to keep that extra bedroom as a guest room or office—they hadn't decided which. Just because she was the oldest of the four didn't mean she got a room to herself.

They found themselves inviting Ellen out to come see the land for herself, and, naturally, Tia, Eric, and Blaine invited themselves to come

HOME ~ First Nillionaires Club

with her. Even though Bree and Taylor weren't thrilled with that aspect, the four of them seemed to be a packaged deal.

CHAPTER EIGHTEEN

"Gravel—check. Gates—check," Vinnie said as she watched Taylor, amused.

"Sorry, thought you just might run across it faster than Bree could find it on the Marketplace or Craigslist." She smiled as she poured coffee into her friend's thermos for her to take with her to the job site.

"I found someone to work on the basement, and, with the bricks he will install, you can get that permit you're gonna need to put the house on it. He said he'd teach you."

"I thought you told Bree about the decorative bricks? She had no idea what I was talking about." She remembered Bree being totally clueless about it.

Vinnie shook her head, frowning. "No, I never said anything to Bree about bricks. Maybe that was Gretchen?"

Taylor frowned now, trying to remember. It was all any of them talked about these days, the building of Taylor and Bree's new home. Everyone had chipped in their time and efforts.

"Relax, it'll all come together." Vinnie squeezed her friend's arm as she left money on the counter. "Your brain won't implode," she assured her before she exited the door of the restaurant.

"I better write this shit down," Taylor murmured to herself. She rang in the coffee and croissant sandwich Vinnie had paid for and took out the difference for her tip.

It was Gretchen who had the tip on the bricks. After the show up in Twin Rivers, Gretchen and Bree overloaded the trailer with her find.

"Geez, babe, I think you bent the axle. That's going to be expensive to replace," Taylor said when she saw it. Fortunately for them, she was wrong, but they did need new springs. "That's a relief," she admitted.

"I'm sorry, babe. With all the pottery we haul in that thing, I thought it could handle the bricks. I was worried that the owner would change his mind on Gretchen and renege on the deal if we had to make extra trips. I wanted to get as much as possible, as quickly as possible. He gave me bad vibes, and I didn't want to go back."

"I understand, but we need to make our equipment last as long as possible. You know that. Still, those are mighty pretty bricks," she admitted to take the sting off her admonishment.

It was Vinnie who arranged to have Lenny, Gretchen, and Elsie come over to help lay the bricks. It was a rather cool design with cinder blocks to form the base around the decorative bricks that kind of wove an intricate wave pattern.

"This is really pretty," Vinnie admitted after they worked out a system of alternating bricks in each of their areas. Vinnie's friend Greg was showing them how to put rebar inside the cinder block holes to bring the wall up to code. They'd save money on building it themselves, but they had to have a contractor who would ultimately be responsible.

"If I'd known about these, I'd have picked them up," Greg kiddingly grouched about the decorative bricks as he showed Bree how to pound in the rebar to hold up the walls. He was amused at how she had the children working, putting rocks in the holes as filler, a good idea to keep them distracted and engaged. He was pleased to show these women who were volunteering their time how to build with the blocks.

"Yoo-hoo," Ellen called as she and Tia walked up to the basement. "Whoa," she said, pulling back from the side she had almost walked over. "This isn't safe," she complained, looking down at her daughter and her friends. They were all a bit dirty from hauling the bricks, whether decorative or cinder, as well as mixing concrete for in between the bricks.

"Mom? What are you doing here today? I thought you were coming on the weekend?" Taylor dusted off her gloves and stared up at her mom.

"I went by your work, and they said you weren't working today, so we thought we'd come out."

Taylor tried to look pleased to see her mother and sister but failed. "We're kinda busy here, Mom."

"Grandma!" the children shouted and ran from the basement to the level where their grandmother stood. She enthusiastically returned their hugs while Taylor slumped her shoulders and exchanged a look with her wife. She reluctantly followed the children, knowing she couldn't avoid showing her family around the place.

"What are you doing?" Tia looked down at the working women and the one man, who was now measuring out the L-shaped wall on the far side.

"We're putting in the basement. We hope to get it done so we can have concrete poured for the floor," Taylor explained, wiping her arm against her nose and smudging her face with sweat and dust. "We need to have it all set before the house gets here."

Tia looked around skeptically. The place looked a mess, and that swamp they had passed by on the way in was filthy. She stared at the mulch under the trees with grass springing up in random spots. "Don't you worry that the children are going to get lost in the woods or fall into the pond?"

"Oh, that's not a pond yet," Taylor said cheerfully, knowing her sister's words were meant to zing her. "It's a swamp," she admitted with a small smile. She knew everyone in the basement hole could hear her quite well.

"Taylor, aren't you worried about the children?" Ellen asked, now prompted by the thought Tia had put into her head.

"No, because they aren't allowed to go near the water or into the woods without an adult," she said matter-of-factly. She watched as Eric and Blaine got out of the car, gazing around gloomily. She could bet they had hoped to eat at the diner on Ellen's dime and with Taylor's discount, but when Ellen found she wasn't there, they probably had left without eating anything. Ellen wasn't about to buy them lunch without her discount. Taylor glanced at the barbeque on the other side of the basement. It was fired up and ready to cook a late lunch for all her volunteers, the kids, and Greg, too, if he wanted to stay, but they didn't have enough to feed four more people, especially Eric and Blaine. She'd bet her mother would want to stay to watch them work, and, somehow, Tia and her brother-in-law would want to cop a free meal. She sighed inwardly.

"How many acres is this place?" Eric asked, then angrily slapped a mosquito against his leg.

"Ten-point-three acres," Taylor said proudly, but she knew he was just assessing it for whatever stupid thoughts he had.

"Why'd you need so much?" he asked, confirming he had stupid thoughts.

"It came with the barn," she answered dryly and heard a couple of chuckles from the basement.

"Well, it will be nice to hunt on this fall," he said. He peered down the trail leading into the woods on the other side of the yard.

"No hunting here," Taylor told him, but she was certain he wasn't listening.

"Yeah, no hunting here," Bree put in, coming up and pulling off her own gloves. "We posted the land."

"Why not?" he asked, sounding like he wanted to argue.

"Because we have small children and a pet. We don't want strangers on our land shooting off their guns." Bree wasn't intimidated by his so-called manliness, and he knew it. She knew he referred to her and her friends as dykes when he didn't think they could hear. Taylor would go ballistic on him if she heard, and he knew better than to do it around her.

"That's just for strangers, then?" he asked smugly, thinking this would be a great private hunting retreat for him and his friends.

"No, that's for everyone."

"But, I'm family?"

"Doesn't matter. We don't want guns around here," she said firmly, but she knew he'd bring this argument up again at some point. He never listened to a mere woman. She exchanged looks with her wife, who had never considered her brother-in-law family. "No. That's for everyone. With the children here, we really can't risk having anybody hunting in our woods."

Taylor was pointing out the brush Vinnie's machine had cleared to her mother and sister and telling them some of their plans for the land, including a garden.

"No wonder you haven't been around all summer—you've been clearing brush," Tia sneered. The innuendo was not lost on either of the two married women. Both hated how crude she could be.

Taylor was right; Ellen did try to get an invite to their cookout. "Mom, we barely have enough for our friends who we planned on feeding. You can't stay."

"Well, it looks like you have plenty ..." she began in a whiny voice. She'd had them show her the barn, and she was pleased for her daughter, even if it did sting a bit that Taylor hadn't consulted her before buying the place. And she was offended that Taylor wouldn't let her stay to eat, as well.

"Mom, if I had known you were coming out here today, I would have made plans for it," Taylor reassured her while trying to lead her to the car. Bree had gone back down in the basement to help their friends, and she needed to get back to work, too. "Tell you what, after the house is delivered, we should have a small housewarming party, and you are definitely invited to that." She looked up in time to see a bored Blaine throwing rocks at crows who were cawing angrily. "Hey, Blaine! Stop that!" she yelled down the driveway, startling the youth.

Eric, who had been leaning against the car, waiting on the women once he realized they weren't going to feed them, looked up angrily. "Boy! You get your butt over here and in the car." He was embarrassed that someone other than himself or Tia had yelled at his son.

Taylor's children were hustling away from Blaine, who had just been yelled at, certain they were next.

"Aren't you worried about this being so far off the road?" Ellen got in the car, not realizing that Taylor had basically herded her away from the house site to get her to leave.

"We've thought it out, Mom. I'll call you," she assured her. "I have to get back to work. Can't let my friends do it all."

She watched Tia get in the front seat next to their mother, with Eric looking annoyed to be relegated to the back with his son. As they turned the car around, Taylor waved enthusiastically, glad to see the last of them before she turned to her guilt-ridden children.

Before they could say a word to defend themselves, Taylor held up a hand and stopped them. "I know you didn't throw rocks, but you didn't stop him, either. Crows are fierce creatures. Don't you *ever* throw anything at them," she told them. "They are also smart and will remember a kindness. Always be nice to crows."

They walked around the side of the basement hole in order to get back to work.

"What was that yelling before?" Bree asked while Taylor pulled her gloves on. She'd seen the kids looking guilty as they went back to picking up rocks to wedge into the cinder blocks.

"Oh, Blaine was throwing rocks at crows."

"Geez, you should never be mean to crows," Gretchen said. "Did I tell you about that time I got that birdbath you made for me set up?"

The others shook their heads as she continued with her story, knowing the children were listening, too. The two boys, Bryan and Jack, were playing in the dirt and digging up more rocks for their sisters to put in the blocks.

"I'd put that birdbath in so early into the decorations that it got dirty, and I had to clean it out. I thought I was alone there at the client's house, and I heard, 'Hello? Hello?' Scared me a bit as I looked around. There was no one there. I thought I was losing my mind." She put another brick on the wavy wall she and Elsie were building together and used the level to make sure they got it straight. "Then, it happened again. I knew I was losing it. But it turns out that the local crows had frequented the bath I had just started cleaning out. They'd spent enough time around the humans that they picked up both basic greetings and passive aggressive tones." She grinned at the others as she paused for a moment to stretch her back. She saw the children were enjoying her story, even if they didn't understand all her words. Talking crows had captured their attention, so she went on with the story. "By the time I realized where the greeting was coming from, as well as the sense of urgency in their tone, there were three crows on the fence line, waiting impatiently for me to finish cleaning out the bird bath. They were urging me to hurry up, not only in what they were saying but in their agitation to have that fresh water. I figured I better hurry up since they were so impatient. Crows, sheesh!"

Several people chuckled at her story.

"Did you know that a couple of crows is called a murder?" Lenny asked, making sure she sounded mysterious so the children would hear.

"Dontcha have to have three or more?" Elsie asked sincerely, slopping some concrete on top of bricks before gently laying another on top of that.

"A group of crows is called a murder," Lenny repeated back, looking at the children.

"Crows have the biggest brain of birds their size," Bree put in, lugging a cinder block over to Greg, who was listening, amused, while the women worked. He quickly hefted it over some of the bars and slid it down to the next spot on the wall he was building.

"They mate for life," Lenny continued, bringing the wheelbarrow full of mixed concrete closer to Greg and the others who needed it.

"I heard ..." began Taylor, "that older crow chicks will look after their siblings when they hatch from the same nest."

"And I heard," Bree added, "that crows have dialects, depending on where they have lived and change them if they move to another area."

Everyone seemed to have crow stories to share, showing the children that these intelligent birds had value. It hit home why they shouldn't throw rocks at them.

They had to keep working until the last of the concrete in the wheelbarrow was used up so it wouldn't dry out. By the time they

stopped, one entire wall was done. They wouldn't get the whole thing done in one day, but they all knew that and had planned to keep helping.

Over lunch, Greg contributed more crow lore. "I heard of a guy who rescued a fledgling crow that he named Edgar Allan Crowe." He grinned at the adults, who got the pun. "His neighbor had deliberately run over the wee bird," his lilt giving a poignant edge to the story. The children stopped eating to listen, sure it was a sad tale. "The guy took care of the neighbor, but that's a story for another time." He glanced deliberately at the children. "He took that crow and wrapped him in a towel and put him in a box. It took a while for the mama crow to realize why her caws produced no answer. Those crows knew, though. They realized what was in that box, wrapped in the towel. They mourned for that fledgling, all right." He saw Taylor fidgeting and decided not to get too graphic. The children were, after all, very young. "About one hundred crows arrived to mourn that poor wee baby. They sat around the guy's house on wires, cawing out their grief. The racket was tremendous. Then, suddenly, they all left at once. The guy took the babe in the box and buried him.

"Those crows, though, they didn't forget." He pointed to his brain for emphasis and included the women, who were listening, too. "They would show up and follow him when he walked his dog. If he pointed back to his house, they would meet him there, and he'd give them peanuts. Mama Crow would sit outside his front door and make eye contact with him. They seemed to know." He emphasized that last part by pointing at his head and making eye contact with each of the children. He sounded all mysterious and worldly.

The crow stories continued as the adults recollected more of them. Elsie told one about a couple of crows, where the female had somehow broken her beak and the male patiently and faithfully fed her for years.

"How many years?" Melanie asked in amazement.

"Well, I remember seeing them show up when I was twelve. She crashed into a car when I was about sixteen, and I thought for sure she would die. But, when I was in college and came home to visit my Mom, they were still there. I was twenty-four, so that's twelve years. and he took care of her for at least eight of those years."

The child was astonished, as were many of the adults.

Soon, they'd finished lunch, and the building of the walls continued, along with more talk of crows.

"Have you ever seen what a crow baby looks like?" Taylor asked her daughter affectionately. Melanie shook her head. "Well, you've seen baby chicks? Imagine one of those golden chicks completely black and fluffy. Even the eyes are black." The girl looked enraptured. Barbie was pleased, too.

Taylor saw the tired looks on the boys' faces, so she had them help her set up a pup tent in the shade of a nearby tree. They were tired from playing and being in the sunshine all day. She could see they wouldn't need a blanket, with this heat, but she put a sheet over them to protect them because the pup tent wouldn't provide much protection from the sun. The boys crawled in and took a nap. Later, Melanie and Barbie would join them, despite their claims that they didn't *need* a nap.

"I didn't know half of that stuff about crows," Bree commented after the children were all asleep. She wished she could crawl in the pup tent and join them. Lifting bricks was hard work.

"I have one that I didn't share with yer chicks," Greg put in. "Crows hold grudges." He nodded to emphasize his words. "They are so smart that they remember things and teach their friends who to hate. They teach their chicks, too."

"That would be like having a blood feud against you." Lenny laughed.

"Dive bombers from the sky," Vinnie added, laughing as well.

"A murder of crows with a blood feud until the end of time," Gretchen put in, chortling at her quip.

They all enjoyed the sharing of stories, and it helped the time go by pleasantly. By the second day, they seemed to be done with talk of crows and sick of the monotony of the work.

"You girls are getting the hang of this right well," Greg put in, slathering cement on the last of the concrete blocks that formed the L-shaped basement. He had been very particular that everything was aligned correctly because it was his reputation on the line here, but he owed a favor and was willing to work it off for his friend. Her friends had been surprisingly good company, and he'd enjoyed his time working with them all. "I might have to hire ya'll a time or two," he teased good-naturedly, saluting them with his beer at the end. They'd done a fine job, and he was pleased.

"You couldn't afford us," Vinnie quipped with a grin. "We're expensive girls." In her butch-ness, she didn't look anything like a girl, but she didn't mind. And it didn't bother her when people didn't know whether to address her as 'sir' or 'ma'am', which was most of the time.

"I remembered another story about crows, guys. It was when I was working a neighborhood on the north side of town," Vinnie said later as they were cleaning up. They'd finished the L-shaped wall frontage, all with cinder blocks. The wavy walls were inside and holding back the dirt in various places, creating a neat pattern that was pleasing to the eye.

Now, they were on ladders, putting concrete on the very top, over the blocks, to prevent rainwater from building up inside the walls. "That is, if you all aren't sick of hearing crow stories?"

Encouraged by the others, she explained she was working the neighborhood, which meant she was cutting lawns for several people. "One of the homeowners said there was huge drama in their neighborhood, and I thought it might be one of those neighbor things over a tree or property lines or something. Turned out it was the crows versus the squirrels. This lady had been leaving out food for the crows, and the crows got pissed …" she saw Bree frown at her choice of words and glance at the kids, who were now fully awake and listening intently to the story. "… er, uh, angry," she corrected herself, "at the squirrels for taking all the food. Those crows found all the nests where the squirrels were hiding their ill-gotten gains and cleaned them out. Full retaliation for their thefts. They went from tree to tree, the squirrels watching in horror while the crows ate it all," she finished with a grin. Several of the adults chuckled at the story, but the children sat, wide-eyed and imagining the scene playing out.

On their way home that night, Melanie asked if they could have a bird feeder when the house was built.

"What kind of bird feeder?" Taylor asked. She was tired, and she knew everyone was, too. After two days of sun and lifting rocks and brick, they were exhausted. She glanced at Bree, who looked sunburned and equally as tired.

"One for crows," Barbie piped up.

"What about the squirrels?" Taylor asked to tease her daughters.

"Maybe a separate one for those?" Bryan asked earnestly.

"We will see; we will see," Taylor said noncommittally.

HOME ~ First Nillionaires Club

CHAPTER NINETEEN

"We have a date," Bree told Taylor joyfully.

"A date?" she asked stupidly in return, wondering if she'd missed date night or something equally important to her wife.

"The contractor called. He got all the permits to deliver the house to our basement! The inspector told him we'd done a good job on the basement walls, and the plumber put in the pipes to the septic correctly. I'm going to bake Greg cookies!"

"Wait a minute. Greg was just supervising; he didn't do all the work," her wife reminded her, not wishing to miss out on some home-baked cookies.

"I'll make sure at our next gathering everyone gets cookies and lots of praise," she answered, delighted at the news. She gave a little victory dance.

"What date did they give us?" Taylor asked, amused at her wife's antics.

"September eighth," she said, showing the penciled-in date on the calendar.

"Wow, that seems so soon and yet …" she mused, having thought the house would never be put in.

"I know, right? We have a house coming!" Bree twirled her wife around in her arms.

"Hey, that means the kids will be back in school."

"And?" Had Taylor thought of something she hadn't?

"We won't have to watch out for them while they put the house in place." It was aggravating how much time was spent distracting the children when they had to work. They were both used to it, but it curbed how much they actually got done. Still, they wouldn't have given up their children for the world. They loved them too much.

Looking farther down the calendar, Bree pointed out, "Hey, the tenth is Jack's final court date."

"Oh, wow. A Wednesday and a Friday," Taylor lamented. "My boss isn't going to be happy."

"He never likes you to take off," her wife pointed out, grinning. She hoped they got enough business so Taylor could quit that job someday. "You may as well take Thursday off, too."

"We still need to get the well inspected and the plumbing for the water hooked up. Don't we need a pump?"

"I have that scheduled here and here," she said, pointing out the dates on the calendar, well ahead of the delivery of their house.

* * * * *

"Look at this," Bree said a few days later, smacking the computer monitor, which was flickering again. Taylor came to read over her shoulder.

Level 3 Handbuilding Package includes the DRD II/24G Gear Reduced Slab Roller with 51" Table,
Standard 4 Extruder, and Standard Die Kit, an 8-Piece Do Woo Pottery Tool Kit, Apron, Xiem
Wedging Board, 15" Turntable, (1) 44lb Box of Tucker's CCS Speckled Cone 6 Stoneware and the
Bailey TL2322-10 6.0 Cu Ft Kiln with Furniture Kit and Free Extra Relays and Thermocouples. This
is a great grouping of equipment for the serious potter.

She whistled softly, imagining what they could make with that. Serious potter indeed. "Who would buy something that new and not use it?" she wondered aloud while she read the rest of the ad. It went on to say the seller had ordered it, but it was too big for his shop. The two wives exchanged looks, wondering what kind of competition they had in the local area. He was only in the next village over.

"He's asking full price," Taylor pointed out.

"I won't offer that much. He should lose a little for his mistake," Bree said sensibly in return.

"Can we afford it?"

"After that last show, you bet your britches we can," she said and reached for the keyboard to type out a reply. She knew deals like this didn't happen every day, and someone else could get it if she didn't act fast.

It took several weeks of negotiating, back and forth with emails and messages, but Taylor felt Bree just wore him down. He probably hadn't gotten any other offers because these were very specific items for a very specific purpose. Unlike the seller, they did have enough room in their shop for the equipment, and she cheerfully waved off Bree and Gretchen, who Bree had asked to help her pick it up. She herself got in her Jeep and headed to her waitressing job, wondering when the day would come when she could quit. She only had a four-hour shift today, but it might be good with tips during the lunch hour. She was out at the property when the two women returned with the kit, and she helped them unload it.

"You two go play with your trucks," Taylor warned the younger kids away. She saw that Bree was handing select items to the girls to carry into the barn. The kids weren't big enough to carry most of the things, but between the three women they managed to get it all put away.

"What took so long?" she asked. She'd come home and been surprised as the children came off the bus and Bree wasn't already there. She'd loaded them into the Jeep and came out to the property.

"Oh, he wanted to renegotiate the price. Trying to say that now that I saw it, I could see it was practically brand new and should be full price." Bree sounded disgusted. "He also wouldn't help us load it; it took us forever to figure out how to get it into the back of the truck."

"I hope you two didn't hurt anything," Taylor fretted, knowing how heavy the equipment had been from having off-loaded it.

"You two owe me," Gretchen teased, holding her back as though she were an old woman.

They were just coming out of the barn when yet another yahoo came roaring up the drive. When he realized there were people at the end of it and it wasn't a road, he quickly turned around, waving cheekily as he went.

"I always worry about the children," Bree lamented.

"I thought you two were exaggerating about how often that happens, but when we helped with the basement, what were there, six, in those two

days?" Gretchen asked, stretching to ease her back from the strain of unloading heavy things from her truck.

"I counted eight," Taylor said, a tone in her voice letting the other two know she was angry. They needed a gate, but she had gotten a quote of sixteen *thousand* dollars for a steel one that worked with a door opener or actuator. That was way beyond their budget.

"I'm so sick of it, but, really, what can we do?" Bree asked, but didn't expect a reply.

There really was nothing they could do. They couldn't afford a new gate, and, while their friends were keeping their eyes open for a used one, only one that had been hit by a truck had come up in the time since they'd bought the place. It simply wouldn't do. Building a wooden one could end up being their only option.

"I'd like something classy," Taylor said to Bree as they discussed it in bed one night.

"I know what you'd like, and I agree. But we simply can't afford it. We will need something. Maybe a stock gate might do in the meantime?"

"That just seems so … redneck," she complained, turning over in their bed, exasperated at being so poor.

"It might be what we will have to make do with."

* * * * *

Gretchen, not Vinnie, was the one who solved their driveway drainage problem. Instead of gravel, she pointed out the rocks she'd found a deal on would provide a firmer base, but they needed to remove them from the farmer's field as soon as possible. They enlisted Lenny and Vinnie, both women who owned trucks, as well as Gretchen herself, to load a lot of rocks, most the size of a fist, into the truck beds. They couldn't fill the truck beds since the weight would be too much, but they half-filled the three, loaded the kids into the Jeep, and headed back to the property to unload the rocks along the driveway and go back to the farmer's field to load more rocks from the piles that had been there for a millennium.

"How'd you find this?" Lenny asked Gretchen curiously as she lifted another rock and threw it into the bed. The satisfying sound of it landing on another stone soothed her worry that it might be scratching her bed liner. She shrugged; that liner was tough.

"I thought about their gravel problem and remembered how many farmers in this area made piles of rocks they've taken out of their fields in order to plow. I've seen these piles and thought, why not use them?"

"If we can get the farmers to give us the rocks, it really is a win-win for us, and I thank you for thinking of us," Taylor put in. She was sweating as they finished cleaning up the pile in this farmer's field. Bree and she both had their hands full with keeping the children out of the way because they wanted to help. The rocks were too heavy for the youngsters, and they certainly couldn't get them in the truck beds. Their attempts to help had nearly busted out Gretchen's back window so they were to stay out of the way.

"I think I know of a farmer out by my place we can go talk to," Vinnie mentioned, admiring Gretchen as she reached for one of the last stones near them. She quickly looked away.

"Well, it won't be every day all three of you have your trucks available, and we cleaned up these piles in no time," Taylor pointed out. Bree was already shooing the children back into the Jeep.

"I'll drive near my place and ask him if he wants us to remove them. Then, I'll meet you out at your place," Vinnie stated as she headed for her cab door.

"We'll see you out there," Taylor agreed with a smile. She hoped Bree had more than soda in that cooler in the Jeep. She wanted a gallon of water and maybe a beer, and she was certain everyone else was just as thirsty. She was looking forward to the ham sandwiches they had packed that morning, even though a barbeque would have been better. There hadn't had been enough time to plan one.

They carefully rolled the stones and rocks along the driveway until they began to show out of the water. They continued down the drive, widening it by several feet until they ran out of rock.

"I can't believe how much that took," Taylor gasped as they heaved the last stones onto what was a pretty deep pile.

"There's Vinnie. Maybe she has good news," Bree pointed out.

"Sure. She shows up after we finish," Taylor teased.

"Better late than never," Gretchen returned, moving to her truck to make way for Vinnie's.

"Hey, my neighbor said we were welcome to his piles. Let's get this unloaded and go get them?"

"I think we better unload this one and eat some lunch before we go out again," Bree objected. "You all are going to faint, otherwise."

It was a sensible idea, and they made quick work of the stones in the back of Vinnie's truck. Sitting on the open tailgates, everyone munched on their sandwiches and drank to their hearts' content.

There were individual chip bags, and, when Bryan went to chuck his on the ground, Bree corrected him. "That's littering, and we never *ever* do

that," she explained gently. "Bags like that can harm the birds and wildlife. We don't want that."

Remembering all the crow stories, he looked around fearfully, as though the birds and animals would be mad at him. He crumpled it up and made sure to put it in the trash bag Bree had started.

Between the three trucks and five women, it took them three trips to empty the other field. There was enough rock to make a pretty substantial base along that section of the driveway.

"We should stack some at the end of the driveway and build pillars," Taylor joked. "Then, if we ever put up a gate, it will look nice."

"That's not a bad idea," Vinnie mused, envisioning it. "You could put up lights and have it all on solar power."

They heard a tremendous crash at the end of their driveway by the roadside. They couldn't see the car involved because it sped around the curve in no time and was out of sight. Hurrying down to the end, Taylor saw someone had hit their mailbox. "Goddamnit," she said angrily and then looked to see if the children had heard her. They weren't as fast as the adults and were still coming down the drive.

"Whoa, they really f—" began Vinnie but, glancing at Bree and back to the kids, "… screwed that up." She reached for the brightly colored mailbox that had been intentionally knocked off its wooden post. It was too far back from the road to be anything but deliberate. The post the two women had mounted it on was halfway out of the ground with the concrete still intact. The post was cracked and unusable.

"Should we report it?" Bree asked, biting her lip. She wanted to cry, but that wouldn't set a good example for the kids.

"Yeah," Taylor agreed. "In the meantime, we better prop this up so we can still get our mail." She looked down the highway and mumbled under her breath. "Bastards."

"*Taylor*," Bree said, glancing at the kids.

Taylor nodded, but she wasn't going to apologize. She wasn't sorry, just pissed. She took several pictures with her phone before they managed to jury-rig something to hold it up. "We're going to have to replace the post, even if we can get the mailbox pounded out."

"Why do people have to be so destructive?" Gretchen fretted, shaking her head as they all walked back up the drive.

"Probably teens joyriding," Lenny put in sagely.

Whoever did it, it proved to be expensive. This was the first of five attacks on their mailbox, and they would have to replace it time and again. Taylor took pictures, but their driveway was too long for them to hear all the crashes, and, while the post office was sympathetic and took a report each time—the police as well—unless they caught them in the act or had visual proof of who was doing it, there was nothing the officials *could* do. And theirs wasn't the only rural box getting hit.

CHAPTER TWENTY

The widening of their driveway, though, was a happy event, and it proved to be advantageous when the house was delivered. Both Bree and Taylor wanted to be there and waited impatiently for the trucks and trailers to arrive, carrying their new home. The wide load signs on the trucks made them realize their driveway was fairly narrow. Without the added stone they had put in near the swamp, the trucks may not have made it up the long drive.

The builders brought a crane to offload the modular home in sections onto the concrete walls. The slab in the basement and the pad for their garage were finished just two weeks ago, and it had hardened into a nice, white slab in both places. The L shape of the house gave it a huge space in the walk-out basement. The contractor put up a type of plastic sheet on top of the walls of the basement to provide a vapor barrier, then wood on top of this. It was all bolted down into the walls before they lowered one side of the L.

They started at the back of the house, where the bedrooms would go, lowering that section, where the raw wood intermixed with partially finished vinyl siding. The windows were already installed in most of the rooms. It amazed the two women how the men easily used ropes and other equipment to control the load while the crane slowly lowered each section.

Taylor turned and saw that Gretchen, Vinnie, Elsie, and Lenny had all joined them, their trucks and cars parked along the drive, well back from the contractor's trucks and trailers.

"Amazing," Elsie breathed, staring in awe at the huge trailers holding her friends' new home.

The contractors offloaded steel support beams and laid them out in the basement to help hold up the house sections.

Some of the men helped direct the bedrooms into place. The process went slowly, with them pulling with lines attached to the section and getting the house in place. It was amazingly accurate, and, pretty soon, they were using pneumatic nail guns to attach the section to the boards they had lain on top of the basement walls.

"Don't get any ideas," Bree teased Taylor, who seemed especially interested all the tools being used.

"What?" Gretchen asked.

"Taylor sees power tools, and she starts to get excited," Bree further teased, and all their friends looked. Taylor did seem especially animated. "If we could afford it, she'd buy tools that we have no idea how to use."

"I could learn," Taylor stated, staring as some of the men began getting another section of the house ready for the crane.

The friends exchanged some good-natured ribbing and enjoyed the show. It was amazing how the house looked so heavy, and, yet, the crane lifted it so easily. The second section went up next to the first and included the other half of the bedrooms. They lifted the supports and nailed them to the house in both sections. Once they'd finished that part, the first trailer left, followed soon by the second. Within half an hour, two more trailers arrived with the second part of the house, half each on their trailers.

"Wow, this is incredible!" Lenny mouthed over the intense noise. She noticed the men all wore earplugs, and she wished she'd brought her own. No women were on this team, of course.

As one crew put the third section in with precision, another crew went down to the basement to attach the supports, but some were already using their nail guns to attach it around the edges. Still others were on the roof, lifting it to a V and placing two unseen sections that would support the previously flattened roof into an angle to make it shed water.

"That is so clever," Taylor stated when things were quiet for a moment, and the women beside her who stood with their arms crossed all agreed.

The crane lifted one side of the roof, and the crew rushed in to lower wooden supports on both sides. Then, the crane lifted the ends one by one, and the men quickly locked them into place. It was all detailed, premade,

and fit together amazingly well. The women were all captivated as they watched.

The fourth section, the front of the house, went on just as well. The men obviously knew their jobs and were in place, ready and waiting, for each step. No one was hurrying, and the crane operator knew exactly where to place whatever was attached to the end of his crane cable. It was endlessly fascinating, and the women didn't feel the morning hours slip by as they watched the men work like bees at a hive, going over the prefab house and nailing it together. There was even a power box at one end of the side of the house, where the power was already run through the house when they built the sections and walls.

"God, and I didn't even think about the plumbing," Bree murmured, watching the men effortlessly piece the house together.

"I did," Taylor said in an aggrieved tone. "I couldn't do that," she admitted, nodding towards how easily someone applied a nail gun.

"That looks like fun," Vinnie said in a tone that hinted she would have liked to try it.

"It's so quick," Elsie commented. "I mean, it's taking hours, but even that isn't much when you consider how much there is to do." She nodded towards the totally changed landscape. Around them, there were several trucks and a crane. An entire house stood where only hours before was just an open basement.

The crane lifted first one side of the V at the top of the house, finishing out the last three feet or so on the bedrooms and creating the V roof. Two men on man lifts began taking up shingles to finish off the roof, where the last three-foot section had been applied. They would repeat this on the other side, and then both sides of the front of the house where the final two section had been put in place.

Walking around to the back of the house, the women watched the workers putting the shingles up. They made it look like they were just reaching under the previous shingles and sliding their hands and arms along, when, in reality, they were pressing the trigger on their nail guns in a rapid-fire motion and installing the missing shingles. They were so neat and tidy as they worked. When they were done, the roof looked flawless.

"They really got this down pat," Vinnie murmured. "Maybe in my next house, I'll have them do this."

"Your next house?" Taylor asked, amused.

Vinnie had bought a large piece of land two years before. The place was big enough to have her business at one end, away from her home, but near enough that she didn't have to travel far to her work barn before going out on jobs with the right equipment. She stored the equipment,

locked up, on her own land. She'd built a beautiful custom log house for herself and a mother-in-law's house a short distance from it for her mother to live in. Taylor speculated that Vinnie regretted that decision. Her mother refused to drive and expected Vinnie to take her places any time she wasn't tied up with work. Luckily, the bus stopped at their place, and her mother's house was close to the road. Another house could mean even more problems for Vinnie.

Vinnie grinned unrepentantly. "Well, maybe not, then."

Gretchen looked at her miserably. She'd wanted ... no, it was better not to think that way.

Elsie saw the look and exchanged one with Lenny. They both diverted their eyes back to the progress on the house. It was absolutely fascinating, and whatever was going on between Vinnie and Gretchen was none of their business.

One of the crews were now putting up insulation on the outside of the basement walls to stave off water. Because it was a walk-out basement, the women could see them at work.

"That's why Greg wouldn't let us put the dirt against the brick!" Bree exclaimed, understanding finally.

"Yeah, they would have covered up your beautiful wavy brick design if it didn't have the room it does now. You'll be able to put dirt down there against the insulation," the contractor said as he overheard the owner. He'd introduced himself as Marc Copeland, the foreman, when he had arrived with his men. He'd driven a big king cab truck full of tools. He headed into the walk-out basement. It was a bonus for his workers as they wouldn't asphyxiate from the insulation, some of it would be sprayed on in this job. One of his men was making stringers for the steps leading up to the first floor. They'd brought in several kinds of saws and were hard at work.

"I can't believe they did this all in one day," Bree marveled to Taylor as they walked their friends to their vehicles. "Wonder what they will do tomorrow?" She looked up in time to see the school bus dropping off their kids at the end of their long driveway.

* * * * *

"I won't be here to see tomorrow," Taylor pouted. She was frustrated because she had enjoyed watching them put the house together, but she hadn't been able to get the three days off in a row she'd wanted.

The workers would soon be gone for the day. The trailers and the crane had already gone, but the contractors were still gathering tools and materials they weren't leaving on site overnight.

"Well, you'll see it after work?" Gretchen tried to console her friend. She knew Taylor couldn't take off too much time; the two women couldn't afford for her to lose the job.

"Yeah, but it isn't the same as watching them work," Taylor whined, smiling as the children caught sight of them.

"Well, I wasted a whole day," Vinnie pretended to grouch. "Mow that lawn!" The grass was getting quite long, but it looked luxurious. She could see where they had raked aside the hay that had protected the seeds. In other places, the grass was growing up amongst the matted hay.

"Yeah, yeah, in my spare time," Taylor grouched back teasingly as she shut Vinnie's door for her. "Thanks for coming."

"I'll wait until the munchkins are out of the way," Vinnie informed her, looking in her side view window at the children pelting themselves up the driveway towards their moms.

"It's here! It's here!" Barbie shouted as she outpaced her siblings.

Taylor looked back at the house with admiration. The day had truly been transformative.

One by one their friends left, using the round drive to circle around and leave, followed by the contractors as they finished up for the day.

"Now, don't go in yet," Marc warned. "Everything isn't nailed down, and I don't want anyone hurt." He could see the kids were chomping at the bit to go exploring.

"We won't. And thank you," Bree informed him, holding Jack in her arms on her hip. They all watched as Marc was the last to leave.

"Wow, that's amazing," Barbie breathed, looking in awe at the house. It hadn't been there the previous day, when their moms had let them play in and around the basement. They were all good and didn't try to climb the walls, stayed away from the plumbing and pipes, and didn't hurt themselves, and it had been fun to pretend that they had a house. But now … today … there really was one.

"Can we go in?" Melanie asked, eager to find her promised room.

"No, you heard Mr. Marc. He said not to go in." Bree saw their disappointment. "But we can walk around the outside and check it out." She held hands with the two youngest, and Taylor took the other two, and they walked and talked as they explored around the house.

"It's so big!" Bryan marveled.

Taylor wondered when they would realize it was really quite a small house, but, coming from their tiny apartment, she supposed it did look

huge. It was all so new. Would they someday look back on it and think how small it was?

CHAPTER TWENTY-ONE

Taylor was quite grumpy when she headed off to work the next day. She managed to leave from the house. All the children had left quite reluctantly on the bus that morning from the apartment. Jack was in the regular kindergarten all day this year and no longer in kindergarten half-days. He felt like a big boy, and they were proud of his progress.

Taylor and Bree watched as the men began building the walls of the garage on the slab to the right of the house. It had a thick, sturdy all-weather door between the two buildings. The garage was big enough for two and a half cars, which meant that they could park their two inside and have room for a lawnmower, if they were so inclined. Some homeowners used that extra space for tools and other storage. The garage was also deep enough that if they ever bought a Suburban—and they hoped they would someday —it would fit.

Taylor managed to see all four framed walls of the garage and two of the trusses go up before she had to leave. She was cutting it close, and her boss wouldn't be happy if she was late. He'd already been pissed that she missed yesterday and would be out tomorrow for court, but she had no choice—no one had been able to switch shifts with her.

Bree was as fascinated as she had been the previous day. She really should have been throwing pots but couldn't tear herself away. The machine, a kind of pallet lifter on steroids, lifted the trusses up one at a time, putting them in place as a man on each end slid them where they needed to go and nailed them in place.

It seemed no time at all before they were putting down sheets of plywood to sheath the trusses, then unrolling the underlayment, and then some guys were hauling shingles up to put on top of those. As one guy was cutting off the excess plywood from the edge, a couple of guys behind him came down the slope of the garage, putting on the shingles.

Inside, she could hear thuds and hammering. She had no idea what they were doing; she hadn't been inside yet. She watched as a couple of guys began building out the porch, making it look so easy as they measured and put up large boards, nailing them together in even and divided sections to form the floor and then putting down supports over them. One step, then two, and now there was a way into the house from the front. It would later be enhanced with landscaping—including concrete, gravel, and even more grass.

Bree slowly walked around the house, surprised to see how quickly the siding had meshed together from the different sections. You could no longer tell this house had been shipped here in four sections. She walked down around the hill to the walk-out basement and was shocked to see windows, where there had previously been openings in the concrete. They even had a steel door painted to look like wood, and, if you didn't know it was steel, you would have thought it a nice attractive wood door with glass panels imbedded in it. It didn't have the lock or handle on it yet, but it looked amazing to her eyes. She looked up from the basement and was surprised to see how seamlessly the house now was from the basement to the sections, as though it had always been there.

In two days, they had managed to put all this together, and it was making her crazy to see the interior. But Bree managed to wait for Taylor to return, although it was difficult, as Marc had found her and offered to show her around. She held him off, explaining her wife would be returning from a short shift at work, and she wanted to see her face when she saw it, too. She had plenty to entertain her, though, watching them finishing up in the garage, including putting up pink sheets of insulation and using spray foam in between them and the wood to seal the corners. They had opted for a finished garage, and there were guys putting up drywall sheets, mudding them, and finishing that off, too, but not painting them yet because other guys were installing the roll-up doors and garage opener.

"Here are your two car fobs to the garage doors, one for each side … and here are the clickers for them," one of the men told her as he offered them to her.

"Thank you," she said in awe. She had never had a home that had such luxuries. Every time she was tempted to go inside the house, she whispered to herself, "Wait for Taylor. Wait for Taylor." She wanted to share the experience with her wife—and with the kids, of course.

When the school bus came and dropped off the kids, they sprinted up the driveway, leaving Jack in tears, struggling to keep up. Admonishing the others for leaving him back—and not for the first time—Bree told them they couldn't go in the house until Taylor got there. She could still hear interesting noises coming from inside the house. She'd seen plumbers and electricians go in, and their crews were still hard at work. Some of Marc's crews had already left, and she wondered what more there was to do. The one crew had finished the garage except for painting it, and you couldn't even tell it had been built separately from the house because the roof went across the whole front of the house and onto the garaged section.

"Please, Mommy, please, can't we go in?" Melanie begged.

"Yes Mommy, please?" Barbie tried.

"No, we will wait for your mom to get off from work so we can all see it together," she told them firmly.

"Can't we just sit on the porch and wait for Mommy?" Melanie tried to compromise.

As tempting as it was to Bree to do just that, she shook her head, disappointing both girls.

She was so pleased with how the house looked. The front had real bricks on the outside. Only a couple had come loose during the move, and Marc's crew had effortlessly reattached them. Above the bricks was vinyl siding that looked like real wood. The combination was beautiful. On the roof, the black shingles looked fresh and oh-so-new. One endless stream of tar. There were waterspouts attached along the edges to catch the rain and route it to the corners of the house. Bree was looking forward to finding chairs so they could sit on the porch. Maybe rocking chairs or a big swing. It would be lovely, and she couldn't wait to move in. Marc said they could begin moving in over the weekend. Everything was already dried in, and they had some few finishing touches he would point out when they toured the house. The construction crew would finish tomorrow, and the landscapers would start on Monday.

Finally, after what seemed like a lifetime, a Jeep appeared in the driveway, but it wasn't Taylor's Jeep. The driver was a stranger who gaped at them and the contractor's trucks with wide eyes and then tore out of there, spinning his tires as he went around the circle and sped down the drive. Bree sighed. She'd gotten her hopes up, and now they were dashed.

The next Jeep was Taylor's, though, and Bree was so happy to see her. She practically pulled her from the vehicle as she hugged and kissed her.

"Whoa, baby, whoa!" Taylor said in defense to her wife's enthusiasm. "Let me go change and ..." she began, but she could see neither her wife nor children were going wait for her change out of her waitress uniform. She looked at the house, amazed at the transformation from when she saw it earlier in the day. She hadn't expected it to be fully roofed or for the water spouts to be added on, much less the garage doors installed. It looked ... finished. "What more do they have to do?" she asked as Bree and Melanie began pulling her towards the porch.

"I have no idea, besides the landscaping. But *come on*," Bree replied, pulling her along. "I've waited hours, when I could have gone in without you. I wouldn't let the kids go in until you got here."

"So none of you have seen anything?" she began, but she was being dragged across the porch by then. She barely got a glimpse of the concrete made to look like wood planks before the front door with its beautiful etched glass was being opened.

The entry opened into a front hallway. There was slate tile flooring in various colors that would inspire the children to play hopscotch over the coming years. Immediately behind the front door was a large double walk-in closet that would hold coats, jackets, and boots, and shoes could be put on its carpeted floor. It also had the incline for the stairs that led to the basement through the left side of this closet covered in drywall and painted. Going towards the living room were two planters on top of half-walls, and that led through an L-shaped room that ended at the dining room. From the dining room was a doorway into the kitchen. From the front hallway, they were facing another closet. It was not as big as the one behind the door, but it, too, would be perfect for jackets and coats. To the left was a powder room with a toilet and a sink, and its floor was already covered in tile.

"Can I use it?" Jack asked, suddenly clutching at his privates.

"Jack, go use the tree," Bree ordered, not sure if the plumbers were done hooking them up to the septic tank. In the months leading up to the build, they'd had to use a bucket out in the barn for number two, and the children had learned to squat if they were girls or pee against trees for number one.

Jack ran back out the front door, still holding himself.

There was a short hall that had a door to the basement or to the left of this, the door out to the garage. This short hallway led to the other side of the kitchen, creating a block and in the middle of the block was the powder room and closet. To the right of the kitchen and the short end of the L,

behind the garage, was a small family room with a fireplace, where they intended to keep their television. Between the kitchen and this family room was an open area above the countertop with cupboards that opened from both sides. Off the family room was a set of glass doors that led out onto a deck over the walk-out basement.

"Oh, look at this," Bree breathed, admiring their fine, new kitchen. "It's so clean!" There weren't any appliances yet—no refrigerator, dishwasher, or microwave. Looking at the empty spaces where they would go, she heard Marc approaching.

"The appliances will be here tomorrow. We have them at the shop, the ones you picked out. I plugged them all in, and they all work."

"Even the washer and dryer?" Bree asked, enthused.

"Yep," he said, smiling at the family's excitement. Jack came running back in, then, and his pants were still unzipped.

"Jack, your barn door is open," Taylor told him meaningfully.

He turned and stared out the front door, thinking she meant the actual barn until he realized what she meant and turned around to zip up his jeans.

Marc turned away to hide his laugh. He stood back so the family could walk down the longer arm of the L shape of the house. The hallway was off the far side of the kitchen, next to where the refrigerator would go. Finishing his earlier statement to the two women he added, "yes, it's standard procedure to unpack the appliances and make sure they work. Just in case we need to replace any."

The hallway led to three of the four bedrooms in the house. There was a small bedroom on the left, and they all peered in. They'd chosen green carpeting for this smaller room. Next, on the right was the laundry room with space for a side-by-side set of appliances with cabinets above it. There was also a small closet, and a washout tub. The back door to the house was through this room, and it led to the deck above the basement.

"What's this sink for, Mom?" Barbie asked either of the moms.

"Sometimes you need to wash things out by hand, and it can also be the overflow for the washer," Taylor explained. She turned to her wife. "I can soak my restaurant clothes and not smell like grease anymore."

"You won't need that," Bree told her, nodding towards the sink. "With the settings on washers these days, it should be able to presoak those clothes for you."

Taylor smiled. She hated always smelling like grease, but she knew it came with the job.

"This is tiny," squeaked Jack, opening the closet.

"That's for an ironing board," Bree told him, amused.

"A what?"

Bree realized they never bought clothing that needed ironing. With four kids, who had time to iron? "Never mind," she mumbled, amused and sharing a grin with Taylor.

Across the hall was a bathroom with two sinks, a toilet, and a full bathtub. It was all so fresh and clean; the children were in awe. At the end of the hall was a large bedroom with a red carpet. This would become the girls' room. It had a large closet to the left of the door, and there was plenty of room for two single twin beds, maybe even full sized if they ever bought them, as well as dressers. Outside this bedroom was a linen closet between the girls' room and the bathroom. Next to the girls' room was a room with a plush, deep blue carpet. Beside the door was a large closet with sliding doors and then there was a small bathroom with a toilet, shower, and sink. The room itself was very large, definitely the master bedroom. On one wall was a set of patio doors that led to the deck. The deck continued past the laundry room and then turned for the family room. The deck covered the walk-out basement. Each end of the L shaped deck ended on firm soil with a short set of stairs. One end in the back yard, one end in the side yard beyond the garage.

"I want this room," Melanie said enviously. She was looking out the patio door and then back at the large room. There was plenty of light from the south facing window on the end.

"And yet, you'll be happy in the red room," Bree firmly corrected her, sharing an amused look with her wife.

"Who wants to see the garage?" Taylor asked, heading off a temper tantrum from Melanie.

Easily distracted, the kids rushed out of the room.

"Hey, the house rules still apply. No running!" Taylor called, stopping them steps from the end of the carpeted hall leading into the kitchen.

The kids didn't realize the doors to the garage and basement weren't just more closets. Taylor opened the sturdy door on the left of the family room. The step down nearly tripped the children, but they caught themselves.

"Nice," Taylor commented, wishing they had better vehicles to park in this nice clean garage. It seemed so light and airy with its west facing window, and she couldn't believe the contractors had built all this in one day. But then, realizing they'd put a whole house here in one, wasn't really surprised. The unfished drywall even looked wonderful. The light from the windows on the garage doors was muted, but that was because they faced north. "Are we going to want to paint this, or are they?" she

asked her wife. Marc had disappeared, letting the family enjoy their explorations.

"No idea," Bree responded, looking at how large the garage seemed. The door on the far side attracted the children's attention, and Bree had to stop them from opening it because there were still a crew working on the other side of the house.

"Let's take a look at the basement, shall we?" Taylor asked and they hurried out of the garage.

Opening the basement door, Taylor refused to let any of the children go first down the stairs. Instead, she stepped out in front of them onto the steps and slowly descended. She saw where the crews had insulated the concrete on the inside, knowing where the wavy, decorative bricks were. The insulation was only on the outside in these sections, still effective, and holding out the moisture. Already, she could see where drywall had been hung along portions of the basement, finishing it off, as per the plans. In the corner, under the master bedroom, was an enclosed room, the fourth bedroom to their ranch-style home. It had a large west-facing window to allow for escape in case of an emergency. Across from this room was a basement door space they couldn't use as of yet as they would have to dig down into the hill on that eastern side of the house. It was odd to see the door space in the concrete without a door, and there wouldn't be one unless they knocked it out. They hadn't wanted to cut out this door with the huge walk-out basement across from it, but maybe, someday, they might have to dig in the hill on the east side to open this up. They had future plans for their house, but right now they were content with what they were seeing.

There was another basement door under the patio door from the family room and below the deck that led out of this walk-out basement. There were large windows for viewing on both sides of the L before ending with the bedroom which was below the master bedroom. There was so much room, now the basement was enclosed and insulated and had unpainted drywall over the insulation.

"Wow, another house is down here," Melanie marveled, looking around at the many changes. They'd all played in and out of the basement since they'd built it, then the pad had been laid in both the basement and the garage area. That was fun since their toys and bikes rode well on the dried concrete.

"Almost," Bree agreed, pleased with how it looked. "Have to decide if we're going to paint down here, too," she murmured to Taylor, who grinned. She was pleased—very pleased—with how it all looked.

They slowly returned to the main floor, and Marc was waiting for them. He could see the kids were thrilled, but he gave Bree and Taylor an expectant grin.

"Can we go look at our bedrooms again, Mom?" Melanie asked, and Marc wondered which one of the women she was addressing. He knew they were married, but which one was the mom, and did they call them both that. The girl looked at both of the women hopefully.

"Yes, but no jumping around or cartwheels," the blonde, Taylor, answered with a grin, and the children hurried off, being careful not to run.

"Will the drywall be painted?" Bree asked before Taylor could, but both looked at Marc curiously.

He nodded. "We'll be painting the basement tomorrow and installing all the appliances up here. The color will be a generic white that you can change anytime, but it's a long-lasting enamel. We'll then finish the garage off. On Monday, we'll be back to finish the landscaping around the immediate house, and then we're done."

Both women marveled at how efficient the modular house had come together. They'd known it would happen like this, but it had all been on paper for months—now, reality was setting in.

"The plumbers and electricians finished today. Have you flipped any of the switches or turned on the water?" he asked, amused. He'd seen reactions like this for years. People never realized how quickly they could work until they saw his crew in action. He gave them a quick tour of the systems that worked—lights, water, and the garbage disposal, which was the only appliance already installed. The whir of the disposal sounded foreign to the women's ears, and the kids came running when they heard it. They didn't have one in their apartment and weren't allowed near the one at Grandma's.

"Everything is working fine, and the solar will be installed tomorrow," Marc informed them, pointing at the roof.

"Only on the south and west facing roofs, right?" Taylor asked, suddenly remembering that. She'd forgotten they'd opted for that when they bought the house. It would be a tremendous savings on taxes when they filed next spring. The state encouraged new home owners to install solar.

"Yes, that's right. That's where the most sun is. That's another crew. I don't understand the technology, but that's okay; they do. They'll drill through to your crawl space in the attic and run the wires down to the basement."

Taylor had noticed the furnace and other electronic items in the dark corner farthest away from the open walk-out. She thought that might be a good place to have a small tornado shelter. They were, after all, in a state that got them occasionally, and it would be wise to put one in. But she hadn't thought to ask when they were designing the house. After a moment, she asked Marc, "How hard would it be to enclose the furnace and those electronics in a small room? Maybe put another small room next to it, enclosed with the same concrete blocks?"

He looked at her thoughtfully and asked that she accompany him to the basement so she could show him what and where she wanted it. He promised to get back to her on the price but couldn't tell her when they would be able to do it. "You understand, we schedule these things," his hands encompassed the house they'd installed above them, "months in advance."

"Oh, of course. It just occurred to me that we don't have a room in case of a tornado, and we should."

He nodded. "It would be better that it was separate from the water heater, furnace, and all these electronics for the solar?"

"Yes, nothing fancy, just separate and big enough for the six of us."

"I'll mock up something and get back with you by Monday on that, when my crew returns to do the landscaping," he promised.

"What was that about?" Bree asked as they locked up the barn and got the children in the cars. They didn't want to go, seeing no reason they couldn't stay in the house that, to them, was finished.

"We're going to need your beds and food," Taylor pointed out to the excited children who laughed. Answering Bree, she told her about her thought for a tornado shelter.

"They'll charge us an arm and a leg. It would be better if we built it ourselves," Bree pointed out in return.

"Probably, but it would be interesting to see how much they would quote us."

Bree agreed and got in her own car, taking the two boys while the girls piled into the Jeep to ride with Taylor, and they all headed home. They all looked back at the remaining contractor's trucks and at their beautiful—and almost finished—brand new home.

HOME ~ First Nillionaires Club

CHAPTER TWENTY-TWO

The next day they had to go to court to finalize their adoption for Jack. At five years old, Jack didn't fully understand what went on during family court. He'd been many times and been asked questions so the judge could hear what he thought about living with Bree and Taylor. Other times, he'd had an hour or two to play with his birth parents. That hadn't happened in a long time, and he'd almost forgot about them. This time seemed just like the others to him but with one special exception: it would be the last time. After the judge signed the adoption decree, the moms hugged and kissed their little boy, expressed their thanks to the judge, and made arrangements for follow-up visits with Mrs. Henderson, who had been a huge help to them since being assigned to their case.

"Well, my boy, this means no more court," Taylor told him as she carried him out of the building. It was a relief for them, as well. It had been a long time coming. They would still have the few follow-up visits from Mrs. Henderson, especially now that they were moving into their new house. She was happy to hear it had been delivered and looked forward to seeing it when they were settled.

"That's good," he said pragmatically, not really understanding but accepting what his mom told him.

"Why don't we go to the apartment and load the cars with those boxes we've been packing?" Bree suggested to her wife.

"That sounds good, and we can change out of our good clothes at the same time. Right, Jack?"

"Right," he agreed, but then he would have agreed to anything his moms said. He was just happy to have some alone time with the two of them without his siblings.

And that's exactly what they did. They'd been packing for a while, getting boxes from the local grocery stores, good sturdy liquor boxes or fruit boxes that seemed extra thick to protect the things they packed inside.

"We'll empty the trailer and get the furniture over my days off," Taylor predicted. "See who we can rope into helping us move in."

They packed box after box into the cars, barely leaving room for Jack's booster seat. Even the front seats of both the Jeep and the minivan were full as they made their way to the house. When they pulled up to the driveway, they found the crew painting their garage, so that answered one of their questions. Before they had gotten out of their vehicles, they saw Marc hurrying out to greet them with a worried expression on his face.

"The house was broken into last night."

"What?" Taylor asked, a box already in her arms after releasing Jack from his car seat. He'd run off to play on the Little Tykes items Bree had found on the internet. She'd cleaned each of them carefully before placing them about their property.

"What do you mean?" Bree asked, her own arms around a box.

"Apparently, someone left a door unlocked and they got in and graffitied the house," he told them sadly. He saw their horrified expressions and quickly added, "We're here to paint the drywall in the garage, as well as put in the appliances, so we'll take care of it." He shook his head at the mess they had found. "We have the equipment, and my men are cleaning it up now."

The two women exchanged looks, and Bree glanced over at the barn to where Jack was playing. She saw they had tagged the barn, too. "Oh, crap!" she murmured, putting her box down to go see what damage was in the house.

Taylor put her box down, too, and followed her wife.

It was just graffiti—no insults or threats—but the black spray paint on their white walls made it show up rather well.

"Fortunately, they didn't hit too much of the woodwork," Marc said consolingly. At their looks he added, "We wouldn't have been able to get the paint off the woodwork as easily as painting over this," he indicated the sheetrock. He had to talk louder over the sound of an air compressor as his men painted. "I'll have them bring in another paint machine, and

we'll get this done in no time," he promised. He hoped they wouldn't be angry. There was no way to know who had left the door unlocked.

"Let's unload the Jeep into the barn, for now," Taylor suggested. "I can't be late to work." She'd appeased her boss by agreeing to come in for an extra dinner shift.

Bree sighed, completely bummed, as they surveyed the damage to their beautiful new home, going from room to room where the house had been invaded. Still, Marc was right, his crews would clean it up and paint it over in no time. It was just so unnecessary. Why couldn't whoever did this have left them alone? "We're going to have to paint the barn again," she mumbled as she followed her wife outside.

"We can do that, too, if you get the paint," Marc offered generously, anything to keep the client happy. He suspected one of his men had left the door unlocked, and this was unacceptable.

"We appreciate the offer but I don't know if we have the extra money to go buy the paint," Bree admitted. "Red paint is the most expensive."

Marc thought for only a second before saying, "Tell you what, I'll have one of my guys pick up a few gallons to cover that up. It's the least we can do." He knew with their contractor pricing he'd get a better pricing.

"That would be very nice of you," Bree said graciously, relieved they wouldn't have additional expenses.

"Let's get this unloaded," Taylor repeated with a broad hint. She was really bummed, too, now that they had seen the damage.

Between the two women, they managed to fill a pallet with what had been in the Jeep. Taylor went to help with the minivan, but Bree stopped her. "I'll do this. I have Jack to help," she said as the little boy manfully lugged a small box over to the pallet. "You, go to work and earn that paycheck."

"Are you sure?" Taylor asked, taking her in her arms. "I'm sorry this happened. We were so happy to be moving in."

Bree shrugged. "It happens. I notice Marc and his men didn't call the police, and I wonder about that. I hope they took pictures."

"Why don't you get your camera and take those pictures." She nodded towards the barn graffiti and then back towards the house, where even now the damage was being covered up. "We might need that evidence at some point." She was beginning to get a bad feeling about all this. Those who had used the hill and this land for so long hadn't like that they'd moved here, but she'd hoped, with a house as evidence they were here to stay, they'd stop trespassing and causing damage.

"Yeah, I'll do that," Bree snuffled into her shirt. "It was all so pretty, too!"

"It will be again, and Marc is cleaning it up. Take the pictures and unload the van," she advised. "I'd stay but ..."

"You have to work," Bree finished for her, getting herself in order from the momentary cry she'd had. It had all been so new and pretty. Marc and his crew would fix it. They were taking responsibility for it. She'd make sure it was all locked up tonight herself if it was the last thing she did.

"The kids know to take the bus out here today?" Taylor confirmed as they walked towards the Jeep, eyeing Jack to make sure he was okay. He'd found a toy they had packed and was working it out of the van.

"Yep, told them this morning," Bree confirmed and held the door for Taylor to get in.

"I'll see you later," she said, and they exchanged a kiss.

Bree watched Taylor turn around in the circle they'd made of their drive and sighed. She looked back at the barn, straightened her shoulders, and went for the camera on her phone.

* * * * *

"They did what?" Lenny asked, horrified, when Taylor told the little group that had arrived at the diner.

"Hang on," Taylor answered and rushed off to welcome a new group that had walked in. Only after she had given them water and menus and checked for any orders that came up did she have a minute to go back to her friends.

"Yeah, they tagged all the white walls in the house. They didn't go down in the basement, thank God." She thought about all that nice concrete—the blocks and the wavy bricks—and mentally shuddered. "But they also got the barn again."

"What did the police say?" asked Elsie, who looked concerned. Her friends had worked so hard towards this moment, only to have it ruined by some vandal.

Taylor shrugged. "I don't think the contractor called the police, but I told Bree to take pictures. Be right back," she said, hurrying off to take an order.

"Geez, I know what I'm giving them as a housewarming gift," Lenny said to Elsie.

"What? I wasn't sure what they needed," she answered, looking interested.

"A security camera. One of those they can tie into their phone and call the police."

"That's a good idea. Will only one do, though?"

"I have no idea how much those cost. Do you?"

"We have a system at work, but it was there when we moved into our space. I have no idea what a personal security system costs. I haven't bought them anything; let me go with you when you shop for one, and maybe we'll split the cost?"

"Split what cost?" Gretchen asked and took the seat next to Lenny. She had planted her son Aaron, who had just come from an orthodontist appointment, at the counter. There was no way the near-teen wanted to be seen with his mom's friends. Already, one of the other waitresses was taking his order.

They quickly told her about what had happened at their friends' new home.

"Oh, that sucks. I'm in if you want to go three ways," she offered immediately, but then she wondered if it would be a problem with her husband, who would rather she didn't spend any time with her friends, much less buy them presents. Still, she was earning her own money with her plants.

"Didn't you say you were getting them trees as a present?" Elsie asked, reminding her.

"Oh, that's right," she remembered. She'd already ordered them, too. If Barry found out, he'd go ballistic. Spending money that she wouldn't recoup was a bad business decision, in his mind. He didn't like her friends. The close-knit group of friends, known as The Nillionaires Club, bothered him because most were lesbians.

Taylor made sure her other customers were taken care of, then brought sodas for her friends since she knew their preferences. "Hi, there," she said, greeting Gretchen. "The usual?" At her friend's nod, she quickly wrote up the ticket and gave it to the cook, who also happened to be the owner. It was a good thing her friends always ordered something because he didn't appreciate their socializing, otherwise. She returned with Lenny and Elsie's food. "Hey, you guys, I'm off on Tuesday and Wednesday next week. Wanna help us move?"

"Will the house be ready by then?" Elsie asked.

"Well, the contractor and his men were already painting over the mess when I left. I have a feeling he felt responsible somehow for the unlocked door, so I'm certain everything will be ready far before my day off," she said. Talking about it with her friends had lifted her spirits.

"I'm game," Gretchen said, stealing one of Lenny's French fries.

"Hey!" Lenny said, swiping at her with her fork and deliberately missing. "I'm in. I have the fair over in the eastern part of the state this weekend, but I'll be back in time to help."

"With your truck, maybe we can get Vinnie's help, too?" Elsie asked the table at large.

"Any help will be appreciated," Taylor added and quickly hurried off to welcome another customer.

"Damn, those two never stop," Gretchen admired.

"Hard working moms," she agreed. "I hope whoever did the graffiti doesn't come back," Lenny mentioned, spearing another French fry and glaring at Gretchen distrustfully.

* * * * *

Bree was pleasantly surprised that the painting crews had the first coat of paint up over all the graffiti in the rooms in no time. The garage had been particularly hard hit, which led them all to believe that was the point of entry. They had to do more than one coat, with primer first over most of the black paint because it bled through the white. Still, whoever Marc had called had sent another sprayer and more paint and even went and bought more than five gallons of red paint for the barn. A third sprayer arrived and was set up near the barn by the time the children got off the bus.

"The barn is getting painted, too?" Melanie asked, amazed and wanting to explore the house, but there seemed to be a lot of men about. They made her nervous.

"Well, someone was mean and came and painted the barn with bad words. They got in the house, too, through an unlocked door and did the walls there, too." She'd gotten some work done in the barn while the crews worked diligently to cover up the walls inside, but she had seen the different coats covering it all.

"Unlocked door?" the little girl worried, looking around.

Not wanting any of the children to feel unsafe, Bree hurried to clarify. "They won't bother us once we live here. They just took advantage when one of the crew," she nodded towards the contractors, "left a door unlocked. They won't be back," she assured her daughter, hoping it would be true.

By the time the crews left for the evening, the children watching avidly as the appliances were hauled in the front door of the house, Bree had finished for the day, too.

"Who wants to go see how the house looks now?" Bree asked. "I don't know if the walls are completely dry, but I don't want you touching *anything*," she stressed.

The children were really quiet as Bree unlocked the front door. The front, back, and side doors were keyed the same. Bree had two sets, one of which she would give to Taylor when she saw her, and the third set was held by Marc, who had made certain the doors were all locked. They were behind on this house because of the graffiti, but having the extra sprayers had caught them up in no time. His landscaping crew would be there on Monday. Already, the photos of the empty and now pristine painted walls had been taken.

Bree was pleased to see the walls no longer bled the black paint. All the light switches were in place and worked. They would have to have lamps in a few spots, but that would be something she could shop for on Marketplace. Taylor had insisted they get a new computer when the house was done, and now it was done. She knew just where it would go, too—in the family room. In the corner, there was a lower part of the countertop that had been made specifically as a built-in desk. The computer would look lovely there. If that didn't work out, maybe it could go in their bedroom. She thought the new computer should have a nice desk or table to accommodate it. The kids could use the desk in the family room to do their homework as they grew up. She was already envisioning a bigger table in the kitchen and a nice dining room table in the space allotted for it. She would have to see what they could afford and what they could find, but she was already looking forward to the search.

The entire house smelled of paint, and Marc had cracked the windows open to air it out. Because of the designs of the windows with the bug screens built in, only if the intruder broke the windows could he or she get in.

"When can we move in, Mom?" Barbie asked, awed once again by the house as they walked through.

"Mom and I brought over some things today," she admitted. "We'll keep bringing things over and then move all the furniture at once with the trailer."

"Will it be like when you moved the storage unit?" Melanie asked, sounding important.

"Probably, and I think I should ask our friends. We could have a barbeque out back," she said, looking forward to the idea. She stepped into the laundry room and lovingly ran her fingertips along the edge of both machines. They returned to the kitchen and checked out the new refrigerator, microwave, and stove. Bree sighed, thrilled with the new dishwasher.

"All this is ours?" Bryan asked.

"Yep, Bryan, this is going to be our home," Bree reminded the little boy.

"Marmalade likes it." Jack pointed at the orange cat who hesitantly sniffed at the garage door. She must have followed them in.

"Who left the front door open? You have to learn to close doors to the outside," Bree told them, admonishing them. She wasn't certain she wanted that cat to be an indoor cat in their new house, but it didn't look like she'd have too much say in the matter. She'd discuss it with Taylor later.

"I'm hungry," Bryan put out there, gazing at the empty kitchen.

"Well, then, we should get home and get dinner going. Mom is working late today, and we should really pack up the van some more, if we can." Bree leaned down and scooped up Marmalade, who purred and cozied herself in her arms. She checked that she had her keys to the house and that the front door was locked before setting down the cat. "I'm going to check the side door," she called as the children headed towards the van, but they all tramped after her as she turned the knob and tried to open the door to the garage. Next, she went around to the back of the house and onto the deck to check the patio doors to the family room, the back door to the laundry room, and then the patio doors to the master bedroom. Man, that room looked big through the window. With the children and cat still following, she went down around the incline to the basement and checked those doors, too.

"This is a big house," Bryan declared as they climbed the incline to the side of the house again and began to troop around the garage.

"Sure seems that way," Bree agreed with a smile. There had been times during this whole process when she was unsure they'd made the right choices, but, now, she was so pleased with the result.

Just then, a car turned down their driveway and sped up as it got closer to the house. As the family stood their trapped in the car's headlights, the car idled and its driver revved the engine. He or she—it was impossible for Bree to see through the glare—sat there for a moment just watching. After what seemed like a lifetime, the car spun around, revealing a bunch of gawping teenagers, who were surprised to find them there. A sense of relief washed over Bree as the intruders' car blasted down the driveway, but her relief was quickly replaced by anger. For all she knew … Bree was annoyed, they had to do something about these invasions to their privacy. For all she knew, that had been last night's graffiti artists.

"Let's get back to the apartment," she said, deliberately omitting the word *home* since this house was soon to be that.

CHAPTER TWENTY-THREE

Their friends all chipped in on Taylor's days off to help them move the last of their furniture from the apartment. Some couldn't make it until later in the day, but everyone helped when and where they could. Taylor and Bree had filled their vehicles with every item, every box, they could possibly fit in them themselves.

"I'm so sick of that shit," Taylor said as another car came up the drive, saw what was at the end of it, and turned around. The people in it stared at the group moving furniture from the trailer as though they had never seen such an event before.

"Yeah, you definitely need a gate, and I have a line on one," Vinnie told her as she walked backwards, the table they were moving necessitating the two of them.

"Yeah?" Taylor asked, immediately interested. Bree had told her of the visit the night after the graffiti incident and how unsafe it made her feel and how she'd had to reassure the kids.

"I'll let you know," she said as they were walking up the steps to the open front door.

"Oh, leave that in the living room," Bree directed. At some point during the move, she had just taken charge of house design to simplify things. Everything from the storage unit that had been in the barn was now someplace in the house, waiting for her and Taylor to unpack. The food from their apartment had been brought over and swallowed up by the much larger cupboards and cabinets in their new house. After they threw out expired food and cleaned out their apartment fridge, the remaining items made their new fridge look empty and sad, but at least things had been brought over. Lenny and Gretchen had been putting their beds together so the family could sleep in their new home that night.

"I've got to check on the barbeque," Bree suddenly said, walking out the patio door of the family room onto the deck.

"Well, the apartment is clean!" Elsie came through the front door carrying a bucket full of cleaners in one hand.

"Thank you so much for the carpet cleaner," Taylor told her, walking over to give her a hug.

"Well, it made a difference, but you've all lived there quite a few years. I'm certain your landlord will find a reason not to give you all your deposit back."

"That doesn't sound fair," Vinnie put in, leaning against the table. "Isn't there some law about replacing carpets every four years, anyway, if it's a rental? They've been there longer than that and never had the carpet replaced."

"I'm sure they'll stick it to us somehow. We'll go by tomorrow with the keys for the walk-through."

"The carpet should be dry by then. I checked the cabinets and closets all one more time," Elsie assured her.

"You and Bree, both," Taylor teased. She, too, had the compulsion to keep checking they had all their stuff. Even now, with everything in the house, she wasn't certain everything was even here. There was so much more room.

As they sat around eating off paper plates and discussing the house, Gretchen piped up, "They did a nice job on the landscaping, but they should have gone farther out."

"The contract was for only ten feet around the house," Bree mentioned, biting into her hamburger.

"We can expand from that," Taylor added, spearing a piece of fruit on her fork. "I've enjoyed cutting the lawn as it came in."

They'd teased her, Vinnie especially, about cutting the lawn.

"I'd love to find something to cut more of that brush back around the woods," Taylor confessed.

"A brush cutter?" Vinnie asked. At Taylor's nod she added, "You'll never get all ten acres cleaned up, you know?"

"Well, we have so many other projects with the swamp and expanding the business," Bree pointed out.

They discussed what the two wanted to do with their mini farm, from raising their own chickens to possibly getting a dog.

"Ixnay on the ogday," Bree made sure to state before the kids could overhear her wife. They had enough settling in to do. She slapped at a mosquito. The children had plenty of sores from bites. "Jack, quit picking at that mosquito bite," she warned and then explained to her friends, "They'll scratch them raw if we don't keep up on them."

"I don't have the tools to build a coop, much less a doghouse," Taylor teased back. She'd be in the doghouse if she brought home a dog without her wife's say-so.

"What are they building back there?" Elsie asked, hearing the sounds of hammers and saws towards the south of the house.

"That's the new mini-mansion subdivision we told you about," Bree told her, having learned to tune out the noise all summer.

"Oh, I read about that in the papers," she admitted. "That is backed up to your place?"

"They even stole our fence," Taylor told her, amused.

"Stole your fence?"

Bree looked up in surprise at her wife's words but Taylor went on. "Yeah, I went back there to check to see if our signs were still up. Most of them are, but someone removed the barbed-wire fence that used to be there."

"The nerve!" Elsie stated.

Taylor shrugged. "It was old, rusty, and probably an eye-sore to the people buying those houses." Her head nodded towards the noise they could all hear. "They wouldn't want to tarnish their beautiful places with a barbed-wire fence that was sitting there, falling down."

"But it isn't on their property," her friend pointed out.

"No, it isn't, and it was ours, but I'm glad it's gone. We are, however, gonna have to watch for them stealing our wood, even if it's on the ground," Taylor pointed out.

"How do you keep them from doing that?"

Taylor shrugged. "We put up signs, I guess. We can't physically keep them out unless we catch them at it. People have weird concepts of ownership sometimes."

* * * * *

It was only after they delivered several toasts, most with water or soda with plenty of, "Here's to the First Nillionaires Club," that the party wound down.

"Thank you, thank you," they kept saying to their friends as they left them in their new home that first night. They left, one by one, after making sure Bree and Taylor didn't need any more help.

There were boxes stacked everywhere throughout the house, furniture in every room. "This is going to take forever to get straightened out," Taylor commented, but she was so pleased to be finally in their new home.

"But I don't *want* to go to bed," Barbie whined, but Bree insisted. After all the running in and out of the house today, they had to be exhausted. She'd allowed the girls their first bath in their new home, hoping to tire them out further, but now they were over-tired.

"You have school in the morning. Remember, you get to catch the bus from the driveway for the first time! We don't want to be late, right?"

"We won't go to the apartment ever again?" Bryan confirmed, standing by the door.

"You get back to bed, young man," Bree told him. Her tone had him scooting back to his room.

"I'm not used to not having my bunk bed." Barbie was changing tact to drag her bedtime out.

"With all this space in your new bedroom, we thought you'd like it like this." Bree gestured at the new layout, with the beds side-by-side.

"People can see in the windows," the little girl tried next.

"Nonsense, no one is near the house, and we have the woods between us and the next house. No one is even living there yet," Bree pointed out. She was right, too; the McMansions weren't built yet, just in the various stages of their builds.

"Quit arguing with your mom. We made sure your lava lamp was plugged in and on your dresser," Taylor said, coming into the room and turning it on for the little girl. "We even turned it on early so you can see the lava balls floating up and down. Now, hop in your bed. It has nice, clean sheets on it, and you'll sleep wonderfully in this new house of ours."

Barbie knew better than to argue with Taylor, and Melanie, who was already in her twin bed, waited for her moms to kiss her good night.

Bryan was back in the green room, where Jack was already half asleep in his own bed. Bryan was excited to have his family in their very own home, knowing they wouldn't be going back to the apartment, ever. Marmalade was waiting for Bryan on the top bunk, his tail slapping out a pattern of contentment as he shed his orange hairs on the blanket. Taylor stopped to kiss both boys, watching the wax balls in the lava lamp for a moment. She laughed at the cat who seemed to be mesmerized by it.

* * * * *

"Everyone tucked in?" Bree asked, as Taylor returned from checking on the doors to the house, the patio ones, as well, and looking into each room, where snoring children belied the young girl's assurances that she hadn't been tired. She turned from putting a box away in the closet. Their clothes had been easy to move, but the trinkets and other things in boxes that they had packed away for years would prove harder. They needed display cabinets and more shelves, things she was looking forward to acquiring. They had a show this coming weekend and would have to hurry to fill the trailer they had used to move most of their furniture. It hadn't taken the two days that Taylor had off, after all. The move had gone very quickly, leaving them plenty of time to barbeque and socialize.

"Yep, and I think you should stop, shower, and join me," she said, locking the door behind her, wrapping herself into her wife's arms. "We're here," she breathed happily. As she buried her nose in Bree's neck, Taylor inhaled her wife's musky scent. Her hair felt wonderful against Taylor's face—familiar.

"Mmmm," Bree murmured against her skin, loving the feel of her strong body and closing her eyes at the sensation. "I should put away …" she began to protest but immediately forgot, as Taylor had begun to undress her.

"These clothes need to be washed," Taylor said softly, removing them piece by piece. "You can even use our new washing machine."

Bree giggled and removed Taylor's clothing as they slowly made their way into the bathroom, caressing each other's exposed skin.

Taylor reached for the shower, pulling Bree with her, but gasped at the cold water that shot out of the sprayer. "Oh, God!" she exclaimed, and Bree erupted into more giggles. Quickly, she turned the nob to the hot side and then fiddled with it to adjust to a comfortable temperature. The whole time Bree was giggling while she finished stripping Taylor's clothes off. "Um, I'm trying something here," Taylor noted.

"I'm trying something here, too," Bree countered, her giggles dying as she reached up for the liquid soap in the automatic dispenser and pumping some into the palm of her hand. She lathered the soap and then began rubbing it all over her wife's skin, taking great delight in reaching every curve, ever muscle, all the crevices. The grin on her face told Taylor how much she was enjoying herself.

"So, that's the way it is, is it?" Taylor asked, reaching for the pump herself but getting shampoo and beginning to lather Bree's long hair in her hands, using her fingertips to scrub her scalp.

"I think I'm feral," Bree admitted, closing her eyes to the feeling of her Taylor's fingers in her hair, the nails gently scraping her scalp.

"A feral housewife?" Taylor taunted.

"Nope, I'm just loving the feel of your nails on me. I must be feral or something. And I'm not a mere housewife."

"No, baby, you are not a mere housewife," she agreed lovingly, reaching in for a kiss as she cupped Bree's head and held it place under the spray.

Deeply and passionately, they kissed, a familiar feel of each other's lips against the other's. Hesitantly, Taylor opened her lips and licked at Bree's, who opened hers immediately. They caressed each other's' tongues before Bree began sucking on Taylor's.

"Mmmm," Taylor moaned into her wife's mouth, enjoying the sensation. The water spray washed any and all suds from their bodies as they got distracted. Remembering where they were and what they were supposed to be doing, Taylor backed slightly away and pumped soap into the palm of her hand to rub against Bree's body, first lifting her arm up and over her head so she could reach the underside, her underarm, and then down her rib cage to her hip. As the bath grew more pleasant, she could see Bree was anticipating more, so she pumped some more soap into her palm and began to wash the other side.

Bree was becoming heated, not from the water, but from her wife's actions, and figured two could play at this. She again pumped some soap into her palm when Taylor finished her other side and slowly slid her body against Taylor and down to where she was kneeling at her feet. She rubbed her hands together to work up a lather and began washing Taylor's long legs from the bottom up, completing with the water spray to get everywhere before it was washed down the drain.

Taylor spread her legs so Bree could get between them, but Bree teased her by stopping to get more soap, rubbing her body against her as she stood. "You tease!"

Bree turned her so she could get her back and rubbed the muscles at Taylor's neck, using her fingertips to get deep in them, while the water spray helped her relax as she rubbed down her back. Taylor loved the feel as Bree washed and kneaded her buttocks, leading to more interesting thoughts, but her wife was being frustratingly thorough in her desire to clean her and continued on down her legs and then back up to make sure she got all the suds rinsed off.

"Okay, that's—" Taylor began to say, but cut off what she had been about to say when Bree pushed her fingers between her wife's legs and

began washing the folds there with no soap, just water. She sputtered in surprise at the attack.

Bree grinned, knowing she'd surprised Taylor and hoping she could stay upright in the close confines of the shower. It would be a horrible first night in the house if Taylor fell. To be safe she only *washed* her with the one hand, while the other reached around to grab a butt cheek and hold her in place under the shower spray. As a curtesy, her mouth made sure her wife's nipples were clean as she tongued them under the water.

It was a curious sensation, the water relaxing her, but, at the same time, her wife and her actions causing her to be strangely tense. She spread her legs as wide as she could so Bree could access whatever she wanted. Soon, she felt a rubbing that built a delightful tension in her exhausted body. She wanted to do the same to Bree, but her arms were clamped around Bree's shoulders to hold her balance.

Heat that wasn't from the warm water of the shower began to focus in one spot on her body, and soon it was radiating outward, as though all her blood had drained from everywhere to this one point. As her body released the warmth, it shot through her veins with a delicious languid feel to it. She was suddenly very, very tired.

"Did you like that?" Bree murmured, reaching up for a kiss as Taylor began to focus. She was grinning.

"Did you?" Taylor countered, returning the grin with a delighted smile. "I want to hear you come," she continued, pinning Bree against the shower wall.

"You don't have t—" she began, but the woman was already kneading her breast and a buttock at the same time, a curiously erotic sensation, while she slowly slid down her body, the water enabling this and causing friction, despite the slick feel of their bodies from washing. Two fingers roughly thrust inside her, but it didn't hurt—she was too wet for that. The mouth that captured her clit, though, was hot; it felt almost molten. Maybe she was worked up from what she had done to Taylor, but Bree didn't hold out for long and began to buck soon afterward, the juices that spurted out of her and onto her wife's fingers rinsing off in the shower spray. "Jeez, that was quick," she complained but smiled down at the view of her wife kneeling between her legs and felt more contractions in her. Taylor thrust a few more times to make sure Bree was satisfied. When she smiled up at Bree, the shower sprayed right into her face, causing her to sputter, and they both shared a laugh.

They quietly finished showering together and helped each other to dry off.

"I think I'm going to sleep well tonight," Bree complained, but she didn't sound upset about it as she wrapped her hair in a towel and curled up around her wife.

"Me, too," Taylor said, "A perfect ending to a perfect day."

CHAPTER TWENTY-FOUR

Taylor forced herself to get up the next morning as the alarm went off. She ached from constantly lifting heavy boxes and furniture over the last few days, always on the move, and was disoriented for a moment when she looked about the unfamiliar bedroom. Her eyes opened wide when she remembered the previous night and that they were in their bed in the new house, in their own bedroom. She felt around for the damp towel that had been around her hair and pulled it out of the bed.

"Hey," Bree murmured sleepily as Taylor began to move deliberately to turn off the alarm.

"Hey, yourself," Taylor murmured back and leaned in for a kiss. Before it could get too interesting for either of them, she decided she had to brush her teeth. Bree's breath was horrible, and she could only imagine her own. "Have to pee," she said, swinging her legs over the queen-sized bed and shuffling off to the bathroom. She was pleased with this small bathroom of their own, only wishing it was a little bigger and it had a bathtub she could share with her wife. Still, their home was lovely, perfect for their growing family. She hung up her towel and looked into the bathroom mirror as she brushed her teeth, toothpaste already around the edges of her lips, she smiled to herself at what they had achieved.

"Almost done?" Bree asked at the door, hopping from foot to foot as she waited her turn to use the toilet. She was carrying her own hair towel.

"You can come in," Taylor told her, cocking an eyebrow.

"Can't ... need privacy," she answered, clutching at pajama bottoms where they met at her crotch. "Gotta go!"

"C'mon, we've been married forever. You can pee in front of me." She finished brushing her teeth and spit into the sink, quickly washing it out. She hated seeing toothpaste build-up and wiped it down under the flow of fresh, clean water.

Bree knew that and quickly sat down, hunching over to hide her stream and laughing up at her wife. Her hair was tousled, a mess from going to bed with it wet, and she looked like a naughty, little girl, which made Taylor laugh, as well. Taylor leaned down to give her a peck on the mouth. "Morning."

"Oh, gawd. Bet I have Sasquatch mouth," Bree murmured, enjoying the kiss but realizing she could smell her own morning breath.

"Well, it's just the hair that gets me," Taylor replied, straightening up and scooting out of the small bathroom.

Bree smacked her on the ass on her way out and then turned to grab toilet paper. Ready to start her own morning, she hung up her towel next to her wife's.

Taylor quickly changed into clean blue jeans and a polo shirt, slipping her bra on underneath it. She never understood why she couldn't remember the damn bra before she put on her shirt, but her contortions were the stuff of legends. She looked out the patio doors and saw a deer beyond the landscaping that Marc's crew had put in. It took off with her appearance at the glass, and she smiled, pleased at seeing the wildlife. All the construction hadn't scared them off; it would be back, probably to eat the sod grass. She could see it would take a while to blend in the sod with the grasses they had planted. There was a gap all the way around the house, like a sleek Persian green carpet next to straggly Kentucky bluegrass with a six-inch gap in between. Both Gretchen and Vinnie had suggested she fill that gap with the rich black dirt from the pond and plant some more grass. It would eventually blend. She could see she needed to cut the grass again, and this didn't displease her.

"Enjoying the view?" Bree asked, coming up and hugging her from behind. Her hands started to wander, and Taylor turned in her arms, looking down at the shorter woman with delight.

"Yes. Yes, I am," she returned, but they both knew she didn't mean the trees and grasses beyond their patio windows. Taylor looked down at her wife and leaned in for another good morning kiss. "I am so happy."

"Me, too. Let's get the kids off to school so we can get this place in order!" she answered with a return kiss, squeezing her.

Bree quickly changed, while Taylor made their bed. There was so much more room to do so here. She wasn't smashed up against a wall, trying to lay out the wrinkled sheets and blankets. She could actually snap them into place and smooth them out without contorting herself with only an inch or two to spare. She fluffed up their pillows and smoothed out their coverings.

"Nice," Bree murmured, seeing her wife's ass bent over the bed. She stood there for a moment in her bra and panties as she halted the pulling on of her own jeans to admire the woman.

"C'mon, last night will have to do you for a while," Taylor teased, wiggling her ass suggestively.

"I'd rather you do me for a while," she responded but then heard the unmistakable sound of the door knob rattling.

"Hey, Mom, the door's locked," came a voice.

"Yes, because you don't enter your parents' room without permission. Can't you knock?" Taylor called, finishing up by fluffing the pillows and glancing at her wife, who was now hurrying to get dressed. Her bare feet felt good against the new blue carpet as she walked across to unlock the door. Checking to see that Bree was actually dressed, she opened the door to Barbie, whose face was riddled with worry. "Yes? Can I help you, miss?" she asked formally but with enough humor in her voice that the six-year-old knew she wasn't in trouble.

"Do we have to go to school today?"

"And why wouldn't you?"

"We could stay home and help," she pointed out with perfect logic.

"And ... you could go to school and do your job."

"Job?"

"It's your job to get an education, and it's our job ..." she pointed at Bree who was putting her hair up in a ponytail with her thumb, swinging it back and forth between the two of them, "to provide you with a roof over our heads." Her hands encompassed the newly painted ceiling.

"Huh?" the girl asked.

"Get ready for school," Taylor advised. "Get your sister up." She called over her shoulder to her wife. "I'll get the boys up and start breakfast."

As they were all sitting down at the kitchen table, Bree smiled over her bowl of cereal. It wasn't fancy; it wasn't expensive; but it was home—their home. "Now, remember," she said, "we aren't going back to the apartment, so don't take that bus. Always take the one here to the house from now on."

The children nodded solemnly, and Bree looked at the time. "You all better clean up, brush your teeth, and get ready to catch the bus."

They watched as the children trekked off down the long driveway and then waited for the bus. They had plenty of time, but Bree had been afraid they would be late and miss it. Both parents walked part of the way, but didn't want to embarrass the children by walking them all the way to the bus. The two women waved as they turned one last time before trooping up the steps.

"Well, that's the first of many," Taylor stated, pleased to see them off to school.

"Well, we should get started unpacking," Bree advised. They had planned to move both days of Taylor's days off, but having got it all done over the past few days and finished early yesterday, they had a full day to do whatever they wanted.

"I was going to cut the lawn and maybe start planting those trees Gretchen gave us if I have time," Taylor put in. She really didn't want to decorate the house. Bree could ask her five questions for every item she wanted to hang or put on a shelf, and it would lead to a fight.

"You don't want to help put our things away?"

"Babe, you know where you want them to go. Just remember where you put things, so when I ask, you know."

Bree laughed, not really disappointed. She'd enjoyed helping with cutting the grass over the summer once it got long enough, but they'd been pretty busy of late, and it was overly long. There were impressions where the bigger trucks and the crane had stood that might need to be smoothed out, too, but, overall, that was Taylor's job, and she loved it. She'd helped out Vinnie often enough over the years that the woman had offered her a position, but Taylor knew she couldn't come home always smelling of cut grass and full of dirt. Plus, she knew working for Vinnie might put a strain on their friendship. The tradeoff was grease in her pores and hair and uniforms full of various stains. Bree knew she would have preferred the grass smells to the grease. With that in mind, she gathered up everyone's clothes from the past few days and started the first of a couple of loads in their new washing machine. Then, she stacked their dirty dishes from breakfast in the new dishwasher.

Taylor was happy. The smell of fresh-cut grass was wonderful in the cool morning air. It wasn't fall yet, but it was almost in the air. It was going to be a hot afternoon, but, for now, it was early enough that she was enjoying cutting the grass around the place. One of Bree's finds, the John Deere was older but sound, and they'd replaced the filter, tightened the bands, and sharpened the blades. It worked wonderfully for them. They

kept a five-gallon gas can in the corner of the barn next to the tractor and lawnmower. It was a pleasure as she walked along over the lawn, cutting the grass they had planted. She made sure to let the clippings fill the gap between their grass and the new landscaping. She hoped it contained seeds that would grow. It was such a pleasure to cut the lawn, pushing the mower or using the bar to let it turn itself and basking in the sunshine as she tanned under its glare. When the immediate lawn was done, she went around the trees at the edge of their woods, encompassing part of it into their now well-established lawn. It helped to cut down those saplings that had sprung back up over the summer.

"What the heck did you do?" Bree asked Taylor, concerned when she caught her later.

"I tied the bar down on the lawnmower ..." she began, watching her clever work with a grin.

"That's not all you did," her wife interrupted, concerned. "What if the kids get in the way."

They were both watching the lawnmower, which was also tied to a tree, cut smaller circles around and around the tree as it wound tighter. Each pass made the circle smaller. "That's why I'm supervising."

"I'd appreciate it if you just cut the lawn like other normal people and walked behind the lawnmower."

"This is why I want a riding lawn mower. Our lawn is too big."

"But if the rope breaks, you're going to have a potential tragedy on your hands."

"I'm supervising," she repeated with a smug smile. "Besides, the kids are at school."

Bree sighed, looked at the lawn mower for another moment, and went back in the house to work. She really couldn't argue with her wife.

Next, after all the lawns were done, Taylor filled the wheelbarrow with dirt from the garden area, the small piles of leftover and very rich swamp dirt easily filling it. She carefully shoveled out the dirt in the gaps around the whole house, and Bree joined her for the last of it to spread seed and cover that up. They filled all the dips caused by the wheels of the cranes or the contractors, trying to smooth out the lawn.

"Job well done," Taylor gasped when they finished around noon.

"Should we water it right away?" Bree asked.

"You just want to try out the new spigots on the house," she accused, laughing.

"Guilty!" she laughed back and then added, "I'll get the hose."

They were both a little sunburnt and damp when they went in for lunch.

"Hey, you got a few boxes emptied," Taylor noticed, seeing them piled up by the garage and basement door. She went over to the kitchen sink and washed her hands.

"A few," she admitted non-committally, slathering some mayonnaise on their ham sandwiches. "Cheese?"

"Not today—made me gassy the other day," Taylor admitted, putting her hand to her belly.

"Becoming lactose intolerant?"

"I hope not. I like a nice glass of milk," she said as she filled two glasses for their meal and then reached for the chip bag to put some on each plate. "Ketchup?" she teasingly asked her wife.

"I don't know why you would ask," Bree said prissily. "Yuck!" She watched as Taylor poured out a small pool of the red sauce onto her plate to dip her potato chips in.

Over lunch, they discussed everything they wanted to still do that day and all the things they still needed to buy for the house. "All in time, all in time," Taylor admonished her eager wife. She was worried they would use up their savings too fast, but she knew Bree was very thrifty. Looking at the things Bree had found for their home already, she liked how clever her wife was in her hunt for things to make it a home, and she looked forward to seeing the other things she would find.

"I know, but, when I see deals, I don't want to always consult you. And waiting sometimes takes forever. What if I miss a deal?" Now that she was in their home, she wanted to make it all cozy.

"That has only happened a few times," Taylor pointed out. "Don't we have to meet with the landlord back at the apartment?"

"I told him one-thirty," she said, looking at the clock and finishing her sandwich.

"Could you go alone and I—" began Taylor but stopped at her wife's look.

"You could go alone, and I ..." Bree mimicked back and then grinned.

They both had plans for their new home, and neither wanted to leave. Not to mention, they still had pots to make for their customers and hadn't worked on that in days because they were so occupied with the move. Having it all here, at their fingertips made them both ambitious.

Reluctantly, they loaded the empty boxes into the Jeep to take to the recycling center and piled in it. Bree had called repeatedly for a rolling bin to recycle cardboard and plastic, but they hadn't delivered it yet. Meanwhile, their garbage bin was on wheels, at least, to be taken down the long driveway.

The landlord wasn't thrilled to be losing a long-term tenant, but they had made an effort to clean the place. The carpets looked fairly good after Gretchen's washing, but they would still have to be replaced. He had looked for signs of the cat that supposedly had been living with them, but he found none. With nothing negative to note, he signed off on their walk-through checklist and promised to mail their security deposit back. Bree and Taylor thought there was a fifty-fifty chance they might actually get it.

"Well, that's done," Bree said with a sigh, pleased to be out from under that obligation. "Would you like to stop at Home Depot on the way home?"

"No, it's just too tempting, and there is that sale on tools. I don't want to torture myself. What we have will do for now."

Bree smiled. She knew Taylor wanted to try building things, and the pitiful tools they had in their toolbox weren't adequate for some of her more ambitious plans. Still, as she had said earlier—all in time. Plus, she didn't mind getting used things from Marketplace or Craigslist, and there were other sources, as well. Frequently, when Taylor was at work and the kids were in bed, she would use her alone time to hunt for household treasures. Now that they were in the house, she could budget for these things. Meanwhile, they still had a lot of boxes to go through.

* * * * *

"Mom? Mom?" the voices could be heard coming through the front door as the two women unpacked and put away what they could. There were a few things that would have to remain in boxes until they had more of an idea where everything would go, more shelves, and more furniture. Bree was looking forward to the hunt.

"Hey, how was your day at school?" Taylor asked, scooping Jack up in her arms and swinging him around.

The children talked a mile a minute, both moms giving them plenty of attention while they had an after-school snack. Then, Bree sent them off to change their clothes and go out to play. Both moms warned them away from the swath of rich dark black dirt around the lawn, now drying to a matte color in the early fall sun, they had just planted it with grass seed.

"I never thought this day would come," Bree said joyfully, watching the kids play on the used Little Tykes plastic playground toys she had managed to find. She'd watched them many times over the summer as they waited for their house to be delivered, but, now, from the comfort of their deck, it was different.

"It's only just begun," her wife reminded her.

CHAPTER TWENTY-FIVE

"Okay, it's taken a while, but I have a line on a gate and some fencing for you." Vinnie called Bree one evening soon after they moved in. "But you have to come and help me pull it out."

"Pull it out?" Bree asked, confused. "Taylor, too?"

"The more the merrier," Vinnie advised. "Can you meet me at six?"

"In the morning or …?" she asked stupidly.

"Of course, in the morning, when else …?" she asked in return but then realized. "What time do the kids go off to school?"

"The bus picks them up at seven-twenty." Bree laughed at the disgruntlement in her friend's voice. "I don't know if Taylor can make it or not; let me check the calendar." She perused the well-worn paper pinned with magnets to the refrigerator. "I can come, but Taylor has to be at work by noon and she's working until nine."

"Damn. Wonder what Lenny is doing?"

"Is it a three-woman job? What about Gretchen?"

"I'd rather not bother her, and Elsie can't get out of the office."

"Look, you two need to have out your differences. This has been going on for years, and it's getting old."

"Stay out of it, Bree," her friend advised, and not for the first time.

"I know, I know. I don't know the whole story," she lamented. "I'll be ready by seven thirty and over at your place?"

HOME ~ First Nillionaires Club

"Please."

* * * * *

"What are you doing with Vinnie?" Taylor asked sleepily the next morning. She'd worked four afternoon and evening shifts in a row and wasn't too keen on getting up to get the kids off to school while her wife went off with their friend. On her only day off, she had planted the trees Gretchen had given them along the driveway on the west side near the field their neighbor, Eric Norman, owned. His cows had drawn plenty of flies all summer long, and it was nice to think of these many trees growing up and blocking the field, especially if Eric eventually sold the field to some developer. She could still hear the sounds from the current development behind their place—saws, hammers, and—worse yet—big trucks and construction vehicles. Every. Single. Day. And it started at eight A.M. She couldn't have slept in if she wanted to. And, she wanted to. Many times, she wanted to.

She'd seen the stakes out in the other field that Eric cut the hay from, having delivered the round bales in payment to them. Even now, those round bales were alongside the barn, covered in plastic and waiting for Taylor and Bree to use them somehow. Those stakes in the ground had turned into a few basements, but only a couple of model houses had been built in the subdivision going up to the east of their land. It was behind them that most of the noise occurred with the McMansions.

"She said she needed our help, but I'm meeting her over at her place since you have to work. I don't want to be late," she said as she pulled on her socks and tugged on her jeans.

Taylor didn't fully understand, but, before she could put two coherent thoughts together, her wife kissed her and left with one admonishment. "Don't fall back to sleep, or the kids will miss the bus."

Taylor grumpily got up, splashed cold water on her sleepy face, and got the kids going. She got them dressed and their hair done while they ate their cereal and fought over who got to read the pictures on the boxes. While she watched them walk down the driveway, she began to put together her day. She'd have to be at work by noon, but that meant she had a few hours she could paint and draw designs. She wouldn't throw pots because she'd be covered in clay, and she'd been warned about looking like that at work a few times over the years. As she washed down the table and stacked the dishwasher, she could feel her resentment building over having to juggle multiple jobs. How would she ever get

anything done? She returned to the window to watch the kids getting safely on the bus, then headed off to the barn to get to work.

She painted Amazonian designs she copied from a book that translated them as well wishes and good deeds. She had once been accused of cultural appropriation for using foreign designs, and, even though she'd defended herself by saying she wanted to recreate their beautiful artwork, the accusation still hurt her feelings. "Bree can just fire these later," she muttered to herself, remembering the incident. *And why did Vinnie need Bree today, anyway?* she thought.

An hour before work, she had showered and was headed to work in plenty of time. She locked up the house, which now had cameras at each door, inside and out, thanks to her friend's generous housewarming gift. They still had riders come up their driveway occasionally, but it really gave them peace of mind to see on their phones who came and went at their place. At least they could see who it was, take a picture of any plates, and tell if they were men or women. The vandals hadn't returned, as far as they knew.

* * * * *

"What's going on with these?" Bree asked as she and Lenny got in Vinnie's truck, which was towing one of her flatbed trailers.

"So, this guy is getting fancy new fences and gates for his property, and I *magnanimously* offered to remove the old ones," she said with a grin. "Bart is meeting us there with the backhoe since we'll have to pull some of them out of the ground, and the concrete may want to prevent that."

"He won't mind us taking them?"

"I already have the signed contract to remove the old fence and gates and dispose of them as I see fit."

"How hard is this going to be?" Lenny asked.

"Now, Lenore, we won't ruin your manicure," Vinnie teased.

Lenny snorted. She hadn't had a manicure or pedicure in her life and wasn't likely to. "Look, Alvinia ..." she began menacingly and laughed as Vinnie winced at the use of her proper name. Turnabout was fair play.

"Enough of that, you two," Bree put in, laughing at their discomfort. Neither of them suited their formal names—both of them butch—although Vinnie was soft-butch. It was hilarious when someone discovered they had rather pretty proper names. Lenny's last girlfriend had never even bothered to learn.

Bart already had the backhoe unloaded from the other trailer and was digging carefully around the posts that held up the rather large gate.

"You mentioned gates, plural?" Bree asked, watching with fascination as he worked.

"Yes, he has another one over there," Vinnie pointed with her chin and then went to grab a shovel.

"We only need the one," she fretted, not wanting to appear greedy. This iron fencing would more than suit and it looked so stately.

"It's an all or nothing deal."

They spent hours walking sections that had to be loosened with drills, then the backhoe would dig up the posts and concrete and pull them out of the ground.

"Save those nuts and bolts," Bree entreated, producing a plastic baggie for the many pieces and helping carry and load smaller sections by hand onto the empty trailer. Most were larger sections and had to be moved with the backhoe, the women drawing them down and stacking them carefully. They had to use both trailers for the many large sections, putting the two gates at the top of each stack when they were done.

"Shall I leave the holes or fill them in, boss?" Bart asked from his seat on the backhoe.

"Leave them. We'll fill them when the new fence sections arrive, and that should be tomorrow or the next day. I know the installers might appreciate them, so, if the owner gets mad at the view," she indicated the scar on the landscape where they had pulled up the many concreted-in posts, "tell him that."

"I'll pick up the backhoe later, after we offload," Bart agreed, helping to ratchet down the sections to the trailers.

Taylor wasn't home yet when they got there, but they made it in time to meet the children a few minutes after they got off the bus. Bree was nervous the whole ride home, not being there to greet them for the first time, but Vinnie had assured her they would be fine.

"What's this, Mom?" more than one voice was heard saying as they began to offload the first trailer. Lenny had pulled around the circle and backed up to the barn.

"It's a gate for the driveway and fencing," she answered, while she, Lenny, Bart, and Vinnie lifted the heavy sections together. "Stay back," she cautioned the children, who watched, fascinated, as they leaned the gate up on one side of the barn and then, one by one, stacked the sections against the other. "This won't be too heavy against the barn?" she fretted, not wanting to have to fix any damage.

"No, it just feels heavier because of the concrete still attached to the steel posts. We'll knock as much of that off as possible and plant them whenever we can," Vinnie promised, envisioning it.

"I can't thank you enough, and I'm sure Taylor will say the same." She huffed and puffed, lifting her fair share. "Are you sure I shouldn't get my tractor out?"

"You've said that, several times," her friend teased, also out of breath from the manual lifting. "And, no, the four of us can do this." Despite her assurances about the removal of the concrete, the steel *was* extraordinarily heavy. They'd all gotten quite the workout. However, Vinnie felt the four of them lifting was much faster than using her tractor.

Once they were done and the two gates were leaning against the front of the barn, Vinnie teased Bree further. "Does your tractor even work?"

"Ha! I'll show you," Bree promised, heading to move the first gate away from the sliding door on the barn. "Um, a little help here," she puffed, trying to move it herself, and her two friends laughed and helped to move it back on the trailer.

"I can do that, ma'am," Bart offered once he saw the tractor she revealed.

Vinnie grinned, waiting for the fallout from her employee's misguided chivalry.

"I assure you—Bart was it?" she asked him frostily, and, at his nod, she said, "I can work my tractor very well. You just run along."

They didn't bother fastening the one gate for the quick run down the driveway, so Vinnie threw her tie-downs and chains in the bucket on the tractor. She rode on the tractor's step, and, when they got to end and parked, she directed Bree to dig a hole on the south side of the driveway.

"Do you think we could get this thing in place and hung today?" yelled Bree.

"No! No time, but at least you'll have the hole dug and we can put another post over there!" Vinnie yelled over the noise, indicating across the wide drive. The children had followed, watching wide-eyed as their mom dug the hole. "We can put the gate here for now," she called, indicating leaning it against a telephone pole on one side. "We need to measure."

"Well, that's ready," Bree said after the hole had been dug and she'd turned tractor off.

"You'll have to get concrete, maybe that Quikrete stuff." Vinnie banged her hammer against the end of the post to knock small bits of concrete off it.

"I'll see if we can work it into our budget. If nothing else, we can put up one section at a time, as we can afford it," she admitted honestly, not ashamed to admit that money was tight. Her friends would understand.

"We'll want to measure another section from this south side first so that you can block off this," she pointed to the side of the driveway nearest to the cow field. "Then continue along there."

"Will look odd to have a swamp enclosed," Bree teased, pleased with the steel fencing, even if it was second hand. Free was free.

And Vinnie was pleased to help her friend. They brought two more sections down to the end of the driveway so they would be there and ready to install. It was getting late, and it was time for them to go. She didn't want Bree to feel obliged to invite them to dinner because she knew how tight things could be. She'd packed lunch for them in the form of ordering Subway sandwiches, and they'd all done a full day's work.

"See you," Bree waved her friends off, Bart in the second truck and trailer and Lenny riding with Vinnie as they left. She started up the tractor and headed back to the barn, Jack riding with her and the other children running down the darkening drive as they headed for the house.

* * * * *

The headlights of Taylor's Jeep shined like a spotlight on the three sections of iron-looking fencing leaning against the telephone pole. The arch on each section made them look very expensive to her, and Taylor hoped no one would steal them where they lay. She could see someone had hit their mailbox, and she stopped in the driveway to pick up the pieces once again.

* * * * *

On Taylor's next day off, Vinnie helped her and Bree to set the posts for the actual gate. "Can we put stones around this and make it look like those hoity toity places?" Taylor asked her friend.

"Sure, you can put faux stone up, too," she advised, and then, realizing her friends probably didn't have the money, added, "I can show you how to build a wood form that you can move up as you put the stones on and concrete them in."

"Can we use the Quikrete?" Bree asked, more familiar with that.

"Yes, but, with the form, you're gonna get that perfect square, and in the middle will be the actual steel post," she said, demonstrating with one hand in the hole Bree had dug and using a level to get it upright. "By adding the stones around it, you'll make it stronger."

"We need to do that for the mailbox," Taylor muttered, annoyed that she kept having to replace it.

"I think I have a spare piece of steel I can give you to use as the base for that. It will look like you planned it," Vinnie told her, imagining the number of stones they would need to do each post. "You can have the kids collect the rocks."

"We still have a bunch from widening the drive." Bree pointed to where the grass had grown up and hidden the piles of rocks they'd left for this very purpose down at the end of the driveway.

"Oh, that's great!" Vinnie exclaimed, pleased they wouldn't have to go to any additional expense.

They disconnected the gate from its' two posts, and Vinnie made a box from some wood left over from when the contractors built their house.

"Can't tell you two are potter-er … ers," she over-emphasized. They exchanged smiles as they slathered on the concrete in between the stones against the deeply seated post. "Pour some of that concrete in here." Vinnie pointed to the top of the steel post. She was on a ladder at this point and would cap it off once the concrete had hardened. She and Taylor had run electric lines through the empty post before pouring the concrete inside. They mixed the concrete a little runny to make sure it filled the length of the long post, and Taylor ran a piece of rebar inside the post to get out any air pockets. "That should hold. Great work!" Vinnie complimented her friends as they finished the first post and set up for the second.

They got four posts in that day but couldn't hang the gate until the concrete had time to set. They used Vinnie's scrap steel post to set their mailbox more securely.

"You're going to have to buy a new one of these," Vinnie mentioned as they placed the rocks, one by one, around the pole. The mailbox itself had seen better days.

"Well, this time, at least, it shouldn't be batting practice for whoever is beating the hell out of it," Taylor quipped. She placed a particularly pretty stone and set it so the sun shone on it. "Ain't that purty?"

"Wish we had cameras down here," Bree muttered, bringing a few more stones in a bucket.

"That's not hard to do," Vinnie told her, laying out stones for Taylor.

"We can't run the lines," Bree answered, imagining how expensive that would be.

"No, they're all Bluetooth these days, just like the ones at the house," she explained. "We can run them off solar," she pointed to the tops of the gate posts, where the couple planned to run lights off solar, too.

"It all costs money," Bree groaned.

* * * * *

But when they went by the hardware store for more Quikrete, Bree looked at the cameras Vinnie recommended and bought a two-pack. They weren't as expensive as she had thought, and Taylor had just collected a large check for an order of pots.

"That is really nice," Gretchen complimented them when she saw the hung gate. "Is that going to be a problem with the snow?" She motioned how the large gate split and swung inward toward the cow field and then their woods.

"Well, I'm hoping to keep it clear with the front-end loader on the tractor," Taylor explained, but they hadn't experienced snow out here and that was a large field next door. The snowdrift might be bigger than she thought, though, with nothing to stop it. The new trees hadn't had much time to grow, and it would be years before they blocked out that field. Gretchen's gift had been quite practical, and the hundreds of saplings were now placed evenly along that row by the fence. The fence had provided them with a measuring stick of where to place the many saplings. They'd pushed back the overgrown grasses to dig a hole with enough room so the roots could grow. Their neighbors, the cows, merely chewed their cud and watched the humans behaving so oddly at each and every planting.

There was room enough for a car or truck to pull off the highway and push the button to ask to be let in. Both the Jeep and the minivan had a device in them that automatically triggered the gate before they even finished getting off the highway so the gate would split open.

"And there." Bree measured so they knew where to stop in the driveway if the gate didn't split open promptly. They didn't want the cars to get hit by the swinging gate.

They'd had one minor hiccup, having forgotten to put a small gate for the children before the first fence panel, but they solved the issue by putting one in before the next panel. "I want to put up a snow house for the kids to wait for the bus," Taylor added, imagining her babies freezing on those cold winter mornings. "We can heat it with solar, too."

Bree knew Taylor was getting a kick out of planning builds, even if they only had crappy tools for her to work with to accomplish her dreams. "Hey, we need to invite your mom over, now that the house has been delivered and we're living here. She's called a couple of times," she reminded her wife. She handed her a small hand saw to finish cutting the scrap wood they were using to build the snow house behind the walk-in gate. They had built it on stilts since this section was in a ditch and would

be swampy with run off from the road and driveway. They'd also built a short gangplank for the kids to scramble into and out of the small building.

Taylor sighed. She'd wanted to see her mom and show her the new house, but inviting her mom meant Tia would come, too. If Tia came, she'd bring Blaine and Eric, and she really didn't want to see them at all. "I want to put up stone around this building, too." The kids had been in and out of the small shed, and it allowed them to sit or stand as they waited for the bus. This would be especially important in inclement weather, and snow season wasn't that far off.

"Get it over with, like pulling a bandage off," Bree advised, driving in a nail. She knew Taylor was changing the subject to distract her.

When they were finished, there were three sections of fencing in, including the gate. One section was at an angle and met up with the fence for the cow pasture on that one side. The other side went along far enough that someone could not drive around the gate without going into the woods. The foot gate was now in place with stone pillars on either side of it, and the small snow house was awaiting winter for the kids' use. Taylor hadn't been able to enclose it in stone, but the wood looked nice.

"We can continue on down the road until we run out of sections," Taylor said enthusiastically, but it had been so much work and she knew Bree was exhausted from it. She was, too, but she loved the look of the wrought iron. Bree had touched up all the scratches on it with black paint, making it look shiny, black, and rich. It had definitely stopped the incursion of random vehicles driving up their remote driveway, even when they left it open for deliveries. Some days, they left the gate open so the deliveries they were expecting didn't have to stop and push the call button on the gate, and, still, there were no intruders. The problem that had plagued them from day one on the property was finally solved.

HOME ~ First Nillionaires Club

CHAPTER TWENTY-SIX

"Ooh-la-la," Tia mocked upon seeing the gate and then the house. "Aren't we fancy?"

Taylor just smiled at her sister's obvious jealousy and greeted their mother with a hug and a kiss on the cheek.

"Oh, Taylor, this is lovely," Ellen complimented her daughter. After releasing her, she went to hug Bree. "You two did good!"

They showed their guests around the house and watched patiently as they looked into every closet and cupboard, repeatedly exclaiming over the amount of room the two apparently had. With very little furniture, there was a lot of room to spare. The children excitedly pulled their grandmother from room to room, showing off their rooms, their toys, and the features of the new house.

"Solar? Does that even work?" Eric asked scornfully, looking at the electric boxes in the basement. He could see where they had started laying more cinder blocks to create walls enclosing the electronics. "Why'd you bother with a pour if you're gonna dig it up?" he asked, pointing to where they had cut down in the slab to put rebar before putting the blocks over it and laying more concrete.

Bree could understand why Taylor got so exasperated with her brother-in-law. The questions, while real and seemingly innocent, all sounded like accusations when he said them with a sneer. "We didn't realize how big

the room for the electronics would be," she found herself defending their decision. "Then, we realized we wanted a storm shelter, but the bid for that from the contractor was astronomical." That was true. They'd been sticker-shocked when Marc sent them the paperwork with his bid. "We'll build it when we can," she said airily. "We have plenty of time."

The basement was mostly empty except where they had worked on rainy days. The cinder blocks were heavy, and lifting them over the rebar gave Bree and Taylor quite the workout. Putting in the fence had delayed this project, but they didn't mind.

"It's like having another house down here," Tia put in, looking speculatively at the spare bedroom. "You could even put in another bathroom."

"We had them install the piping for that. Someday, we will put one in," her sister told her, pointing at the capped pipes. She heard herself bragging and knew she'd regret it. Her sister was already scheming.

"That fence makes it look like we're coming on someone's estate," Ellen told her daughter as they shared a meal together on their deck, despite it being a little cold. Their view of the woods was nice, but the leaves had already turned and, soon, the wind would be ripping them down.

"We're so lucky the guy wanted them gone and that Vinnie picked them up for a song," Bree told her mother-in-law, not admitting they had gotten it all for free, except for their hard work. She knew Tia and Eric were listening avidly. As Bree watched, the much older Blaine tried to bully her daughters, telling them what to do and physically pushing them around. "Careful there," she called, trying to make light of his behavior, knowing that his parents were touchy where their only son was concerned.

Somehow, someway, during the course of casual conversation, the subject of Blaine being the only "true" grandson came up.

"Not being biologically related to a child doesn't make you any less family. Being a real family isn't in the DNA; it's in the heart," Taylor asserted stoutly when her sister stated her twaddle.

"Yes, well, he is Mom's only direct descendant," Tia tried a different tact.

Taylor waved her off, but it irritated her that her sister thought like this. Looking over at Eric, Taylor wasn't too impressed with his pedigree. It was things like this that had made her not want to invite her family over in the first place. But it was almost over, and she would get through this.

"We should have Christmas here," Ellen stated happily. "You have all this room. and we can decorate properly. Much better than at my little

place. I can leave the family ornaments here, then, and you can store them, with all your room."

Tia's eyes narrowed, and she seemed to smolder at the thought. Taylor's smile froze on her face, but she would agree to make her mother happy. Bree was the only one actually pleased at the idea of having their first Christmas in the house together with the whole family.

After they had left, Taylor breathed a sigh of relief. Bree laughed at her for how tense she had gotten over the idea of their visit. "It wasn't *that* bad," she consoled, having lived through all the snipes made by her in-laws. "Your mother was really happy for us."

* * * * *

A few days later, Taylor got the call she was dreading. Ellen had left a message on Taylor's phone, asking her to call back.

"Hey, Mom. I just got off of work. What's up?" It was late, and Taylor was tired. She'd dropped a full platter of hot, greasy food during the dinner rush, and it had taken forever to clean it up. She was ready to get home and relax.

"Darling, I was thinking about that big house of yours. I know you have plans for the basement, but how about we speed those along and get it finished now instead in the distant future?"

"We're in no hurry." As she drove home in the dark, watching for deer and other critters on the road, Taylor wondered where Ellen was going with this.

"I was thinking you could put in a couple more rooms down there since it mirrors your upstairs. Finish that bathroom and put in a kitchen. With that view to the woods, it will be lovely."

"Well, maybe in a few years—"

"How about I pay for the remodel, and you can eventually pay me back by charging rent?"

"Charging rent? Who would we charge rent to?"

"Well, Tia and Eric. I know they would love the new apartment."

"What new apartment?" she asked, confused. It had been a long day.

"The one we will build in the basement. You have all that unused space, and you yourself said you would be putting in the bathroom. We just need to put in another couple of bedrooms and finish off the space, and it would be perfect for them."

Taylor blinked, unsure of what she had just heard. She was glad her mother couldn't see her face. Her immediate thought was to scream "NO!" but she knew that wasn't the mature way to handle the situation.

"I'll discuss it with Bree, Mom, but I just got off work, and I'm really very tired." She just wanted to get home, and, right now, driving was going to require all her concentration.

"Of course, darling. You discuss it with Bree, and I'll call you in a few days." Her tone suggested she had won something. Taylor was leery, but she purged it from her mind to focus on her driving.

Once home, Taylor was hesitant to talk with Bree about the phone call. She knew she didn't want her sister, her useless husband, and their bratty kid moving into their new home. She knew they would sow seeds of discord in their tiny family. Having the unruly Blaine around all the time would be terrible for their own young brood, and Eric—who seemed to excel in being fired from dead-end jobs—she knew his condescension would be too much to take. As with many things related to her family, she happily pushed it from her mind, forgetting to tell her wife until a few days later when she got a call at work.

"Taylor, why was Tia over here with a measuring tape?" Bree asked through clenched teeth into the phone.

Taylor could almost hear the bristling of her wife. "Oh, gawd, you let her in?" she hedged. She glanced around, hoping for a rush of customers so she could get back to work, but sadly it was a slow moment at the diner.

"I had no reason not to," Bree pointed out.

She had just stopped for lunch when the doorbell rang. Seeing her sister-in-law looking cheerily into the camera, she hadn't suspected anything was amiss.

"Hi, Bree. Did Taylor tell you I was coming over?" she asked brightly, her tone suggesting something was settled.

"No?" she asked, heading back into the kitchen with Tia following. "I just stopped to have lunch. Do you want a sandwich?" She hoped Tia didn't because she needed to go to the store and only had enough bread for one sandwich.

"No, I just came to measure," she said, holding up a dilapidated tape measure that had seen better days and indicating the basement door.

Frowning, Bree nodded, wondering what that was about. Taylor must have forgotten to tell her that her sister was coming over—which was odd—but they had both been busy. Bree, trying to make pots for current orders and for the last fall show, and, Taylor, taking extra shifts to get ahead on house payments. Still, they weren't doing too badly and had gotten their deposit back on their old apartment, arguing that the wear and tear the manager tried to ding them with was common. They were saving that money to fall back on if they needed it for their mortgage.

Before long, Tia was back upstairs. "Got it," the woman said happily, waving the tape measure which seemed to be permanently extended by a foot or more. "I'll talk to you later," she said, then waved at Bree, who was rinsing her dishes from lunch, and made her way out the front door before Bree could ask her any questions.

That led to their current conversation where Bree, after finishing her clean up and heading back out to the shop, called Taylor.

"She said you knew about it."

Taylor shook her head. "No, I knew nothing about Tia coming over. Mom called me a few nights ago, and I forgot to tell you." Her shoulders sagged. She hated the position this put her in. She'd thought about it and knew there was no way that Tia and her family could move into their house, even if it would help out her mother, who was tired of their freeloading. They did nothing to really contribute to her mom's household, and she knew their supposed rent payments were sporadic. There was no reason to think that their behaviors would change if they moved in with Taylor and Bree.

"What did your mother call about?" Bree was beginning to get an odd feeling. It was as if her family were conspiring against her. A long time ago, they had pushed Bree until she'd actually considered not marrying Taylor. But Taylor had proven to be the woman she thought she was. It was shit like this that could have driven a wedge between them—if they let it. Well, she wasn't going to let it. Those people didn't have the power over them they sometimes thought they did.

Taylor explained the phone call and quickly added, "I meant to tell you—to warn you—but I blew it off. I know we don't want them in the house."

"Taylor, Tia was just here measuring. She must think she's moving in!"

"I'll call and tell my mother under no circumstances will we allow that. Don't let her in. How'd she get past the gate?"

"I had the gate open for deliveries," Bree pointed out, knowing she should have left it closed. They'd spent a little of their miniscule cushion of savings on extra cameras, having found those beautiful solar lanterns that were also cameras for the gate. Taylor had figured out how to install them, and Bree had helped her. They'd been zapped once because they'd forgotten to turn off the solar. It had been funny, but they'd felt a sense of accomplishment when the gates swung wide on the push of a button from their phones. Each of their vehicles had a sensor in it so the gates would recognize them and open automatically when they approached.

Taylor sighed loudly, knowing how determined her sister would be, now that she had this idea in her head. She'd bet Eric was already planning to hunt on their property this fall, and who knew what mischief Blaine was up to. "I'll call," she promised again. "Why can't they just leave us alone?" she mumbled wearily.

"Because you don't want to cut your mom out of your life, and, with your mom, comes Tia and Eric."

Taylor nodded and sighed into the phone, admitting her wife was right. She felt bad for her mom, who was going to receive the fallout from this little plan. She wondered if it were all Tia's idea, right down to their mom financing the basement remodel. She'd know soon enough, but she had to wait to call her mother until her next break. A customer came into the diner, and she had to wait on her.

* * * * *

"Look, Mom! Look!" Bryan held up a shiny, new dime to show it off to Bree.

"What is it? Oh, a dime. That's nice," she said, not really impressed.

"Allan brought it to me!" he said, even more excited.

"Is Allan one of your friends at school?" she asked, disinterested as she tried to work, but concerned that he was taking money from his friends. She'd surely get a call from an annoyed parent or the school for that behavior.

"No, Mom! It's from Allan Crowe."

"I don't think I know Allan Crowe."

He was getting upset at her apparent confusion. He had a shiny dime his friend had brought him, and his mom didn't understand. "He's a crow, Mom! A crow! Remember the story about Allan Crowe? I named him after the story."

It took Bree a few seconds to remember the afternoon of crow stories with their friends. It had, after all, been in late summer, back before the house had been delivered. It took her another second to remember the pun-like name that had been in the one story. Edgar Allan Poe became Edgar Allan Crowe. It just proved the kids *had* been listening, even if they didn't get all the nuances of it. Then, the sense of what Bryan was telling her began to penetrate Bree's brain. "Wait ... you're saying a crow gave you this dime?"

He nodded enthusiastically, the cowlick on his head bobbing as he nodded so hard.

"Why would a crow give you this dime?" she asked, alarmed that a wild creature might be coming so close to her son.

"I've been cawing to them as we walk up the driveway. I save some of my bread, and, when I see Allan, I throw it to him. He knows me now and jumps up and down when he sees me. He gets really excited when I give him the bread."

Bree blinked, not sure if she should be upset or not. Were the stories they shared so long ago influencing her son, or was her son smart enough to realize he had trained the bird to come because he would give him some bread? Who was training whom here? After all, the bird had brought the boy a dime in payment for his offerings. "Wow, that's really nice," she said, sounding enthused but not sure if that was the correct way to respond. The crow was a wild animal. She would have to discuss it with Taylor when she got home so they could come up with a plan of action.

* * * * *

Taylor was having a bad day at work. First, there was her wife's phone call. After she made the call to her mother (it hadn't gone well), Gretchen and Barry had come in with their son, Aaron, who was turning thirteen soon. Taylor was surprised to see Barry, but it wasn't long before she'd had enough of him.

She held her tongue when he gave the soon-to-be teen a hard time, but when he started in on Gretchen about why feminism shouldn't even be a "thing," Taylor let him have it with both barrels. "Look, women are 51% of the population, but 70% of the poor and 83% of single parents, doing 66% of the work, and producing 50% of the food, but earn just 11% of the pay, and only own 1% of the land. Just in case you wonder why we still need feminism." she asked sarcastically. With that, she walked away without even taking his order.

Her boss gave her hell as Barry complained, but Taylor explained who Barry really was and why he wanted to get her in trouble. Still, he was a paying customer. She didn't care if she'd insulted the man; he treated her friend Gretchen and their son terribly.

On her way home she thought about her conversation with her mother.

"Hey, Mom. I only have a few minutes," she began, a convenient excuse so she didn't have to stay on the phone long, but also, since she was calling on her break, quite true. "I said we'd think about turning the basement into an apartment, and Bree and I decided not right now. We've only just moved in and want to get used to the place."

"Oh, dear," her mother said wearily. "I know Tia was counting on it."

"I'm sorry, but she will have to live with the disappointment. We only just moved in and are still getting settled."

"You don't know what she's like, and I know they've already made plans."

"I do know what she's like, and you should stand up for yourself. It's your home, not hers."

"Isn't there any way I could talk you into fixing up the apartment space?"

"No, Mom, not right now." She thought to herself, 'and not *ever*.'

Ellen sighed, totally defeated. "I'll tell Tia." It was obvious to both of them that she was not looking forward to the conversation with her other daughter.

"I've got to go, Mom. My break is over," Taylor fibbed, ending the call. She didn't want to deal with this, and it was completely not of her making. She couldn't help them making plans around something she was not even willing to consider.

* * * * *

"No worries. Tia will get the message," Taylor told Bree when she got home. She was wearily stripping off her outfit which reeked of grease. Some kid had flung his macaroni and cheese everywhere, and her uniform had gotten the worst of it.

"I mean, if it was your mother, that would be one thing," Bree began indignantly, having thought about the whole situation as she worked on pottery all afternoon.

"No, because if Mom moved here, Tia would have an excuse to visit. I don't even want her on the property anymore," Taylor decided. "With Tia comes Eric, and you know he hasn't given up the idea of hunting on our land."

"Oh, shit! You think?" She was worried about that, which was why their entire property was posted. She knew they'd have to repost in several areas where weather (and, perhaps, people) had destroyed the signs. She'd noticed many of them were faded when they took their walks.

"I'm certain of it. They are kind of hard-headed. I don't envy the conversation with Tia that my mom was going to have to have."

"Shouldn't you have told Tia yourself?"

Taylor shook her head, her hair coming out of the bun she wore for work. "No, I have a feeling Tia manipulated Mom into the whole idea, and I wasn't getting in the middle of that."

After Taylor relayed what she'd told her mother, Bree was certain the matter was closed. Ellen would tell Tia and Eric, and they'd have to live with their disappointment.

* * * * *

It was nearly ten at night when they heard the chime that indicated movement at the gate. Taylor stopped on her way to the shower to check it out on her phone, and Bree picked up her phone at the same time. They both looked up at each other when they realized Tia was in her car, reaching for the buzzer on the keypad. Taylor briefly remembered as they put in that steel arm for the keypad. The buzzer jarred her.

"Should we answer?" she asked her wife.

"She's only going to keep pressing it until we let her in," Bree pointed out.

"I'm so not ready for a confrontation," Taylor whined, her shoulder sagging in defeat as the buzzer went off again.

"Better get it over with," Bree advised, equally defeated at the idea. She didn't press any of the buttons on her phone as she watched Tia's anger over their lack of immediate response.

"What?" Taylor barked into her phone, pressing the communications button to speak. "We're getting ready for bed, Tia."

"You let me in, NOW!" her sister ordered her.

"No, I don't think so," Taylor taunted, trying to keep the sound of triumph from coming through her voice. Tia had no idea how many times Taylor had been sickened by the way she treated people. "I'm not having you upset the children. We're going to bed. I've had a long day, and Bree is already in bed." She glanced at her wife who was certainly *not* in bed.

"I don't want to know about your sexual deviations," Tia said spitefully, pressing the button a few more times. The buzzing was annoying. "Let me in, you coward."

"No, Tia, go home. Mom knows why we won't let you move in, and I think you do, too. I won't listen to your arguments or spite. Go away before we call the police for your trespassing."

Bree pumped the air, encouraging her wife. She couldn't have been prouder than she was in that moment, and she was ecstatic they had put up the extra fence panels, despite the extra cost. Tia couldn't drive around the gate and wouldn't take the chance of ramming it because it would do a lot more damage to her precious car than anything else.

"Tresp—" she began, but Taylor shut off her app and turned to her wife. "I'm going to take a shower. Watch that?" She thumb-pointed vaguely towards the gate.

"Do you really want me to call the police if she tries anything?" Bree asked dryly, watching as Tia became unglued. She hadn't turned on her sound, so they could only see her facial expressions, which were alarming in themselves. She wondered if Tia knew all this was being recorded.

"Yes," Taylor responded with a small mischievous grin. The thought of how her sister would react to the police really improved her mood as she went into the little bathroom to take her shower. By the time she returned and picked up her dirty laundry to presoak the mess, Bree was watching her phone avidly. "Is she still here?"

Bree shook her head. "No, she left, but I'm watching the idiot who just hit our mailbox."

"Again?" Taylor asked mournfully, reaching for her own phone to pull up the camera.

"Yeah. Looks like we got a good shot of his license plate this time."

"Can we deal with it in the morning?" Taylor asked wearily.

"Nope, I already called the police." Bree got up and pulled on clean jeans and a t-shirt.

"Crap! Let me set this in the washer," she indicated her gathered uniform. "I'll be out in a minute."

The police didn't come, but the county sheriff did. He took a long time observing and documenting the damage to the column that housed their mailbox. The stones had come loose, but the steel pipe in the middle hadn't even moved. He took pictures of the paint on the stone, all the time Bree watched this from the comfort of their home. When he pressed the buzzer on their keypad, she immediately pressed the button to open the gate which swung wide and greeted him at the door.

"Good evening, Officer," she said quietly. "Would you like to come in?"

He looked around at the new house, having not known anyone lived back here. It was very nice, if a bit bare in terms of furniture. She welcomed him into the lit kitchen, where another woman joined them, carrying some paperwork. "Good evening, Sheriff," Taylor said in a teasing voice, recognizing the officer from the diner. "Or, should I call you Deputy?"

"You? You live here?" he asked, sounding awed as he recognized her. He couldn't believe she was the same waitress. Her hair down and out of the waitress uniform, she looked much prettier.

"Yes, and this is my wife, Bree. Bree, this is one of the deputies who eats at Tweety's."

Bree nodded, but then ruined it with a barely concealed yawn. It was getting late, and the stress of Tia, followed by the truck hitting their mailbox, was getting to her.

"Your wife?" he asked, perplexed, before realizing what she was saying. "Oh, you're ..." he began but stopped himself, becoming completely professional. "You stated on the phone that you have video evidence of the accident?"

"That was no accident," Taylor stated, indicating the papers she had printed out. "That's the fourth time someone has hit our mailbox since we put it up last spring."

"There is only damage to the rock work ..." he began.

"But we've had to replace the box three times. The only reason it isn't gone this time is probably because of the steel post we put it in it. We only put up the rock to conceal—" she began but thought better of her wording, "um, to match the posts on our gate."

The deputy looked at the papers where it was clear that the truck had appeared to aim for their mailbox, and he could clearly see the license plate.

"I believe hitting a mailbox is a federal crime, Officer?" Bree asked sweetly.

"Deputy," he corrected her automatically, sounding official. "I'll run the plate and proceed with an investigation."

"Deputy Mendez," Taylor said in a steely voice. "We want this prosecuted to the fullest extent of the law. As my wife said," she indicated Bree, "it's a *federal* offense, and we have been greatly inconvenienced previously in having to retrieve our strewn mail, as well as replacing the mailbox several times."

He nodded absentmindedly as looked over the papers. "May I take these?"

Bree and Taylor both nodded. "Do you need the video?" Taylor asked, holding up a small flash drive.

"Probably," he said, holding out his hand. "I'll let you know what he says."

"You know the truck and who owns it?" Taylor pressed, handing him the drive.

He hesitated before nodding. "He's a local boy, and I'll go give him a talk." He didn't want to tell the two women no charges would be filed, not if the boy's daddy had anything to say about it.

"Deputy," Taylor said warningly, having read his expression. She waited until he looked up. "Do we need to file federal charges with the post office? Those are only copies." She pointed to the drive and the papers he was holding.

Swallowing, he shook his head. "No, I'll handle it," he promised. Daddy or no, the boy had done wrong, and he would have to follow through. Taylor may only be a waitress at Tweety's, but she was right; it was a federal offense. Daddy wasn't going to get the boy off this time. He promised to call them and went to his car. As he left, he glanced around as his patrol car lights revealed a new lawn, a freshly painted barn, and an all new, raw, house that was coming along nicely. He didn't think a waitress could afford a place like this, but, seeing the swamp, he swallowed and vowed to look into that aspect of it. He'd bet this place had been a dump, but he couldn't remember. As the gate closed behind him, he turned onto Restlawn Highway and headed for the boy's home address. He didn't even need to enter it into his GPS.

"Think he'll do anything?" Bree asked, not impressed with the deputy Taylor apparently knew. She knew a lot of people from working at the diner.

"He knows he better or we'll be filing charges against him, too," Taylor said angrily. She had a strong suspicion who owned that blue truck, and she wasn't going to let this go.

CHAPTER TWENTY-SEVEN

When the sheriff's vehicle showed up at their gate the next day, Taylor's was helping Bree stack pots onto pallets for transport to their next show. Tia was still furious and had blown up their phones with nasty messages all night, so they knew better than to leave the gate open now. They'd been looking for the patrol car all morning and popped the gate before the Sheriff could even stop to let them know he was there.

"Hard to believe that was only yesterday," Bree murmured. She checked her phone and found three new messages had come in on her phone in the last hour. She assumed Taylor's phone would have even more threats from the deranged woman.

"And now we have to deal with this," Taylor said, watching the deputy drive through the gate and up towards the house.

Bree closed the gate behind him, never knowing if Tia was waiting to get onto the property. Taylor had already said that Tia would never walk up the driveway, so they weren't worried about her just showing up. Taylor had flatly ordered her mother to call off her sister, saying it was inappropriate for her to show up, not to mention the phone calls and texts and her threatening to call the police. Maybe, if Tia saw the sheriff's car, she would stay away.

As she came out of the barn, Taylor waved to the Sheriff and respectfully wiped her hands on a rag. Fall in the air, and, to lighten the mood, they had been talking about Jack's upcoming birthday. With Halloween past, they had gone into some new neighborhoods, driving to find trick or treating for the kids. Now, they needed to worry about Jack and have a conversation about it.

"I asked Jack what he wanted for his fifth birthday."

Bree sighed. She was afraid to ask but then figured *what the hell.* "What did he answer?"

"He said he wanted unicorns, rainbows, and fairies." She giggled as she told her wife.

"That's not unreasonable, is it?" Bree was desperately thinking of how they could decorate so the boy would get exactly what he wanted.

Taylor lowered her voice and added, "My first thought was we'd get all of that if we took some LSD."

Bree snorted through her nose before she collapsed into giggles of her own.

"Hi, Sheriff!" Taylor called, while Bree tried to collect herself. They grew sober as church mice as they watched the man get out of the car and walk up to them, clearly annoyed.

"Do you know what you two have done by convincing my deputy to file those charges against Kyle Longuard?"

"Is that the owner of the blue truck that's been hitting our mailbox?" Taylor asked, clearly not intimidated by the sheriff.

He looked around, noting the new house and the freshly painted barn, something his deputy had mentioned. "No, it's owned by his father, but you can see on the video Kyle was driving. We could have handled this privately, but, no, you had to mention the federal charges, and Derek is pissed."

"Derek is Kyle's father?" Bree asked to clarify, irritated by the sheriff's tone.

"Yes, Derek Longuard is pretty important around here—if you didn't know!"

Neither woman did know, but they didn't particularly care, either. "Is he offering to make restitution for his son targeting our mailbox?" Taylor asked reasonably.

"He's freaking pissed!" the sheriff repeated angrily.

"Look, we reported those other hits, and now that we have it on tape …" Taylor began, just as angrily.

He hitched up his pants, but the leather belt with his handcuffs and other paraphernalia pulled it back down. "We could have handled it in-house! But, no, you had to make it a federal offense."

"It was always a federal offense, Sheriff," Bree put in quietly. She laid her hand on Taylor's arm, not sure whether she was trying to keep Taylor or herself from lunging forward.

"Mr. Longuard is very unhappy."

"What about us?" Bree asked reasonably.

"What about you?" he repeated stupidly.

"We let your department know about the times our mailbox had been taken out. We also reported it to the postmaster," she said, still keeping an even tone. She could see it aggravated him. She could hear Taylor breathing angrily beside her, ready to do combat with the sheriff, verbally at least.

"You reported it to the postmaster?"

She nodded. "Of course. From what I understand mailboxes are protected by federal law, and crimes against them and what they contain are considered a federal offense. Violators can be fined up to $250,000 or imprisoned for up to three years for each act of vandalism. The post office has on record the four times our mailbox has been hit, so that's ..." she hesitated here as though to give it time to sink in, "a million dollars and twelve years in a federal penitentiary."

"You already reported last night?" he asked stupidly, sounding even more angry.

"Oh, yes. They're used to us coming in by now," she said in a chirpy voice she knew would anger him further. "And, with the mail that was strewn about, if he picked it up, it's a separate offense to take a letter. I filled out the forms with the postal inspection service. I'm sure an agent will be out to talk to Mr. Longuard."

"As if he'd see them," he muttered, sounding triumphant.

"It would be Kyle, not Derek," she pointed out. "He would have no choice, even if he is a minor. Daddy's money wouldn't save him."

"You're taking law enforcement into your own hands!" he accused. "I'm not certain those cameras are legal, either."

"We put in the cameras at the end of our driveway to see who is coming up to our gate. They are on our land, on our property, and pointing at our gate. He came onto our land to commit a felony."

Taylor stared at Bree in delight, surprised by her reasoning. She had only known about the first time where they went to the post office to ask what they could do. The police had said it was the sheriff's jurisdiction, and the sheriff's department hadn't really wanted to take a report, passing it off at first as the police's duty. They had reluctantly taken a report that first time but not the other times. They only came this last time after Bree mentioned they had film and evidence of the person who did it.

"We could have handled it!"

"Oh, no, sir," Bree continued in her chirpy voice. "You are to immediately report theft, tampering, or destruction of your mailbox to the postmaster." She sounded like she was quoting something, and both the sheriff and her wife looked at her. Her face was a mask of innocence.

"Mr. Longuard could cause you a lot of trouble," he warned.

"And I expect you to handle that for us if he does," Bree continued. "After all, Sheriff, you're here to protect us, aren't you?"

He glared at her but didn't reply. Finally, he grunted and turned to leave.

"Can I get the report number so I can come down and get a copy?" Taylor thought to ask as they followed him back to his car.

"They'll give it to you at the desk," he snarled as he got back in his car. "If I want to see those tapes," his head nodded toward the end of the driveway, "you'll give them to me." It wasn't a question.

"If you wish to see the copy, I gave your deputy …" Bree began, but he was shaking his head.

"No, I mean any tapes. Anytime I want them." He started the car and sped down the driveway.

"That sounded like a threat. Can he even do that?" Bree asked Taylor, frowning.

"No, but it sounds like he is going to try. Wonder why he wants to see our tapes?" They weren't really tapes. They were digital recordings, but it was easier to say.

* * * * *

Later, before the kids got home, Gretchen stopped by to pick up some pots she'd ordered for her clients. They told her what happened with both Tia and the sheriff the previous night.

"Nothing like some excitement around the old homestead," she teased. "That sheriff sounds like he might be out of line," she mused. "I'd ask Elsie if she knows anyone you can ask."

"Why Elsie?"

"She knows a lot of people and might know what you can do. I would hate for you to have to hire a lawyer. That sounds expensive."

They both exchanged looks, agreeing it would be expensive.

"Are your business permits in order?" Gretchen further asked.

"Yes, we took them out for this place as soon as we knew we were moving things into the barn," Bree told her, now worrying about the

threatening attitude of the sheriff and the apparent warning about Derek Longuard. They had Kyle dead to rights on the video.

"Just make sure you have all your insurance up to date and that your permits are current," she warned. "Talk to Elsie—I think she knows someone at the local TV station."

"What's that going to do?" Taylor asked, her stomach churning at the thought of all this.

"If you show that tape to the TV station, that's news. The Longuards won't touch you," she pointed out.

They'd sent a digital file to the postmaster, or so Bree had explained to Taylor. They had it in the cloud so it could be given out to anyone they chose.

"This is turning out great," Gretchen complimented them. She admired the new designs they had sitting out. "I have a spider plant with your name on it," she told them as they loaded the pots into her truck.

Back when the family had finally settled in their new house, Gretchen and Elsie had gone with them and picked up a camera, as well as helping them to pick out their new computer for their business. They'd waited so long to buy the computer. Both of their friends had enjoyed showing them how to use their new programs. The computer in the shop was connected to the one in the house, and Taylor was learning to put pictures of their pots online. They'd put up a black drop cloth behind the pots and then found a green one, so they could change the backgrounds. They wouldn't ship individual pots, but they would meet with people at shows or they could buy them through the businesses that were carrying them, including Gretchen's.

"You've already given us a lot of housewarming presents. First the camera and help in learning how to use the programs on our new computer, and then those," Taylor protested, pointing to the trees along the property line she had spent an entire day planting. They were willows and would probably do well, with the water table being so high from the swamp. She'd planted them along the far side of the driveway next to the barbed wire, hoping they would grow fast and block the view of the fence, maybe the smell from the cows and the eternal flies that accompanied the beasts.

"No, this isn't a housewarming present. This is an idea for you to draw on some of the pots I want you to make," she said, making it sound reasonable. "I can't learn macramé for the life of me, and I thought, if my pots had pictures of plants on them, they might sell even better in the greenhouse." She wanted to hang some of the lighter pots and that string art would look marvelous.

"I think Lenny knows how to do crafts like macramé," Taylor pointed out, looking at the spider plant speculatively.

"Lenny?" Gretchen asked, surprised. That butch was always doing things that didn't seem to conform to people's expectations. She mentally chastised herself for selling the woman short.

"Yeah, who'd a thunk, eh?" Taylor teased, already seeing how she could make the lines to the variegated leaves.

"Hey, are you two hosting Thanksgiving this year?" Gretchen asked, looking at their house with pride in her friends.

"We hadn't planned to," Bree said, suddenly alarmed. They'd been going to the diner for years and had assumed they would this year, too, mostly because Taylor would be working the holiday again.

"We could have the First Nillionaires Club bring dishes to pass."

Bree laughed. That club had grown over the years, and they'd be at the diner, too. "I don't want to have to cook or clean," she said, pointing a finger at Gretchen for emphasis.

"How about a Christmas feast?"

"How about New Year's?" she countered.

"That sounds good. We'll all bring dishes to pass, so you don't have to cook."

"Not one of the children will be able to stay up that late."

"Good, then we can have adult beverages and pass out on your furniture."

"What furniture?" Taylor teased in return, much to mutual laughter.

"Will Barry let you stay?" Bree asked.

A brief shadow passed over Gretchen's eyes, and she stopped teasing. Bree immediately felt bad for bringing it up. She knew their marriage wasn't the greatest.

"Why don't you plan on bringing Barry and Aaron," Taylor put in, hugging Bree to lighten the suddenly somber mood.

"Oh, yeah, that would be fun," Gretchen grouched but then laughed. "Aaron would like it, but I don't think Barry would."

"We could always play walk on the swamp ice and see how far he gets?"

"Shhh, if he ever disappears, I need to have an alibi!"

They all laughed, but it didn't erase the fact that Barry liked to control Gretchen. All their friends knew it but had no idea how to help her other than to just be there when she needed them.

Bree made up an invoice for the pots Gretchen had ordered as soon as she left and emailed it off. Having the new computer was such a wonderful thing. She had never thought they would finally get to this

point. They'd dreamed of it for so long. Taking pictures of their work meant a lot more steps in their production, but the brochures and business cards Elsie produced for them meant their customers bought more. Elsie had loved working with them to make ideas they had talked about for years a reality and teaching them how to market their product.

"So, we're hosting New Year's?" Taylor asked dryly after Bree closed out QuickBooks.

"I guess so," she said but laughed at how that had come about.

She loved that they had a place now and could host their friends. She didn't want to have Thanksgiving here, since they always went to Tweety's, but Christmas was just for them and the kids. Taylor's mother, Ellen, had wanted to join them and bring her sister and her family, of course, but Taylor figured that was off, considering the incident with Tia. Yes, a New Year's celebration with their friends in their new home, with their children all snug in their beds, sounded perfect.

* * * * *

"This is lovely," Mrs. Henderson commented, glancing around the new home as she signed off on their final inspection. She'd given them each time to get settled in their new home, and each of the children were thriving. Jack was now their son legally, and the paperwork was in order to change his last name. She would miss seeing this couple and had already fielded pressure from the sheriff and a Mr. Longuard to check into the welfare of the children. She saw no cause for concern, and, when the couple had explained about the mailbox drama, she had understood. She'd made note in their file that the complaint was submitted as an attempt to exact revenge on the couple and not due to any actual problem over the children. She looked at each of the bedrooms, where the mothers had put a wall for each of the children to pin up their artwork. The wall was covered for each of them, filled with drawings, trinkets, and posters. She'd seen the Little Tykes toys and equipment out the back of the house, a nice play area they could resume using in the spring. It was becoming too cold to play out there, with icicles hanging down from the swing set.

"We can let them have their tricycles down here to race around," Taylor bragged, showing off the basement, where they were putting up walls to keep them away from the furnace and then another for a tornado shelter. There was plenty of room, wide open areas for the children to play during the winter. The two women didn't have too much to store down in their basement, so the children would have plenty of room over the cold months.

"How about that fireplace?" she asked, pointing it out in the family room.

"We've only burned in it once, and then followed the directions to get it 'broken in.'"

"Broken in?"

"Well, you have to burn really hot for four hours, and we have plenty of wood," she pointed to the woods. She'd been using a hand saw to cut chunks for the fireplace, which was a lot of work. Still, she loved having their own fireplace and their own woods. Their hikes around the property line and on a few trails going through the woods had been a lot of fun.

"You two really deserve this," she said sincerely, making notes. "Would you consider fostering another?"

The two moms exchanged looks. "The problem with that, Mrs. Henderson ..." Bree began hesitantly for both of them. "We never just foster; we always end up adopting. We think four is plenty. We just got this," her hands encompassed the house. "We're comfortable, and our mortgage is less than our rent was on the apartment. We want to give the kids we have a good life."

"You are," she assured the mom. She was disappointed she couldn't place another child with them, but she understood that four was all they felt they could handle. But she would have had no qualms about these two if they were willing.

"And, what about that swamp?" she asked, pointing to the front of the house, where it was on one side of their driveway. The water had receded from the drive, and she'd seen where they had filled it in with rocks on that side, widening it. It still looked eerie to her, and she worried about the children.

"They aren't allowed near it and stay to the drive when they walk to and from the bus," Taylor assured her.

"We're hoping to dig down and maybe put in a pond to help drain more of it," Bree confided. She smiled. "It will take time ..." Then both moms said at the same time, "... and money." They looked at each other and to Mrs. Henderson, then all three of them laughed.

Mrs. Henderson left, closing the file completely on the two women. She was pleased for them. They were making a really nice home for their family.

CHAPTER TWENTY-EIGHT

"What are you doing Taylor?" Bree asked, trying not to laugh.

"We're clearing the snow off the van, hon," she replied, gently pushing Jack across the hood of the minivan. He was giggling the entire time as the snow built up along his body, and she stopped to catch him from falling off. "There we go," she told him. "Now, the other side."

"Me, me, me!" Barbie and Bryan demanded.

"Nuh-uh, you wouldn't help me when I asked, and Jack here is just right for this job."

The snow was still coming down, and the four inches of it already on the van were being slid off the van easily by Jack in his snowsuit. Occasionally, he got a face-full, but he was giggling too much to care.

"There you go, sport. You were a real help to Mom," she told the Kindergartener as she brushed off the snow from his suit. As soon as he was clear, she opened the door to help him in.

"You really think CPS is going to look on that as positive interaction with your adopted son?" Bree murmured. She handed Taylor her hot chocolate and gave her a kiss as thanks for clearing off the van. She'd forgotten to put it away in the garage, still not used to having one.

"Can't say I won't do it again," she answered just as quietly with a grin. "And we no longer have to worry about CPS, remember?"

She did remember, having been so pleased that Mrs. Henderson liked the new house. Their finances had been scrutinized, and she understood why. The sheriff and Mr. Longuard had tried to make waves for them but couldn't. They had saved for years, and—while it had been difficult—they owned their land and were paying on the house. They weren't doing anything illegal, and she hated that an elected official had tried to manipulate the system for a rich man. It had been weeks, and Kyle Longuard had been in the papers and on TV. Their camera footage had led to an explosive story, and Elsie assured them they were probably protected now from retribution. Well, most of it, anyway.

Taylor smiled at her wife. They were taking the children for a Christmas surprise. They didn't know, but all their presents were already made or bought and hidden in the house. This present, though, this one was for all of them. Taylor had wanted one for a while, but they couldn't justify it when living in the apartment. Their Christmas show had netted them an unprecedented bonus, but maybe it was because of the orders they had taken before the actual show, putting them up on the new website Elsie had helped them create. They'd had to take the Jeep, pulling an extra U-Haul trailer to bring it all, while the minivan pulled their regular trailer. Their booth had been enormous and they'd been run off their feet, but it had all been worth it. They'd been able to send two extra payments to their mortgage to get ahead and had paid off all their minor bills. They'd even picked up another store to carry their pots and paid for the oncoming Christmas with the kids. They were very, very happy with all their hard work.

Today, they were going to the pound to pick out a dog. They had no idea what they were doing, having never owned a dog between them. But they had the room, now, and the two moms had excitedly discussed it time and time again for months. They'd considered getting a puppy, which would be nice, cute, and precious, but also aggravating and a lot of work—just not what they were looking for. It wouldn't be fair to Bree, who would be home with it most of the time and get stuck doing all the housetraining and cleanup. Instead, they had decided to get an older dog, one that was manageable but young enough to play with the kids. They would adopt it and save it. They hoped the children would agree.

It was depressing to see all the dogs behind the tall cages. Each were in their own run that led to the outside. Many were barking, and the place echoed with their howls. The smell wasn't very nice, either. The children were excited when they told them where they were, but the pound didn't live up to any of their expectations as they listened to the noisy and excited animals. They saw Labradors, mixed breeds, Chihuahuas, and many

others. Finally, one drew the attention of three of the four children, though. They had already walked by him at least three times looking at the other dogs.

The children pointed him out to their moms, who exchanged looks. He was hiding and looking miserable in the corner of his kennel. Bryan, who had been the only one to ignore him, finally noticed him. He stared, his fingers flat against the cage because his moms had told them never to put fingers, which could be nipped, inside the cage. They'd gotten plenty of pets in, licks, and snuffles from the eager dogs, but this one was trying not to be noticed. As Bryan stared, his siblings tried to encourage this shy dog to come up to them. The dog made eye contact with the boy and stared back hard.

"Look, he's stalking the boy," Bree cautioned. The dog had cropped ears, short, brown hair, and a stocky build. "Is that a Pit-Bull?" she worried, having heard terrible things about the breed.

"It says here," Taylor said, reading the card that was attached to the cage, "he's a Staffordshire Bull Terrier."

"Isn't that a fancy name for a Pit-Bull?"

"I don't think they can sell Pit-Bulls in our county."

"What?"

"I remember reading something about outlawing them. If he isn't a Staffordshire, he certainly isn't a Pit-Bull."

"That sounds like breed prejudice," she said defensively, but she was watching the dog, who was hesitantly approaching the door of the cage where Bryan stood, transfixed. The dog raised its nose to smell the boy.

"It says his name is Staffy. Probably a play on the breed's name."

"Hiya, Staffy," Bryan said, hearing his mom.

"Here, Staffy," Melanie said, and her siblings quickly echoed her, adding to the noise in this concrete building.

"Hang on, let him have room," Bree cautioned, not sure about this. She'd have thought they would want a big, curly-haired or fluffy dog and had been looking forward to a mixed breed, maybe a labradoodle or something like that. There was even a pure-bred poodle in one cage, but it was a toy poodle, and she wasn't sure she wanted anything that small. Staffy wasn't too big, but he looked solid. She watched as he thoroughly sniffed the boy, as much as he could through the cage, and then his tail started wagging. He looked intelligently at the boy; his cut ears raised.

"Mom, can I pet him?" the boy asked, looking up hopefully.

Bree exchanged a look with Taylor, who wasn't sure, either. The dog *looked* friendly, but one could never be sure. She pushed her own fingers through the fence. "Hiya, boy," she said in a calm voice. The dog barely glanced at her, his tail still wagging, he was intent on Bryan's face. "You try," she encouraged her son whose smaller hand immediately went through the fence to offer it to the dog. It's solid-looking muzzle opened in a smile as he sniffed the hand and allowed the boy to pet him. His tail wagged harder.

"He's nice," Bryan exclaimed, and the others crowded in behind him.

"Hey there, wait. Take turns," Taylor cautioned. "You don't want to overwhelm the dog."

Each of them got to pet the friendly but shy dog. It was pointed out to them how shy he was when one of the caretakers at the pound came down the line, and the dog ran to the back of his kennel and turned his back on the worker.

"He's an old grump," the young man complained.

"Can we see him in the run?" Taylor asked, pointing to the area where they allowed people to socialize with their potential adoptee.

"You want to see *him*?"

"Yes, we do," she assured him. She watched as he reluctantly took a spare leash with a loop on the end from the wall and approached the cage. The shy dog retreated further to the other end of the cage, despite the children calling to him. He hid his head from the young man, who held the leash as he came in and approached the dog carefully.

"He doesn't look like he likes that," Bree murmured worriedly.

"He was perfectly fine before that guy went in there," Taylor pointed out, watching closely. She was reserving judgment, but there was no way she'd let a dog that powerful in their house if he was a threat to the kids.

After some dashing back and forth, the young man captured the dog who obviously didn't want to be caught or walk on the leash that looked like it would choke him.

"Stand back," Taylor warned the kids, pulling two of them back into her arms as Bree caught the other two. They both watched as the dog was taken, pulled actually, to the other run. The dog did not like it at all. Once released inside it, the leash left on, the caretaker signaled to the two women.

"I don't know if you should take your children in there yet. He needs to calm down," he warned.

"You stay outside for now," Taylor warned Bryan and Barbie, who she'd been holding. She opened the gate and went inside. The dog glanced her way but looked decidedly at the wall, ignoring his captors. Taylor hunkered down and watched him, noticing that he was shaking. "Hey there, Staffy," she crooned, holding out her hand. He glanced around, saw her and the eager group behind her on the other side of the

fence, and turned back to the wall. Taylor watched her family; the man having gone outside the fence but staying close by if needed. The children looked so hopeful. She turned back to the dog. "Hey there, boy," she began again and scrooched closer, doing a duck walk as she stayed crouched. She got closer, close enough to reach out and pet him. His skin shuddered as she ran her hand down his soft coat. "Hey there," she repeated, petting him. "It's okay. We're not going to hurt you," she reassured him. She peeked at her family, the children looking very hopeful. He relaxed marginally, but she could tell the dog was not happy. Why couldn't they have fallen for an outgoing, fluffy dog?

Taylor looked at Bree and glanced at Bryan and Barbie meaningfully. "Bryan, you and Barbie can go in first," Bree told them and cut off the protests from Melanie and Jack that immediately came up. "You'll get your turn. Let's not scare the dog."

Taking their cue from their moms, the young boy and girl came in the pen and approached the dog while their mom was gently petting down the shaking dog's back.

"Hey there, boy," Barbie said, reaching out to duplicate her mom's pats.

"Hey there, Staffy," Bryan said.

At the boy's voice, the dog's head came up and around, realizing that the children were in the pen with him. He visibly relaxed as he began to turn around, giving a side-eye at Taylor before starting to sniff the two children thoroughly. As they both eagerly petted him, his tail began to wag, smacking against the side of the pen loudly. He snuffled them thoroughly, seeming to like the smell of the children. He even gave a gratuitous huff at Taylor in his exuberance. Taylor smiled back at the dog. After a while she suggested calmly that the Bryan and Barbie give their siblings a turn.

"But, Mom ..." they began whining, and she turned a stern look on them. "If we decide to adopt Staffy, we have to let everyone meet him," she pointed out. She waited as they reluctantly made their way to the gate of the pen, the pound worker growing irritated by how long this meet-and-greet was taking.

When Melanie and Jack slipped into the run, Staffy seemed just as pleased to meet them as he had the others, but his eyes kept straying back to Bryan. His peek at the pound worker made the dog quickly turn back to the exuberant children.

"I'll trade with you," Taylor offered Bree, so she too could meet the dog, who seemed to tolerate adults as long as the children were around.

"He's sweet," Bree said as Taylor watched her pet the dog. He hopped around as if he wanted to play, but there weren't any toys in the pen.

"Can we adopt him, Mom?" Melanie asked for all of them. All the children immediately turned their attention to their moms, their eyes pleading in unspoken hope.

"What do you say?" Bree asked Taylor, wondering if this was too much of a dog for them.

"I don't know ... it's going to be a lot of work," she grouched.

"I'll help," three of the four children immediately offered, Barbie was still petting the dog.

Taylor chuckled and nodded to Bree, who smiled in return. "What do we have to fill out to adopt Staffy?" she asked the worker.

He returned the Staffordshire to his cage, and the dog resumed his dejected posture and immediately retreated to the back of his pen.

"Aww, Mom, he's sad," Barbie said as she viewed the dog.

"Well, we have some paperwork to fill out, and he'll be happy again soon."

"Can we stay?" Melanie asked, sounding like she was about to plead.

"No, you kids have to come with us," Bree told her firmly, shepherding them out of the passageway and into the office areas of the pound.

The paperwork seemed to take forever, but, with perseverance, their identification, and a check, they finally were the legal owners of Staffy the Staffordshire Bull Terrier.

"You may want to keep a copy of that somewhere," the clerk advised, pointing to their paperwork that showed what breed the dog is. "There will be someone, somewhere, who will think that dog isn't what he is." There was enough insinuation in her tone that both Bree and Taylor took note.

"Would you mind making two copies of this?" Bree asked. "We'll pay you for them, of course."

"I'll be happy to," she replied, pleased a family had adopted the shy dog. "No charge."

Bree and Taylor both tucked a copy in their wallets. The form showed they had officially adopted a Staffordshire Bull Terrier from the city pound and that his name was Staffy.

"Now, I'd advise getting him microchipped at your vet," the clerk also advised. "It's not mandatory, but, if anything were to every happen to him or he got away from you, it's a way to identify him."

They both nodded at her advice and waited for Staffy to be brought out to them. One of the pound workers, not the same one as before, was dragging the dog on a lead. He was very reluctant until he saw the

children and their moms waiting for him in the office. Then, he nearly took the worker's arm off as he lunged towards the group.

Taylor took control of the lead as the dog showed how happy he was to see the children again. Each of them got a bit of slobber on them as he kissed and showed affection.

"Easy, boy, easy," Bree crooned, attempting to calm the exuberant dog.

When Staffy realized they were taking him with them, he walked eagerly with the children out the door and readily hopped in the minivan with them. It wasn't until everyone was in and the doors shut that Bree released the leash holding the solid dog.

There was an argument about where he was going to sit, as there were still three car seats in the car for the children and everyone wanted the dog next to them. Taylor solved the debate by decreeing he should sit in the middle seat, where Melanie and Jack sat.

Barbie and Bryan were ready to argue, but Taylor was ready for them and assured them they'd all get their turn. Staffy didn't mind, sitting proudly and looking out the front window, ready to go.

"We need to get dog food and things," Bree mentioned under her breath as she belted herself in after making sure the children were.

"Petco or PetSmart?" Taylor asked quietly as she put the car in gear. She probably couldn't be heard over the children's exuberant talking to the happy dog, but she didn't want their input on what they needed for the dog.

A new area across town had built up with a lot of shops, including the two big chain pet stores. Bree and Taylor had avoided the development, for the most part, and had only gone to one grocery store there. They'd never been in either pet store, never having a reason to visit either store, although they had been there for at least two years. They'd bought Marmalade's food at the grocery store.

"How do you think Marmalade will like our new addition?" she thumb-pointed at the alert dog who was watching and apparently judging Taylor's driving.

"I forgot Marmalade!" Bree exclaimed, suddenly worried. "We didn't ask how Staffy was with cats."

"Well, we'll have to figure it out."

Petco and PetSmart were eye-opening experiences for the moms as they determined which had less expensive food and accessories. They'd never been in stores that allowed you to walk a dog. Taylor held tightly to the lead, a cheap choke chain around the neck of the dog. Bree insisted the children help pick out a nice nylon collar and matching six-foot lead for

their new adoptee. The word adoptee seemed to really engage the children since they all knew they had been adopted by their moms. They added a stainless-steel bowl and a bag of kibble to their cart, choosing the food from a sample that Staffy seemed to like.

"No, no, you can't hold his lead yet," Taylor had informed the children, who all crowded around the dog. He was enjoying the attention and smiling at everyone.

"We have to have this," Bree informed her wife, picking out a tag where the dog's name could go on it on one side and, on the other, it read, "My family is stupid crying if I'm lost, please call:" and had a spot for their phone number on it. She read the directions on the machine that would carve the dog's name.

"That's hilarious," Taylor murmured, agreeing with her wife.

"I'll make a phone call to Marmalade's vet to take him in," Bree also promised as she chose the tag they wanted and fed dollar bills into the machine.

Staffy was really happy to get back in the minivan and go home with his new family. He smelled every scent around the outside of the house as Taylor held his new lead attached to his new, bright red nylon collar. He really looked sharp as he pulled her along. When she pulled back hard against him, he looked up at her, still smiling and happy. It only took a few times for him to realize not to keep pulling her as they walked along. *What a smart dog,* she thought.

"I'll take all this in?" Bree offered from where she watched by the van while she indicated all they had bought for the dog. She could see how happy they had made the children, who all wanted to walk the new dog.

Each had taken a turn, and Staffy was learning that Taylor was alpha and the children could be pulled along until Taylor, who still had the end of the lead, pulled him up short. He was smart as a whip and soon figured out the difference of Barbie holding his lead and Jack, who was easily pulled off his feet if the dog wasn't careful. Once inside the house, he sniffed every corner before settling down in the family room, panting happily, with the children petting him. Finally, with a loud sigh, he fell asleep.

"You've worn him out," Taylor told the children with a chuckle. She'd let go of the lead once inside and behind a closed door so that the children could show the dog his new home. He was tired out, probably from the stress of living in the pound.

Bree proved she was thinking along the same lines as her wife as she murmured to her, "I wonder how long he was in the pound?"

They would never know, but Staffy would prove to be a good dog for their family. Taylor made a concerted effort to train the smart dog. She took him out at least twice a day and directed him to one corner of the yard where he could poop. The kids took him out many more times, but weren't as concerned to get him to go in 'his' corner. He peed everywhere, marking his territory. They did not let him off-lead for months until he knew his territory and they felt they could trust him. Both moms looked forward to a time they could walk with him off-lead, but, in the meantime, he was learning his family.

Bree hadn't thought about how good a companion he would be for her during the day when the children were at school. He lay in the sunshine on the concrete of the shop, hanging out and waiting for her to take a break for lunch. Together they would head back to the house, where he'd eat some of his own kibble while she talked to him in between bites of her sandwich.

"Look at this," Bree said to Taylor, pointing out the blanket they had laid out by the patio door for the dog. On it, Jack was napping, his arm wrapped around the sleeping dog.

Marmalade, while not thrilled to have a dog in *his* home, taught Staffy that sticking his nose into him uninvited would earn him nails across his sensitive nose. The first time it happened and the dog yipped, the children rushed to comfort him, but Taylor held them back. "He has to learn. Marmalade was here first, and he'll teach Staffy some manners," she warned.

The only accommodation they had to make was to feed Marmalade on top of the refrigerator. The delicious cat food was too tempting for Staffy to resist, even at the risk of feline retribution. Staffy wasn't pleased when the tomcat helped himself to his own kibble, put out in the stainless-steel bowl and waiting whenever the dog was hungry. Catching Marmalade sampling his kibble, he'd do a little dance of displeasure, looking up at his humans as though to say, "That's unfair, he's eating *my* food!" But they ignored it, figuring the animals would work out their differences. For the most part, they lived companionably in the house together, tolerated each other, and got along fairly well.

CHAPTER TWENTY-NINE

"Mom, Mom, Mom!" Melanie called importantly.

Taylor looked up from the bookkeeping Bree was forcing her to double-check before they gave it to their accountant. "What's up?" she asked the girl, smiling slightly so her accounting-hating face didn't show.

"If you see someone do this," she said, holding her arms out in front of her and walking like there were lead weights in her feet, "they're a zombie, and you have to kill zombies."

"You do, huh?" Taylor asked, completely forgetting the work she had before her. "That's how you know?"

The girl nodded solemnly.

"Good to know." She nodded, showing she had been paying absolute attention. She glanced around the family room, where she was working at the desk, hoping for another distraction. Melanie went back to the dolls she was positioning, possibly as zombies, with Staffy looking on sleepily. She could hear the other children playing in the basement, the tricycles they hadn't been unable to play with outside put into use on the concrete floor. Taylor heard Bree coming down the hall from the bedrooms and quickly went back to her paperwork. It was a good thing they had QuickBooks or both of them would have trouble when they took it all to the accountant. They'd had a lot of expenses this year with buying the land, having the house added on, and moving everything. They'd gotten their permits and new equipment, so they would have to deduct quite a few things this year. They'd also attended a few more shows and picked up a couple more stores to sell their pots, so their income had increased. It had been a good year. Taylor sighed, rubbing her eyes as she thought about the work she'd done in the barn, something she loved, but then she remembered she had to go back to the diner tomorrow and sighed again.

"Something wrong?" Bree asked, seeing her rubbing her eyes and wondering if she had screwed up some of the paperwork.

"I don't want to go back to work tomorrow," Taylor confessed and then glanced at Melanie, realizing they shouldn't be talking about such things in front of the children. She looked back up at Bree, who understood immediately.

"We'll talk about that later," she said meaningfully.

Later, they did talk about it. "Is something going on at work?" Bree asked after the children were in bed. They were sitting in the family room, alone after picking up after the children. It was nice that they had this cozy room, where they could look out on the deck and enjoy their time alone. It was dark now, so they couldn't see far. They could have started a fire in the fireplace if they wanted, but neither wanted to make the effort.

"No, it's the same," she admitted ruefully. "I'm just tired of being on my feet all day. I love it here," her hands encompassed their house and she gestured towards the barn where they had worked together on her day off, "but I'm not enjoying it the same way I used to."

"What's changed?"

"I think it's me," she said, smiling slightly. "I think I just want to stay home and work here. Wait for the kids to get off school, so we can play and walk and enjoy each other." They hadn't walked too much lately, with the snow on the ground, but she eagerly anticipated the spring, when they could walk in the woods again together. She'd enjoyed their explorations as the children discovered their new home. The woods always had something new for them to find.

Bree smiled and sighed as she cuddled into Taylor. She was glad it wasn't anything serious, but she knew Taylor had to earn that extra money until they built up the pottery business. It was a buffer against harder times as their tiny business slowly took off. They'd spent a lot of money this year, almost all of their savings, to buy this place and build it up. They needed that outside income, or Bree would have to go find a job again. But they didn't have the time to have her work outside the home, too, and run the pottery business. "Maybe it's just the time of year?" she asked.

"Probably," Taylor agreed, but she knew it wasn't that. She had worked there too long, and it had gotten old. She no longer enjoyed playing the characters as she had in the past. Something was missing. She was sick of the smell of grease. The only thing she would ever miss about that place was seeing her friends on a regular basis. Her world was complete when Bree would pop in, which wasn't as often since they'd moved out here, and she could entertain here at home with her friends and wife.

CHAPTER THIRTY

The snow didn't last long, but then something new came up which they had anticipated and dreaded. Taylor was holding Staffy's leash, this one a twenty-foot cable so he could run and play with the children as they played in the afternoon sun. It was still early on a Saturday, and Taylor didn't have to be in for a few hours. Staffy turned and stared intently towards the woods, beyond which came the sounds of construction machines and vehicles, even now in late fall. Taylor assumed there must be some work going on she couldn't hear and ignored the dog's concerns. After she and Staffy had walked around a couple of trees, the dog always checking back on the kids, he stopped in his tracks, turned back to the woods, and growled.

Taylor looked at the dog with alarm, making sure he wasn't growling at any of the children. He'd been so good with them. The vet had been pleased with his health when he examined the dog. "He could put on some more weight. He probably lost a bit from being incarcerated, but he's healthy otherwise," he told them with a grin. He checked and explained the dog's shots were all up to date, put a microchip in his neck, and showed it was active with a scanner. He registered it to both Bree and Taylor and put both their cell-phone numbers on the registration they had to send in. "This is one lucky dog," he said as he watched the children mauling the happy dog, each reassuring him the exam was all over and

they loved him. Bree and Taylor were pleased Staffy was already neutered and they didn't have to pay to have that done. Right now, though, he stood motionless, his stocky body alert, tense except for his twitching muscles. Taylor followed his look and was astonished to see two men stepping out of the woods.

Taylor reeled in the leash as she walked rapidly towards the dog to get in front of him and the children. "What are you doing here?" she called out in a firm voice.

"Oh, we're hunting," one of the men responded in a gregarious *let's be friends* voice. He gestured to his rifle. He was dressed in camouflage with an orange vest, and, when he turned to look around, she saw that it had his hunting tag on the back.

"We have children here, and the land is posted. No hunting or trespassing!" she barked. The children froze at Taylor's tone. She glanced back at them and ordered, "Get back to the house, now!" The now was added to avoid argument, but she needn't have worried. The kids took one look at the hunters and scurried off towards the house. Taylor turned back to the men with guns, glaring holes through them.

"Oh, we didn't know. We've been hunting these woods for years," he said, continuing in his same tone.

"You walked by at least a couple of the signs to get into these woods." She kept a secure hold on Staffy's leash. He had already tested her a couple of times, ready to lunge at the trespassers.

"Well, we had permission of the owner …" he began, seemingly hurt by her own stiff tone and eyeing the cropped-eared dog warily. He exchanged a look with the man beside him.

"No, you don't have that permission anymore," she said, sounding ominous. Her ears pricked up at the sound of her children going into the house. All her own protective instincts were aroused. "My wife and I bought this property last summer. We've been building ever since, and one of the first things we did was put up the signs that you walked by. Get off our land, and don't come back. Tell all your friends."

"Look, this is simply a misunderstanding …" he began, trying to reason with the angry woman.

"No, you walked by several signs telling you clearly you weren't welcome, and now I suspect your lying to save face. Get off my land before I let my dog loose on you!"

Both men looked alarmed at the dog whining and tugging at the end of the leash. One of them shifted his gun, almost protectively.

"If you use that gun on my dog, I'm going to shoot you," Taylor bluffed.

"What's going on here?!" Bree called from the back door, where she had just come outside onto the deck.

"These *gentlemen* are just leaving!" Taylor called back without turning away from them.

"You're *hunting*?! On *our* land?!" Bree asked, alarmed. All her initial fears which had led to them posting the land returned in an instant.

"Apparently, they can't read, and the owner gave them permission!" Taylor mocked as she held a menacing stare. She addressed the two hunters, who were looking decidedly uncomfortable. "Get off our land!" Then she called up to Bree, still not taking her eyes off the two. "Go get my gun, now!" She didn't see the startled look Bree gave her, but she heard the back door close, and the two men turned as one and hotfooted it back through the woods.

"What the hell was that about?" Bree asked as Taylor came in five minutes later, pulling Staffy.

"Trespassers," she answered shakily. She unhooked the leash and let the dog run off to check on the children.

"The kids came running in, saying there were men in the woods with guns!"

"I guess until people realize that we mean it, we will have to be diligent."

"The kids can't play out there without one of us," Bree decreed, gesturing to the playset she'd been so happy to acquire piece-by-piece over the summer.

"It was really Staffy who let me know someone was there."

* * * * *

In the coming days, the two moms took the time while the children were at school to walk the entire ten acres and found that several of the signs had been pulled down and some had grown faded. They replaced the signs they could, rehanging ones they found in the brush or grass, but they could see some people were going to ignore their posts and do what they wanted, anyway. In some places, even their pink topped stakes were missing. Neither mom liked thinking they would have trespassers, but ten acres was too big for them to be everywhere all the time.

A couple of days later, Taylor was on her way back from an early shift and found a truck parked on their property near the highway curve. She stopped, parked her Jeep behind it, and marched into the woods to look for them. The area was pretty overgrown, and she couldn't see anyone. She finally gave up and went back to the truck to see if she could figure out who the owner was. As luck would have it, the owner hadn't locked the doors, but the glove compartment was empty and there weren't any other papers in the cab. She laid on the horn for about five minutes, when someone finally came rushing out of the brush.

"What the hell are you doing, lady?" he asked, aggravated. The man had heard the horn for a while before it registered it was his own truck horn. He had come running, though, missing a chance at the buck he had a line on.

"This your truck?" she asked, unnecessarily. He'd come out of her woods, after all.

"Yeah?" he asked belligerently, frowning at her in her waitress uniform.

"You're trespassing!"

"What?" he exaggerated, looking around as if he was seeing the sign he was parked next to for the first time.

"Don't lie," she said next, righteously angry. "I catch you here on my property again, and I'm gonna take an axe to your truck. You're trespassing!"

"I ain't hurting nothin'!" he pushed back, just as angrily at her threats.

"You're trespassing, and it says," she pointed to the sign, "No hunting or trespassing. I have kids! What if they were in the woods?"

"Well, maybe you should keep an eye on your kids."

"And maybe you should get the hell out of here!"

They went back and forth long enough for him to get in his truck and slam the door in her face. He started the truck, put it in gear, and spun his tires on his way out.

"Goddamn it," Taylor swore as she headed up their drive. It was too cold and the ground too hard to put in the rest of their fencing, but she was so angry these hunters were coming onto their land. They'd stopped three now—who knew how many more there were—and these people couldn't be reasoned with.

* * * * *

"Babe, I need your help," Taylor said, coming into the barn in her waitress uniform.

"Why, what's up?" Bree asked reasonably. She looked up from the pot she was painting, its beautiful flower pattern in distinct contrast to Taylor's mood.

Taylor told her what had just happened and what she wanted to do about it.

"But if we lay them there, won't it look shoddy?"

"I don't care. At least, it will establish our property line, and we can put up more of the No Trespassing signs. They can't say they weren't warned."

"Do you really think we have enough fencing for the front line?"

"We've discussed that before, and I think we do."

"Well, I'll get these in the oven while you go change," Bree offered weakly. She wasn't thrilled at the idea Taylor had, but she, too, was worried about the kids. If they weren't safe on their own land and near their own home, where would they be safe?

Taylor went in the house, cursing the grease on her uniform. She was so angry, she nearly ripped it from her body. She changed into jeans and a sweatshirt, put on a winter coat Bree had found for her at Goodwill, and then slipped on boots and gloves.

The two of them hooked up two of the long fence panels, ones they still hadn't gotten all the concrete off the ends of the posts. They'd both intermittently banged on them with a sledgehammer and regular hammer, splintering off the occasional piece, but it was hard work and neither was too enthused to make much headway. Then, concrete and post and all, the long fence panels were taken by tractor to the end of their driveway, through the gate, and laid one-by-one approximately where they would be put along the highway portion of their land. They were lucky to be able to prop some of them against trees, thick brush, or even the occasional phone or power pole, but some of the brush couldn't hold up these heavy pieces.

When the children got off the bus, they were excited to see their moms working in the late afternoon dusk.

"Whatcha doin'?" they asked.

"We're getting the fences down here, ready to put up," Taylor told them, ushering them away so Bree could come through the gate with the next two panels. It was slow work, and they'd only gotten a half a dozen or so put where they could prop them. "Do you remember where we put the last of the No Trespassing signs in the barn?" she asked Melanie.

The little girl thought and then nodded. At almost nine, she was very cognizant she was the oldest of her siblings, and she craved responsibility. Both moms were careful how much they gave her so as not to overwhelm the little girl, but they knew it helped her build character. "When we go back up to the barn, we'll need a bunch of those, as well as some zip ties," she saw the other children eagerly awaiting their own involvement, "and maybe the others can help you grab those things?"

By nightfall, they put up ten sections, using the lights on the tractor at the end so they could see to zip tie the signs to the iron bars. "We're going

to have to paint this next year," Bree called as she noted the scratches and the obvious signs of rust on the metal.

It took them two days to get the last of the sections along the front of their property, working around Taylor's insane holiday schedule and fighting the cold weather. They even put the second gate to use by leaning it up against trees to block the other entrance where the lone hunter had parked. Bree was right; it looked shoddy, but it clearly defined their property. They still had more sections they planned to use in the field along the woods, but that could wait until spring, when they put all these in the ground. Each section had a sign on it. Even if the panels weren't secured in the ground, the leaning fences clearly showed the owners' intent: stay away.

CHAPTER THIRTY-ONE

"So, what happened in school today?" Bree asked now seven-year-old Barbie.

"I took Carl down in a headlock," she said proudly.

"And why would you do that?" Taylor asked, trying not to laugh. Bree glared at her. She, for one, hadn't appreciated the phone call from school.

"Be ... cause ... because," she stammered, starting to twist the hem of her dress as she realized she just might be in trouble with her moms.

"Because what?" Taylor asked gently, trying to keep a straight face but wanting to know the details. Bree had taken the call from the school, but their version was way too official, too cut and dried, and she wanted to hear the child's version. Taylor found it amusing.

"He said ..." she began, starting to swing her hips back and forth, and Taylor reached out to get her to stand still and answer them. "He said that I had to marry him."

"Did he *ask* you to marry him?"

She nodded and then added, "But I said kids don't get married."

Taylor could have corrected that but thought it would be too much for a seven-year-old to understand. "And what was your answer?"

"I put him in a headlock and took him down to the ground," she answered with perfect logic and then smiled proudly.

"Well," began Bree, also trying not to laugh, "that is not the way we handle things like that, okay?"

"But he said—"

"Because what if you had hurt him?"

Barbie considered, suddenly thinking hard. "Then I would have had to take care of him."

Taylor nodded consolingly. "Do you want to marry him?"

"Not now," she said passionately, swinging again.

"Good, then that's settled. You don't wrestle with anyone, okay?"

The little girl nodded emphatically, and Taylor let her go, smacking her lightly on the butt to hurry her off. "Get ready for dinner."

"Taylor," Bree began in an aggrieved tone.

"What?" she asked innocently. She could see Bree, too, was finding humor in the situation.

"Don't you *what* me," she began, shaking a finger warningly at her wife.

Taylor grinned. "What's a girl gonna do when a boy asks her to marry her?"

"Did a boy ever ask you to marry you?"

"Of course, especially when I'd been helping out Vinnie. Hot and sweaty and full of dirt. I was a catch!"

"I know how you look when you're like that, and I'd have to agree."

"Oh, you do, do you?" she flirted and grinned.

"You clean up good."

* * * * *

They got out of having Thanksgiving with Ellen because Tia was still pissed at her sister and her wife for not giving into her bullying. Ellen had made several gestures of reconciliation, but it was slow going.

The Nillionaires Club met, as always, at Tweety's, so they could see Taylor while she worked. So many people didn't like to cook that the diner was packed, and many of them were regulars. The women had a reserved table, but Taylor didn't get a chance to eat with them because she was run off her feet serving the other tables. The children were wearing their best clothes and tried to be on their best behavior, with a little prodding from Bree.

Melanie was earnestly telling Lenny about Staffy, who the woman hadn't had the pleasure of meeting yet. Several adults listened, amused. "And she poops in a corner of the yard. Mom said if we take her to the same spot, she'll get used to it being her toilet."

"That's not appropriate to talk about Melanie," Bree corrected her, and when the child looked ready to argue, she added, "not at the dinner table."

"Did you get Taylor what you talked to me about?" Gretchen whispered to Bree while everyone else was occupied with conversation.

"No, I found a better deal," she whispered back and then told her what she had gotten.

"What are you two whispering about?" Elsie teased, and they included her in it, and, before long, everyone except the children and Taylor knew what Bree had gotten Taylor for Christmas.

"How do you know it isn't stolen?" Vinnie asked, when she heard what the gift was.

"I don't, but I don't think anyone is going to run the numbers on them," Bree pointed out. That was one of the things she did worry about when buying off Craigslist or the Marketplace. Used items could possibly be stolen items. Still, the story behind them had been believable, and the deal too good to pass up. She knew Taylor was going to love them.

"Have you tried them out?" Vinnie asked, curious.

"Yes and no. You can't play with them."

"Play with what?" Taylor asked, coming up to fill water cups and to ask if anyone needed anything.

"Oh, just ..." Vinnie began and then pretended to get distracted by some noise across the restaurant.

Taylor looked, too, and promptly forgot the question. "Everybody okay?" she remembered to ask. They all were, so she hurried off to serve her other tables.

"Damn, she works hard," Elsie marveled.

"Too hard," Bree agreed. Just then, she saw a male customer grab Taylor's ass, and she would have gotten up from the table to go off on the guy, but Gretchen saw it, too, and held onto Bree's arm. She eye-pointed at the children, and Bree settled down. She watched across the room as Taylor *accidentally* dumped a pitcher of water over the man's head. Carl yelled from the kitchen when he saw his customer sopping wet and outraged.

Vinnie chuckled and shook her head, having seen the whole thing play out. This wasn't their first Thanksgiving at the diner, and things like that happened often enough. Taylor could handle herself, but Vinnie saw Bree scowling until the man finally left. "He's lucky she didn't punch him," Vinnie commented in an aside to Bree.

"Don't encourage her," Bree murmured back, glancing at the children who seemed to hear everything.

* * * * *

"Should we cut one of our own trees for Christmas or go buy one?" Taylor asked Bree, helping her stack pots on her day off. Staffy was tied by the door and chewing on a soup bone Bree had given the dog. Marmalade was eyeing the bone, wondering if any of that marrow would still be left when the dog was done with it.

"Oh, let's find one on the property and make a big to-do about cutting it down with the kids. Do you know where there is one that might do?" she enthused. Taylor walked in the woods a lot more than Bree did.

"A couple," she admitted. "Across the creek."

That's what they did the next day. It was Taylor's last day off for a while with the holidays, and they waited for the kids to get home from school and hurried them into jeans and jackets, changing their school clothes to something more appropriate for the woods and getting dirty. Taylor took her poor hand saw to cut the tree, and they made their way across the creek, the moms helping the children across over a downed tree.

"This would make a great place for a bridge," Taylor noted as she balanced herself on the tree. Jack was in front of her and going so slow and careful she could have carried him. Staffy was waiting on the far side, smiling happily at being included on this hike. He'd practically run across the tree, scrambling up the bank as though he did this all the time.

Bree smiled in return, holding out her hand to the small boy and helping him the last few feet.

They found a tree that was at least six feet high and gathered 'round as Taylor sawed at it. Bree took a turn with the semi-rusty and very old saw, and finally the tree toppled. "We should plan on planting more of these for future years," she noted to Taylor.

"Maybe in our field," she nodded towards the field they let the neighbor Eric Norman raise hay in.

"That's a good idea," Taylor responded thoughtfully, pulling the Christmas tree along on the ground and letting Melanie carry the saw for her. She wasn't sure how she was going to get the tree across the creek without getting it wet. "We can look into buying fingerlings or something like that? Ask Gretchen to grow us a few hundred trees?"

"She'd love that, and she can get them wholesale," Bree responded.

"What's wholesale?" Barbie asked, skipping along with Staffy.

"It's when you don't buy at the listed price," Taylor tried to explain, but she knew from Barbie's blank expression she hadn't understood.

"You know when we sell our pots at different prices?" Bree asked her daughter. At her nod, she continued. "The prices we tell you not to repeat?" Again, a nod. "Those are wholesale prices and for businesses. The prices we sell at the show are retail prices. It's a different price because a business will buy many, but retail—they usually buy only one or two."

"But that one woman bought six," Bryan pointed out, remembering the last show.

"Yes, and we sold it to her, anyway," Bree said dismissively, trying to end an in-depth conversation the children didn't have a hope of understanding. She didn't want to lecture but to enjoy their walk. "Oh, look! Are those rabbit tracks?" she asked when Staffy chose that moment to start snuffling at them.

As expected, they couldn't manage to get the tree across the creek without it getting wet. They leaned it up on the porch so it would drip dry before they could put it up in the living room.

"Your mom called me and brought these by the other day," Bree confessed, showing Taylor several boxes of her family's ornaments. "If we can find some of those plastic, red and green totes, I would love to put some of these in them for safekeeping." She indicated the many ancient-looking cardboard boxes, some of them from Ellen's mother's family and collectible.

"Isn't Tia going to be pissed?" Taylor marveled.

"Your mom, I think, was worried that Blaine would ruin them all eventually," Bree whispered.

There were a lot of ornaments, many of them antiques, including a large bag of plastic ornaments that the children could hang without damaging. These, too, were decades old, and Taylor could remember putting them up when she was a little girl. Once the tree was relatively dry, they hauled it in and set it up on its stand, they put on a tree skirt and filled the water reservoir in the stand. They had to chase both Staffy and Marmalade away from the outside-smelling tree as they all decorated it. The kids really liked the lights, the tinsel, and the stories behind some of the ornaments that Taylor told them. The more expensive, fragile, or treasured antique ornaments were put higher on the tree, away from wagging tails, curious children, or anything that might cause them to fall. Since the tree was in the living room, which they rarely used and hadn't furnished much, it was out of the way and special for the children. Their first Christmas in the new house was going to be extra special.

"Do you want to do Elf on the Shelf?" Bree asked Taylor trepidatiously.

"Oh, hell no. Don't you find that creepy?" She was hanging garland along the mantle in the family room, bringing some of the Christmas decorations into this part of the house.

"Yeah, but I thought I'd ask, just in case," she said, putting the elf back into the bag she had found.

"Bury that bugger," Taylor advised, agreeing that they needed totes to store all these decorations. "You know, there'll probably be a sale on those totes. Plus, you could find them online, maybe."

Bree laughed and gave her a kiss on the cheek. "I'm already on it, babe."

CHAPTER THIRTY-TWO

Taylor was so angry, sick of her job, sick of people in general, but her mood shifted when she came home and found the table set for two, with a homemade menu propped up at her place that read:

MENU

DINNER
Ravioli……...one hug
Fettuccini……one hug
Lasagna……. free

DRINKS
Lemonade….one kiss
Mikes hard lemonade…one kiss, again

DESERT
Ice Cream & sprinkles…one squeeze

Damn, that woman was aggravating … and romantic. While Taylor was still angry, she also loved her wife to bits. She looked around in

wonder at the romantic table setting and heard the children shushing themselves from the back hall. All her anger melted away at the touching scene.

"You can come out now," she called. They rushed out, and Bree, all dressed up, followed behind them sporting a huge smile. Taylor smiled in return, going into her wife's arms, pulling back—to Bree's surprise—and then hugging her again and kissing her twice. She squeezed her, earning a squeal in response.

"What was that about?" Bree marveled, pleased at the hugs and kisses and the surprise squeeze.

"Just following the menu," Taylor answered, indicating the lit kitchen table.

"Happy anniversary! Happy anniversary!" the children chanted. "We helped," more than one said as Taylor looked around.

"Well, I better change to something more appropriate," she said, gesturing to her waitress uniform. "I'm a little underdressed. I'll be right back," she promised, heading for the back hall.

"Come, help me put dinner on the table," Bree told the children, distracting them from following their mother.

Taylor's anger had followed her home from the restaurant, only to see someone climbing around their fences over by the second gate. But that had dissipated, and she wouldn't' mention it to Bree—no point in ruining her carefully created ambiance. She kept thinking of the romantic dinner waiting for her as she quickly showered, washing away her anger and the smell of grease, and quickly drying off to throw on some nice clothes.

Even though having four children kept them from being alone for their anniversary, Taylor and Bree stared meaningfully into each other's eyes, remembering the first time they met. Taylor had been working part-time for Vinnie and was covered in fine dust from head to foot. Little bits of grass were in her hair and on her clothes. She looked up from where she was unclogging a lawn mower and saw a young woman staring at her, transfixed.

For Bree, she had never thought she had seen such a physically fit young woman. Vinnie had mown their lawn many times, and she was buff but more of a soft-butch. It was almost ... expected when she saw the work the woman did. This creature—even with her hair tied back in a ponytail—was suave, with a hint of muscles along her arms, and the muscle shirt showing off her back where it had ripped and no surplus fat showed. Instead, the muscles rippled as she bent over the lawn mower. Sure, she could use a shower, but the skin that showed, despite the dust, made Bree's fingers ache to trace patterns in it.

They both shared smiles as they remembered their first meeting.

"The lasagna is delicious," Taylor complimented her wife, toasting her with her fork.

"Stouffers, on sale at the store," Bree responded, toasting with her water.

"Don't do that!" Taylor cautioned.

"What?" Bree asked, looking around.

"Don't toast with water; it's bad luck."

Bree chuckled, the First Nillionaires Club toasted with water or whatever was at hand all the time. She got up from the table and headed for the refrigerator. She was so proud to have it well-stocked for the children, but tonight she pulled a chilled bottle of wine and waggled it side to side suggestively to her wife. Taylor nodded, and Bree closed the door and grabbed a bottle opener. She peeled back the gold tin-foil and began to screw in the cork, turning and turning until it was deep within, and then she used the handles to pop out the cork.

"Let it breathe," Taylor suggested as her wife brought it, and two wine glasses back to the table.

"May I have some?" Melanie asked, eyeing the bottle.

"Me, too?" Barbie echoed.

"Me, too?" echoed Bryan and Jack, although they didn't know what they were asking for.

"When you're older," Taylor said in a stern voice to groans of disappointment.

Bree was pleased when the children had eaten their full and went off to play. She quickly put their dishes in the sink and returned to sit next to Taylor and enjoy the last of their dinner and some wine. "Maybe next year we can find a babysitter?" she asked suggestively.

Taylor smiled. "This," she said, pausing for effect, "... was lovely." They touched glasses before taking a sip of the wine.

"Mom!" screeched Melanie. "It's Marmalade!"

Both women got up and rushed into the family room, where the children had congregated, pulling out toys to play with before bedtime. The cat was sitting at the patio door, looking proud of himself in his orange fluffiness. Staffy was wagging his tail, ready to greet his buddy. He had realized the cat wouldn't allow himself to be chased and had learned to respect the sharp claws at the ends of his paws.

"What the heck?" Taylor murmured, staring hard into the darkness.

Bree flipped on the deck lights, and they all stared. Marmalade had *caught* his dinner and brought it home.

"How do you think he managed to pluck and ready his dinner?" Taylor asked, trying not to laugh at the large cat attempting to be let in through the heavy door. He was getting impatient, too, as he rose up and stretched.

"How did he manage to carry that thing? It looks heavy," Bree asked, peering at the sight of their big orange cat who had brought home what looked like a large, prepped chicken. It hadn't been cooked, but was naked and white, lying there on the deck.

"Can we still use it?" Taylor wondered, reaching for the door to open it.

"Eww! Imagine how many times he had to put it down and where it was before he got it here."

"Who the heck did you steal that from, mister?" Taylor asked the proud cat who, was mewling how happy he was to see his humans. Taylor reached down to pick up the large chicken, surprised at how heavy he really was and how solid. "No, Staffy." she said as she lifted it up and slipped out the patio door.

Bree frowned at her wife as she took the chicken and went down the steps. "No, Marmalade," she cautioned the cat while the children leaned their cheeks against the glass to watch their mom slip around the corner of the house.

"Where's she going with it?" Bryan wondered aloud.

"Probably the garbage," Bree answered practically. Marmalade was rubbing against her legs as though he had done something good. "You, mister, are going to have to stay home!" she warned him, wondering who had lost their dinner to this cat. But she knew it would prove impossible to keep him home. He was a bum, but he was *their* bum, and he always came home. They had made sure he was fixed, so, at least, he wasn't populating the neighborhood.

"Can't we eat it?" Barbie asked.

"No, ewwww!" Melanie parroted Bree. "Germs."

Taylor had taken it to the garbage can they kept inside the garage, locking the garage door behind her and wondering how long it had been unlocked. They always kept it locked because of the graffiti artist who had tagged it before they'd even moved in. She would have to remind the children not to unlock doors like this. It was hard enough to keep up with the kids when they played about the house, but, now, they had to worry about the pets. She threw the chicken in the garbage can, giggling at the thought of someone looking all over their kitchen for a meal that had simply disappeared. She wondered if Marmalade had used someone's cat door, maybe at one of the McMansions behind their woods. That was a long way for the cat to have carried the heavy bird.

CHAPTER THIRTY-THREE

Taylor was certain Christmas was going to be tense. Ellen had assured her she had taken all the blame for Tia's snit over the *misunderstanding* about the basement apartment. Taylor knew her mother had probably been berated and mentally abused since the twit got the idea. She wished they could offer her mother an out, but she could only help so much. It was up to Ellen to throw Tia and her useless husband out of the house. She knew how much Ellen was looking forward to watching the children open their presents, so Taylor agreed to them coming over.

She and Bree had agreed years before not to overindulge their children. Each got one present from their moms and two from Santa. Ellen always made sure to bring them two presents and told them one of those was from Tia and Eric. Everyone knew Tia didn't have the money because Eric never made enough to give away presents like this, but they took the credit for Ellen's thoughtfulness, anyway.

"Don't you let them open their presents until we get there," Ellen had exacted a promise from her daughter and daughter-in-law. They didn't have the heart to disappoint her. She had been so generous with the ornaments they now had on their tree, and their own decorations blended with the antiques.

"Hey there, my darlings!" Ellen said, hugging each of the grandchildren and then handing them presents. "Now, go put them under the Christmas tree until it's time to open them."

Tia ignored both of the women to march up to the tree, look at it critically, and put the other presents she had carried in for her mom underneath it.

"That driveway is going to be full of snow," Eric said as he took off his coat to hand it to Bree. He glanced fearfully towards Taylor, who was holding Staffy back by his collar. Staffy wasn't behaving aggressively, but he wanted to greet the guests enthusiastically.

"Yes, that's why we have the tractor," Bree said sweetly as she went to hang up his coat. She glanced outside at the snow that had started the night before, feeling a tiny curl of excitement. They'd gotten a few dustings since October, but this was the first real, sustainable snowfall, and it was beautiful. Just in time for Christmas.

"You got a dog?" Ellen asked unnecessarily.

"Yes," Taylor answered with a smile. He was a little hard to hold with his muscular body and exuberance. "Sit, Staffy."

"That's a Pit-Bull!" Eric accused.

"No, it's a Staffordshire Bull Terrier," Taylor told him with relish, enjoying correcting him. He turned and went to sit down, ignoring her.

"Blaine, you go help yourself to some of the food," Tia encouraged her son, seeing it laid out on card tables in the dining room which was attached to the living room. The two rooms were part of an L shape, with a bathroom in between that had entrances from the front hall and the kitchen.

Taylor exchanged a look with Bree. They had laid out the snacks and cut cheese and sausage for their guests, but a teenager—especially one with Blaine's personality—would inhale those.

Ellen must have noticed them because she countered her daughter's edict, "Not too much, though, Blaine. I can smell something cooking in the kitchen, and you don't want to ruin your appetite." She ignored Tia's indignant look.

Melanie, Barbie, Bryan, and Jack had all waited patiently since they had discovered Santa Claus had come. They had been allowed to take down their stockings from the mantel in the family room, but only to look at, not touch, the presents they contained. They looked hopefully at their moms now.

Bree laughed and nodded. "You can start with your stockings."

Each of the children ran to get them and started unloading them, finding candy canes, nuts, and fruit, but also little wrapped presents containing trinkets.

"Oh, look! I have an ornament with my name on it!" exclaimed Melanie.

"Me, too!" Barbie spoke up, reaching for hers.

The two boys echoed their sisters.

Taylor watched from where she stood in the entranceway. They didn't really have furniture in these rooms yet, and Tia and Eric had confiscated the two chairs they did have. She watched her children, as well as her nephew. She didn't know why, but something about that boy always made her nervous. He was sneaky and conniving and never had to be held accountable for his behavior. Her sister and husband always indulged him, and, as a result, he was a brat.

"Mom, are you going to do your stocking?" Jack worried, looking at Bree and then over at Taylor to include her.

"Moms don't need—" Tia began importantly, but Ellen interrupted whatever she had been about to say.

"Yes, Jack, why don't you go get your moms' stockings, so we can see what Santa brought for them."

The little boy, who had emptied his stocking into a pile on his lap, quickly got up to run and fetch the stockings. "What about the ones for Staffy and Marmalade?" he called from the family room.

"One of you had better help him carry all that," Bree teased the remaining children. She laughed as both Melanie and Bryan ran off.

"Can we open these now, please?" Barbie asked, pointing at the presents under the tree.

"Why don't you hang your ornament and wait for your siblings to come back with the stockings," Bree advised, smiling at how anxious the little girl was.

The grownups and Blaine all watched as she very carefully hung the ornament with her name and the year on it. It was a tradition that the two moms had started years ago with each of their foster children.

Soon, the children had the other stockings in the living room, and Bree and Taylor pretended to be surprised by the ornaments and other trinkets inside. The children had slipped in handmade gifts, including drawings and craft projects. They oohed and aahed over these, hanging them carefully to show their pride in the children's work. They let the children unpack the dog's and the cat's stockings for the animals.

"Okay, Barbie, reach for a present not your own and hand it to the person that's name is on it," Bree advised.

"Oh, do we have to do it that way?" Melanie complained. "It takes so long."

"Then we can enjoy it longer," her mother said sternly.

Taylor had let go of Staffy, and he was chewing happily on the Kong he got from Santa in his stocking, along with a light up collar and other treats. She sat down on the floor next to her mother and watched as the children read names and handed them to the recipients.

Tia was surprised at the matched set of gloves, hat, and scarf she got from Taylor and Bree, graciously thanking them.

Eric also got the same, but a manlier set. He grunted his thanks and put them aside to watch the children.

"What's this?" Blaine asked, not understanding the nice writing set he opened.

"Your mom said you were starting English classes, and I knew you'd want to be prepared for all the writing you'll do," Taylor told him evenly. She never let on that she knew he would probably hate it, but it was a useful gift.

The kid didn't thank them, and, like his dad, put the gift aside before continuing to gobble up the snacks.

The children loved all their gifts, grateful to their moms, to Santa, to Grandma, and to Aunt Tia and Uncle Eric for their gifts. They were really easy to please at this age.

"Let's gather this up," Bree said, grabbing the large garbage bag she had ready for the wrappings.

"You should burn that," Eric said importantly, getting up to reach for the bag.

"Oh, no, that stuff flairs up, and it's awful to put in a fire," Bree said, turning slightly so he couldn't get the bag.

"Yeah, whatever." He shrugged and went over to the two card tables they had set up for the snacks. "You ate all the sausage," he accused his son, rearing back to backhand the youth, who got ready to move out of the way.

"We have more," Taylor assured him coldly, irritated that he was bringing that crap into their house.

He grunted and went through the doorway into the kitchen, heading for the family room, where he could see a TV. They could bring him his food.

Taylor exchanged a look with her mother and wife before helping her mother up from the floor, where she had been helping her grandchildren.

"Why'd you get a dog?" Tia asked, pulling her feet away from where Staffy was enthusiastically chewing on the Kong.

"He's adopted," Barbie said proudly. "Like me!"

"Me, too," Melanie added, and the brothers echoed. They were all proud of the fact they were chosen to be in this family.

Tia, not willing to be mean to the children, saved her barbs for the adults. "Take a plate in to your father," she told Blaine.

"He could have gotten his own plate," the youth protested. He was relieved he hadn't been hit but not willing to forgive his father for embarrassing him.

"Take a plate in to him," she said warningly, and the boy started piling things on a plate.

"I'll go cut some more sausage," Bree said airily, knowing her chirpy voice annoyed Tia. She headed into the kitchen, stopping Blaine when he went through for several slices of the summer sausage to be added to the overfilled plate. He might have remembered there were others who wanted to eat, too. She was just glad they had made special pancakes early that morning for their children, knowing their guests would inhale whatever was put out for them.

The women tended to sit or stand around in the kitchen as Eric and Blaine channel surfed. After playing with all their new toys, the children headed downstairs to ride their tricycles and play with other toys they kept down there. Staffy went with them, and Marmalade finally stuck his nose out from wherever he had been hiding. He decided to stay hidden with all these people in the house.

"Whew, look at that," Tia mentioned, "look at the snow being blown off the roof and onto the deck."

"Yeah, I think we're going to be shoveling the deck at some point," Taylor mentioned, her eyes twinkling at her wife. She was still so pleased with her gift. Somewhere, Bree had found a set of Milwaukee tools that contained a drill, an impact drill, three different types of saws, two rechargeable batteries, and more. Even now, the batteries were on the charger so she could try them out. She wished she'd had them when she built Bree her Christmas presents.

"Does that mean you won't be hanging my bird houses and bird feeders?" Bree teased, smiling at her wife. She'd known she was building something, but she'd been told not to look under the drop cloths in the garage. She'd been tempted, though, and had avoided Taylor's work space altogether.

"Oh, yes, I'll hang them for you, my love," she said, leaning in for a hug and a kiss. She was so pleased with her wife; she would have loved if her family wasn't there so she could take her back to their bedroom to show her appreciation.

"I love my Christmas gifts," Bree said quietly into her ear, whispering it close so her breath was warm against Taylor's skin. She felt Taylor shudder slightly and smiled at how she affected her.

"And I love mine. Do you think they're stolen?" she teased but then saw the disappointment in Bree's eyes. "I was just kidding, really. I don't think they're stolen at all."

"I did worry about that, but how could I know? He said he'd gotten them and just didn't use them."

"They're mine now, and they will be well-used. I hated using that hand saw; it was so old and rusty."

"I know, and I'm glad you have decent tools now. Vinnie said Milwaukee was one of the best."

"You know it's not made in Milwaukee anymore, right."

"Yeah, that's disappointing that none of the good tools are made in America, but it's still a good name, and I thought the fact that they were rechargeable a good bonus."

"I'm going to love building things with them." She gave Bree an extra squeeze before releasing her.

"You two shouldn't act like that around the children," Tia said prissily, watching them.

"The children are downstairs, and maybe you should have done more of that around yours," Taylor said firmly, challenging her sister to say more. She was pleased to see her back down.

Dinner turned out to be nice, but only because Eric found a football game to watch, and Blaine, who didn't care about sports, was stuck watching it with him in the family room. Bree kindly brought them serving trays to eat from, but the rest of them were crowded at the kitchen table.

"Worn out, honey?" Taylor asked a sweaty Melanie, who she had heard trying out her new skates, clomping back and forth on the basement's concrete floor. It was a sound that would get on Taylor's nerves over the winter, but the little girl loved her present. The others watched enviously, hoping that someday they, too, would have a pair of their own. If not, maybe they could grow into their sister's pair.

The little girl nodded, thankful that she had also gotten pads for her knees and elbows because she seemed to fall a lot. She was catching on, little-by-little, that skating was more like gliding than walking. She ate her meal in silence and was very sleepy afterwards.

"We better head home," Ellen stated, seeing how fast the snow was building up.

"I better go plow the driveway," Bree said happily, reaching for her winter things.

"Any way I can help?" Taylor immediately asked.

"Just shovel around the edges where the front-end loader can't go."

"Do you need help getting the loader on?"

"No, I removed the pallet forks yesterday in anticipation of this," she said happily, pulling on her snow pants and hopping up to pull the suspenders over her shoulders.

Taylor knew that Bree had been really looking forward to plowing the driveway with the tractor.

"Can I go?" Bryan asked excitedly.

"No, sport. It's important you stay in the house so Mom doesn't haven't to worry about you," Taylor told him. "Mom, can you stick around and watch these guys? I think some naps might be coming on, and I don't want to leave them in the house alone."

"Sure," Ellen agreed immediately, always happy to help with her grandchildren. It was such a relief to deal with *normal* children instead of the constant turmoil with Blaine.

The children watched avidly while Bree plowed a path from the barn towards the circle drive, before continuing around it to Ellen's car. She carefully pushed the snow from around it so that, when their guests were ready to leave, they could easily pull out of the spot. Next, she pulled snow back from the garage, using the front-end loader at an angle and pulling it off the pad, and then pushed it to the side. Then, she started on the long drive, pushing the loader along and dumping it to the side when it filled the front bucket. A month ago, Taylor had come down the long drive with the pink flags they'd saved from the property markers and marked off the edge of the swamp, and these were still visible. Bree was relieved they were there. Her biggest fear was driving off the drive into the swamp since they didn't know how deep it really was.

Taylor shoveled off the porch, the walkway, and the edges as Bree had suggested. She continued around the side of the garage to the back door and then back to the deck, where she shoveled the billowing snow over the edge, clearing it all. By the time she was done with all that, Bree had made two complete lengths of the driveway and was working on a third and final. The snow was coming down harder, filling in where she had already plowed, but she'd cleared the gate. After the third swipe, she parked the tractor back in the barn, backing it in so she could plow out of it, if need be, and shut down the tractor, closing the large garage door behind her. She came into the house, stamping her feet, and left her boots on a small carpet near the door.

"Ellen, I think you should stay the night. It's coming down hard, and I don't think driving on the roads is going to be ..." she began, but Eric heard her.

"I can drive on any road," he bragged. He finally got up from where his butt had been glued to their comfortable easy chair, watching the games for the last few hours. "Come on, boy, get ready to go," he told Blaine.

"I don't know, Eric. If Bree thinks the roads are bad—" Ellen began.

"Eric will get us home, Ma!" she defended her husband proudly and went to get her coat on.

Taylor exchanged a look with her wife and shrugged. Her mother hesitated but dutifully began pulling on her outer clothing. Bree grimaced, but they were adults and there was nothing she or Taylor could do to force them to stay. Taylor gathered some leftovers and put them in a bag for her mother, knowing the odds were she wouldn't get to eat any of them, even her favorites.

"You come by anytime now, ya hear?" she whispered in her mother's ear as she hugged her goodbye. Even quieter, she added, "Alone." She exchanged a knowing look with her mother, hoping she would be safe on the wintery roads.

They all watched as Eric stuffed everyone in the car that Ellen owned, taking the wheel importantly. He spun the tires getting out of the snowbank that had formed around the car, but Bree had done a thorough job on the driveway, and, once clear, he was able to continue without a problem. Ellen waved at everyone as the car went around the circle and then down the drive.

"Think they'll make it?" Taylor asked Bree.

"I don't know," she admitted, sounding worried. "Turn off the gate so we can get out of the drive," she reminded her wife and watched as she went to do that. They'd discussed that long before the snow had come down and decided that having an open gate would be important during snowstorms so they could plow out the snow around it.

"Hey, you kids, let's take a nap," Bree said eagerly. Although they were sleepy and protested when Grandma Ellen tried to get them to go to bed, now they had no choice. She told them to rest their eyes for a little while, and soon they were all snoring in their beds. She checked on them one last time, tiptoed out, and closed their doors.

"Now what?" Taylor asked.

"Let's clean up, and then you and I can neck on the sofa," she offered. They did exactly that, getting rather stimulated in their necking, but it was only a tease for their bedtime later that night.

The children played with their new toys when they awoke, and Taylor was relieved when Ellen called to say it had taken them a good hour and a half to get home but they had made it. Normally, it was about a twenty-minute drive, but Taylor didn't ask what had taken so long. She was just relieved her mother had made it home safely.

* * * * *

Bree got up early the next morning to get at least get one car-width plowed on the driveway so Taylor could get the Jeep out and go to work. She was working on a second row, plowing and stopping, piling it up, when her wife went by her and waved, blowing her a kiss as she went. She grinned, remembering the kisses and more that they had exchanged the night before. Bree got the entire driveway done and was back in the house before the children were up.

It was a fun day for the kids, playing with their new toys and Bree joining in when she could. She was baking more cookies for the New Year's party and looking forward to a First Nillionaires Club meeting. Elsie had phoned to ask if she could bring a potential club member, which meant she had a date. Bree laughed and agreed heartily, glad to see her friend dating again. She'd dated Lenny now and again, but nothing seemed to catch for either of them and they remained friends.

It was two days before New Year's when things reached a tipping point. According to Taylor, she quit her job; according to Carl, her boss, he fired her ass. As Taylor told the tale, she put a bowl of soup in front of a customer's son, warning him that it was hot. He immediately put his hands around the bowl and burned himself, crying like a banshee with pain.

When she came back with ice in a napkin for the young man, his entitled mother demanded an apology.

"Sorry," Taylor said automatically. The boy was really too old to be crying, and she suspected he did it so that his mama bear would defend him.

"I don't believe you're sincere," the woman stated angrily.

"What's going on here?" Carl asked, having come from the kitchen because of the commotion.

"Your *waitress*," she said disparagingly, "deliberately burnt my son's hands!"

"What?" he asked, shocked at the accusation. He looked to Taylor for clarification. Today, she was dressed to look like Flo. Carl hated the costumes she wore, but it brought in the customers and they loved it.

- 263 -

"I wouldn't do that," Taylor gasped. "I warned him the bowl was hot. He put his hands around it himself."

"She did not," the woman accused, "and she didn't apologize."

"I did both," Taylor insisted, aghast at the accusations. The woman was lying.

"Apologize," Carl insisted.

"I already did," Taylor said dryly, outraged at the turn this had taken.

"She didn't mean it," the woman accused further.

Taylor's eyes narrowed, and she automatically said, "I'm sorry." There was no emotion in her voice as she said it.

"You see? She is insincere. I demand that she apologize!"

Carl really didn't know what to do and turned furiously to Taylor.

"I'm sorry," she said with a modicum of inflection in her voice, but the woman wasn't having it.

"Is this the type of employee you have? One that causes harm and doesn't acknowledge that she's in the wrong?" the woman asked Carl who, she could sense, was siding with her.

That was it as far as Taylor could see. The boy had smiled behind his mother's back, obviously pleased at the scene she was making. His crocodile tears had even dried up. She turned to the woman. "I'm sorry," she said and then leaned towards the woman and in a sterner voice added, "I'm sorry that you don't understand a sincere apology for something I didn't do. I'm sorry your son is too stupid to know that soup is hot, especially when I distinctly told him the bowl was hot. I'm sorry you're too stupid, as well, to realize he's playing you. You're the reason that boys like this grow up with a sense of entitlement and think the world owes them. I'm sorry you're too stupid to see it." She'd said it firmly and too fast for the woman to interrupt. Both the customer and Carl were left with their mouths open in shock. A couple of customers started to clap. Taylor removed her apron, fished her tips out of the pockets, and handed it to Carl before he could recover. "I quit."

Taylor went to the waitress station to get her jacket and get out of there as quickly as she could. As she left, she could see Carl arguing with the awful mother. She walked out, feeling like a weight had been lifted from her shoulders, waving to the other waitresses, who she knew would be overworked in her absence. She didn't care anymore. She'd been unhappy at this job for too long, angry she had to work there just to keep food on the table. But this was the wrong time of the year to be looking for another job, and she'd regret it. She thought about it all the way home. The Jeep needed to be replaced—hell, their minivan needed to be replaced. They wanted a new trailer for the pottery business, and they

were in their slow season, to boot. What a stupid time for her to quit her job.

"I am sorry," she repeated to Bree for the thousandth time after she told her what happened. "I should go back and beg Carl to give me my job back."

"No, you shouldn't. If you have to work at McDonalds, or wherever, I don't care. You're good at anything you set your mind to do, and I don't care where you choose to work. But don't you go back to Tweety's; you were miserable there."

Taylor looked up at her wife's encouraging words. She had started to cry in her weariness and mental fatigue. "Thank you."

"Honey, I'll go get a job if it helps. We're okay for a while."

"No, we agreed you were here for the kids so we don't have to put them in daycare. We agreed you could manage the pottery business, with me helping on my days off," Taylor objected. "We don't have to have you work at another job yet. I'll find something.

* * * * *

The First Nillionaires Club began to arrive for the big New Year's party, in the afternoon of New Years Eve, parking in front of the garage and along the sides of the rounded drive. They all planned to drink, had brought alcohol for their own tastes and to share, and planned to stay the night. Sleeping bags and pads were brought into the house for the sleepover.

They all met Claire, Elsie's newest girlfriend, and she actually fit in well with the others while they chatted, ate, and played not only with the children until they went to bed but with the dog, who had found all these wonderful new people to throw toys for him to fetch. A couple of them helped build a snow fort outside with the kids as well as sliding on the sleds along the hill. Returning to the house, Bree had hot chocolate for them all.

After feeding the kids and playing cards, the adults put the kids to bed, leaving the grownups to snack and talk for a while.

When Taylor told them the news, they were all sitting in the family room, watching the fireplace. Bree had found a DVD that projected a fireplace, and that was on the TV, as well. The room was cozy, the food was good, and the booze flowed well.

"Well, then, come work for me," Vinnie offered. "I need snow removers."

"That's okay, Vinnie. You don't have to ..." Taylor immediately began.

"I'm not doing it out of pity. You've worked for me before. I can stand you, and you won't be trying to show me up because of what's hangin' between your legs."

"Vinnie!" Gretchen admonished, wincing at her crudity.

"It's true. Half the guys I hire seem to have a chip on their shoulder, working for a woman."

"And the other half?" Lenny asked, grinning as she started biting down on a carrot stick.

"They're good eggs and I'll keep them, but I do need someone I can trust to back me up. Women don't tend to apply to plow snow."

"And when the snow is gone?" Taylor asked, worried about providing for her family.

"Then, you start cutting lawns. That is," she hesitated here, glancing at Bree, "if you can still handle it."

"If I can handle—" she began blustering before she saw Vinnie was teasing her. She grinned and told the story about tying off the lawnmower last fall so it circled the tree.

"Yeah, we discourage that," Vinnie told her with a grin. "You talk it over with Bree, and, if you two want, the position is ..."

"She doesn't have to talk it over with me. If she wants the job and you want her ... I just want her to be happy." Bree wasn't going to let her wife be unhappy.

"You haven't been happy at Tweety's in a while, love," Elsie pointed out. "I know you were playing a part, but that many years is a bit much."

Taylor nodded and looked happily at her wife. She'd enjoyed the times she'd worked for Lenny in the past. They were friends first, and, if any conflicts came up, she knew that Vinnie would be more than fair. She loved the variety and being outdoors. "I accept," she agreed.

"Good, because a snowstorm is on the way, and I'm going to need you tomorrow. We're both going to have to stop drinking soon so we're not hung over," her new boss advised, deliberately finishing off her last beer with those words.

"Well, I wanted the New Year's week off ..." she began, but at Vinnie's glare, she smiled to show she was kidding.

"Wait, wait," Gretchen said, getting up. She'd been able to leave Aaron at home with her reluctant husband Barry. She'd needed a girls' night, and she was pleased to be out with her favorite friends. "Here's to the First Nillionaires Club," she said, raising her glass. The others soon followed, clinking glasses with beer bottles and all saluting each other.

A few minutes later the clock chimed twelve. It was one of Bree's estate sale finds, a Seiko motion clock whose face broke into pieces and spun around as it went off on the hour. It put itself back together, and all eyes were drawn to it as the pieces fell back into place.

"Amazing! Here's to a fabulous New Year!" Lenny said, raising her beer bottle.

Both Taylor and Vinnie had to borrow some alcohol for a few more toasts, but they didn't mind, and they'd stopped early enough and eaten enough to prevent hangovers in the morning. By one o'clock, everyone was in their bed or sleeping area, dozing off or thinking about the prior year and/or the year to come.

HOME ~ First Nillionaires Club

CHAPTER THIRTY-FOUR

The next day, Taylor rode with Vinnie to go pick up the vehicle she'd be using for work.

"Oh, ohhh, ohhhhh," she groaned as Vinnie showed her the truck she would be driving. "Are you sure this is mine?"

"Yep," she said proudly at the F350 that she was giving Taylor to use. "It's just like mine," she said, pointing at a nearly identical set up. The trucks both had plows on the front and a walking snow blower on treads in the bed. There were shovels and a leaf blower to use on lighter snow attached with locking quick grips on racks at the sides of the bed. There was even a ramp rack down the back in place of a lift gate so the snow blower could be driven in and out of the bed.

"When did you get these?" Taylor marveled admiringly. She knew this was some expensive equipment.

"I've been wanting to do these racks for a while," she said, slapping the ramp and showing Taylor how it worked. "I picked up the two F350's at an auction a month back. Lenny found them for me and helped me drive them home. Pete drove my truck," she nodded towards where she had parked her personal truck in the four-car garage she had at her place. She'd built this all a couple of years back. It was really too much, but Taylor knew Vinnie deserved it; she'd worked hard since she was twelve years old to make this landscaping business a success.

"Have you used them?" Taylor asked, marveling at the simplicity of the ramp rack and how easily it opened.

"Just the one snowfall at Christmas, but I think Mother Nature is just clearing her throat. Let's take this one out," she slapped the one for Taylor to use, "and see if you remember how to plow."

Taylor got into the driver's seat, and Vinnie climbed into the passenger seat. For an auction purchase, it was amazingly well maintained, but she would bet Lenny had helped Vinnie detail both trucks before she put in the rack and equipment. "Why didn't you convince Lenny to work for you?" she asked as she started plowing Vinnie's driveway, being careful to stay within the barrier posts that had been put in to outline the curvy drive.

"I was going to ask her but she got busy with something, and then the opportunity of you working for me again came up. I couldn't pass that up," she said, pleased with how it worked out. They were both her friends, and she'd give Lenny a job if she asked. Right now, though, it was important to get Taylor set up and going. They had a list of places that needed plowing, both residential and commercial. She saw that Taylor was being extra careful, and that boded well. After she finished her own driveway, she had Taylor drive her back up to the garage. "Let me go get you a list of addresses. Gimme a few minutes." she said, hopping out.

Vinnie ran inside to her office, where she had printed pages from her spreadsheet of customers, separated by location. She assigned several to Taylor then called a couple of her guys who had her equipment and would handle addresses in their area that she assigned and verified that they were out there doing their jobs. Grabbing Taylor's list and a company credit card, she went back outside and handed both to Taylor through the window. "You get into any trouble, call me," she said, waving her cell phone.

"You got it, boss," Taylor answered with a smile, pleased with Vinnie's confidence in her. She backed up and turned around in the driveway, stopping for a moment to check for the closest address. When she looked up from the spreadsheet, she saw Vinnie pull past her and turn the opposite way she was heading.

Turning up the tunes in the truck on the radio, she soon found her favorite station. The truck drove so much nicer than her Jeep, which was getting old. The first stop was a quick one, clearing a little, old lady's driveway and shoveling around her car and walkway, as the spread sheet indicated. Quite a few of the places were driveways only, no shovel work. She realized why some insisted on the blower when she saw those on the spread sheet—shoveling alone would take too long and was labor intensive. All of it was a lot of hard work, rattling her muscles, and she

was exhausted when she went home. She sent a text after each driveway she cleared, taking pictures and sending those, too, as that had been Vinnie's way to prove the work was done. Each picture had a time and date stamp that Taylor had to turn on her phone, but it would be worth it if a client said they hadn't done the job. Taylor knew Vinnie would later sit down and enter all of them into her computer.

By the time Taylor got home, she was exhausted. Vinnie had told her on the phone to use the credit card and fill up the truck before she took the truck home and parked it in her garage in preparation for the next storm that was due in two days. Taylor texted Bree to move the Jeep to the half parking spot beside the garage, so she could just pull in and get into the warm house.

"Tired babe?" Bree asked when she came in. The kids were already in bed, and only Bree and Staffy were there to greet her. Bree put a plate of hot stew in front of her wife after she removed her outer clothes and boots and slumped down wearily at the kitchen table.

"Yeah, but I'll adjust," she said happily as she looked up at her wife. "Thank you," she added, gesturing to the stew.

"You sound happier already." Bree tore off a piece of the bread she had baked just for this stew and handed it to her wife.

"I am. It was a long day, and using the snow blower by hand is back-breaking. But that truck ..." She told her wife about the F350 and its features, and Bree, curious, went out after Taylor's dinner to take a look. She whistled low at how impressive it looked.

"Now, you don't get any ideas," she shook her finger at her wife but smiled.

Though fatigued, Taylor had definitely enjoyed her first day at work. She'd plow snow any way the customer wanted rather than work at that stupid diner and serve one more ungrateful customer.

* * * * *

That day of snow removal was the first day of many. It was as though Mother Nature, who hadn't sent much snow that fall or early winter, was making up for it after the holidays. It had snowed on both Christmas and New Year's, but nothing like it did the rest of January. Sometimes she had to do some places on her route twice because of the amount of snowfall. They didn't get paid extra for these *touchups*, but it kept the clients happy. Taylor was loving it, even if it meant eighteen-hour days sometimes, and she almost resented having to stop to eat or fuel up the vehicle.

Bree found that many times she had to drive the van down to the bus stop because there was simply too much snow and it was too cold for the children to wait for the bus. She felt better watching them go straight from the warm van to the warm bus.

There were enough days off between storms, though, that Taylor had time to help Bree in the barn, filling orders and stocking up pottery for their next show, which was after Easter. They still had some stores to stock, but this was definitely their slow season.

"I can't believe I found this," Bree stated as they took Taylor's first paycheck and bought furniture for their living room. Bree found a Victorian couch with matching chairs. It was formal and beautiful, and she warned the children they were not to play on these. She should have warned Marmalade and Staffy, who seemed to love the coolness of the satin. "I'm going to be removing cat hair forever," she complained as she used the brush on the furniture.

Taylor laughed at her wife. Bree hadn't wanted to spend the money but deals like this didn't come along every day. With all the hours she was clocking, her checks from Vinnie were quite impressive, and they tried to sock what they could away against extra payments towards the house and any unexpected bills. With the income down from the pottery business, they didn't have a lot of extra money, but she was earning more than she had at waitressing. And she was definitely happier.

"Let's save towards a new truck," she commented as they discussed their money one late night in bed.

"We can't afford a new truck," Bree said automatically.

"But if we have enough for a decent down payment and I sell the Jeep ..." she began, but Bree cut her off.

"You are becoming a truck snob, driving that souped-up monstrosity of Vinnie's."

"No, I'm serious babe. If we can somehow save up a good down payment, we can get a truck to pull the trailer. Maybe a new trailer if you find a deal. You're always finding good deals," she pointed out, knowing that was one of the ways Bree entertained herself, looking on Craigslist and the Marketplace at the pictures.

"I don't want to go into further debt ..." she began cautiously. "You know how I hate to worry about the bills."

Taylor nodded, petting her wife's hair as they discussed this. "Okay, but saving towards buying the truck outright, if we find a deal ... then we can get it? What kind should we watch for?"

"I'd love one with a camper on the back," Bree admitted, now they were playing pretend.

"Oh, yeah, with bunk beds for the kids?"

"Ohhh," she breathed, imagining how that would work. "I'd say an RV, but I don't think it could pull the weight of our trailer."

"Maybe we should get a newer trailer first."

Back and forth they discussed it, always it was going to be used—nothing new, but at least they knew what they were working towards, saving towards. In it together.

HOME ~ First Nillionaires Club

CHAPTER THIRTY-FIVE

Carl asked Taylor to come back to Tweety's and even apologized profusely for not backing her up. But then he ruined it by saying he had no choice because the customer was always right. Taylor was kind and didn't gloat, but she told him she already had another job that paid much better. She thanked him for the offer but let him know it wasn't going to happen. He said he understood, but she found out later he was bad-mouthing her to her friends, and they stopped going to Tweety's after that.

Instead, they began showing up at Taylor and Bree's house whenever they could. Bree welcomed them and always had a coffee pot on. They brought soda, sometimes beer, and groceries to feed them all, more interested in company than food or drinks. The children enjoyed having the First Nillionaires Club members coming around because they always entertained each other. The guests teased them, played games with them, and listened to their stories.

By March, the storms were less frequent and intense, and there was no more plowing by April. Vinnie had her employees take the plows off their vehicles, and they winterized the snow blowers and stored them in Vinnie's equipment barn for the season. They put lawnmowers and rakes, as well as shovels, weed eaters, and blowers, on the trucks and in the trailers. They were ready for spring, and, as the snow melted, they began raking lawns and preparing them for the coming season.

"Ready to work away your summer?" Lenny teased Taylor.

"Gonna work on my muscles and my tan," she teased back.

Lenny had provided her with polo shirts with the company logo embroidered on the front and a screen print on the back. She'd also advised her to buy those cool new long-sleeved shirts that would go under the polos to ward off sun rays on their arms. "Have to prevent skin cancer," she advised.

The receding snow also meant the swamp was filling up and spilling over onto the driveway again. The children were advised to stay to the high part of the drive and well away from the dark water.

Lenny's business wasn't the only one getting ready for spring. Taylor and Bree could hear contractors gearing up on the McMansions behind them, and they were also prepping to pour foundations on the few basements dug in the field next door. Gretchen had ordered the trees they wanted to plant to block the view of the new building site.

* * * * *

On Thursday, Taylor was on her way home from a half day of work and looking forward to a rare thing in her life—an entire weekend off. When she drove up to the driveway, she was surprised to see the gate open. Maybe Bree had left it open for some deliveries? But she was puzzled to find an excavator blocking the circle driveway. Had Bree hired it? They'd talked many times about what to do with the swamp. Making it into a pond seemed safer since they couldn't tell where the swamp started and ended. The pond would drain some of the land, and maybe the extra dirt could be used around the edges for something good.

This excavator was brand spanking new. It still had plastic on certain parts, and Taylor got excited at the idea of using it. She hurried to change out of her landscaping clothes and into her regular everyday, around-the-house clothes, putting on a jacket—as it was still kind of cold—before going out and climbing up the enclosed cab of the machine. Familiarizing herself with the controls, she tentatively started it and tried out the various features. Slowly, she drove it back and forth on the driveway, trying things out, before venturing off to the edge of the swamp to begin digging. She tentatively began pulling up dirt with the bucket, getting more aggressive as she became familiar with the machine and its controls. She dug farther and farther out, extending the bucket its entire length and feeling the power of the machine as it dug for her. Piles began to build up along the swamp as she dug deeper and piled higher, and she was fascinated to watch the muck and water sluice off the piles she was

making. She waved at Bree when she saw her come home, giving her a thumbs up in her excitement over what she had rented. She was having a blast. She didn't want to stop, even when Bree got out of the van and watched her for a while.

Almost every minute of her long weekend could find Taylor out in the cold, spring sunshine, using the machine to dig out the swamp and build up piles along its banks, moving deeper into the swamp and woods as she rounded out their new pond.

She thanked Bree for renting it, but Bree claimed no knowledge of it. She'd have then thanked Vinnie, but she was out of town for the weekend. The children stood and watched, captivated as she dug up the rich, black earth, some clay, and few rocks. Large digs with muck, water pouring out the sides of the bucket, and roots helped line the piles she made. Out of the swamp, she eventually carved out a large bowl filled with silt and muck and black earth atop the piles, the beginnings of a pond.

By the time she went back to work on Monday, she had practically finished all the work excavating she wanted to do on the pond and was wondering what other projects she could use the excavator for. Vinnie had disavowed any knowledge of it, so its origins were still a mystery. When she got home, she changed out of her work clothes, preparing to do whatever she could with the machine, only to get a call from the gate from a very concerned-sounding construction foreman. The mystery was solved; the excavator had been delivered to the wrong property.

"Holy cow! How many hours did you put on this thing?" the man exclaimed as he examined the gauges on the instrument panel. There was a lot of dirt along the tracks from where she had driven and dropped dirt from her bucket as she went.

Taylor looked guilty because she felt guilty, having worked long hours to get as much done as possible. But she had been excited with her new toy. "Well, I did have to add diesel a couple of times," she admitted, feeling foolish. No one had lent it to her, no one had rented it, and she'd done a lot with it. To answer his question, she'd put in a *lot* of hours and had intended to add to it this evening.

The man surveyed the pond before him, astonished at how much work had been done using the new machine. He re-checked the gauges and the hours put on it. His bosses were not going to be happy. He'd gotten the address wrong, seen the gate, and thought this was part of the housing development next door. When asked about the machine, he'd gone looking, but he hadn't expected anyone to actually use it.

"Please don't tell anyone," he begged her, after putting it on his trailer and using chains to tie it to the bed.

Taylor nodded and watched him drive away with her excavator. She was glad she wasn't in trouble, but a little sad to see it go. She'd hoped for a few more hours of working with it. She'd wanted to dig out more of the pond she had built in those three-and-a-half days. She'd had to work today and thought about what she could do with her big toy, but she had hoped, with lights, to work a little this evening. She was looking sadly at the taillights as he drove away with the big machine when Bree came out of the house.

"What's wrong, baby?" she asked, putting her arm around Taylor's waist. She'd seen how obsessively her wife had worked all weekend long—to the exclusion of everything else—but she thought she understood.

"My new toy is gone," Taylor answered gloomily and then turned in towards Bree's arms and explained about the mistake.

"So, Vinnie didn't rent it for you?" Bree laughed. "Oh, my God, look at all you got done!" She gestured at the piles of dirt, some of them quite high, with even a few trees in the mix. "How are we ever going to smooth that out?"

"I guess with the tractor," she said sadly, feeling like a fool.

"Aw, babe, don't be like that. Look at all you've done," she repeated, gesturing again. "We'll manage."

Taylor began to feel better, but she thought about her humiliating mistake all the next day. She cleaned up other people's yards in the cool spring air in preparation for grass growing, raking up lawns that had gravel and grass dug up from plowing. When Vinnie came by for a periodic check-in, she told her what had happened with the excavator.

Vinnie had a good laugh. "I bet that guy was relieved to get out of there!"

"I'm gonna have to rent a bulldozer to get all those piles in order. It's a mess," she lamented. Both her wife and one of her best friends had laughed at her. This did not bode well.

"C'mon, finish up here and go home. I want to follow you and see it," Vinnie cajoled her and hopped out of her truck. She picked up a rake and started working to help her finish faster. "It could be worse; you could have broken it or something."

When she got home, though, things had gotten worse. To make up for laughing at her wife, Bree attempted to take down one of the piles. Not judging the edge of the pond correctly, she pushed through, and the tractor had teetered and then fell over the edge. Bree had climbed back in and tried to reverse it out of the mess, but it wouldn't budge. It was now up to its wheels in the middle of the mucky pond. She'd gotten a rope around

the scoop and was attempting to pull it with the Jeep when the two trucks pulled into the yard. The children turned from where they were raptly watching their mom.

"BREE! WHAT ARE YOU DOING?!" Taylor yelled.

"Don't worry, I got this," she called back as she put the Jeep in gear and went ... nowhere. The Jeep wasn't heavy enough, and all she accomplished was to pull the rope taut and then break it. The two approaching adults ducked and fell to the ground in time as it came apart and whipped through the air over the Jeep. Bree stomped on the brake and stared in horror at nearly hurting her wife or her best friend. She quickly put the hand brake on, turned off the Jeep, and got out.

"Are you two okay?" she asked, glancing at the children, who were up on the lawn and away from the piles of dirt. They came closer, now that all the adults were there and the machines off.

"Yeah, we're fine," Taylor said as she got up, brushed herself off, and looked at Vinnie for agreement.

"The Jeep isn't strong enough to pull that out," Vinnie pointed out. "You need these," she said, thumb-pointing to the two trucks. "And, chains," she added, sneering at the rope in disgust.

"Oh, God, I'm sorry," Bree said, bursting into tears.

Taylor hurried over and gathered her into her arms. "What happened? How'd the tractor end up in the pond?"

"It's a good thing there isn't much water in there," Bree hiccupped, shaking her head. "I got too close to the edge, and it looked like it was going to fall over and I jumped. It righted itself but went in." She was crying but trying hold herself together to tell her woeful tale.

Taylor tried not to snicker, but a small snort snuck out, and Vinnie couldn't help but turn away to hide her own laughter.

"Don't you two laugh at me!" Bree ordered, and the two tried to get it under control.

"I'm sorry, honey," Taylor said, her face a mask of soberness. "I'm not laughing at you. It could have happened to any of us," her thumb pointed at Vinnie who nodded in agreement and then back to herself. "Could you move the Jeep so we could try to get the tractor out?"

"I think I better untie the rope from the hitch first," she stated and stomped away, her ears burning.

"Do we have any chains?" Taylor asked Vinnie, still trying to keep the laughter spasms from her face in case Bree looked back.

It turned out Vinnie did have some chains in the back of her truck, having used them to pull her own equipment when necessary. They positioned both trucks, using their hitches to hook up, not on the arm of the

tractor, but below it on some hooks. With the heavy-duty trucks, they were soon pulling the tractor out of the muck. It took several tries and a kind of back-and-forth motion to wiggle it out, but it eventually was back on shore and pulled into the driveway. Amazingly, it started up. Using a garden hose, Bree washed off the black muck before putting the tractor away.

"Good thing you didn't have more water in that bowl," Vinnie pointed out as she dropped her chain in loops inside the bed of her truck. "It would have gotten in the engine and carburetor, for sure."

"Well, I don't feel so bad now with my own snafu," Taylor mentioned, handing off more of the chain to Vinnie.

"That's a helluva dig you have there," Vinnie admired speculatively as Bree walked up. "I bet I know a couple of my guys who can use the Cat to smooth it down. Over time some of that dirt will settle, anyway, but you are going to have to haul a few loads away."

"Where to?" Taylor worried, wondering how much this was going to cost them.

"Call Gretchen. I'm sure she'll take a few truck loads for the plants she grows, and I'll store some at my place. We can always use black dirt like that, but you're going to want to keep some of it for yourself." She went on to venture how the guys would do the work.

"Can I use one of the Cats?" Taylor asked eagerly.

Vinnie ignored her. "This requires specialized work. You were lucky that you didn't wreck that excavator."

"Its operating system was easier than video games," Taylor assured her, remembering how exciting it had been.

"Why isn't there more water in the pond?" Bree asked Vinnie, relieved the tractor wasn't any worse for wear. She'd already imagined calling the insurance company to explain what had happened and why their tractor had ended up in the middle of the pond.

"There will be when it fills from the springs." Vinnie pointed to where bubbles were coming up at places in the standing muck. "You are going to have to file a permit to dig a pond," she added low so the children couldn't hear. "I'll have a couple of my guys come out with the Cats and tidy up, but go get that tomorrow."

* * * * *

It wasn't as easy as all that. Taylor had to work, and the chore fell to Bree. She had to bring in the plat of their property, showing the large swamp that encompassed most of it, and explaining where they wanted to dig, that they wouldn't be impeding the flow of the creek. It was hard for Bree not to state in the present that it was already dug and instead imply the permit was for a future build. It took many hours of her time, hours she had planned to throwing pots, now that it was spring and business was picking up. She'd wasted several hours the previous day trying to smooth out the piles Taylor had dug, only to end up in the pond. She could still feel how scared she'd been about having to jump off the tractor and then see it roll inexorably into the muck. Dealing with bureaucrats to get a pond digging permit was almost too much for her, but she channeled her anger and anxiety from the previous day into a determination not to quit until the process was done. After several hours of jumping through hoops, she finally got the permit and thanked them sweetly. She went home with a sense of relief.

The pottery business was invited to a show the following weekend because a vendor cancelled at the last minute. Bree and Taylor agreed to take the spot on the spur of the moment. It was an unexpected precursor to the big spring show they'd been planning for, but at least the family would get their feet wet about the process of shows after not having been to one since the fall.

"We need to get a stronger truck," Bree admitted as the minivan protested the weight they were pulling behind them. They hadn't been able to bring as much variety as she wanted for this show, but they already planned to rent a U-Haul—as they had for the fall show—for the big show in a couple of weeks.

"That's what I've been saying," Taylor sympathized, having traded off driving and realizing that the trailer was unbalanced. They needed a stronger, heavier trailer, too.

Sleeping with four growing children at the show wasn't much fun, either. It was cold, they were bigger, and their elbows seemed to be sharper. Complaints were louder, and now they had Staffy with them in the van, too. He stayed near the trailer during the day, guarding it for his family, but at least they could take him with them so they didn't need a sitter.

When they got home on Sunday, cold, tired, but now broken into the yearly cycle of shows that had just started, they were astonished at the amount of work Vinnie and her crew had done around the pond. The driveway was an entire car width wider in the section next to the pond and over the rocks they had laid earlier. No more worrying about falling off into the swamp. Extra dirt was smoothed out among the formerly swampy area of trees Taylor had wanted to dig up but hadn't gotten to. The ground nearer the house was at a steep incline, and Vinnie had somehow gotten a

truckload of sand and poured it to even the area out. She was still there and clearing the bigger rocks out of it with a hard rake.

"Hi, there," she yelled over the noise of her Cats that were smoothing down piles of muck on the east side of the pond. Trees that Taylor had mixed in with the piles were now pulled out and stacked neatly on part of the trail.

"Oh, my goodness, Vinnie! You've done so much!" Bree exclaimed, widening her arms to encompass it all. It didn't look at all like the muddy mess they'd left on Friday.

Vinnie turned back to look at the beach she was creating. The sand still had a lot of fist-sized rocks and a few bigger ones, but her raking had helped to even it out. It was walkable now. She had three more loads coming in exchange for some of the rich dirt. She'd used a front-end loader to load the truck back up with the rich dirt. She knew these two wouldn't mind getting the shorter end of the deal. The guy she'd traded the sand for had salivated over the black earth. "Yeah, another day or so and they should have that all spread out. The trees on that side," she pointed, "shade the pond quite nicely. My friend Jeff came out and said you hit a few springs, like I said, and it should fill the pond eventually. But it's supposed to rain later this week, and that will help, too. I told my guys to hurry up and finish." She nodded towards the piles they were carefully smoothing out, making sure to level out the edges so there were no abrupt drops along the pond. "So, erosion shouldn't be an issue."

"How can we ever thank you?" Taylor said gratefully.

"Oh, you're working for me; you'll pay me back," she assured her with a devilish grin and a wink. "Slave labor."

Taylor smiled. She knew she went the extra mile for Vinnie, mostly because she loved the work. Waitressing was already a long-ago nightmare, although she did miss the interaction with some regulars. She'd run into a couple of them while running errands, but, then, it was a small town.

"About erosion, should we plant grass again? Even in the pond a bit?" Bree asked.

"That wouldn't be a bad idea. Eventually, you'll have fish in here ..."

"Oh, no, we don't want fish in there. We want to be able to swim," she assured her.

Vinnie chuckled. "You won't have a choice about the fish. Birds will drop them in, and they will breed."

"They will?" Bree asked, sounding stupid. "How in the world would they know to drop them in?"

Vinnie shrugged. "I don't know how it works exactly. Some say it's accidental. They're carrying a fish they caught home to their nest, and it wiggles out of their talons, and—plop—it falls in a random lake, river, or pond. Voila, you have a fish in your water! If it's pregnant ... you get the idea."

Both women stared, astounded at their friend's information. Then, they all turned at the growl of a large truck coming up the driveway. "There is some more of your beach. You might want to move your trailer and van."

Taylor rushed to pull the van around the circle and back the trailer up to the barn, well away from where the trucks needed to go. She could see they'd really rutted up the lawn, but she didn't care at the moment since they were dumping sand for a beach at their pond. Vinnie then directed them to the nearest pile of swamp dirt, and they began using her front-end loader to fill first one truck then the other.

"Wow, that's amazing," Bree stated when Taylor walked up next to her. The children were utterly spellbound as well.

"We better get them inside and washed up. They have school in the morning," Taylor reminded her, wanting to stay and watch just as much, but it was getting late and they were all exhausted. They hadn't expected all this.

Bree and Taylor ushered the reluctant, tired, and whiny children inside, pulling on Staffy's leash as he, too, wanted to stand guard. They took turns, Taylor washing the two youngest in the bathtub, dressing them for bed, and then feeding them; while Bree fed the two oldest and then washed them. They all ended up getting tucked in at about the same time—clean, dust-free, and with full bellies.

"Mom, can you read us a story?" Jack and Bryan begged Taylor as she turned on their lava lamp. She obliged as she always did, but they were both out before she finished. Comparing notes with her wife, she found Bree had similar results with the girls.

"Good. Let's go see what they've done," Taylor said eagerly, waving towards the front of the house.

She hoped to see what they were doing, with all the machine noises they could hear, even though it was so close to the dark, but they were too late. By the time they got out there, Vinnie had her men packing up. They'd earned extra this weekend, which was why they had agreed to work, and the moving of dirt had been pretty straightforward. Jeff recommended digging a little more, and they could use the Cats to elongate the pond and smooth out the dirt they dug up to trade for the sand. That could all wait until tomorrow, in the daylight, when they came

back to smooth out all the piles among the trees and the bumps that were still swampy.

"See you at work tomorrow!" Vinnie called as she got in her truck and waved goodbye.

"I can barely see to walk," Bree complained, and Taylor, chuckling, turned her around to go in the house. "Here, Staffy!" she called the dog, who had been snuffling in the weeds next to the house between the cow pasture and their land. He looked up, surprised, and bounded towards his humans.

"Hey!" Taylor grabbed her wife's shoulder as she went in the front door, nearly bowled over by the solid dog. Taylor turned and locked the front door, shutting off the lights on the porch they had hoped would give them a view of the work on the pond. "We still have to get cleaned up," she pointed out. "Wanna conserve water … together?" She waggled her eyebrows outrageously.

"I'll race you," Bree offered, but she stopped to make sure the garage was closed and then felt obliged to check the side door.

Taylor made sure the patio doors were locked for the night, letting in Marmalade, who wound around her legs and nearly tripped her, as he purred loudly and welcomed them home. He'd been inside when they got home, but obviously one of the kids had let him out.

Showering together proved … interesting. They had dust from the fairgrounds in the most interesting places, and they got them all. But they didn't conserve much water because they took a long, hot shower together. When they were done, Bree and Taylor snuggled in bed, and, like the children, they dozed off within minutes.

CHAPTER THIRTY-SIX

Taylor groaned when the alarm went off the next day. She'd forgotten over the winter how those weekends taxed her muscles. She was stiff from the cold of sleeping in the van in uncomfortable positions with all those kids. She would bet they would all be grumpy this morning. As she got up to wake them, she heard Bree groaning on the other side of the bed.

Still, she managed to get off to work on time, giving the children a ride to the end of their long drive and watching them get on their bus. She waved at Mrs. Schlieve, the bus driver, who had proven to be a nice woman, always watching out for the little ones. As Taylor turned onto Restlawn Highway, she looked at the fences that still needed to be put in the ground. Depending on how high the water was, maybe they could set those posts soon. She hoped most of it had drained away and they could dig the post holes without them filling with water. She'd better come out here with a sledge hammer soon and take off as much of the old concrete as she could.

It was a hard day at work for Taylor. Her muscles had done too much over the weekend, and this work was demanding of the same muscles. She worked slowly and steadily.

For her own part, Bree had thought she might slip in a nap, but it wasn't to be. The weekend sales had to be tallied, the deposit made, and the trailer and van emptied. Normally, Taylor and the children helped with some of these chores, but she was determined, despite her aching body, to do it all by herself. She knew how much Taylor did for Vinnie—already the muscles on Taylor's arms, back, and thighs were getting toned. Her butt didn't look too bad, either, and it would continue to tone the longer Taylor worked for the landscaper. Bree was determined to do as much work as she could, herself.

She was surprised when the two guys who had worked the Cats came back that afternoon right before the kids got off the bus. She'd already gotten the trailer cleared out and parked in its spot, cleaned out the van, and stopped at the bank, but she hadn't done their weekly shopping, worried she'd miss the children when they got off the bus. Instead, she found herself, after parking the van in the garage, wasting time as she watched the captivating work these men were doing for them.

"Hey, there," she said in greeting to the children as they came running up the driveway, their heads pivoting toward the big machines moving dirt. She had brought Staffy outside with her, and she let him off-leash to run out and meet the kids. After a day away from his children, he was eager to let them know he didn't hold any ill will for them leaving him. Bree noticed Bryan stopping to leave bread for Allan Crowe. She'd been packing an extra slice every day for months after the boy told her he was saving back part of his lunch for the bird. The crow watched for Bryan and hopped over to get the treat, and soon another crow, likely his mate, joined them. He must have been young because it wasn't just one crow he shared it with anymore. She'd have to remember to pack two slices from now on and maybe some seed. She would talk to Taylor about setting up a crow feeder somewhere near the pond so they wouldn't chase any of the birds from the feeders in the back of the house.

"Here's the mail, Mom," Melanie said importantly while Bree absentmindedly began reading through the letters, brochures, and newspaper ads that came every day. She frowned at one envelope and opened it. It read:

Dear Homeowner,

This is to inform you that there is a scheduled association meeting for the Rolling Ridge Estates homeowners. We expect everyone to attend as we hand out our new homeowners' rules and regulations.

Good neighbors follow rules that we can all live by.

The letter was on stationery with letterhead from the contractor for the McMansions behind their property and signed by someone Bree had never heard of, and she frowned at it, looking on both sides of the relatively short letter. Shrugging, she decided it must be junk mail and started going through the rest of their mail to look for bills, which reminded her she needed to go pick up the business mail from the P.O. box the next day. The homeowner's association letter was promptly forgotten.

* * * * *

"Oh, isn't that lovely?" Taylor breathed as Vinnie and she used rakes to pick out rocks and stones from the sand around the pond. It made a nice beach, and they'd gotten some extra truckloads in trade after the guy Vinnie traded with saw the quality of the dirt.

"You can use these rocks for your fence posts," Vinnie suggested.

"You know you're not going to be able to swim in this for at least a year." Vinnie's pond guy friend, Jeff, was over checking out the pond and talking with her and the two homeowners while the children gamboled about on the now-mounded dirty sides around the pond and through the trees. "I wouldn't want to swim where there were springs, anyway."

"Why is that?" Taylor asked, disappointed, as though this had all been a waste of time. She wanted to enjoy their pond with its lovely sandy beach extending out into the water. It had taken weeks to build.

"Have you ever dipped your foot into a spring?" he asked with a grin and exchanged a look with Vinnie who started to grin herself.

"Maybe," she shrugged. "When I played in the creek in my youth."

"Ever notice how ice cold it is coming out of the earth? That water is going to be cold," he pointed to the pond, "until the sun has a chance to heat it up. Maybe, by the end of summer, you can swim in it, but I still wouldn't go on the shaded side under those trees."

"Why is that?" Bree asked, alarmed.

"I'm betting you have leeches in that mud, and it will take a while for them to disappear, move, or whatever they do." He laughed. He had also talked to Taylor about putting in a dam so they would have a spillway for when the pond reached its maximum depth. The springs would overfill it, and the water would have to have somewhere to go. "With that creek running through your woods, that's a natural place for the water to spill into."

Taylor felt pleased they had something going in their favor as they discussed what kind of dam, how to build it, and what materials they would need.

"We have to buy a lot of Quikrete, anyway, to finish our fencing. Would that work for the dam, too?" Bree asked, wondering if they could buy it by the pallet load to save money. But maybe it would be cheaper to buy regular concrete and mix it.

"Yes, but you are going to want to build the dam before more rains come and fill the pond in, along with the springs," he warned. The guys had hit a few more springs when they elongated the pond to fill in more of the swamp area, but there was still a significant amount left with a few trees poking up here and there. Hopefully, the pond would settle over time, and some of the swamp would drain into it. Some of those trees would die and others would thrive, but it would create a beautiful oasis for wildlife.

* * * * *

For a fun game with the children, they collected all the rocks they could find from the beach and built them up in little piles, digging down into the sand to find them where they could. There was a lot of extra sand, and the children could only play in it if the moms were present. The children were not allowed anywhere near the pond without supervision. Taylor started filling five-gallon pails with the rocks to collect for various projects they had around the place, having to tip out water more often than she liked as spring rains came in.

As spring heated up and the grass grew, Taylor was enjoying her job more and more. She'd come home in the late afternoon or early evening, peel off her mucky work clothes, and head directly for the shower. Having a washer and dryer in the house was a bonus since her jeans and polo shirts got so dirty.

"I found these at the Goodwill today. Could you try them on?" Bree requested, showing Taylor a pair of jeans, she had bought her.

"Oh, thanks, babe. I was starting to worry about wearing everything out." She stepped out of the shower and pulled on some clean underwear. "I'm going to have to buy some new sports bras," she confessed.

"Those will be expensive," Bree lamented, having had to buy some for herself recently. She watched, unabashed, as her wife tried on the jeans. "Looks like you're losing weight."

"I think I might be, but I love the exercise," she answered, flexing a muscle for her wife's amusement.

"You're so much happier working for Vinnie," she commented with a touch of sadness.

"Hey, what's wrong with that?"

"What if we make enough pots to support us? You won't want to do that full time anymore."

"I've done both," she pointed out. On her days off she cut the lawns here at home, and now that they had the pond, they'd spread grass seed right up to edge. They were smoothing out the sides and raking it out so it could be cut as a lawn even amongst the trees. There were still big chunks of dirt that needed to be pounded down and smooth, despite the Cats pulling and pushing it relatively smooth. It would take months, years even, to get it all the way they wanted.

"It's just ..." she started then picked at the bedspread in her agitation.

"What?" Taylor frowned at her wife, worrying.

"You're so busy," she put out there, her hands spreading helplessly as she tried to explain herself.

"I'm trying to make up for the money we would have lost." She still remembered that sinking feeling when she quit her job from Tweety's. "Do you want me to quit with Vinnie?" She sure hoped not. Taylor enjoyed running lawnmowers, weed eaters, and other equipment. The way Vinnie had her truck set up was brilliant. She could work completely autonomously on virtually any job.

"No ... that's not it," she answered, squirming and still not making eye contact. "Actually, I think you're making more." She *knew* Taylor was. "It's just that if you like it more than our pottery business ..." she hesitated again, unsure how to make it clear.

"Hey, I want to make as much as possible so we can buy that truck, that camper, and a new trailer." She came over to crouch down and force Bree to look her in the eye.

"I do, too, and our savings are back on track. Heck, our house payment is ahead. I don't know ... I guess when we struggled a little more, you needed me more and ..."

"You don't think I need you?" Taylor asked, incredulous. She stood up, and the used jeans bagged a little because she *had* been losing weight. She waited until Bree looked up. "I *need* you. Who else is going to take care of this tribe of hooligans?" They could hear the children playing on the Little Tyke's equipment out back with Staffy right there in the middle of them, barking and playing. She'd brought home some things just today she would need help unloading and hoped the children would like the idea, she couldn't wait to show them. "I thought you liked staying home, but, if it's bothering you, we can make other arrangements." She said the last part quietly as she cupped Bree's jaw to get her to look at her.

"I'm sorry. I do love being home and working in the barn at my convenience. When the kids are in school, I can get so much done." She shook her head. "I guess I thought … you out there," she gestured to the world at large. "That you were having too much fun."

"It's no different from when I was waitressing. I actually see less people, and I have a lot more time for thinking."

Bree stood up to hug her wife. "What do you think about when you're working?"

"I think about designs for the pottery. I think about improvements I want to make around here. And I've barely used the tools you gave me for Christmas." She had made and hung a lot of bird houses and feeders. They'd discovered a bear nosing around the feeder in the yard and chased it off. More importantly, they'd watched from the windows as Marmalade had chased one off! "What do you think about when you're working?"

"I think of more designs, but for some reason I think of making them on the computer instead of free hand."

"Well, see, we're working towards our strengths." Taylor gave Bree a warm kiss and waited a few seconds to ask, "Are we okay?"

Bree chuckled. "I guess we are. I don't know; I just suddenly felt weird."

"Well, voicing it always helps. Feel better?"

"I do."

"I have something in the back of the truck I need help unloading," Taylor admitted. "Maybe I shouldn't have showered first." She looked down at the used jeans. They were nice, and she decided to keep them even if they were a bit big on her now. She might need them if she bloated up.

"Then, you better put on a shirt. As fetching as you look right now," she caressed along the edge of her wife's bra, "I don't think we should shock the children."

But Bree was the one shocked. Taylor had begun to salvage junk at her work sites and bring things home to repurpose them. Today's prize took the cake, though. It was a frame for a trampoline and a rather small one, at that. Melanie, as the oldest, recognized the trampoline frame for what it was and was excited they were getting a new toy until Taylor told her it was to use in a building project.

She came home another time with two satellite dishes and Bree was alarmed. Some of the stuff Taylor brought home didn't make sense to her. "Um, babe, I don't want to complain, but what are you going to do with this junk?" She didn't want their yard ending up looking like some junkyard.

"Remember, you asked what I was thinking when I work?" She waited for Bree to nod. "I was thinking we need a chicken coop," she said with

perfect logic. Bree had just helped her put the first of the two satellite dishes on the trampoline frame. It fit, if a little off because of the concave dish, but Taylor was confident she could make it work.

"I don't get it," she admitted.

"You will," Taylor said mysteriously. "I need you to pick up some things the next time you're at the Home Depot." She named off a few things including metallic paint, black paint, and then asked her to look on the Marketplace and Craigslist for some bulbous glass? I think we're going to need at least a dozen of those."

"What in the world are you making?" Bree wondered, shaking her head, but she dutifully wrote out the list things needed.

"I told you: we need a chicken coop. And don't you be buying any chicks for Easter." She shook her finger at her wife. "So many of those are surrendered after Easter that we can put our name in at the pound and really make out."

Since Easter was fast approaching, along with their biggest spring show, they were more concerned about that, but Bree still wondered what kind of chicken coop her wife had in mind.

Taylor removed all the cables and any protrusions from the first satellite dish and, with some help from the children, painted it silver with black lines and 'rivets.' Then, they painted the trampoline frame in silver, too.

At Taylor's request, Lenny brought over her welding equipment and showed Taylor how to use it. They cut a flap from the satellite dish and secured it back onto the dish with a hinge. Now, the flap hung down but could be latched and locked. Protruding from this flap was a gangplank of sorts. They cut a simple frame and a circle out of plywood with the Milwaukee tools Taylor had gotten for Christmas and made a platform inside the dish. Since this project took weeks, Taylor frequently had to dump out the dish as it filled with water from the spring rains.

"I still don't see what you're building there," Bree stated after they had spent a lot of Taylor's day off on the project. The children were captivated and helped wherever they could.

"No, don't touch the power tools," Taylor warned the kids, time and again.

"Give me that hammer," Bree commanded after someone decided to use the tool to do a band solo. "Don't stare into the light," she repeated a couple of times, pulling children away from their allure as Taylor learned to weld.

"I told you we need a chicken coop," Taylor repeated with a grin, the grime from welding making a shape on her face around where the mask had been.

They painted the second satellite dish with metallic silver paint and drilled large holes around its edge in equal parts. Bree eventually found the bulbous glass Taylor had asked for, and the structure look even weirder than before until Taylor painted a darker gray ring around the caulking seals to make the glass look like port holes. Bree was starting to get an inkling of what Taylor's creation would be. They affixed the second satellite dish on top of the first one with huge hinges and added large handles and a prop so the whole thing could be opened when necessary. Taylor installed white landing lights where the two dishes came together and a string of green lights over the ramp.

"You made a UFO chicken coop?" Bree asked dryly, but she was thrilled at her wife's creativeness. Taylor had also built in some nesting boxes that could be easily accessed and some wide roosts so the chickens would have a safe and dry place to sleep.

"Yeah, isn't it great? I saw it on Facebook once, and it always stuck with me. When we got this place, I knew I wanted to build this but didn't know how until I saw these babies." Her hand slapped the repurposed satellite dishes. No one has these huge dishes anymore, and they would have ended up in a landfill unless someone could recycle or upcycle them.

"That really is great," Bree admired. The lights worked off a small solar panel, so it wouldn't draw power from the house. "Now we need fencing."

She shouldn't have worried, though. With all the properties Vinnie serviced, they soon found a six-foot-high dog fence that was long enough to cover the entire chicken pen. They reinforced it with hardware cloth to keep out dogs and other large critters and buried two feet of hardware cloth all along the fence line to keep out swamp varmints like weasels, mink, raccoons, and opossums. Chicken wire was used only on the inside or top to keep birds where they ought to go.

As they worked on the large pen, Lenny snickered and said, "I have a crow joke for you."

"Oh, no. Not you, too," Taylor groaned before even hearing it. With Allan Crowe and his brood around regularly, they heard a lot of crow news in her house.

"Before the crowbar was invented, crows simply drank at home," Lenny said without cracking a grin.

Slowly, Taylor started to laugh as she realized the pun. She shook her head at her friend, warning her with her finger as she shook it at her. "Don't tell that one to the boys; they won't understand it."

Lenny chuckled as she helped finish laying wire across the top of the run. The older and larger trees around the place had housed more than their fair share of owls and hawks. It only made sense to enclose the chicken house completely.

Bree loved how the enclosed coop looked with its UFO inside of it. She wanted to go out and get chicks immediately.

"We can't get chickens until after Easter," Taylor repeated for the umpteenth time to her wife and children.

"But we have the show right after Easter," Bree pointed out. It was the show they'd been making pots for since December.

"And we have no one to take care of the chicks while we're at it." Everyone wanted to go look at chicks but Taylor had resisted all the hints and begging because she knew they'd want to come home with every last one the store had.

"Why don't we just look?" she asked, a gleam in her eye. "You know, just see what they have? I promise we won't bring any home.

"With those kids?" Her thumb pointed over her shoulder at the children playing. "They will whine and plead until we give in. Nuh-uh, no chicks until we are home from the show."

Defeated, Bree smiled at her and kissed her on the cheek. "Okay, no chicks." She grinned at how that sounded and added, "Bock-bock." She started to laugh as Taylor chased her back towards the kids.

* * * * *

The spring show was one of the largest around, and in some years, they'd gone in the snow. They'd gotten their feet wet at the show weeks before, and now worked together like a well-oiled machine. They took a large tent, a second U-Haul truck, and laid out more pots than they ever had brought before, months of work for customers to peruse.

The children helped where they could, and customers were thrilled when Melanie and Barbie could answer questions about the pottery. They knew their moms' stock pretty well and could find almost anything the customers were looking for. Jack and Bryan stayed out of the way for the most part, but they knew the routine well and frequently checked up on Staffy who was *guarding* the trailer, using the coolness inside to doze out his long day. Bree was pleased to have the dog with them because she

could leave the trailer open to replenish stock as they sold, but the U-Haul was a little harder to get into with its roll-up door and ramp.

"Do you like the little cave I made in here?" Taylor asked on their first night. The kids were all in the minivan, butted up to the U-Haul so they weren't alone or too far away from their moms. Staffy was with them, but the adults had given them plenty of room by laying their own sleeping bags in the rented truck. With the stacks of pottery around them it was almost like they had a blanket fort as they snuggled together down the aisles they had made.

"Mmm-hmm. How much you want to bet they end up in here with us?" Bree responded, snuggling closer to her wife.

"Oh, no bets there." Taylor laughed and held Bree close as they drifted off to sleep.

Sure enough, one by one, the children joined them inside the truck, climbing like monkeys up the ramp and ducking under the roll up door, snuggling deep in their own sleeping bags they'd brought them with them. Bryan was the last to climb into the trailer, and Staffy followed to be near his chosen boy as well as the whole family, who also fell under his guardianship. The family all slept in a space about half the size of the minivan, despite Taylor and Bree's efforts.

"Well, today is the big day," Bree announced early on Saturday as she fought off the bed head she'd slept in, brushing out her hair after taking care of the kids.

"So, no fooling around," Tayler warned as she pulled bowls out of the cooler, along with milk and cereal.

"You always say that, Mom," Melanie complained, reaching for a bowl and a spoon.

"It bears repeating."

The kids were really well-behaved, considering their ages. By the afternoon, Bryan and Jack could be found with Staffy, dozing in the trailer. Bree kept a side panel of their tent up so she could keep an eye on them, while Taylor and the girls helped people carry pots to their cars. It was an endless day—long and hot—but both moms were pleased with the net results. Sunday would be a short day, and they'd have to take down in the late afternoon. They would be one of the last to leave, and they would barely get home in time to scrounge dinner and prepare for the next day of work and school.

Both Lenny and Gretchen were vending at the show, too. They had waved and popped in to chat with Bree and Taylor for a few seconds now and then, but the show was really too busy for extended conversations.

When they were about halfway done with packing on Sunday afternoon, Gretchen caught Bree's attention. "Hey, could I stop over tomorrow?" She looked at her hopefully, but her face was haggard.

"Sure, anytime," Bree said. "Something up?"

"I'll talk to you then," she said airily as she hurried back to her booth.

* * * * *

Back at home that evening, Taylor and Bree watched the chickadees fight off bigger birds for their share of the bird seed.

"What did Gretchen say she wanted?"

"I told you; I have no idea," Bree repeated what she'd said earlier when she told her that Gretchen was coming by the following day. "How can you see anything out there?"

"I left the porch light on so they can see the feeder for a bit longer. Hmm … why would Gretchen say something so mysterious?"

The kids were in bed, asleep practically before they laid their heads on the pillows, but they had earned their right to sleep. Baths and showers had cleaned off the dust, and full bellies meant they slept soundly.

"God, I'm tired," Taylor admitted. They'd had car trouble with the minivan and not for the first time. She was glad they'd unloaded the U-Haul and returned it in the dark, but she was tired, so very tired, from all the work.

"Come on, let's shower and head to bed."

"But then tomorrow comes, and I have to go to work," Taylor moaned, grinning to show she didn't mind. This was part of their routine.

* * * * *

"Gretchen!" Bree gasped as she held her gloved hand to her chest in surprise. She had left the gate open for a delivery and unloaded the trailer so it would be ready to organize for the next show. Gretchen had appeared out of nowhere and scared the bejeezus out of her.

"Hey, there. Sorry about yesterday. I couldn't stay and explain, but can I stay with you and Taylor for a while?" she blurted out.

"What?" Bree asked, blinking stupidly at the question. It wasn't like Gretchen to ask for help, much less something that involved, but, as part of the First Millionaire's Club, she was welcome to ask any favor. "Sure, but what—"

"I'm leaving Barry," she interrupted, "and I need somewhere to move my stuff. I remembered that incident with your sister-in-law and hoped …" she left off, biting her lip. *Was she asking too much?*

"Uh, okay," Bree got out, concerned for her friend. *Wow, leaving Barry after all these years. What had happened to bring it to this point?* "Do you have your stuff with you? Do you need help moving out? What about Aaron?"

"I have some of my stuff in my truck. I loaded what I could after he left for work, but I should go get more," she worried her lip, causing it to bleed. "I need to get some of my plants, too."

"Hang on. You start moving your stuff into the basement," Bree said, taking charge. Gretchen was a disorganized mess, and Bree could see her truck bed was crammed full of things she'd tossed in it at random. "I'll go unlock the basement door if you'll carefully drive around? Just go easy on the lawn, and watch out for toys and the chicken coop. You may have to move some stuff."

Gretchen looked relieved to have someone telling her what to do. She nodded and turned back to her truck to get in. Bree rushed into the house and down the steps, pushing aside Staffy, who tried to race her to the bottom. She unlocked the patio doors, as well as the regular door, directed Gretchen where to back the truck to, and then helped Gretchen bring her things into the house. She asked no further questions and left it to Gretchen to explain in her own time.

"He keeps taking all my money." She sobbed as she laid down boxes of clothes, odd trinkets, and an occasional plant. "Then, he gets angry when I have to work and don't make dinner. I can't have him taking his anger out on Aaron."

"I'm sure Aaron sees him for what he is, at this age." She could vaguely remember a thirteenth birthday party for Aaron none of the club had been invited to. At the time, she had guessed it was probably because of Barry, and now she was sure of it. "If you'll help me finish emptying the trailer, we can use that, too. Let me make a few calls."

"Don't tell Vinnie," she warned immediately, putting her hand on Bree's arm.

Vinnie had been one of the calls Bree would naturally have made, but, seeing the stricken look on Gretchen's face, she knew she couldn't. And she knew why. Gretchen and Vinnie were involved more than a decade ago, but Gretchen had bought into the heteronormative programming of her parents and went out with Barry to prove it. Only Barry had gotten her pregnant, and she'd married him to right a wrong. He'd made her life hell ever since.

Her first call was to Taylor, but she was almost glad when she didn't pick up. It would have been tough on her to keep a secret from Vinnie all day, so Bree didn't leave a message. They would have to figure out how they were going to handle it later on. Next, Lenny answered and met them in town with her own truck. Elsie agreed to come by after work with her new girlfriend to see what she could help with.

They started with the house, taking the things Gretchen wanted, and that went smoothly enough. The five of them sorted and packed clothing and other things Gretchen wanted. Then they carried boxes and furniture out to the trucks and trailer. She took the bed from their guest room and all of Aaron's things from his room so Barry couldn't destroy it all when he returned home.

The greenhouse, though, was a mess. Barry had taken a baseball bat to the windows, and there was glass everywhere—across the floor, in the plants, and in the compost bin. Plants were strewn about the place, dirt thrown down, and bags of various additives slit open with a knife.

Before they got started, Lenny insisted, "No, you have to have pictures of all this." She popped out her phone and began taking pictures left and right.

"I'll never get the glass out of all this," Gretchen lamented over her plants. They were her babies. Barry had even broken all the pots she had bought from Taylor and Bree to use for display and to sell. Still, she gamely collected those she could salvage and filled one of the truck beds. Worried that Barry would come home at any time, they headed back to Taylor and Bree's, closing the gate behind them.

Gretchen and her friends lined the side of the barn with the plants she was able to save, hanging and otherwise, so they could catch the rain when it fell off the roof. Even the dew would benefit some of the hothouse plants that had been damaged in Barry's rampage.

"Did he hurt you?" Elsie asked, her new girlfriend Jemma looking on in alarm. Jemma knew all these people from the First Nillionaires Club but had socialized relatively little with them. She knew they were important to Elsie, so she wanted to get along with them. By helping this relative stranger move out of an abusive relationship, she strangely hoped this would make them all closer.

"No, but his rage was something to behold," Gretchen said shakily as memories of the night before came back to her. She'd relived it all night long—the breaking of the glass, the impact of the baseball bat on her plants and her pots, the ripping open and throwing of the fertilizer and other things—as Barry ranted over her getting home late from the spring sale.

Her trailer was now hidden beyond the barn on the far side, the plants and pots inside of it yet untouched. But Gretchen knew she would have to start over.

It had taken so much to think about leaving Barry. He'd raged at her on Friday, thinking he'd ruin her weekend, forgetting about her packed truck and trailer, and then, shown up and counted her change box, using that lack of funds to continue his rage. An excuse to abuse her. When she got home from the show, she'd found where he'd taken the baseball bat to her greenhouse. She was certain he'd really enjoyed batting the hanging pots, smashing the ones about on the floor, and using his knife to open the bags. The fight he'd started had scared her, and she could see Aaron had gone and hid in his room.

The police had come out. A neighbor had made a complaint, so they had to at least show a response. The officers were Barry's friends, though, and they did nothing but ask Barry if everything was all right. He assured them with a friendly grin that everything was fine. Knowing she would get no help from them, Gretchen nodded agreement with everything Barry said. She didn't want him terrorizing Aaron any further; she just wanted him to calm down. She'd already decided at the show to leave him, and this was just icing on the cake. She would leave in the morning after he went to work.

After helping to unload the trucks and the trailer into the basement, Elsie asked "Can I call a friend of mine? He's a lawyer, a damn good one."

"I don't know ..." she began hesitantly.

"Do you want me to pick up Aaron at the junior high?" Bree asked helpfully. She glanced at the clock in the kitchen across from the family room, where they were all now sitting, sipping water or Kool-Aid.

"No, nooo. He won't understand, and I better be the one to pick him up." She, too, glanced at the clock, trying to determine how long it would take her to drive to the junior high. Aaron had been just been relieved to get away to the show with his mom, hoping that next week he could go visit a friend at least one night to avoid his father and his rages.

"Well, you consider this your home for as long as you want," Bree said generously, getting up, going to the desk, and handing Gretchen a key that read, 'Do Not Duplicate' on it, as well as a sensor for the gate that she could clip to her visor. "I don't want to leave things unlocked."

Gretchen understood because she knew about their issues with Taylor's sister, not to mention the random strangers driving on their property last year. Now, they could add Barry to that list. She got up to go get Aaron.

"Think she'll call that lawyer?" Lenny asked Elsie, glancing at Jemma to include her. It was always hard to bring an outsider into their group of friends because they were all so close. Some hadn't been able to understand.

Elsie shrugged. It was completely up to Gretchen, but they'd support her whatever decision she made.

* * * * *

When Taylor got home, she found Gretchen's truck in the driveway over by the barn and Bree in the kitchen with Gretchen, cooking dinner.

"Well, hello," she said, stopping to kiss her wife and including Gretchen on the hello. She peeked into the living room, where Aaron looked up at her from playing with the younger children. Nine-year-old Melanie might have a case of hero worship for the young boy, or perhaps he was her first crush. Taylor nodded and smiled to him before looking at her wife in puzzlement. She hadn't known they would be visiting.

"Didn't you get missed calls?" Bree asked, returning the kiss and trying to say so much with her eyes.

"No, we were on a property on the north side, and it had a dip between hills that I'm certain blocked any calls. Why, did something come up?" she asked, her own eyes trying to figure out what Bree was trying to convey. She looked to Gretchen for an answer, but Gretchen avoided eye contact.

"Gretchen and Aaron will be staying with us for a while," Bree said meaningfully.

This took Taylor aback, but she didn't show it on her face. She just nodded thoughtfully and said, "Cool. I'm going to go take my shower before I join you to help with dinner."

"Oh, we got it," Bree assured her. "Gretchen knows how to make a roux." She pointed at the white gravy they were slicing pieces of chicken into.

"Oh, that looks yummy!" Taylor assured her. "I'll hurry."

"We have at least half an hour for the pasta and other things."

Dinner was crowded around their kitchen table with eight instead of six, but they made it work with a couple of folding chairs. The children were clueless to the tension emanating from Gretchen. They were so excited to have visitors for the first time, they hadn't even questioned Bree when she told them the basement was off limits for now. Aaron had figured out he and his mom were staying for a while, especially after Gretchen showed him their things stacked up in the basement.

HOME ~ First Nillionaires Club

Aaron watched his mom. He could see she looked tired, but they were both relieved to be away from his father and out of their house. Dinner was pleasant, but there was still a tension. At least there wasn't going to be any explosions of temper.

After dinner, Taylor took a call from Vinnie. She didn't dare ignore a call from her boss and friend.

"What's going on?"

"What do you mean?" she asked, glancing at her wife and guest.

"I just got a banging on my front door from a very drunk Barry, looking for Gretchen. Do you know where she is? Apparently, she ransacked their house, broke ever window in the greenhouse and every pot, and left him."

"That's not exactly what happened," Taylor said tightly, her head gesturing to her wife and friend to pull them away from the children, who were watching some TV in the family room. Aaron looked up at the phone with a question on his face.

When the three adults had gone into the master bedroom and closed the door, Taylor put her phone on speaker. "Gretchen is staying with us," she informed her boss and their friend.

"She is? She's okay then?"

"I'm here Vinnie," Gretchen spoke up. "I've left Barry."

"Yeah? He was here. Drunk as a skunk and making up stories. Did you really take a baseball bat to your greenhouse?"

"No, and I'm disappointed that you would think I'd do that to my livelihood. You know how long I saved to buy that. He also destroyed every pot that he could find around the gardens and in the greenhouse."

"Sorry, I didn't know what happened, but he thought, for some reason, that you'd be here at my place. How'd he even know where I lived?"

Vinnie had built her home a few years before to house her and store her equipment for her lawn care and landscaping business. She had added a mother-in-law home on the property for her own mother, with an extra bedroom for her companion that took care of her, now that she was getting up there in years. A large barn on the property held her lawn care equipment to keep it out of the elements, store it out of season, and to do repairs when needed.

"It's not like your business isn't known around the area," Gretchen pointed out.

Vinnie, realizing she was on speaker asked carefully, "Does he *know*?"

Gretchen nodded, glancing at her two anxious friends before answering. "Yes."

"How does he know?"

"I told him years ago. I thought it would make us closer."

"Did it?"

She shook her head as she answered, "No."

Vinnie didn't know what to say.

"Did you let him drive that way?"

Vinnie winced at the tone of worry she heard in her friend's voice; the guy certainly didn't deserve her loyalty. "I tried to stop him, and, when he went to his car, I called the police. I saw flashing lights down the road, so maybe they stopped him." She waited a count of five to hear a response and then, "Do you want me to come over?"

"No, that's not a good idea," she said tightly, feeling conflicted.

Both Bree and Taylor exchanged looks, and Taylor walked over to the darkened patio doors. She couldn't see far into the back yard, but she could look across into the family room, where the children were watching TV.

"Well, if you need anything, give me a call," Vinnie said, her own voice sounding a little tight.

"I'll do that," Gretchen said, emotion starting to fill her voice. She could tell Vinnie wanted to get off the phone and quickly added, "Vinnie, thank you."

"Anytime," she returned and meant it. She disconnected the phone.

"You okay?" Bree asked, concerned. She knew there were a lot of unresolved emotions between those two.

Gretchen looked up with a rueful expression and shrugged. "I think that it's time Aaron and I went to bed."

"We have to get the children down, too," Taylor said. It was a little early, but everyone needed something to do. Having guests screwed up their routine.

The kids protested, of course, but their moms cajoled them into brushing their teeth and going to bed early by promising two stories instead of one. The girls came into the boys' room to hear the first one, and Jack was out before they even finished the first story. Bryan was close to falling asleep, so they started the second one, the moms trading off reading until he fell off. Conspiratorially, they all snuck out to the girls' room and piled into some big, comfy chairs Bree had picked up. Both girls were yawning and stared at the lava lamp while Bree's voice filled the room as she read. By the time she finished a second story, this one about dragons, they were both soundly asleep. She carefully got up, putting the book on the comfortable chair, and they slipped out of the room.

"That was nice," Taylor admitted, her head bobbing back to where they had read to the children. She let Staffy out, and he immediately went to

the edge of the backyard, watching something. He huffed and puffed but did not bark. He left whatever is was and used his bathroom corner before toddling back to the door. "Remind me to clean up Staffy's corner this weekend," Taylor said to her wife as she locked the patio door behind him.

"I gave Gretchen a key and one of the sensors," Bree told her, changing into her pajamas.

"Good idea. I hope that asshole doesn't come here."

"Taylor ..."

"What? He is an asshole. Always has been. He doesn't like a lesbian jerk circle, as he called it," she reminded her.

"He just didn't like finding out about Vinnie. Why Gretchen ever told him, I don't understand."

They both checked the front door, accompanied by Staffy, who watched them make the doors fast, unlocking and relocking them. The side door was never opened, but Bree checked anyway because the children didn't always ask permission. She liked that Taylor still backed her work truck into the garage, something she'd started so she could plow right out the garage door, if needed.

"We should think of getting rid of the Jeep," she mentioned to her wife in a whisper as Taylor checked the patio door to the family room.

"What? Get rid of my Jeep?" she protested, but she understood. She had her work truck, and they needed money to buy a trailer or another truck.

Bree checked the back door to the laundry room. Taylor had installed a chain latch, high up where children's fingers couldn't reach without a ladder, and it was always kept latched so they would know the children hadn't gone through the door. But it didn't mean they didn't try.

"Have you found anything that we can use?" Taylor asked as they got into bed. It was Bree who found the furniture and anything else second hand that they were slowly accumulating.

"No vehicle, but I did save a dining room table I liked." At her wife's look she added, "Saved it—didn't inbox them about it."

"What's it look like?"

Bree described it, and it sounded perfect for the dining room. They'd been using card tables and really needed a nice table in there.

"Does it have chairs?"

"No, which is why I think it's a bargain."

They discussed it a while as they snuggled in to sleep.

CHAPTER THIRTY-SEVEN

Some of the things Gretchen brought from her destroyed business were buckets of seedlings she had purchased for her friends. She showed them to Bree the next day.

"Oh, this will be fun to plant around the place," Bree said in her chirpy voice, looking out from the barn at the dismal rain coming down. "I guess I better tell the neighbor that we won't let him cut hay anymore."

"Won't let him cut hay?"

"Yeah, Taylor and I wanted to plant trees, not only around the pond," she gestured towards where they were watching the plops of rain on the water filling the pond, "but on the field where that guy cuts the hay." She pointed down the track through the woods.

"Well, you might also want to put netting around some of these fingerlings so the rabbits don't eat them."

"Oh, that's a good idea."

They discussed the planting as Bree got back to work firing up the kiln for her pots. They also discussed what Gretchen was going to do about Barry. She had an appointment with Elsie's friend who happened to be a lawyer.

Gretchen left for her appointment, and Vinnie arrived ten minutes later, looking for her.

"You just missed her," Bree said around the mound of clay she was putting into her molds. "She went to see that friend of Elsie's who's a lawyer. She had an appointment."

"Shit." Vinnie stared off into space, wondering what she should do.

"I don't think she wants to see you yet," Bree said carefully.

"I know that, but …" she began, and then her shoulders slumped. "It's not about her and I. The police came out again, looking for her. They hoped I'd know where she was, at least. They wanted to talk to her." She put her hand up to stop Bree from interrupting. "No, I didn't tell them where she was. You think I want those dingleberries, friends of Barry's, to know where she is hiding?" She waited for Bree to nod. They all knew the system had been skewed in his favor. He was friends with the right people, so when he made her life a living hell, he'd gotten away with the abuse. "No, I finally got them to tell me why they wanted to talk to her. Barry was in an accident early this morning, apparently looking for her." She could see Bree listening avidly. "He didn't make it."

Bree's eyes rounded as she realized the statement her friend had just made. "He's dead?!"

Vinnie nodded and turned around. One of her company trucks was pulling into the driveway, and she watched it slow and back into the garage. It was Taylor, and she gave her a quick wave.

Startled, Taylor waved back at her boss, parked, and ducked through the garage door before it shut.

"What's going on?" she asked, jogging through the rain into the barn. "Something up? I couldn't work because of the rain," she quickly added.

"Yeah, I kinda figured." Vinnie sighed and checked with Bree, who nodded. "Barry's dead."

"What?!" Taylor asked, glancing at her wife, who nodded again. "How?"

"He was out this morning, looking for where Gretchen was hiding. I'll bet that son of a bitch checked out everyone's house that ever knew her. Strangely, they said he wasn't drunk, so it must have worn off from when he came by my house and they stopped him."

"So it was him they stopped?"

She nodded. "They probably let him go, too—you know how tight he was with his friends."

The three of them agreed and were silent for a moment, thinking about the impact Barry's death would have on Gretchen.

"Do you think she'd answer her cell?" Vinnie asked, knowing she should be the one to tell her.

"She doesn't have her cell," Bree spoke up. "She left it in the house so he couldn't trace her."

Gretchen knew Barry had enlisted his friends to track before. It was why she had come here; she didn't think Barry knew where their new home was yet.

"Then, I should wait for her to return," she said sadly. She knew Gretchen had loved the guy at one point. Hell, she'd had a kid with the bastard.

"We could tell her," Taylor offered lamely, clearly uncomfortable with the idea.

"Should we call Elsie? She could call her lawyer friend," Bree asked.

"I got this. I'll just wait to tell her in person," Vinnie asserted, her sense of guilt coming through in her voice.

"You do realize that Barry did this to himself?" Taylor asked.

Vinnie looked distinctly uncomfortable. "I know, but I …"

"Never stopped loving her," Bree finished, coming forward and wiping her hands on a rag.

Vinnie looked up, startled, almost as though her friend had found out a secret. "You knew?"

"We *ALL* knew," Taylor assured her.

"Does Gretchen?"

"I don't know," Taylor admitted. "She's fooled herself for years that her marriage was worth saving. The only good thing that came out of that marriage was Aaron. I just hope he isn't damaged."

"He seems like a good kid," Bree added, finishing up her hand cleaning. "It isn't up to you to tell her," she said, turning back to Vinnie who looked gut-punched.

"Yeah, but I don't want those friends of his to tell her. You know what hell they gave her when she tried to report Barry for his abuse."

Taylor frowned. "Isn't your house out beyond their jurisdiction?"

Vinnie chuckled sardonically. "Yeah, and they didn't like that I told them that, either. The sheriff was the one who pulled Barry over, but I'll bet he dropped some names to get out of it."

"I'm not too impressed with the sheriff's office, either," Bree commented. "He told us we had to turn over any video he asked for."

"Whaaat?"

"Oh. yeah," Taylor agreed. "Threatened us."

"What the hell …?"

"We won't be voting for him next election, I tell you," Bree added, and Taylor nodded in agreement.

"What is going on with our law enforcement?"

"The cops were nice to us when they came out, but I didn't know that the sheriff runs things out here," Bree continued.

"No, you're on Restlawn Highway. That's part of the police's area of patrol," Vinnie told her. "I needed to know that when I built so I knew where to go to get permits. Didn't you say your permits were from the town, not the county?"

"Yeah?" Taylor asked, clearly puzzled.

"Then you're with the town and the police. If it was county, it would be the sheriff's office."

"That bastard scared me," Bree put in, remembering his intimidation tactics.

"Probably because that Longuard was involved. Did you hear anything on that?"

"The feds got involved. So, no, we didn't hear another word. We should sue him civilly to get the price of our mailbox replaced," Taylor put in.

"Actually, I put in for four of them when I filed my paperwork," Bree stated with a little grin. "We'll probably hear from that in three to five years," she added drolly.

"Good for you," Vinnie answered.

"Hey, do you think we should tell anyone else so they can be here for Gretchen?" Taylor asked.

"Who else?"

"Elsie? Lenny?" she named the remaining members of the First Nillionaires Club.

"Maybe we could tell them afterwards. I don't think Gretchen would want everyone knowing before she did that her husband is dead."

"She's going to feel guilty," Bree said astutely.

"Guilty? For what?" Taylor asked incredulously.

"Because she didn't love him anymore. He treated her so badly, and I'll bet she wished he was dead more than once. She's going to feel guilty about that."

Her wife and friend stared at her and realized Bree was probably correct in her assumption.

They were standing in the family room, having abandoned standing in the barn, closing it up against the rain which was coming down harder. They were looking out over the deck, watching the metal grill get rained on, the drops of water splashing up off the metal, and discussing things Taylor wanted to build or learn to build.

"After that UFO you built there, I'm sure you can make anything," Vinnie teased. She was still amused by the chicken coop and its accoutrements.

"Well, we already have the grill; we don't really *need* another one," Taylor pointed out. I'd really like one of those grills that you see in public parks with bricks and the chimney."

"Yeah, but you could put in a pizza oven in that," Vinnie added with a grin. She was drinking cherry Kool-Aid, and it was making her lips very red. "And, if you build that kind of oven or grill, you won't need a burning pit." That had been another idea from Taylor.

"Before you build any of those things, we have to get the rest of the fencing up in the front of the property. Grass and weeds are growing through the grating," Bree reminded them.

"If it would stop raining, I'd say let's go dig the holes," Taylor shot back.

"You spent days on the pond and then weeks on the UFO. We've procrastinated on the fencing due to the weather, too. It's not a sexy project anymore. No more excuses," Bree said in mock command.

"I know, but the UFO does look cool," she said, pointing at it.

"It does look cool," Vinnie agreed.

They heard the kids making noise on the front lawn, and, soon, they burst through the front door. "Mom, Mom, Mom!"

Bree caught them before they were more than a few steps in, knowing they'd soak the entire house if she wasn't quick about it. "Take off your outer wear that's wet," she called, heading for the voices. "Carry it into the laundry room so it can be hung up to dry. No, don't leave it there! Do not walk on the living room carpet!"

Vinnie exchanged a grin with Taylor, who moved to go help her wife corral the exuberant youngsters.

"Mom!" they said in surprise at seeing her home so early.

Taylor helped Bree get jackets and pants hung up, boots turned over the register so they could dry off, and kids dressed in other clothes so they could play.

"Hiya, Aunt Vinnie," more than one voice greeted her when they saw her. Vinnie left the family room, still wondering where Gretchen would be. It had been hours.

"She's probably waiting for Aaron at the Junior High for him to get out of classes," Taylor mentioned.

"Yeah, she probably got out with the lawyer and whatever he had to say and went right to the school."

They found they were both right, and they stood in the living room, waiting and chatting while the children played in the family room.

"Gawd, I'm nervous," Vinnie admitted, pacing. Waiting for hours had made her jittery, despite talking about everything under the sun—except Barry's untimely death. The house was far enough back from the highway they couldn't hear any cars, but every set of lights she saw on the crossroad made her stomach jump until they turned either left or right onto the highway instead of continuing on to Taylor and Bree's driveway. She could only imagine what it had been like before they put the gate up. The rain still hadn't let up. The weather was dark and gloomy, lending itself to her mood.

"You don't have to stay," Taylor pointed out. At Vinnie's outraged look she hastily added, "I just meant, we *could* tell her."

"No, I feel like I owe her this."

"You don't owe her anything," Bree said delicately, trying to soften the words. "That was over long ago."

"Maybe for her," she admitted, seeing another car pull up to the highway and willing it to be Gretchen's. This one did cross over and begin the trip up the long drive. "That's her," she said fervently hoping it really was. They all turned to look, and it was.

Gretchen saw the landscaping truck by the barn but figured it was Taylor's. After all, the one Vinnie drove was almost identical. She didn't see the three adults stepping back from the front window, where they had been watching for her.

"Don't forget your school bag," she warned Aaron. "And, don't tease those kids so much!"

Aaron grinned. He enjoyed playing with the smaller kids. He didn't have to act his age, and there was no one yelling at him or his mom. He lost his smile slightly, wondering how long they would be here before they had to go back home. Grabbing his bag, he ran with his mom to the front porch. "Man, that rain is coming down."

"It sure is. I thought my windshield wipers were going to come off at one …" her voice left off as she went to open the front door, but Bree was standing there holding it for them. Beyond Bree, Taylor and Vinnie were standing there, both looking serious. "Hey, guys. What's going on?" she asked cautiously.

"Hey, Aaron," Bree said brightly. "Would you like an after-school snack? We have Kool-Aid," she said enticingly, putting her arm around the young man.

Aaron looked at his mother, who indicated with her chin that he should go with her. He turned and followed Bree into the kitchen.

"What's going on?" Gretchen asked.

Vinnie swallowed and spoke up. "It's Barry. He's dead."

Taylor grimaced at Vinnie. She hadn't needed to be so blunt. She turned back to see that Gretchen was about to faint. She was too slow, but Vinnie expertly scooped the woman up in her arms and gently lowered her to the carpet in the living room instead of the hard stone of the entranceway.

"Hey, there," Vinnie crooned. "Hey, there."

Gretchen's eyes fluttered, and she looked up into Vinnie's deep blue-brown eyes. She reached up slightly to caress Vinnie's jawline, but then, appreciating where she was and what she thought Vinnie had said, she stopped herself. "Wh-what?"

"Do you recall what I said?"

Gretchen thought for a second and then nodded. Once she realized where she was—on the floor in Bree and Taylor's house and in Vinnie's arms—she gently pushed Vinnie away and tried to get up.

"Easy there, easy," Vinnie cautioned, unwilling to let her go.

Taylor stepped forward and attempted to help her up. "Slowly."

Gretchen stood, blinking as Taylor held her arm. "Did you just say Barry is dead?"

Vinnie stood and nodded at Gretchen cautiously, waiting to see how she'd react.

Gretchen looked down and then around, pulling her elbow from Taylor's grip. "How?"

"He got in a car accident." Vinnie stood waiting, for what she wasn't certain. Perhaps to catch Gretchen if she fainted again.

Gretchen refused to look at Vinnie. She eyed every corner of the room as though she were looking for something she had lost. "When?!" she barked.

"This morning," Vinnie answered warily, wondering what Gretchen was thinking.

"How do you know?" She turned her back, gulping hard to keep from crying, and so she could look at the nearly empty room of her friends.

"Barry came by my house earlier—drunk, of course—and I called the sheriff. I saw flashing lights after he left. They must have let him go because he didn't get in the accident until later. The police stopped by, looking for you."

"But why you?"

Vinnie was getting tired of talking to Gretchen's back, which was now starting to hunch over as if she were waiting for a blow. Maybe Gretchen was crying? She exchanged looks with Taylor. "I think because I was his last known contact point?" She shrugged at Taylor, who was looking at Gretchen in concern.

Gretchen nodded and walked aimlessly through the empty L-shaped room before going into the kitchen and taking a seat at the table.

"Wha ...?" Vinnie said to Taylor, who shrugged, as they watched Gretchen walk out of sight. "Well ... I better be going. Call me on my cell if you need anything."

"Don't go," Taylor hissed, but Vinnie was already reaching for the door.

"No, I got to go. I have things to do," she said, going out the door and contemplating the rain coming down for only a moment before she ran out into it and to her truck. She was drenched almost immediately.

Taylor grabbed the door and shut it tightly behind Vinnie. She watched Vinnie get drenched before she made it to her truck, get in, and drive away. Taylor wiped away her own tears, certain that Vinnie was crying, too.

CHAPTER THIRTY-EIGHT

Gretchen wasn't certain what to do. Sitting down, she asked Bree if she could have some Kool-Aid, too. She knew the two moms didn't have a lot, and it was probably straining their finances to have guests. She'd have to remember to go buy some groceries to help out and contribute. She could put that on her charge card until ... then she realized she didn't have to wait to ask Barry to help her pay the card. She wouldn't have to ask him anything ever again. She glanced at Aaron, realizing she would have to tell their son. But she couldn't tell him. She didn't know anything. She'd just heard the information second hand from Vinnie. Vinnie ...

Gretchen got back up and headed for the basement, forgetting the Kool-Aid Bree had just poured her. Bree stared at her as she left the kitchen so abruptly and headed down the steps, closing the basement door behind her.

"What's with my mom?" Aaron asked around the celery stick with peanut butter he was munching on.

"I don't know," Bree admitted, knowing she wasn't the one who should tell the young man.

* * * * *

Gretchen called the police to ask what had happened to her husband. She was transferred to the sheriff's office since they were the ones who were handling this, and she was left on hold and given the runaround until she finally blew up. She stood by the large basement windows so that her cell phone would work, looking out.

"Look, a friend just told me that the police came by and were looking for me," she tried explaining, but the sheriff's office wouldn't tell her anything. She hung up and called the police back. After more runaround, she finally got someone to talk to her. First, he had to verify who she was and why she was calling. After telling her story for the third time, she was getting sick of this. "Look, could you please just tell me what happened to my husband Barry?" Finally, someone told her, and she nearly fainted again as he explained the situation as tactfully as he could over the phone. She eventually thanked him, told him she would arrange for a funeral home to pick up the body, and hung up. She sat there for half an hour before she heard Bree calling everyone to dinner. She didn't want dinner, and she didn't want to be around people.

Opening the basement door, Bree called down, "Gretchen? Dinner is on the table."

"No, thank you," she called back and waited to hear the door close. It didn't. Instead, Bree came down the steps. She looked at her friend and shrugged, shaking her phone to show she'd used it. "It's true. He's dead," she said in a monotone. "I guess I could go home now," she said sadly, looking around at her things.

"No, you'll stay here until you're steady on your feet. That house is no place to be right now, with the reminder of what he put you through," Bree said forcefully, coming to sit on the edge of the bed Gretchen had moved into their basement. "We'll help you," she added, putting her arm around her friend's shoulder.

"I can't tell you how much I appreciate you both. You're right. I don't want to go back to that house. I can't even cry for him," she said, sad at not feeling sad. "I wished him dead so many times."

Bree didn't know what to say to that, having said it earlier, but she patted her friend on the shoulder to comfort her, feeling inadequate. "Well, Aaron is asking questions. You'll have to tell him, eventually. Think about what you want to say to him. I can bring you a plate?"

Gretchen shook her head. She wasn't hungry. She didn't want to tell Aaron, but she really had no choice. "Send Aaron down after dinner. That boy needs his food," she said with a wry smile. "I'll tell him then."

Bree nodded, patted her shoulder one more time and got up. "If you need anything …"

"Thank you," she said without looking up. Instead, she stared out the darkening window at the rain.

* * * * *

The next day, Bree went with Gretchen to pick out a suit for Barry to be buried in. It also gave them an opportunity for Gretchen to go through Barry's papers and find the life insurance policy.

"That bastard didn't even have the decency to buy a bigger policy so we'd be taken care of," Gretchen bitched when she found the paperwork. They'd had to break open a strong box where he kept his important papers.

"What about the house? Anything else?" Bree asked. She'd had to think about all these things when they bought their own house. They'd both taken out larger policies because of the children, but the house would be paid off in the event of one of their deaths. It had been a hard thought to have, but a decision they both agreed upon. Neither could have afforded the debts on their own.

"Cripes, it looks like he took out a second loan!" she said, reading through the papers. "I don't know how I'll pay for it all."

"Then, sell it," Bree said practically. "If you can't afford it, get rid of it. All there are bad memories here. You can start over, and you have your seed stock."

"Where? Where am I going to be able to afford to start over? If I leave here, I won't have my greenhouse, and he didn't leave me anything. I don't have anything more than the little I made last weekend—and he took that too!"

"He couldn't have spent it already. Maybe it's with his ... body?"

"You don't know him very well, do you? Of course, he spent it already, probably making all his friends happy at the local pub. Why do you think the cops were friendly with him? He bought them all drinks. Mr. Big Shot!"

Bree wondered at that. "Is it possible he had anything through his work?"

"I don't know. I just don't know," she said wearily. She was defeated.

"Well, you're welcome to stay with us until you get this mess straightened out and make some decisions."

"Does it make me a bad wife if I don't throw him a funeral?"

"No, I think it would make you an honest person, after the way he treated you and your kid."

"Oh, cripes. I want to cry and not for him. The bastard!"

Bree understood. She'd been angry at the guy for as long as she had known him. She couldn't imagine living with him, too.

"Okay. I'm not going to let this get me down. How much could a funeral cost? Burial?"

When they got to the funeral parlor, they found that the cheapest plan was well beyond Gretchen's means. Hoping to find money to pay for the funeral, Barry's wallet and personal effects were at the police station, where she could go pick them up, and his car was at the police impound lot.

"Oh, gawd. I don't know if I can do that," Gretchen confided in Bree as they left the funeral parlor and headed for the police station.

"I'll go through it. You stay in the car," she indicated her minivan, "and I'll go through it."

The police stared at Gretchen from the moment she walked into the station and identified herself until the moment she left. She guessed they were all wondering what kind of wife she had been to their friend. After all, she hadn't even been at home when he was in a fatal crash, nor had she answered her phone all the next day. They insisted she show her state identification and then reluctantly handed over his wallet and other personal effects, including his wedding ring. She stared at the ring as the officer had her sign some forms. She hadn't seen Barry wear the ring in years, and she wondered why it was even with him.

"Thank you," she said quietly and retreated back to the minivan, away from their rude stares.

She gave Bree directions to the police impound lot, and Bree drove them over.

Bree grabbed a box out of the minivan and headed for Barry's car. The front of the car was sliced into a V shape from its impact with a tree. She wondered if he had been drunk again, but they had been told he didn't have a registerable blood level for alcohol. That had to be a lie; he'd been drunk the night before and there was no way it could have worn off by the time of the accident. She emptied items from the glove box into the box she had brought. When she saw blood on the steering wheel, she nearly threw up but took a deep breath and continued. There was another compartment in the center console, and she opened it to find a checkbook and other miscellaneous things, which she also threw into the box. There was a briefcase in the back seat, and that went into the box, end first. She checked the doors and above the visors but found nothing there. She reached under the seats in case anything had slid under them and found nothing. She opened the trunk and found a gym bag, and, finally, she was done. There was nothing more to gather, and the car was clean.

She took the box and gym bag back to her minivan and showed them to Gretchen. "This is all I found."

Gretchen looked at the few things and nodded. She'd had a lot of time to think while Bree was going over the car, and she'd called the funeral home to cancel them picking up the body, as well as any funeral service. She told them she'd changed her mind.

"Did you want to go anywhere else?"

"No, let's get back to your place. I don't like leaving Aaron alone all this time." They'd left him at Bree and Taylor's house because she couldn't feel good about making him go to school today. He'd cried a bit when she told him the news last night, and then he said he felt guilty because he felt more relieved than sad. She listened for as long as he wanted to talk, then explained to him how she felt the same way and that he had a right to his own feelings. Barry hadn't been a very nice man.

"But he was my father," the boy protested.

"And he was my husband," she contended. "But he wasn't a very good husband. Do you think he was a very good father?"

The boy shook his head and started crying. Not for the loss of his father but for what his father hadn't given him.

* * * * *

"People are talking around town," Gretchen told Bree. She'd been trying to run her business, despite the controversy and having no a place to work from. She made deliveries of plants people wanted, but she couldn't offer them a viewing because she hadn't gone back to the house. Vinnie, Lenny, Elsie, and Taylor had cleaned up the broken pots and glass, throwing it all out in the garbage and putting the bins out on garbage day. Vinnie had hired someone to clean the house, but there were still personal items in it. Gretchen was putting it up for sale as soon as she could.

"People are going to talk," Bree said as she arranged pots on a tray for the oven. She knew they were talking, too; she'd heard that Barry's friends were shocked when she didn't pick up the body from the morgue. The police had gone out to Vinnie's again, asking where they could reach the widow. Vinnie told them they were outside their jurisdiction, again, and to get the hell off her property.

Gretchen told them, in no uncertain terms, she couldn't afford to bury Barry and they should bury him in a pauper's grave. She'd gotten the death certificate before they found out that little tidbit, and she sent it to Barry's creditors, as well as to the life insurance company. She hoped she could collect on the tiny policy he had, but she wasn't holding her breath.

She'd gone to the bank and taken what money they had in their joint accounts and put it in hers to pay bills. Getting the house up for sale was her next step.

"I can't run a business out of your place," she protested. All she had for her business now was the stock she stored in her trailer and truck. Bree was very encouraging, and, when Taylor came home, she helped or made suggestions, too.

"Well, we can't put in a very large hothouse here with all the trees, but someday …" Taylor said speculatively.

"We could move mine over here, and you could put the windows in," Gretchen suggested.

"We couldn't take that from you," Bree protested.

"What if we put it up next to the barn, where we are trying to grow our sad, sad garden?" Taylor asked.

"Hey, I'm trying to grow vegetables there," Bree protested, but she knew her wife was right. The garden was sad. In her enthusiasm, she'd planted some of the seeds too early, and they'd frozen out. Others had burned in the black, rich soil.

"C'mon, I'll show you how to make a good garden," Gretchen offered generously, so eager to make herself feel useful as she waited for the insurance companies to respond to her various inquiries and claims. From life insurance to the household insurance to the car insurance—it was going to take a long time before she could put her house on the market. Fortunately, she had friends helping her through this terrible time.

K'ANNE MEINEL

CHAPTER THIRTY-NINE

"The First Nillionaires Club meeting of this year will come to order!" Bree called from the deck as her friends gathered around.

Today she'd invited everyone for their Easter celebration, and they had agreed to help her and Taylor with building a dam for the swamp. The kids had already had their Easter egg hunt, and all the adults enjoyed watching it. Aaron had participated, even though he felt he was too old, but being included in the family meant a lot to the boy. He'd been having mixed feelings since his father's death, and he and Gretchen had both started therapy. The extended lesbian family that was his mother's friends helped by just being there for them, including them, and treating them as a family should. He wasn't clueless, and he could see his mother had extra affection for Vinnie. He wondered how far that relationship had gone. He thought Vinnie was really cool, but he couldn't help remembering all the disparaging things his father had said about her over the years.

Rock and broken pottery had been hauled out to where the dam was being put in, where extra rain and overflowing springs had raised the level of the pond considerably. Taylor and Bree were kind of in a rush to get the dam in place before it got any higher.

"I'm so glad we found a use for all the damage," Gretchen stated, pulling out the sacks of pottery Barry had broken with a baseball bat.

Cleaning it up hadn't thrilled her, but her friends had generously offered to help, and she took them up on that.

"Let's hear it for the rocks that Vinnie contributed," Lenny teased, grinning at her latest girlfriend, Audrey. The woman hadn't known what she was getting into when she agreed to help build a dam, but she'd dressed in her oldest jeans and a sweatshirt and was willing to get her hands dirty.

"Anyone know how to build a dam?" Elsie asked reasonably.

"No idea," several voices rang out.

"I do, I do," Jeff said, walking up behind Vinnie's truck. He flashed a big a grin at all the ladies.

"Who invited a man?" Elsie's girlfriend Jemma asked in a hiss.

"I did," Bree admitted. She shrugged. "I figured it would cost a few hamburgers for his advice."

Taylor grinned at her wife. Free labor was free labor. It might cost them some food, but the guy had helped create the pond. If he knew how to build a dam, so much the better.

"Who's going in the pond to lay these?" Jeff asked, indicating the pavers Vinnie had recycled.

"Why do they have to go in the pond?" Taylor asked, looking at the spring-fed and rain-filled water that was quite dark from the black dirt underneath it.

"We need these," he indicated the pavers, "to go there," he pointed, "so that the water doesn't undermine the dam you are going to build."

"I thought we were just going to dig and cause a spillway," Elsie put in, holding her shovel expectantly.

"If we do that the water will erode the sides of their pond," he explained.

Taylor agreed to go in, keeping on her old sports shoes so she could walk in the cold water and not hit any sticks or anything else. She did sink a bit into the black muck, but they handed her the pavers one by one and she placed them where Jeff directed her to. He got in the water to help her while others brought them more pavers and stones. The rocks they had collected from the beach were too small for this part of the project, and Vinnie had access to larger stones that they were also using to build up on the muck. Once the stones were stacked above the waterline, Jeff had them mixing cement and using everything left over to fortify the dam—the last of the pavers, the other stones, and even the broken pottery, artistically placed on the exposed edge of the cement.

"You can start digging there," he indicated the middle line of what they had already created.

Back at Jeff's truck, he showed them a drain he'd brought that had two levels to control how much water was in the pond. The drain had a long rectangle shape and was rather clever in its design. After he backed up to the drainage area, it took several of them to lift it from the truck bed and put it in place.

"It's too short," Lenny pointed out when they laid it on top of the dirt.

"Well, I could only get the one, but we can put concrete in at the end and smooth that out ourselves," Jeff offered.

Between all the women, they dug down with their shovels, removing the dirt from the passage that would become the dam.

"You can put the bigger pavers over there." He indicated how they would go over the drain, which was about eighteen inches wide. "Then, you can still drive your tractor or lawnmower over the dam."

It took a lot of joking and hard work for the women to dig out the channel, put in the drain, and set it with concrete.

"I don't want the water to go around the drain," Jeff explained, showing how to prevent overflow with the cement as he sealed the drain with it.

"What is that?" Bree asked, watching Taylor scratching at her leg.

"I don't know." She looked down and squealed like a girl, seeing the blob attached to her skin. "What is that?!" She kicked her leg out, but it didn't come off.

"That's just a blood sucker," Jeff said cheerfully, laughing at her reaction. "No, no, don't pull it. Someone get some salt."

Children were dispatched to run back to the house to get salt.

"What's going on?" Ellen asked, coming out with the children carrying a salt shaker. She'd been invited to the Easter festivities, but Tia had not. She'd been surprised to find Gretchen living there with her daughter and her wife.

"I've got leeches, Mom," Taylor stated, trying not to get skeeved out. It was really unsettling to find more of them. The salt had them peeling back and falling off her legs and onto the ground. Everyone had a good look at them, the children especially captivated. Taking off her wet shoes, Taylor found a couple more.

"It's the black muck," Jeff pointed out, using some salt himself to get a couple off. "Glad we don't have to go in that again. I wouldn't swim over here," he warned.

"Eew. I'm never swimming in that," Melanie put in, seeing the leech peel itself from her mom's skin once the salt was sprinkled on it.

"Me, either," Barbie put in.

The boys seemed unduly spellbound by the leeches.

"They make good bait," Jeff mentioned, and a couple of the woman laughed.

"There won't be leeches over by the sandy beach," Vinnie added and got back to work pressing the broken pottery pieces into the exposed cement. The combination of the pottery and the large stones she'd acquired looked marvelous.

"This will look great when moss or vines grow over it," Gretchen pointed out.

"I think I deserve extra tomatoes on my hamburgers," Jeff proclaimed later after they had finished. He was explaining the rest of the process. "The dam won't be tested for a while. The water level will need to get higher, but that is good because it will have time to set. There is no rain in the forecast for a few days. The concrete will dry thoroughly, and the dam will work for you when the time comes."

"We appreciate your expertise," Bree told him, giving him the extra tomatoes and a couple of extra slices of bacon for his burger. "Can I get you some fruit for a side?"

"I can get that," he told her, blushing. "You don't have to wait on me." He'd enjoyed helping Vinnie's friends. This was a great group of women, and he speculated that Vinnie was in love with the one named Gretchen. He wished he had thought to invite his wife because she would have enjoyed it.

"What's your next project?" Elsie asked Taylor.

Taylor told her of the combination pizza oven, burning pit, and barbeque she was planning in the backyard.

"When are you going to go get chickens?" Lenny asked, pointing at the UFO sitting prominently in the chicken run to the side.

"We wanted to wait until after Easter for those who will be giving up their cute little chicks to the pound," Taylor explained, using her spatula to point towards the chicken coop from where she was cooking on their barbeque.

"Before you build another thing," Bree warned with a finger shaking at her wife, "we have to get up the last of those fences!"

"I noticed the grass and brush are hiding them rather well," Vinnie put in with a grin before she took a sip of the soda. She had found the recyclable pavers a while back and the additional rocks they needed when doing a cleanup of another farmer's field. They would have a lot of stones for making pillars when Taylor and Bree got around to finishing their fence along the highway.

"Don't you start," Bree warned, shaking her finger at her friend.

Ellen enjoyed the group of friends her daughter had made; they made her feel welcome. She told herself she didn't know why Tia couldn't be included, but, deep down, she knew. Tia always wanted to be the center of attention, and a group of women like this didn't suffer fools like her younger daughter gladly. Then, there was her son-in-law and his foolishness. The couple simply wouldn't fit in, and their presence would make for a tense time. Ellen was enjoying herself far too much to let thoughts of Tia ruin her day with her older daughter, her wife, and her grandchildren, as well as their friends.

CHAPTER FORTY

Every night of the following week, Taylor rushed home from work to join her wife and Gretchen in getting projects done around the property. Gretchen, who they were jokingly referring to as their sister wife, and Bree had threatened to do the work with or without her.

"Wait for me," Taylor had pleaded, but it fell on deaf ears. Her wife and sister wife were going to get the job done since she had to work. Working from home meant Bree could set a batch of pots in the ovens and get the tractor warmed up, and the two of them set off for the highway that curved in front of their property.

They'd managed to get one of the fence panels in, yanking it from the grass and brush growing all around and through it. Using the tractor, they set it upright, banged the old concrete from the posts, and dug new holes. They mixed new concrete and set them upright and in place. Since they didn't need another gate, they could go from one panel to the next without worrying about spacing.

"The deer and other wildlife aren't going to like this," Gretchen pointed out as Bree lifted the fence into place with the front-end loader and straps.

Now that the culvert had drained, they could line out the fence properly. Only occasionally did their holes fill with water from the culvert or their swamp. The lines for power, phone, and cable were clearly marked, thanks to Bree's phone calls. The different colored flags indicated where they could not dig, and they were well away from those cables.

Even though their time was limited, Taylor still put in a lot of effort after her work for Vinnie was done for the day. The three of them got several panels done per day. When they finally installed the gate on the far side, where it had lain to prevent hunters from entering their land, it was a satisfying endeavor. It stood there solid—closed, locked, and chained with a big NO TRESPASSING sign posted in the middle.

"Should we keep going? We still have a few of these." Bree indicated some fence panels leaning against the barn. She was considering setting them up along the driveway bordering the neighbor's field. She looked to Taylor for input.

"I think we should to indicate your property line," Gretchen put in, pointing to where the pink flags were still visible, at least the ones that hadn't been stolen, knocked down, or pulled up yet.

"I need to tell that neighbor, damn it." Bree pointed to the new housing development on the land Eric Norman had sold. The McMansions behind them were still going up, but this new subdivision with smaller family homes was developing rapidly. The couple of houses they put up last year as showcase homes had sold well, apparently. Since then, several basements had been built, and construction workers were hard at work from seven a.m. until at least five p.m. daily, sometimes later.

"Tell him what?" Gretchen asked, holding the level against the post to make sure it went in straight. With the aid of the tractor holding it in a sling, the weight wasn't a problem. Bree had mixed the cement and was pouring it around the post. Taylor held the other end of the fence steady so it wouldn't move.

"That we are going to plant those trees in the field." She pointed her chin to where their next project would take place. They'd planted some of the trees around the pond in random spots, but they still had buckets of the fingerlings and a few that were at least a foot in height to plant. Bree had stated the bigger ones would go along the fence line at least five feet back so they knew where their property ended.

"There is no way anyone is going to respect our property line," Taylor mentioned. She'd had to point out to a couple of the McMansion people that the woods were not for public consumption because they were stealing wood from behind their house. She was glad they had put the house where they had because it was far enough away from these people they couldn't hear their backyard conversations, and the woods and brush did muffle the noise, too. When the builder removed part of their fence, one couple went in and cleared brush between the trees without checking with Bree and

Taylor. Taylor had written letters to both the builder and the couple telling them they had been trespassing, had stolen the fence and the wood, and further incursions would not be acceptable. She figured that giving them a written warning would stop others, and it had, for now. Apparently, gossip had spread about the owners of the woods among their neighbors.

The thing was that the woods continued on into another area beyond the McMansions, and it was owned by Eric Norman, who didn't care if they collected wood there. He'd made a mint off his land sales and continued to farm on the other side of Bree and Taylor's place. He wouldn't be so happy next year when people complained about the smell of his cows or the flies that accompanied the animals, though.

"Dammit," Taylor complained, slapping at a mosquito as she worked. It was getting late, but they wanted to use up the rest of the fencing. She admitted they had put it off too long, and some of it was going to need paint to cover up the rust and scratches. They still had the rocks to place around the posts to make it look pretty, but they could do that anytime.

"The joys of living in a swamp," Gretchen teased, slapping at a few herself.

This year was worse than the previous year, or maybe they noticed the bugs more because they actually lived here now. The mosquitos, gnats, and flies had a field day, feasting on the humans when they were outside at the wrong time of day, and bug spray helped but wasn't foolproof.

"Ouch," Bree said, slapping at a deer fly as it bit into her sensitive skin. "How am I supposed to work if these buggers are drinking my blood?" She was also keeping an eye on the children who were playing in the field nearby. Aaron was a great help with babysitting the younger children.

"It's because you're so sweet," Taylor teased, using her shoulder to get the post in the hole correctly.

"Too far," Gretchen complained. She was getting fully sick of putting up fencing. They wouldn't really be done once it was up and set, either. Both Bree and Taylor wanted to put up rock facing around each of the posts and, while beautiful, it was a lot of work. They did it by hand, using rocks they had collected from farmers' fields with Vinnie. Gretchen found the rock work soothing, helping her to forget her troubles as she waited and waited and waited for them to resolve. Only time would take care of some of her problems. She was so grateful to her friends for letting her stay with them while she resolved each issue one by one. One of the problems she hadn't anticipated was how much time she would have to think while she helped out her friends. Her hands and body might be busy putting up fencing or planting trees, but her mind was always able to

think. She thought too much, and it bothered her how often Vinnie was on her mind. It seemed that Vinnie was avoiding her friends' place a lot, but, when she was there, it overwhelmed Gretchen to have her about and underfoot. She wanted to see her, but it was too much and too soon after her husband's death.

Bree brought the remaining fence panels down along the path to the pasture, where Vinnie had cleared a space for the panels last year, and Eric was there, taking an early cutting of hay. Bree flagged him down to tell him this cutting would be the last because they would be planting trees. She nodded towards the panels they had set along the corner of their property line.

"Yes, I was going to tell you that it would be my last time, too." He laughed and indicated the rolled hay he had just ejected from his machine. "They own it now, and this will just clean up the field for them as they build." He pointed to the spec homes already built and the many basements at various stages of completion, probably already sold since they were going up in record time.

He looked at the fence panels, which were really impressive in the corner of the field. He hadn't noticed them along the highway, but on his way around to deliver the bales he owed these two women, he saw how many there were. He hadn't known these two women had the money to buy and put in such elaborate fencing. Waiting at their gate to be let onto the property, he was impressed. The fencing would enhance the property to the east of their place, where the other construction project was going up. He hoped the builders would want to buy the field where he had his cows now, too. The price had just gone up. As his tractor pulled the two bales and the third was on his tines, he looked at the two panels they had put along his fence line. It clearly defined the two properties, and he wondered if they would continue. He saw they had left his barbed-wire fence alone, putting the panels directly behind them. They looked impressive, and he could see where they had planted willows in the middle of all his fences, already they were sending shoots from the rainy spring they'd had.

With their friend's help, Bree and Taylor planted trees all over the property. The fingerlings disappeared in the grass, and Taylor had to be careful when she cut the lawns, especially around the pond. But Bree and Gretchen mulched and put down hay where they could around these small trees to make them a little more visible, adding some wire to help prevent them from being eaten or mowed. As Bree had planned, the foot-tall trees were planted every five feet, with hopes they would spread out and grow along the field property line. They gazed at the buildings rapidly going up, creating an instant neighborhood in what had previously been a hay field.

HOME ~ First Nillionaires Club

CHAPTER FORTY-ONE

At the sound of loud voices, Bree and Taylor froze from putting chicks they had picked up from the pound into the unused chicken coop. Since these were a little older, they didn't need a brooder lamp like they had set up for the smaller chicks they were keeping in the garage.

The voices that were raised were those of Vinnie and Gretchen. After her living with them for well over a month, the two of them were having it out. The sound came from the open windows of the basement, but Bree and Taylor could hear their argument clearly.

Humming loudly, Bree attempted to distract the children, but, as Aaron was helping them with the chicks, he could easily hear Vinnie telling his mother off.

"Then, why don't you move in with me? I have all that room, and you can do whatever the hell you want with your greenhouse and plants?" Vinnie demanded.

"Because I won't take advantage of your generosity, you moron!" Gretchen shot back. "I won't jump from one bad situation into another, no matter what I would like it to be!"

"You're saying living with me would be a bad situa—"

"Look at the speckles coming up on this chick's neck!" Taylor spoke up. The children had stopped admiring the chicks that were fluffing up their feathers as they put them in the coop. A couple of the kids were stretching their necks to get a better look towards the basement.

"Do you think that is a boy chick or a girl chick?" Bree asked, getting their attention back.

Aaron looked stricken, but he answered Bree, anyway. "I don't know what kind that is."

"Me, either," she admitted with a laugh, still trying not to hear the argument.

"I'm saying I can't move my son into your house or my business over there just because you want to be magnanimous!"

"It isn't anything like that, and you know it! I have the room, I love you, and—" Vinnie went deathly quiet, and they all realized she hadn't meant to say that last part out loud.

Taylor glanced at Bree and then Aaron. The boy looked surprised but strangely pleased.

"When will we know what kind they are?" Aaron asked the moms while keeping the younger children involved. He was making sure they all held onto the chick lightly and dipped their beaks in the water and food before letting them go.

"I don't know, but we have all kinds. I told the pound we weren't looking for specific breeds for our mixed flock, just ones that needed a home," Bree answered and exchanged a look with Taylor, realizing what the silence from the basement now meant.

Taylor cleared her throat. "Well, I think you can tell them we have enough now. With these and those in the garage coming along under the brooder, we have enough." She'd been surprised at the number they'd adopted, but a few had already died. They'd had to go through a back yard funeral with each one, complete with a shovel and a short eulogy. She'd planted them next to trees so the family would remember without needing grave markers. She'd been more upset over the cost of a brooder, the adoption fees, and the special feed that chicks needed. She'd thought that corn would be cheap but, apparently, they didn't eat that until older, and then they'd have to have scratch, as well as mixed grains. She really hadn't thought this out when she built the UFO.

They watched the chicks for a while as they discussed the different ones. They had such personalities, and it was funny. Gretchen and Vinnie came out of the basement, holding hands and smiling.

"Aaron, I need to talk to you," Gretchen stated, letting Vinnie's hand go to take her son off around the house to discuss her plans with the boy.

"When are you going to put them in the UFO?" Vinnie asked, trying to act nonchalant, but she was obviously very happy. She was practically

rocking back and forth on her feet, her hands in her jeans pockets, and she looked very pleased with herself.

Bree smiled at her, delighted for her friend. Taylor was the one who answered, trying not to grin too broadly. "I'll put them up at night, and then let them out in daylight. Good thing we put the wire over the top," she said, pointing out a hawk that Allan Crowe and his friends were harassing in one of the tall trees.

"Those alarmists will help you more than you realize," Vinnie pointed out, the grin on her own face never faltering as she pointed at the crows.

"What's an alarm ... larmi ...?" Melanie tried to ask.

"Your friends, the crows will sound the alarm anytime a hunter is around," she said, pointing at the hawk who had given up and flown off, being chased by the flock. "Hawks, owls, or even other animals—they will sound off, alerting you to something that isn't right."

The children avidly lapped up this information. Taylor had made a crow feeder, which Bryan furnished with bread daily. He loved to watch his friends and knew who each one was as they swooped in to eat at the feeder alongside the pond. They let the humans know when it was empty. Bree had put out crusts and even fruit and vegetables for the birds to eat, not only on the crow feeder but on the feeders Taylor had given her for Christmas. They were seeing all sorts of birds they didn't know lived in their vicinity.

*****

"Moving out, eh?" Bree asked with a grin as she watched Gretchen repacking some of her boxes.

"Yeah, Vinnie and I had a talk," she said with a blush, staring down at the towel she was folding so she didn't have to look at Bree.

"Must have been quite the talk," she teased and saw Gretchen's blush deepen.

"Well, you know I've always ..." she began defensively.

Bree put up a hand to stop her. "We've always known. About time you had some happiness."

"Do you think it's too soon? You know, after his death and all?"

Coming up on the two of them from the patio door, Taylor smiled. "I've known that Vinnie has been waiting on you for years. You've made her very happy with your decision." She started to say something about her making it sooner, but stopped herself. The past was what it was, and she knew that Gretchen had made the best of a bad situation. If she hadn't

met and married Barry, Aaron wouldn't be here. So, instead she asked, "How does Aaron feel?"

"Oh, that boy!" Gretchen started to cry, but she stopped Bree from comforting her. "He says even he can see that Vinnie makes me happy. He told her he wants her to teach him how to cut lawns, too. I guess I've told her story over the years, and he's admires her."

"So, you're still selling your house?" Taylor confirmed. That had always been the plan, but she knew Gretchen had to wait for all the insurance claims to be settled, as well as getting back on her feet.

Gretchen nodded. She hadn't even looked at other houses to move to, not sure she could afford them. Barry's parents were furious she hadn't held a funeral for their son, but she simply saw no reason to go to the expense. The only people who would have come would have been her friends and all the cops Barry was friends with. She didn't want to give them an excuse to drink, and he didn't deserve a funeral. The in-laws were further angered because she and Aaron weren't living in the house Barry had provided for them, unaware that he had mortgaged it to the hilt and she would get very little for it.

Moving in with Vinnie did make sense, though. They'd been in love since high school, and, while Gretchen had made other choices, this had been her one regret. She should have defied her parents rather than allow Barry and them to influence her. She'd unnecessarily hurt Vinnie and herself for well over a decade.

CHAPTER FORTY-TWO

"You got a dining room table!" Taylor said gleefully, her voice rising in her excitement as she looked at the beauty her wife had found. She ran her fingertips over its fine wood grain, the tiger oak looking especially beautiful under the lights.

"Now, I have to hunt for chairs to match this baby," Bree said with a grin.

"We could go all redneck and get those nylon weave chairs with the aluminum tubing and place those around ..." she stopped talking at the murderous look her wife gave her and smiled. "Now that we're alone with just our kids, we can have a fine dinner."

"We don't have fine dinners at the kitchen table?" she asked daringly, still annoyed about the chairs.

"We have wonderful dinners at the kitchen table," Taylor confirmed quickly, taking her wife in her arms to keep her arms from flailing about dangerously. "I'm looking forward to our own garden produce, now that you have that in order." She reached down to kiss her wife.

"That's all thanks to Gretchen. I had no clue what I was doing wrong, but she helped me make a couple of raised beds. We put the black dirt, twigs and other things that could rot in the bottom and fresh dirt on top that wouldn't burn off the seeds. Even those mounds down the rows should work out better now," she enthused, now that she knew better. She

would put out pots with dirt in them to showcase her new gardening skills, and the few customers who came out to their barn to pick up orders would see a lush and beautiful garden—all thanks to their friend.

"Let's take the children and Staffy for a walk," Taylor offered.

It was one of Taylor's few days off. With everyone's help, they'd gotten Gretchen completely moved into Vinnie's place, and their basement was clean again. The storm room was finished with Gretchen and Vinnie's help, and the power room separate with the furnace and solar box. The basement had plenty of room for the few boxes they stored there, and the children were using it as their rainy day playroom once again.

"Bring a shovel?" Bree asked, gathering up the children and putting on a hat to keep the sun off her long hair. It had been streaking as the sun got hotter and they crept towards summer. "Here, you need one of these, too," she warned her wife, handing her a straw hat she'd picked up cheap after Easter. They looked beautiful in their bonnets, and Taylor was even wearing a sun dress instead of her usual jeans and polo shirt. Bree was also wearing a sun dress she had picked up at one of the thrift stores. The children skipped along the trail, the dog between them, happy to be going anywhere with his humans.

"What'd I need a shovel for? Taylor asked, catching her hat before it got picked off by a low hanging branch. "I should have brought a hand-cutter," she griped.

"There are a couple of trees that died that I want to pull up. I thought we might need the shovel."

"Already dying?" she asked, surprised.

"I don't know if it's the open field, the sun, or if something got to them," she admitted. "Gretchen didn't know either, but she said she'd order more for us."

"How much is that going to cost us?"

"You know she buys in bulk, and, now, with what she's ordering for Vinnie, it will be pennies."

"Yeah, Vinnie wants to offer trees to her customers that we put in," she grouched with a grin, pleased how happy her boss and friend was these days. She was loving her job.

Before long, they had pulled up all the dead trees and returned to their walk. As the sun was setting, they walked along, holding hands and watching the children run through the long grasses, the dog loping alongside them.

* * * * *

Taylor walked up the steps from the garage into the kitchen and reached for the door knob, which popped off in her hand. "Ouch!"

"What's wrong?" Bree asked, coming out of the kitchen to check on Taylor.

"Someone loosened the door knob, and I just hit myself along my eye!"

Bree tried not to laugh. "What? How did you hit your eye?"

Taylor showed her the loosened door knob. There were obvious scratches where someone had used the wrong screwdriver on the screw. She'd used normal force to open it, but the door was at eye level when she pulled and she'd hit herself in the eye with her own fist.

"You're going to get a shiner there, babe!"

"KIDS!" Taylor thundered, calling to them as she held the doorknob in her hand. She saw the immediate uncomfortable look as Bryan came into the kitchen. "Who's been touching tools they weren't supposed to?" Her suspicions were further confirmed when Barbie snuck a glance at Bryan. Jack immediately put his hand in his mouth, looking worried.

"I didn't," Melanie immediately stated.

"But did you see what your brother and sister were doing? Did you tell them not to touch my tools?" Her eye was still smarting, and she tried to blink away the tears.

Bryan ended up going to bed without his supper, and Barbie got a good talking to that made her cry. The other two heard it all and learned not to touch their mothers' tools without permission.

* * * * *

"No running in the house," Bree said for the umpteenth time since they had moved in. It had been a familiar refrain in the apartment, too. She was sitting at the desk with the computer, trying to enter in receipts. A few minutes later she heard yelling.

"Mom, MOM, MOM!" Barbie called, followed by Bryan yelling the same. There was a certain frantic tone in their voices.

"What is it?" she called back across the kitchen, knowing the kids were down the hall in the girls' room. Sighing, she saved what she was doing and got up to go see why they were shouting.

She found Jack on the floor of the boys' room, holding his knee. "What happened?" When she saw all the blood, she bent down and examined his knee.

The kids blurted out everything at once, so it took her a moment to understand. Apparently, Jack had been running, took a wrong turn, and fell on his knee onto one of their plastic garden rakes. The rake had splintered and poked a hole right into his knee.

"Am I going to need a Band-Aid?" he sniffed.

"Nope, buddy. You are going to need to go to the hospital," she told him, plucking a handful of tissues from the dresser box. "Here, press those on there." She looked up at the other watching children. "Get your shoes on and get ready to go." Five minutes later, she and the other kids had their shoes on and waiting at the door. She scooped Jack up and headed outside. "Hold the door for me," she told Barbie, and Melanie ran to the minivan door to open it for her mom. After strapping in the still sniffling little boy, she quickly got the other three inside. "No, Staffy," she told the dog, having to push him back into the house after he hopped in the front seat of the van. She didn't allow any of the children to sit up front, so he thought that was his place.

At the hospital, she parked and carried the still dripping and snuffling little boy inside, with the others crowding around her. When the doctor asked how it happened, she said to Jack, "Tell them exactly what happened. Tell them the truth." Then she turned away so he wouldn't be influenced by her facial expressions. She knew they would assume she had done something to her kid unless he told them different.

Sniffling hard, he started. "I wasn't supposed to run in the house." He sniffed and made to use his sleeve to wipe his nose but glanced over at his mom and thought better of it. The nurse handed him a tissue, and it was rough on his nose, not like the soft ones his mom bought. "… And I fell on a sand rake," he confessed and looked to see if these adults would yell at him.

"Well, it looks like he's going to need a couple of stitches," the doctor said breezily, making it sound like fun. He was relieved it wasn't more, and, while they had to question the parent, the boy's honest confession and her reaction made him suspect she wasn't doing anything but being a mom. He cleaned and numbed the knee while the other children watched avidly. "Can the other children wait outside?" he asked, not certain they should see this.

"With whom?" Bree asked. "I'm not leaving any of my children alone."

He worked despite his audience. Once the still oozing wound was fully numb, he put two-and-a-half stitches in, cleaned it some more, put an ointment on it, and bandaged it. "You're going to have to sit on the couch the rest of the night, partner." He waited a moment, realizing the boy's age, and asked, "You go to school?" At the boy's nod he asked the mom, "Maybe off tomorrow?"

Bree nodded, glad it wasn't worse or that they hadn't called a police officer. Accidents happened with kids. This wasn't their first, and it wouldn't be their last. But she would always be paranoid about having child protective services called, having her children taken away from her, or some other unknown threat.

Since they'd let her bring Jack right in, with his bleeding knee, the nurse came to get her information. She handed over their insurance card, and a clerk went to go get copies as she filled out paperwork.

"What happened?" a concerned Taylor asked as soon as she got home. After hearing Jack's tale, she could see he was worried he was going to get in trouble. "Won't be running in the house anymore, will you, sport?" she asked sternly.

Nodding, he asked, "What about in the basement?"

"Still have to be careful of the concrete and windows, right?" She reminded him of the rules they had set forth last fall. "And stay away from the plumbing pipes?"

He nodded again, looking thoughtfully at his knee. He felt better when Taylor gave him a hug.

Bree was feeling a little defensive herself, having gone through the scare with their son, but Taylor didn't condemn her in the least. Instead, she took Bree in arms, murmuring that she'd been a great mom and Bryan was lucky to have her as a parent.

"I was so scared," she admitted.

"As I would have been!"

"I had trouble getting the blood out of the carpet, but I remembered that you're supposed to use peroxide and it came up after that."

"Good. We don't want a crime scene," Taylor teased.

"Whew, you better change," Bree said in return, realizing Taylor hadn't changed out of her work clothes. "You're especially ripe tonight. What happened?" As attractive as she found Taylor when she was all sweaty from working, the dust and debris she got on herself really needed to be washed off daily.

"Dog shit," she admitted. "People don't clean up after their dogs, and it gets in the lawn mowers."

"Gross."

Taylor nodded and headed for the shower, dropping her clothes in the washing machine to soak on the way. She hoped to get all traces of dog poop out of her hair—it had flown everywhere.

"Hey, I think you should go with Vinnie and Gretchen when they go to that auction next week," Taylor mentioned to Bree at dinner.

"What auction?" she asked, dishing up Jack's plate. Because of his hurt knee, he got to eat in front of the TV in the family room, sitting on the couch with his leg propped up.

"I guess I thought one of them would tell you. Vinnie is looking for used equipment, and there's a state auction next week. I know Gretchen is looking, too, and I thought you might pick us up a truck or a trailer. Some of that stuff is really good, and you know our finances better."

"Can you get off work?" she asked, intrigued.

"No. If Vinnie's gone, I'll have to stay and do some of her accounts."

"What about the kids?" she asked with real concern.

"Why don't you coordinate with Gretchen. Maybe Aaron can catch a bus here and watch these ragamuffins until I get home from work?"

"Sounds like a plan." Bree wondered what she might find at a state auction. Just this last year, Vinnie had gotten the two landscaping trucks she and Taylor were using, and, the previous year, she'd found a cherry picker she also used for her business. "Do you know what Vinnie is looking for?"

Taylor shook her head as she speared a carrot. "I think she goes to look, and, if there's something she needs—if it's reasonable—she puts a bid in on it. It's all closed bidding."

"What's that mean?"

"You have to write down your offer. That way you don't know if you're too high or too low. You just find out if you won or lost, and they expect you to pay on the spot if you won."

"I don't want to travel with that much cash!" she gasped. She always hated coming home from shows with money like that, anxious to get it into the bank.

"You'll have Vinnie and Gretchen with you," Taylor pointed out.

They discussed it, and then Bree called Gretchen who was now living full-time with Vinnie. Their plans were all settled quickly.

* * * * *

After bath time, they'd had to read their bedtime stories in the family room with Jack propped up there, but Taylor had insisted he sleep in his bed, carrying him there and trading Jack's upper bunk for Bryan's lower so Staffy could sleep with him. The dog seemed to sense the little boy was hurting and cuddled up with him.

As they got ready for bed, Bree though of something she'd forgotten to mention to Taylor. "Your sister called my cell phone again."

"I told you to send those to voicemail," Taylor stated, putting her clothes out for the next day.

"I do, but she always leaves a message, and I hate deleting them all."

"Don't even bother listening to that nonsense."

Since Easter, Taylor's sister had called both of them quite a few times. Mostly, it was to badger them about living with them. Somehow—probably through Ellen—Tia found out about them allowing Gretchen to move in for a while. Once she'd learned Gretchen had moved out, the phone calls started ramping up again. Their mother had also confessed something to Bree and Taylor: Tia was pregnant again. Taylor's first thought was to wonder if she'd done it deliberately. But why? To get sympathy or …? It had been many years since Blaine was born, and she'd *had* to get married. Why would she slip up now of all times?

HOME ~ First Nillionaires Club

CHAPTER FORTY-THREE

They'd decided because Aaron was so young, not to burden him with the four children, even for those few hours, but Ellen had gladly volunteered to babysit the children until Taylor got home from work or Bree got back from the auction. When Taylor arrived home a little late, she found the gate was wide open. Alarmed, she sped up then driveway to find a large moving van in the circle of the drive, and it was backed up to the front door. Her mother's car was parked in front of the garage.

"What's going on?" she asked, parking in front of the large truck as she saw some strange men moving things out of the moving van and into the house. They didn't answer, looked at her curiously, then shrugged and continued with their moving.

"What's going on?" she asked again when she went into the house and saw the living room full of furniture, boxes, and other junk. Their new dining room table was buried under it all. "Mom? Mom?!" she called, going through the house and dodging boxes stacked in the hallway. There were even moving men on the stairwell to the basement.

She found Ellen out back, peacefully watching her grandchildren playing. Blaine was standing outside the chicken coop, throwing pebbles at the chickens. Blaine? What the hell was he doing there? "Mom, who are these men, and what is all that crap they're moving in?"

Ellen looked up at Taylor with surprise. "Tia told me you'd changed your mind ..." she began, puzzled.

"Tia told you?" she asked, confused. Then, she realized what all this meant. "Where is she?!"

Ellen pointed to the patio doors under the deck that led into the basement.

Taylor looked at the basement steps, saw them blocked with the moving men, and headed for the steps off the deck and down around to the basement. As she reached the door to the basement, she saw Tia on the other side locking the door. "Let me in!" she shouted angrily.

"No, you calm down. There's nothing you can do. We have an agreement!" Tia crowed, holding up what looked like a rental agreement.

"No, we don't!" Taylor shouted back. She raced over to the patio doors, but Tia was there before her, triumphantly locking the door and laughing. Taylor hadn't seen her sister in months, and she was very pregnant.

"What's going on?" Ellen asked, walking from the play area to under the decks where her daughters were.

Taylor turned on her mother accusingly. "What did Tia tell you?"

"She said you two worked out your differences and that you and Bree decided they could move in," she said with perfect logic.

Taylor narrowed her eyes in a scowl. Of course, her mother always hoped for the best and believed that little liar. "No, Mom, we didn't change our minds. We don't want them living here, and we never gave them permission."

Ellen looked over Taylor's shoulder, where Tia was holding up the rental agreement. She was perplexed. "I don't think there's anything you can do about it Taylor. She has an agreement," she said, pointing to the paper.

"Then it's forged!" Taylor saw the children starting to come over to see what was going on, and she put up her hand to stop them. "You stay there and play. Grandma will join you shortly." She looked over to where her nephew was still throwing stuff at the chickens. "Blaine, get away from the chicken coop and go find your parents!"

"Dad told me to stay here," he mumbled loud enough for her to hear.

"Go find your dad then!" she told him sternly and saw him start shuffling off. She just detested how he didn't pick up his feet as he walked. She quickly hurried back up the side of the house to the deck, but, as she reached the patio doors, she saw Eric locking them with a smug grin on his face. She hurried to the laundry room which held their back door, but it was locked—something they'd tried to keep that way. She then tried

the master bedroom patio doors, but those were locked, too. Rushing across the two decks, she headed for the garage side door but no luck there, either.

"Goddamn it, Tia!" she called into the house so her sister could hear her. "Get out of my house!" There was no answer, and the movers looked at her curiously. "Stop! Stop bringing crap into my house!" she told them, but they ignored her. Grabbing her cell phone, she dialed 911.

"911. What is your emergency?"

"Someone has moved into my home without my permission. They are in the process of moving in and won't leave."

"This sounds like a civil matter, ma'am, not an emergency," the voice intoned.

Eric must have been watching Taylor because, when he saw her on the phone, he tried to get to her around the movers. Taylor saw him and slipped back into her work truck, locking the doors. Because of the warmth of the late spring day, the windows were all open a crack. "No, you don't understand. These people are moving into my home. They don't have the right, and they're stealing my house!" Taylor pleaded into the phone.

"Why can't you do this for Tia?" Eric shouted through the window, banging on the locked door and then on the window.

"It's my house not Tia's, and we never said you could move in. We don't even want you over here!"

"Let me in the goddamn car, Taylor! Who are you on the phone with?"

"Ma'am, are you in an unsafe situation?" the operator asked.

"Yes! Yes, I am, and he's trying to get into my truck!" Taylor told her frantically. "I'm at ..." she said, her voice sounding afraid as she gave her the address. "He's going to break my window." She could see Tia edging out of the house. She was enormously pregnant, and she waddled rather quickly over to Taylor's truck.

"Taylor! Who are you on the phone with?"

"I'm calling the police," she responded.

"Hang up that phone," her sister demanded.

"You're in my house illegally, and you're trying to steal it," she contended, knowing the operator was getting all of this recorded.

"We have a rental agreement," Eric stated triumphantly, grabbing the paper from Tia and holding it up.

Taylor could see the agreement; it was a form they had printed off the internet and the signatures on it weren't even close to being hers or Bree's. "You falsified that agreement. That isn't even my or my wife's signatures."

He still looked triumphant as he stated snidely back, "Doesn't matter. Possession is nine tenths of the law."

Taylor wanted to roll her eyes. "So, you admit to falsifying that agreement?"

"Yeah, no one's gonna care. We're in the house, and we're staying!"

"But it's my house! It's my wife and family's house. You don't even have a key!"

He held up the 'Do Not Duplicate' key they had lent Ellen. "I've changed the locks. What's the code on the gate?"

"You changed my locks?" she asked to clarify to the operator.

"We have the police on the way," the operator let her know.

He laughed. "It's just a matter of drilling them out," he told her as though he had accomplished something. "Nice Milwaukee tools, by the way."

Taylor was angrier than she could ever imagine being. Those had been presents from her wife, and she cherished the sacrifice Bree had gone through to make sure she had some of the best equipment. It didn't matter that Bree had gotten a deal on them; they were precious to her. That this scumbag had examined them, possibly used them, pissed her off.

"You have more than enough room for all of us," Tia contended, a common argument she had used since she'd first asked to move in last fall.

"No, we don't. And we don't want you in our home," Taylor responded. She used to say it just wasn't convenient and other platitudes so she didn't hurt her sister's feelings, but, once Tia had become so persistent, Taylor had gotten a little blunter. Taylor could see the movers were done and closing up the back of their large truck. One was getting in the driver's seat, but he couldn't drive away since Taylor's work truck was in the way. She glanced behind her down the drive and was relieved to see flashing red and blue lights coming up the drive.

"You called the police?" Tia shrieked and turned around, pulling Eric towards the house. Blaine was on the front porch, and she pushed both of them into the house, locking the door behind her.

"What's going on here?" The first officer came up to Taylor's truck, and the other was slower about getting out of the patrol car.

Taylor opened the door and slid out. "This is my house, and I came home about half an hour ago to find this truck here, moving things into my house. I did not authorize these people to move in. In fact, I've told them no since last fall. They knew my wife and I would be out of the house today, so they took it upon themselves to move in."

"Taylor?" the second officer greeted her in surprise. "Long time since Tweety's."

"Hey, there." She took a few breaths. "Hope you can help with this." Her hands gestured to the truck, where the four movers were jammed in the front seat together, staring back at them. She didn't want to play remember the good times at Tweety's with anyone right now.

"Can you prove this is your home?" the first officer asked, and Taylor reached for her driver's license which showed her current address.

The three of them walked to the front door, and Taylor could see there was a new lock on it, an ugly, mismatched lock that didn't even look like it belonged there. The old lock was still sitting on the floor of the porch, along with Taylor's Milwaukee drill next to it. The battery was missing from the drill.

Taylor told the two officers what had happened since she had gotten home, what her sister had shown her, and how they had locked her out of her own home.

"Your mother let them in the house?"

"She thought we'd come to some sort of agreement. At least, that's what my sister told her. They must have been planning this for when they knew that my wife and I would be out of the house." She gestured to the truck and movers who had gotten out of the cab and were now watching her interaction with the officers. "They set this up to move in, lock," she gestured at the lock on the porch, "stock, and barrel."

"And you definitely didn't want to share your home with your sister?" the first cop confirmed.

Taylor nearly groaned with the stupidity of all this. Having the cop repeat things she'd already told him was frustrating her. Just then her mother came around the corner of the house with the four children trailing behind her. "Mom, I told them I wanted them to stay near the play things."

"What's going on, Taylor?"

"Tia has moved in completely, and no, I never said she could," Taylor told her exasperatedly.

"But she has that lease agreement. She's all moved in. Why can't you let her stay?"

"Mom, you want them out of your house—I understand that. But we don't want her here in our house, either. That lease or rental agreement isn't valid. It's fake. I never signed it, and neither did Bree."

Behind them, two vehicles were coming up the driveway. The police and Taylor walked around the end of the moving truck to see two trucks arrive, one of them identical to Taylor's work truck. Both parked next to the garage, barely fitting with Ellen's car there.

Vinnie popped out of her truck and asked, "What's going on?"

Taylor didn't answer her. She was looking at the second truck, her wife smiling avidly behind the wheel of a Ram 2500 with a crew cab and an eight-foot bed. Bree's smile faded as she saw the police, the moving truck, and Taylor's face. As she opened the door, she repeated Vinnie's question.

Taylor quickly filled in her friend and her wife, and Bree was immediately livid.

"Ma'am, you live here, too?" the first officer asked to confirm.

"I do," Bree admitted. "Hi, Josh," she said to the second officer.

"Do you have any proof, you know, to make it official?"

Disgusted, Bree fished in her pocket for her wallet and showed her driver's license.

"Okay, then," the first officer stated, handing the license back to Bree. He and Josh headed for the front door again.

"What are they going to do?" Bree asked Taylor as they slowly followed, Vinnie trailing behind.

"Mom, take those children to the back. They don't need to see this," Taylor ordered her mom.

The children could hear the stress in Taylor's voice and started trooping back around the garage, at first because they didn't want to get yelled at, but then to see the new-to-them truck Bree had been driving.

"Taylor, they're already moved in. Can't you ...?" she began pleadingly.

"No, Mom, I never would. And, if you'd stop giving in to her, she'd stop walking all over you. They don't have to live with you, you know?"

"I know, but it's easier ..." she began in a pleading voice.

"No, Mom. Stand up for yourself. She'll never get on her feet if you keep molly-coddling her," Taylor said firmly. It wasn't anything she hadn't said before to her mother, but, for some reason, it looked like it was beginning to sink in. She watched as Ellen slumped her shoulders in defeat and followed the children.

The police knocked on the door until Tia answered the door. "Can I help you officers?" she asked in a syrup-sweet voice.

"Ma'am, the homeowners," the first officer thumb-pointed back to Bree and Taylor, "state that they do not want you here, and that you've moved in illegally."

"That's not true. My sister invited us to move in," she lied, "and now that we have a little disagreement, she's called you."

The first officer looked back suspiciously at Taylor, but Josh shook his head. Taylor read the name badge on the man she didn't know. Rodriguez.

"Do you have a written agreement with your sister?" Officer Rodriguez asked.

"Oh, yes," she replied politely, immediately producing the paper. She came out onto the porch; Eric was looking over her shoulder proudly. She looked at Taylor and Bree with a smug, triumphant expression.

As Officer Rodriguez read through the paper, Josh asked Taylor and Bree to produce their driver's licenses again.

"Jose," Josh said as he held the driver's licenses up to compare signatures. Of course, they did not match. They weren't even close.

"Ma'am," Josh said to Tia as he held the licenses. "Do you know how much trouble you can get in for committing fraud?"

"Fraud?" she asked, fluttering her eyelashes, which looked ludicrous.

"Yes, this paper isn't worth the computer you printed it out on," he told her. "The signatures don't match in the least. That's fraud."

"I want to press charges," Taylor spoke up and saw the blood drain from her sister's face.

"This is a simple misunderstanding," Tia quickly said, attempting to step backwards but bumping into Eric.

"These people are illegally in my home," Taylor continued, glaring at Eric, who had been looking so cocky a minute ago. "I want them arrested."

That wiped the smile from his face.

"Taylor," Bree breathed, but she saw her wife shake her head.

"You're going to have to call CPS, too. Their son is underage and has nowhere to go."

"He can go with his grandmother," Tia quickly said as Officer Rodriguez pulled out his handcuffs.

"Sir, you're going to have to come with us," he said, addressing Eric who held up his hands, attempting to step backwards into the house but the officer reached out and quickly whirled him around and against the stone of the house, putting the cuffs on him. Josh quickly reached for Tia before she could escape into the house and turned her around.

"You can't do this!" she told the officers.

They ignored her and made sure the cuffs were on correctly.

"I don't think Mom is going to do that anymore," Taylor said confidently.

Bree turned to the movers, who were standing there with their mouths agape. "Were you hired one way or round trip?"

"What?" they asked her, staring at the couple who had hired them as they were handcuffed and led to the squad car. Tia was struggling but the officer had a firm hold of her.

Tia was practically foaming at the mouth as she spouted off threats to her sister and her 'dyke' wife. She went from pleading, "Don't do this. We don't have anywhere to live," to threatening dire retribution. Josh and Officer Rodriguez noted it all. They closed the door but could still hear Tia screaming obscenities along with, "Are you happy with yourself? You took our home because you're too selfish to share and help out family!"

Taylor started to laugh at her sister. "You've taken all your life. We earned this home for *our* family. You're not getting in on it."

"Ma'am," Josh said, trying to talk over Tia, "may I remind you that everything you say can be used against you in a court of law? We are catching all of this on camera," he indicated the body cam on his shoulder.

Officer Rodriguez gave Tia a few minutes to calm herself before talking with the handcuffed couple in the back seat. Soon, he came back to talk to Taylor and Bree, who were chatting with Josh and Vinnie on the front porch. The movers were still standing there, uncomfortable but unable to leave because of all the cars in their way.

"Your sister," Jose began, unsure if he should be negotiating on Tia's behalf, "asks if you will allow them to move out with all their things and drop the charges."

Taylor exchanged a look with Bree, who nodded briefly. "Every last one of their things out of my house," she clarified, and the officer nodded his head. "I want them to pay for any damages and the locks before the leave!"

Taylor, Bree, and Vinnie watched as they let both Tia and Eric out of the police car, rubbing their wrists after the cuffs were removed. Eric talked to the movers, who nodded and held out their hands. He sighed but removed his wallet and paid them cash, and they headed back into the house to empty the living room, dining room, and basement of the things they had just moved in. Taylor and Bree stood there, glaring across at Tia, who did nothing to help. Eric brought a few things out to the van to help the movers, but he didn't do too much, either. Blaine stood there pouting at his aunts, but Vinnie laughed at the boy until he looked awkwardly away.

"Where is Gretchen?" Taylor finally asked.

"She got a bunch of things that she took home in her truck. I better call her," Vinnie told her and walked away to make the call.

"So, you found a truck?" Taylor asked Bree, sorry her find had been tainted by this incident.

"I was so happy to bring it home. Both Vinnie and Gretchen said I got a good deal." She went on to talk about the auction. Not that many people had shown up, and she'd managed to bid on the truck without

competition. "I thought my bid was too low, but without a competing bid, I got it!" She told her wife how much she had saved. "Vinnie said there's another auction next month across the state. I'd like you to go, and maybe we can find a camper or a trailer."

Taylor glanced to where the movers were still bringing out boxes and loading them into their van. "You better make sure they don't accidentally take any of our things."

Bree hadn't thought of that, and she took her wife's advice and quickly slipped back into the house. It was getting dark, so Taylor joined her, ignoring glares from her sister and brother-in-law. She nodded to Bree, who stood amongst the piled-up boxes in their living room looking incredulous, and headed for the basement, unlocking the door and gesturing to her children and mother to come inside.

"What happened?" Ellen asked tentatively.

"Mom, I want you to go home and change your locks," Taylor told her, as the children gravitated towards their toys. Melanie was standing close by, looking at her expectantly. "What?" she asked

"I need a hug. You usually give us one when you get home."

Taylor softened her face at her daughter. She'd been angry ever since she got home. "I haven't changed from work. I'm still all full of grass. Maybe later? You go play with your brothers and sister."

With a look that told her mother it was completely unsatisfactory, she flounced away. Taylor nearly laughed.

"I can't lock her out," Ellen told her.

"She was willing to lock me and my family out of our own home." Taylor gestured toward the nearly empty basement, where two of the movers were coming down for a few more boxes. "You can't enable her and her behavior anymore."

"Well, where is she going to live now? She'll have to move back in with me."

Taylor wondered if her mother could hear the defeat in her own voice. "Mom, she's a grown-ass woman." Her mother winced at the swear word. "When does she stand on her own two feet? I'll bet she said some things to you as she moved out of the house and convinced you that that paper was real."

Taylor watched closely as her mother thought and saw in her eyes what she had said was true. Tia couldn't have helped herself but be viciously triumphant.

"But … she's pregnant. Where is she going to go?"

"Mom, you didn't get her pregnant. Either time. If Eric keeps getting a woman pregnant, isn't it up to him to provide for his family? That's *your* house. It's time you claimed it for yourself. When else will you get the opportunity? He's probably waiting for you to die so they can inherit it."

Ellen looked at her older daughter in surprise. She spread her hands to take in the whole basement. "But you have so much room here ..." she tried, but her voice had grown weaker.

"Mom, Bree and I worked hard for years to afford all this. We're still working hard to afford it." She had never shared their finances with her because she knew her mother couldn't keep anything from Tia. "Don't you let her situation make you feel sorry for her. She treats you badly."

"But Blaine needs a home—"

"That Eric and Tia are responsible to provide. I bet, if they show up at your home later and you say no, they will survive. They'll probably just try to con someone else. You know what they did today was fraud, right? They can go to jail for that."

"She's your sister!"

"No, Mom. Not anymore. She stopped being my sister when she tried to take advantage. We were only out of the house for eight hours or so today and they moved in. C'mon!"

Ellen looked utterly exhausted. "But where will they go?"

"Mom, I don't care. I care about you and how they bully you into letting them live with you. They will never leave, and they will never pay you back what they owe you." She saw she had hit a button. "Their promises don't mean anything. They will take and take until they break you."

Eventually, she convinced her mother to let Vinnie go with her since she had to stay to make sure that Tia and Eric were completely moved out. Vinnie convinced Ellen to let her stop at the Home Depot and picked up a new set of locks for the older woman. She quickly showed her how to change out the locks and handed her the new keys.

"Why don't we go back to Taylor and Bree's and get your car," Vinnie offered kindly, putting her arm around Ellen's shoulders. She could sense the day had taken a lot out of the woman.

"But Tia and Eric will need my ..." she began. She sounded very, very old after the events of the day. The home truths of her older daughter had finally penetrated her mind, and she was quite weary. She had worried the whole time Vinnie was changing the locks that Tia and Eric would show up and there would be a confrontation.

"I don't think Tia and Eric have a right to your car. Do you?" she asked kindly.

* * * * *

The movers were done and packing up their dollies when Vinnie and Ellen got back to the Taylor and Bree's house. Vinnie marched up to Eric and demanded, "Give me your mother's keys." She held out her hand expectantly and smirked at the man.

"What the hell did you ask me, you dyke?" he sneered. He'd always hated this woman.

"Officer, Taylor's mom needs her keys to her home and her car back, and he's holding them," she pointed out to Josh, who she had met many times at Tweety's back in the day.

"Sir, are they your keys?"

"They're my copies," he lied belligerently.

"They are not," Ellen spoke up for the first time. "My daughter has a set, too," she said pointing to Tia.

"Ma'am, is that true?" Josh said, pulling up his leathers from where they were weighing his belt down, he knew it was a psychological thing and that many people would be intimidated. They'd already had these two in cuffs once today; they wouldn't want to be in them again.

Eventually, Eric and Tia were convinced to take the car key and the house key off their rings, never realizing that the house key would be of no use, anyway. The old house locks were in a bag, stored in a closet in Ellen's house. She was pleased she could put her things out again as she thought about the freedom it gave her to have Tia and her family out of her home. It still saddened her but Vinnie had convinced her to not go home yet.

"How are we going to get home?" Eric muttered as he handed over his keys.

"Mom will drive us," Tia sneered, handing over her set. She looked up as Taylor and Bree came out of the new house where they had been looking for damage. "Are you happy? You've denied us a home because you're too selfish to help out family." Her words were empty and pointless; it was nothing she hadn't said before.

"Oh, no, I've helped out *family*," Taylor countered, glancing at Vinnie who nodded and turned away. Taylor started to laugh. "I help; I don't take. I never offered to share my home with you, and you tried to take it."

"You could have helped out your own sister. You helped your friend; you could have helped *family*."

"You aren't my sister anymore. You and your husband and son are nothing to me," Taylor said cruelly. "I don't want you ever on my property again, or I'll have you arrested for trespassing."

"Girls," Ellen began, but Taylor sliced her hand through the air to shush her mother.

"This is between her and me, Mother. It's been a long time coming. Didn't you ever wonder why we didn't want to come over anymore?" Out of the corner of her eye, she could see the children all watching through the front window, and the movers finally finished and pulled the overhead door down with a bang.

"Where to, boss?" they asked Eric, and he gave Ellen's address.

"Oh, no. You can't move all that in there," Ellen protested, looking at the size of the truck. "That would never fit."

"We got our things from Eric's dad's garage," Tia admitted. "We'll just have to—"

"Move somewhere else," Ellen finished for her. "You've moved out, and you're not moving back in again."

Surprised at her mother's backbone, Taylor turned aside a little to hide her smile. She left them to work it out and get her truck out of the way of the moving van.

"Mom, you can't do that. We need somewhere to live," she said, rubbing her extended belly.

"That's your fault. You told me this morning you couldn't wait to be out of my house. Now, I don't want you back there. She," she indicated Vinnie, "kindly helped to change the locks on my house, and you are not welcome back in there."

"What?" Tia screeched, dropping all pretense of being civil. "You can't do that to me. It's my home!"

"It was your home, but that was before you moved him in," she indicated Eric, who was looking shell-shocked. The movers started to drive away with the moving van.

"Wait! Wait!" he called, but they had been paid and had an address to go to. They weren't waiting around for him and pretended not to hear him. It had been a long day, and they just wanted it to be over.

Taylor turned back in time to share a good laugh with Bree. The vision of Eric running down the driveway after the moving truck was hilarious. He wasn't the most graceful of runners.

"Where are we going to go?" Tia whined again and then turned to her sister with a pleading look.

"Don't look at me," Taylor put up her hands. "I already made it clear you're not welcome here."

Tia started to swear, making her mother's ears turn red.

Taylor had had enough. "Shut up. You're such an entitled brat that you don't even see how you keep taking and taking, and you think people don't see what you are?"

Josh and his partner Rodriguez were only staying to make sure they were off the premises. When Eric returned and started swearing at the women, too, Josh gave him two options. "You either cool it, or I'll put you back in cuffs."

"What for?" Eric sneered.

Josh held up the forged contract they'd had never given back. "If the homeowner doesn't want to press charges, the police might. This is fraud, and, after what we've witnessed here today, I'm sure the district attorney can make the charges stick for both of you." His glance took in the very pregnant Tia, who had been about to stick in her two-cents worth.

"How are we supposed to leave?" Eric whined. "We don't have a ride."

Taylor could see her mother falter and almost capitulate, but Bree spoke up before she could get a work out. "You could call a cab."

"A cab?" he asked stupidly. "Who can afford a cab?"

"The same guy who paid twice for moving today and is going to have to catch up with his movers before they leave everything on the front lawn of his mother-in-law's place?" Vinnie added drolly. She was still stinging at being called a dyke by this moron. It was different if she used the term for herself; she didn't like others to.

"Yeah, wouldn't that be littering, officers? And couldn't people come through and take whatever they want?"

"They better not touch our stuff!" Tia began and looked at Eric horrified.

He started scrolling in his phone for someone to call, not willing to use a cab. He pushed a number and walked away, trying to convince someone to come out and pick them up—and to hurry because they had to catch up with the movers.

Josh and Officer Rodriguez backed Taylor up when she demanded that Eric pay for the locks he had changed.

"You can just put the old ones back in!" he squawked in alarm.

"Nuh-uh, we have to get all new locks since you took the key. I think two hundred dollars should do it."

"I ain't paying you two hundred dollars for locks!"

"Actually, sir, you are," Josh reminded him. "It was a condition of your release and for them to drop the charges."

Eric looked like he was strangling. They could all see when a thought occurred to him. "I don't have the money," he said triumphantly, showing them his now empty wallet.

"Then, sir, you're either going to have to come up with the money or go to jail."

Before the officers would allow Tia, Blaine, and Eric to leave in the back of Eric's father's car, they saw Eric heatedly talking with his father. The man shook his head many times until whatever Eric promised him pried his own wallet open and he handed his son the money. Eric reluctantly handed it to Taylor before joining his wife and son.

"I'm betting that's going to be an awkward conversation," Taylor commented as they watched them go. She looked to the officers. "Do you mind stopping at my mom's so they don't try to break in or give her a hard time?"

She gave them the address, and they followed Ellen down the drive.

"Wow, you don't do things halfway, do you?" Vinnie teased.

'Stay for supper?" Bree offered.

"Thank you, but I have to get home to my family," Vinnie refused, pleased to be able to say those words.

They exchanged hugs, and the couple watched until the taillights were halfway down the driveway.

"Let's get that gate closed," Bree sighed as they walked back into the house.

"I'll make dinner," Taylor offered. She was ashamed at the way her family had behaved, but she felt strangely relieved for her mother.

"You haven't even showered yet, babe. You still have your work all over your clothes." Bree patted her on the shoulder. "I'm going to indulge us and order pizza. Watch the kids while I go pick it up?"

"You just want to drive your new truck."

"Can I go?!" was heard in a cacophony of voices coming from the front door. Bree and Taylor both wondered how long the kids had been listening from there.

"There are no car seats in the new truck. So, no, you can't go," Taylor told them firmly. Her eyes twinkled as she gave her wife the opportunity to be alone for one more drive.

CHAPTER FORTY-FOUR

The truck was a real godsend, worth every dime and then some. Their insurance balked at first, quoting them an outrageous rate, used to their crappy Jeep and very old minivan, but they were homeowners, had a policy for that as well, and were given the multi-car discount which made the difference a little more palatable.

"Now, we'll keep our eyes peeled for a nice camper for the back," Bree said happily.

"Um, hon, we have to pay back our savings and get a trailer as well," Taylor pointed out. She'd loved the deal, but it had cost them money they might need in an emergency. Plus, both of them were always worried about covering a major problem with the house or kids. Jack's accident had scared them, even if insurance did pay for it.

"I know, I know. I'll feel better pulling a full trailer with that," she pointed at the truck, "than with the other vehicles. They're all falling apart."

She wasn't wrong. The minivan was so worn out from pulling the heavy trailer, as well, and it had a ton of rust built up on it.

"We don't use the Jeep anymore. Can't we sell it and put the money in the bank?"

"I'd really like to get rid of the minivan, but ..." She saw Bree was about to interrupt her and sighed. "I know—we need the room for the kids."

Bree settled down, having been about to object, but now they were on the same page. "I guess I'll keep my eye out for a deal on a trailer," she promised.

* * * * *

A few weeks later, Taylor and Bree were outside, checking on the chicks which were all in the coop, now they had grown large enough and the nights were warmer. They threw them scratch and watched as they seem to instinctively know how to use it.

Bree was very impressed at Taylor's dedication to making sure they were all put away at night. Staffy, and sometimes Marmalade, would loyally follow her to the coop to make sure they were locked up just before dark.

"I'd really like to get an automatic door or some sort of apparatus to open that every morning. How cool would it be if the landing platform came out every morning for them to come out of the UFO?"

Bree chuckled. Taylor's creativity had really taken off since they'd gotten the house. She wanted to build the kids a playhouse or maybe a tree house, but one that wasn't in a tree because she worried about broken bones. Two minutes later, the children realized their parents had escaped and came hurtling out of the house, slamming the patio door behind them.

"One of these times they are going to break that glass," Bree fretted.

It was Taylor's turn to chuckle as they left the pen and walked towards the woods, the children chasing after them. Marmalade ran up a tree, but Staffy greeted them enthusiastically.

"Did you hear from your mother?"

Taylor sighed. "Yeah, she's still rattled about standing up to Tia, but I think she'll be okay. I guess I have to continue to back her up in her decision, although I feel like I bullied her into it."

"It was time she kicked that girl out," Bree showed her wife support. "Give your mom a few weeks, and she'll be able to breathe a sigh of relief."

"Yeah, probably. I bet Tia is bombarding her with text messages, though."

"As long as she doesn't send them our way." She'd been surprised when Taylor was prepared to have her sister and brother-in-law arrested

and her nephew put into the system, but she also fully supported her wife. Enough was enough, and they didn't owe Tia anything.

Slowly, they walked around the barn and past their weedy garden. Since Gretchen had moved out, they hadn't had been much time to work on it, and some of the weeds were waist-high. Next, they strolled along their sandy beach, letting the barefooted children splash in the shallows on the sand.

"Are there any roots they need to worry about?" Bree asked as they started along the path into the woods, swatting at mosquitos that loved the coolness.

"No, they can run along this. It's actually very soft," Taylor said, her shoe making a design in the soft dirt.

The water in the dam hadn't gotten high enough to spill over because there hadn't been enough rain. "Should we worry?" Taylor had asked Vinnie, but her boss and friend shook her head.

"Maybe the springs were pressured from the volume of water to stop leaking out? I don't know. I'll ask Jeff when I see him next."

Taylor had taken a hand rake around the edge many times. She had smoothed out the slight hills of dirt keeping the water in the pond. She pulled up roots from trees that stood there last year and raked the grass that she hadn't cut as often as she could. They still only had the push mower, and she really wanted a riding one. The truck had taken precedence, and they really couldn't spend their money frivolously.

"I think we should build a bridge," she complained as they hopped from rock to rock through the creek.

"Gretchen had some marvelous ideas about how we could do that," Bree commented, nearly slipping as she helped the children.

Taylor could imagine Gretchen's marvelous ideas, which would have included a medieval castle, maybe even a drawbridge, but definitely an arched bridge over this little creek. She kind of wanted that, as well.

They continued on their walk through the woods, with Taylor commenting on dead trees she wanted to take down, branches she wanted to cut back, and bushes she wanted to mulch.

"Wow, look how fast those houses are going up," Bree marveled as they reached their field.

"At this rate, there will be a couple of houses at this end in no time." Taylor pointed as the children took off running with Staffy in the tall grass.

"That's a Pit-Bull!" a woman yelled, grabbing her child from where they, too, were walking in the open field.

"No, it's not!" Bree called back. "Hey, guys, bring Staffy back here." He wasn't on a leash, and she didn't want the exuberant dog to scare anyone, even though he already had.

"It is, too. I know a Pit-Bull when I see one!"

"Then you need glasses," Taylor said dryly as she and Bree drew closer to the woman and her child and the dog and children came bounding back. "This is a Staffordshire Bull Terrier. Look it up. It certainly is not a Pit-Bull. Not that there is anything wrong with one of those noble dogs."

"Pit-Bulls are vicious!" the woman declared, pulling her daughter even closer, as if Staffy had lunged at them. He hadn't even looked at them, too excited to be running with his kids.

"Right, lady. Whatever you say." Just then, Staffy nearly bowled Taylor over in his excitement, trying to give her kisses. "Easy there, boy."

"By the way, lady," Bree put in, pointing to the pink property line flags, "you're trespassing."

The woman shot them a dirty look—first for the dog and then the trespassing comment—then flounced away. She yanked her daughter by the hand as they waded through the tall grass back toward the housing development.

"Some people," Bree murmured.

"Let's make sure we keep a leash with us when we are walking Staffy," Taylor advised as they continued their walk towards the front of the property. The two panels that stuck out to enclose their front fence looked odd, but they walked on the inside of the fence, still leaving the dog off lead as he followed the children.

"Careful there, I think it's a little wet from the swamp," Bree called as they walked along the inside path.

"I should come in here and widen it," Taylor pointed out. The fence had been put along their property line in the ditch, and the foliage was trying to overgrow it.

"We still have to put up some of the rocks around the posts," Bree reminded her.

"Damn, I forgot," she replied as they walked along, slapping at mosquitos and gnats. "I want to come in here with a brush cutter and get that." She pointed at a briar patch that would have ripped up clothing and skin if anyone were foolish enough to go in there. "Come away there, Staffy," she called, preventing him from getting scratched or stickers in his short coat.

It took a long time to come out by their driveway, avoiding the damp spots where water from the culvert and ditch drained into the swamp.

"There is always some work that needs to be done," Bree admitted as she noted she had forgotten to bring the black paint and a paintbrush out here.

"Maybe, someday we can paint the iron green. Wouldn't that look rich?"

"It would, but after we get the rocks on the posts?"

They discussed all they wanted to accomplish as they began the long walk up the driveway. Melanie rushed out of the walking gate to stop at the mailbox and get their mail.

"What is this?" Taylor asked, noticing one of the letters and ripping it open.

Dear Homeowner,

This is to inform you that there is a scheduled association meeting for the Rolling Ridge Estates
homeowners. We expect everyone to attend as we hand out our new homeowner's rules and
regulations.

Good neighbors follow rules that we can all live by.

"Oh, that's the second one we've gotten," Bree said, glancing at the letter.

"Second one? We're not part of their association," Taylor pointed out, confused.

"Yeah, that's why I ignored the first one. They've made a mistake."

"But if they think we're part …"

"Yeah, it's a glitch of some sort. They'll figure it out," she dismissed, taking the rest of the mail and sorting it as they walked.

"We're being watched," Taylor murmured a few minutes later. The herd of cows in the next field were chewing their cud and observing the family on their walk.

"Think he sold it?"

"Maybe, maybe not." She scanned the field for surveyor's stakes but found none. "I don't see any stakes or anything, and the cows look like they're in that field to stay."

They could both smell the cows and enjoy the flies they drew, along with the cow plops. When the wind was blowing out of the west, it blew the smell straight up to their house.

"Don't that look purty," Bree teased, pointing at the truck.

"It shore does," Taylor teased back.

* * * * *

The truck came in handy as they went full-time into show and festival season, and Taylor had to give Vinnie back her truck so her other employees could use it. Taylor was conflicted. She loved working for Vinnie, but she also loved the business she had been building for years with her wife. They were busier than ever, and she owed Bree her loyalty.

When their Fourth of July show got rained out, they came home early and called The Nillionaires Club and asked if they wanted to have an impromptu barbeque. Some were planning on going to the town celebration but easily diverted to spend time with their group. Both Lenny and Elsie now had girlfriends they brought, trying to get them to enjoy their group of friends and vice versa. Gretchen and Vinnie brought Aaron, and Taylor called Ellen, who was happy to come and spend time with her oldest child and her grandchildren, not to mention avoiding anything to do with Tia and her family.

As they happily ate bratwurst and corn on the cob, the fireworks from the neighboring housing developments went off from time to time. It was determined that the McMansions didn't necessarily have better fireworks than the new development to the east.

"When are you going to start swimming in that pond out there?" Lenny teased, her arm around her girlfriend.

"That water is damned cold," Taylor admitted. "And I haven't gone in further than my knees since I got those leeches when we put in the dam."

"Has it heated up since then?" Vinnie asked, reaching for some chips and offering them to Gretchen and Aaron.

"Oh, yeah, the sand is nice and hot," Bree put in. "I still don't want to go out too far."

"I'd like to get some ducks," Taylor added. Just then, the chickens set to cackling over the latest screeches of fireworks. Staffy was indoors, looking unhappily out at the gathering but protected from the worst of the noise by the thick patio window. Marmalade was nowhere to be seen.

"If you get ducks, you can't swim in the pond," Vinnie pointed out, gesturing with her beer.

"We can't?" Taylor asked in surprise.

She shook her head. "No, there are parasites or something in the duck poop. You'll end up with skin rashes."

"Eew," Taylor said distinctly, wrinkling her nose. Bree copied her.

"That's too bad," Bree spoke up. "They seem like they would be so much fun to have around." She'd enjoyed growing out the chicks. Most were fully feathered now, and the kids had loved the experience. She was looking forward to having eggs someday.

"Well, decide if you want to swim in the pond or have ducks," Vinnie advised with a grin. "After seeing your pond, I want one on my property, too."

"With all my experience, boss, I expect you could hire me for a few days," Taylor bragged, puffing out her chest.

"Yeah, all I have to do is arrange for someone to deliver an excavator accidentally."

They all laughed, remembering what had happened in the early spring.

Ellen was having such a lovely time, too, talking with her daughter's friends and being entertained by the children. Even Aaron, who Melanie obviously had a crush on, was polite and well mannered. She couldn't help but compare him to her own grandson, Blaine. She hadn't seen him since she'd refused to allow his parents to move back into her house. Taylor had been right, and she was relieved to have her house to herself again, even if it was a little lonely. Elsie had been talking to her about volunteering at the community center, something she had never considered before.

"Well, it's getting late, and you children need to wash up," Bree began, seeing them nodding off in their chairs.

"We should be going," Vinnie immediately said, standing up and holding out a hand to help Gretchen up.

"No, I didn't mean …" Bree protested.

"I move that The First Nillionaires Club adjourn for this Fourth of July celebration," Lenny put in, pulling her girlfriend up and hugging her. "All in favor?"

A chorus of 'ayes' answered her, and everyone took the hint and began gathering up their things. They'd all enjoyed themselves, but it had been a sunny day and a cool night, and the mosquitos had feasted. The food had been good off the grill, and there had been more than plenty of it. Everyone packed a meal to take home, leaving the rest for Bree and Taylor and helping them to put it away.

"Mom, would you like to spend the night?" Taylor offered.

"Oh, no, that's not necessary," Ellen protested while wrapping up food containers.

"That's mine." Gretchen pointed to a Tupperware and helped sort others until everyone had what they had brought with them.

Taylor and Lenny folded the chairs.

"Where did Bree find these, they're so comfortable," Lenny asked.

"I have no idea. She finds deals on the Marketplace or Craigslist all the time," Taylor admitted, carrying the chairs to the side yard, where she put them in the garage and hung them on hooks on the wall.

"Like Milwaukee tools, do you?" Lenny teased again, seeing a new one. "What is that?"

"Bree found a blower so we can keep the sidewalk clear," she admitted, blushing.

"You can blast off the decks, too," Vinnie pointed out, bringing in a couple more chairs. "And blow leaves out from under the trees."

Taylor nodded; she had thought of all that, but, if it hadn't been such a good price, she would have admonished her wife for buying something so frivolous. Still, she loved it and was hoping to find a chain saw eventually.

"She can use it to blow off trucks, too," Bree contributed.

"Naw, I prefer using children," Taylor countered and then had to explain to her friends how she had used her son to clear off the front window of the van.

CHAPTER FORTY-FIVE

Their summer passed happily, the children getting tanned and full of mosquito and other bug bites. The grass was shorter this year because Taylor kept up on it in between shows and her job with Vinnie. Vinnie wanted to expand, but she was in the midst of building a couple of greenhouses on her property—one for Gretchen and one for her business. Everyone went over to her place for barbeques to help out where they could, and it was a good excuse for the First Nillionaires Club to meet.

When school started in the fall, Bree had a hard time finding shoes for all the kids. "They've all grown out of the shoes they didn't wear all summer," she complained. "Now I have to go shopping."

Taylor knew she wouldn't buy new. She'd comb Goodwill and other thrift stores to find good, used shoes since the children would be growing out of them fast.

"Mom, I need *new* ones," Melanie complained. "They'll know at school that these are used."

"Too bad," Taylor said sternly. "If you don't tell them and you keep them clean, they won't know for sure. We don't need to spend that kind of money."

Still, when she wasn't cranking out pots at a rapid rate, Bree was off to the stores, making the rounds, and searching for deals for the children's wardrobe. Books, notebooks, folders, pencils and other things they needed

for school, she picked up in bulk whenever she could, hiding them until they were needed.

"You do not touch that drawer," she warned Bryan who went to help himself to pencils for the third time. "You already have pencils, and I gave you some extra for school."

"But I lost mine," he whined.

"Then, you better find it or take better care of your things," Taylor advised him. "Your mom said to stay out of that drawer."

* * * * *

The moms met the new teachers one by one. Some were surprised to find two moms; while others took it in stride and still others already knew about them and didn't care.

"Do you ever notice it's the younger teachers who are cool with children having lesbian moms?" Bree mentioned as she drove them home from one such meeting.

"Yeah, probably raised right," Taylor casually replied. "Hey, stop a minute," she called, signaling Bree to pull over.

"What?" she asked, surprised as she pulled to the side. Someone had a minivan for sale in their yard. They both got out to take a look.

The vehicle was in great shape, and the owner came out, shushing his dogs that had alerted him to someone in the yard. "Hey, there," he said, looking curiously at the two women.

"Hello," they responded as Taylor peered through the windows at the inside. There wasn't any rust on the outside, a big difference from their own dying minivan.

"That the price?" Bree pointed to the breakdown he had printed out to make it look like a dealership tag.

"Wahl, I might come down a bit. I had it in the want ads, but people kept lowballing me," he confided and unlocked the door so she could check out the interior. He also popped the hood.

Bree was trying to get the blue book value on her phone, and she appreciated the open door so she could put in the mileage.

They talked for a while. The owner said the car had been garaged since they bought it, but he wanted to put a different car in the garage now and had no need for this one. Bree and Taylor took the car for a ride, and it ran smoothly.

"Would you object to us taking it to our mechanic?" Taylor asked. Bree had already indicated it was a good price for the year and make, as well as the mileage.

"Where's your mechanic?" he asked, watching the two women and wondering if they were sisters. Since they looked nothing alike, they would have laughed if he had asked them.

Taylor told him, and he said he'd go with her if she wanted to go right then. Taylor called the mechanic, asking if he would take a look at a car she was thinking of buying. She looked meaningfully at Bree who nodded slightly.

While Taylor went with the car owner to the garage, Bree turned around and went to the bank for a bank check and some cash. The cash was for if they could talk him down, but the check would be the main way to pay the guy if the mechanic felt it was sound.

Taylor and the owner were already there when Bree got back. She pulled up in a hurry and apologized for being late. "Sorry, there was a line."

The owner looked from one of them to the other. He had been certain Taylor was just keeping him talking since the other had taken off in their truck. Taylor offered him a price below his asking, which he considered and refused. She tried to cajole him a little, and, eventually, they met halfway between the asking price and the blue book value. After shaking on it, he went to the house to get the paperwork.

"I hadn't planned on buying a minivan today," Bree hissed as he went inside.

"Don't you want this?" she fretted in return, wondering if she had missed the signal.

"Of course, I do. It's a little higher than I wanted to pay, but it's in great shape."

"Tell you what, we'll sell both the minivan and the Jeep, then."

"You don't want to trade them in?"

"You always get more if you sell them yourself. We can clean them up this weekend and put them up on the various sites."

The man hurried out with a pen in hand and the registration. He filled it out most carefully and signed it after Bree gave him the cashier's check, which she made out to him, using the name on the paperwork. The rest she gave him in cash, surreptitiously hiding the extra she would return to their account.

"Thank you very much," he said, shaking her hand.

"You want to drive the van or the truck?" Bree asked generously.

"Either or," Taylor said with a grin.

"Good, I'll drive the van then," she said, handing her wife the keys to the truck.

The children were all over the van when they got home. Taylor insisted on putting the children's car seats in the new van right away, but only after cleaning each one of them carefully. That proved harder than she'd thought because they had a tremendous number of crumbs all over them, some caked in the creases, and it took them a long time to get them all out. Bree threw the covers into the washing machine while they worked at cleaning and sanitizing the seats. After they had all the car seats reinstalled and the sun had baked the covers dry, they took a ride in the new van.

"I'm going to have to clean the old van before we put it up for sale," Bree complained a little as Taylor took them for a spin, stopping at Gretchen and Vinnie's place for a few minutes to show off the new one.

"You won't be alone," Taylor objected. "We will all help detail the van and then the Jeep. She looked in the rearview mirror at the reluctant kids. "Right, gang?"

"Right."

* * * * *

The children turned out to not be much help, but, slowly and surely, the van and then the Jeep were vacuumed, polished, and detailed. Using old brushes and rags, they cleaned and cleaned and cleaned. It took hours on each vehicle, and, once they were done with each of them, Taylor parked them on either side of the gate at the end of the driveway. On her second trip, Taylor stopped about halfway back to listen to the crows calling to her. She squinted to see if any of them were Allan, Jack's favorite bird, but she couldn't tell one crow from another. She wished the boys were with her so she could ask.

Bree put the vehicles up for sale online, using pictures Taylor took on her cell phone. Before long, they started to get calls, emails, and inboxes. There were so many scams attempted on the deals that Bree was tempted to pull the ads down. She knew about the scam where they asked for your phone number and Gmail account, but she learned a few new ones. She wouldn't meet with anyone without Taylor being there with her because she didn't trust anyone online. That meant it had to wait until Taylor was done with work for the day, which probably lost them at least one sale, but both vehicles were sold by mid-fall.

CHAPTER FORTY-SIX

It was a beautiful fall day with the leaves turning, and Bree and Taylor were enjoying the end of their first complete year in their own home. They celebrated by buying dining room chairs that matched the table Bree had found. Taylor found the chairs, too—not online but at one of properties she worked for Vinnie. The table they actually went with had been damaged, and she was surprised Taylor would buy the chairs without it. They got a good deal and had dinner at the table that night, wearing their nicest clothes and celebrating as a family. Bryan even put a bow tie around Staffy's neck. Marmalade deigned to make an appearance before yowling to go out again.

"He's probably gone to fight with that other cat I saw sneaking around the barn," Bree complained.

"Another cat?" Taylor asked, pouring the last of the wine.

"It's not the first one," she told her. "With the woods, I'm sure there are more hiding. Who knows what Marmalade finds out there."

"Good thing we kept up on his shots, then."

"Exactly."

* * * * *

When it snowed right before Halloween, Taylor was thrilled. She and Vinnie had installed the plows back on the trucks in plenty of time in case of this eventuality. Taylor wasn't driving her usual truck because she was working so hard with Bree to get ready for the Christmas show they did every November that she wasn't working with Vinnie as much. Taylor missed helping out with that first snowfall, but the quality and quantity of the pots that they turned out was paramount.

Gretchen had ordered quite a few pots of various sizes, all with very specific details and her new business logo stamped on them, and this large order had to be completed before they stocked up on their regular array of pots for the show. Packing up the truck and the trailer, they realized their next purchase had to be a new trailer. Taylor followed behind in a rented U-Haul filled with even more pots, their sleeping bags, and a cooler. On the way to the show, Taylor watched up ahead of her as a tire on the trailer blew out and Bree quickly pulled over to the side of the highway. Pulling up behind her wife, she turned off the U-Haul, left on the emergency blinkers, and hurried forward to help her change the tire. She found her wife shaking and upset, bursting into tears as she buried her head in Taylor's shoulder.

"I could have killed the kids," she sobbed.

"I saw you, though. You handled it so well," Taylor told her, holding her tightly, surprised at how upset Bree was.

"All I could think was that the heavy trailer was going to overturn."

"It's not that ..." she began, looking back at the trailer and realizing the tires were a little low. She held Bree until she got herself together enough for them to change the tire. The spare wasn't in much better shape than the one they took off, and Taylor cursed herself for not looking into that. The trailer did not like the weight inside it as the unsteady jack held it up for the change. Eventually, they got it changed, but Bree held to the slow lane and went quite slowly the rest of the drive. As a result, they set up well into the dark, having to make their little cave in the U-Haul in the cold. The conditions made for a miserable camping experience for all three nights.

"It's so c-c-cold. The children must be freezing." Bree shivered. But the kids seemed impervious to the wretched weather. It snowed the second night, making it worse for the adults. The kids got bored much more easily, and Bree snapped at them a few times.

"I've never been so relieved to take down," she confessed to Taylor and Gretchen. Gretchen had been at the show, too, and she had stopped by to place additional orders for pots.

"Was it worth it?" Taylor wondered after they got everything packed up again.

"We have to change how we do this," Bree gestured at the trailer and then the U-Haul.

"At least we have the truck," she added lamely, hoping to have Bree see the silver lining.

After putting everything away and tabulating the three days, Bree was in a better mood. She'd be much happier once they got the cash and checks in the credit union and out of the house.

* * * * *

"Those damn hunters are persistent." Taylor was complaining while Gretchen and Vinnie helped load the latest order of pots into the back of Gretchen's truck. "I caught three of them saying they were hunting rattlesnakes. Can you imagine that? Where the hell are they going to find rattlesnakes up here?"

"Actually, we have Eastern Massasauga rattlesnakes up here." Vinnie corrected her as she lifted a rather heavy pot onto the tailgate, and Gretchen reached for it. "Careful there, that one is heavy."

"We do?" Taylor asked, surprised and then quickly looked around. "Don't tell Bree. It will freak her out and, with the children ..." She shuddered as she imagined what could happen.

"Well, this is the wrong time of year to worry about them. They're pretty shy creatures and avoid humans," she went on to say. "They're known as swamp rattlers."

"Oh, great, and we happen to own a swamp." she gestured towards the pond and beyond it to the wetlands that hadn't dried out or drained.

"You could put in another pond or two," Gretchen teased and then grinned at her when Taylor rolled her eyes.

"I wouldn't worry about it. They're very rare, and they spend most of their time hunting mice. They probably moved on when you started draining your land and put in the first pond." She added the last part with a grin at her girlfriend in reference to building more ponds.

"Gee, thanks for the information," Taylor mumbled, going for more pots. "Any suggestions about getting rid of the hunters who think they can ignore our signs?" She'd ordered aluminum signs screen-printed by Elsie because the printed ones were mostly faded and needed replacing, plus so many had been torn down by trespassers. She wanted her land posted, and those hadn't even lasted a full year. Aluminum should be more weather resistant, but she was going to nail or screw them deep in the trees to make them people resistant.

"You could put in cellular game cameras. They send pictures right to your phone. If you put them in high enough and at an angle, you can catch trespassers," Vinnie responded cheerfully, picking up another pot to put on the tailgate. She held it until she was certain Gretchen had it, then let go. "If it's at human height, people will steal them. And, here, if you have a broken camera, you can put that in a spot they will notice—maybe steal—but it won't matter because it doesn't work."

"If it doesn't work, then why bother?" Bree asked, bringing out more pots and catching the end of their conversation. Taylor was relieved they had stopped talking about the rattlesnakes and Bree hadn't caught that part.

"It's so they get a little paranoid. You could even set up another camera to catch them stealing the broken camera."

"The police won't do much," Bree said.

"I'm not so sure about that anymore," Taylor countered. "After what happened with Tia, they've been a little nicer. Even waving. Now that we don't have to deal with the sheriff. Remember that guy?"

Bree did. He had completely intimidated her with his demands for film footage along the highway. Fortunately, he hadn't been back to ask for it. Then, they found out they were out of his jurisdiction. She didn't care, but she was going to make sure she didn't vote for the creep.

* * * * *

Taylor went back to work full-time for Vinnie after the Christmas show. She didn't get her dream truck back since Vinnie had to play fair with her other employees. She understood, and, anyway, the Ford F-150 Vinnie provided did the job. It had carried the blower and rakes for fall cleanup, and it allowed her to plow when the snows came. Her long hours working for Vinnie returned just as winter hit with a vengeance.

* * * * *

Ellen completely enjoyed Christmas that year without Tia and the tension she created. She absolutely loved living in her home alone without them. Tia had had a little girl, and, while Ellen had gone to see it, she hadn't been welcomed in Eric's father's home. Despite Tia's broad hints, Ellen didn't mention the family moving back with her. Eric's father was rude and surly to Tia, keeping her in her place, and Ellen felt sorry for her but hoped it would motivate them to move out on their own.

Back at Taylor and Bree's house, the four grandchildren loved decorating with their grandmother. She told them stories behind all the ornaments, and they all had a marvelous time decorating the tree in the living room. The Victorian couch and chairs, the beautiful tree in the corner, and the nice dining room set made the two rooms very cozy. Bree was looking for display cabinets to complete the room someday.

Ellen indulged her grandchildren, teaching them to bake, using Bree's still new kitchen, and showing them how to decorate. She sent a big box of treats and Christmas presents over to Tia, but she wasn't certain whether she got them or not: Tia never called to thank her.

They sang Christmas carols, and, for the first time in decades, Ellen thought about going to church. After the children were in bed, she sat by the fire in the family room for a while before standing up and going to the back patio door.

"What are you thinking about?" Taylor asked her when she caught her gazing out the patio door into the darkness. The snow was coming down hard, and Taylor knew she would probably have to go out to plow her clients' driveways and shovel their walkways. She'd asked Ellen to stay with Bree and the children so she wouldn't have drive in the snow.

"You've really made a nice home here, and I'm proud of you," she said, leaning back into her tall daughter's arms.

"Thank you, Mom. That's very kind."

"I know it hasn't been easy. You two work very hard for all you have."

"No, it hasn't been easy, and we have so many plans for the place in the coming years. But there is no hurry. This is home, and we'll fix it up even better in time." Just then her phone went off, and she saw it was Vinnie, texting everyone an hour warning before she expected them to start their client list.

"Oh, do you have to go out?" her mother asked sadly.

"I knew I would."

"You did call it," Bree said from the kitchen, where she was making hot chocolate. She increased the amount so she could send her wife out with a thermos full. She'd made sure that her wife had a new set with a hat, scarf, and mittens that had a rainbow pattern in them. She'd started knitting them last year when she got this job but didn't have the time or the gumption to finish them until this fall. She quickly went into the living room to retrieve the boxes and brought them to her wife. "I think you better open these before you go out."

"Uh-uh. No Christmas presents until tomorrow," Ellen cautioned.

"Well, these Christmas presents I think she better open before she goes out." Bree returned to the stove to stir her concoction, one of the few

recipes she'd retained from her own childhood. She quickly had three cups and the thermos full and dropped marshmallows in the cups. Handing them out to her wife and mother-in-law, she smiled as Taylor planted a kiss on her cheek.

"Thank you, they're beautiful," she admitted, looking at the matching patterns that were so lovingly knitted for her. She put them down so she could drink the hot chocolate. It was delicious, thick, and creamy.

"I almost ran out of yarn, and then I thought I wouldn't find the skeins that I wanted," she said as she told the story behind the gifts she had made.

"Well, I think it's perfect," her wife complimented her, a slight milk moustache on her lip that Bree desperately wanted to lick off. She restrained herself with her mother-in-law present.

"This is good," Ellen agreed about the hot chocolate. "I don't know how to knit, but maybe I should learn. Would you teach me?"

"Well, this is crocheting, not knitting, but I know how to do both."

In the bedroom, Bree watched as Taylor got dressed in long underwear, jeans, and a pullover sweatshirt, then followed her to the door and waited while Taylor put on her boots and coat. She donned the hat and wrapped the scarf around her neck, tucking it into the collar of her sweatshirt. "I'm not wearing these right now as I need to wear gloves," she said apologetically of the mittens she tucked inside her coat pocket. "But I may need them later." She grabbed the thermos, leaned in for a kiss, and headed out to her work truck.

"Don't you worry about her on these roads?" Ellen asked after she left and they could hear the garage door shutting.

"She loves her job. She enjoys it too much for me to let her know that I hate that she goes out there in this mess." Bree indicated the still falling snow. "When she's cutting grass, I know how much she loves the smells and sights. Showering it off at the end of a hard day, she seems reborn. I just worry that she resents coming home to help with the pottery."

"Oh, I don't think you have to worry about the pottery. She loves creating, and I've noticed the different designs you two gals come up with. I bet she thinks about that when she's cutting grass."

"Well, I better clean the dishes up and get to bed." She was pleased with what Ellen said, but she did worry now and then that Taylor might not want to do the pottery anymore. Their business was growing each year, and, one year, it would be full-time work for both of them.

Ellen settled in for the night on their couch, covered in soft blankets and sleepily watching the fireplace until she fell asleep. Bree headed back to the bedroom to get a few hours of sleep before her children got up for Santa Claus.

Out in the cold night, Taylor did her route efficiently. She knew some of the places would require a second pass later on in the day, but she was determined to get home in time to see her children open their presents from Santa Claus.

HOME ~ First Nillionaires Club

CHAPTER FORTY-SEVEN

Spring came later this year, and the deep snows they had gotten that winter stayed around longer than expected. Taylor was kept constantly busy while the snows kept coming. There were times when there was simply no room left to put the plowed snow, so Vinnie took her big dump trucks and the front-end loaders out to collect snow from her customers and dump it on her own property. Eventually, the village's service got approval to dump snow in the river and the lake. She didn't have permission to do that, so the mounds of snow in her field grew higher and higher.

"When spring finally comes, we are going to all float away from the melting snow," Vinnie bitched to Gretchen and then to Taylor.

Taylor thought about that when she saw that Bree had pushed snow off the driveway and into the pond and swamp. She wondered if the melting snow would finally push their pond to use the spillway through the dam.

* * * * *

As Vinnie had predicted, the whole area had floods that year. Bree and Taylor's driveway was flooded, too, despite all the reinforcements, the pond, and the spillway. They were both careful when driving down it in case it got washed out, but it was exciting to watch because the water

continuously moved and churned. The woods were full of water, which kept the family from having their evening walks. Their few attempts sucked the boots right off their feet. The creek was full, but the spillway on the pond finally got its test. They opened the two slots on it fully, and the melt rushed into the flooded creek. Bree warned the children to stay out of the mud puddles every evening when they got home, and she'd even had to drive them out to the bus stop and back for several days because there were no places dry enough for them to walk without wading through the swirling water.

* * * * *

"This, is a mess," Vinnie warned her employees, but she could see that Taylor, like her, was excited to get to their spring work. Every year was different, but they looked forward to raking the lawns of dead debris that had gotten compacted under the snow. The green grass would, they hoped, arrive soon enough and send up shoots through the debris of last year. Gravel was raked back to the driveways. Vinnie now had a rake attachment that fit a couple of her tractors, and she used it judiciously around the melting snow to rake up dead grasses in preparation for the new growth.

"God, I wish the snow was completely gone," Bree bitched as she kept the ovens fired up and full of pottery. She and Taylor were getting ready for the big spring show.

"I think we don't need this rain, but it will help melt the snow," Taylor pointed out, painting sunflowers on the pots she was working on.

"What's with the vines?" Bree asked when she saw some finished pots.

"Just trying something."

"It's pretty, but don't we need some bright colors?"

Taylor added a few flowers to the design, carefully putting roses and bougainvillea, leaf by leaf, amongst the vines in various colors, changing the design on several pots.

"Too bad you can't put all that on each pot."

"Some of it would clash."

"And they will want multiple pots in each color," she added with a grin, realizing that was how it worked. "If they see red flowers on one pot and orange on another, they will collect multiple pots to match the red even though the pots are identical."

"You're working too hard," Taylor pointed out as she finished up painting for the day. The lights were on in the barn, and Bree had put in a final batch to bake.

"How about you? You come in here after a full day working for Vinnie." Her wife pointed back at her with a stick.

"We have to have as much stock as possible for the show." It was something they said every year as they got ready for the spring show.

"I don't know if that's going to last." Bree pointed to the trailer, which looked like it was sagging in the middle and ready to collapse.

"Yeah, that should be a priority," she agreed miserably. "I did have a thought …"

"You did?" Bree teased, pretending amazement. "Uh-oh …"

"Cute, real cute. Do you want to hear it or not?"

"Okaaaay." She stopped what she was doing to listen.

Taylor cleaned her brushes and watched Bree out of the corner of her eye. "Now, before you jump down my throat, hear me out," she warned.

"Am I not going to like this?" she asked cautiously, suddenly wondering if she should worry.

"I think—when you hear it all—you might think it's a good idea."

"Okay, lay it on me," she answered with a come-on gesture.

"Why don't we, after the spring show, go to the credit union and refinance the house." At Bree's opening of her mouth, she knew she was about to interrupt. "Wait, wait. Hear me out?" She stopped talking until her wife nodded in agreement. "If we have the money from that show in the account, which shows us to be good business people and dependable, they are much more likely to refinance the house. Rates are good now, and it would improve both our credit."

Bree could see Taylor was checking off a mental list of arguments and stood there silently, waiting for her to finish. Inside, she was seething at the idea of getting further in debt. The financing they had taken from the builders didn't count since they'd had paid rent at their apartment for years. It was more like trading one debt for another.

"Did you know that financing with the credit union will look better on our reports?" Taylor asked and waited for Bree to shrug. "The builder just shows up as a bill, not a mortgage; anyone looking at our credit wouldn't realize that we are paying off our house. An actual house loan through the credit union would look much better, and we might get a lower rate." She looked hopefully at her wife to see if she was enthused or not, but Bree's face was impassive. "We could also borrow a little more." She winced as Bree's face tightened in a scowl. "Get the camper and maybe the trailer? Not new, of course. Maybe we don't have to wait anymore?" She stopped talking, waiting for the explosion she knew was there and simmering. Tentatively, she added, "At least, think about that?"

Bree nodded tightly. They were comfortable. Although buying the truck and the van had eaten up their savings, they didn't have any major bills and they hadn't missed any of their house payments. But Taylor was right; the bill didn't look like a house payment on their credit report. It simply looked like a large bill, and it would be regarded differently when anyone looked at their credit history. Bree bit the inside of her lip as she thought about it while helping to clean up and getting ready to head into the house.

"Can I get back to you on this?"

Taylor nodded. She'd had a lot of time to think through the idea and how to best introduce it to Bree. At least Bree hadn't given an outright no.

CHAPTER FORTY-EIGHT

Over the next week, Bree did think about the conversation over and over again while she prepared the molds to make pots. She tried her hand at free style and enjoyed the experience, as always, but envied how effortlessly Taylor was able to do that aspect of their business. Some of the pots she threw were absolute works of art, and they priced them accordingly.

"You know, it would be foolish not to refinance," Bree eventually conceded. "But …" she added, seeing Taylor's face fall as she braced herself for bad news, "not until after the spring show."

Taylor pulled her into a big hug, appreciating how they could talk through most of their ideas and problems and rarely argued.

The small spring show they usually did to get geared up for the big one wasn't to be. Bryan came home with chickenpox, and it soon spread to the other children. Having four sick children was not how they planned to spend their weekend, and they were glad when Ellen came by to spell them so they could take turns sleeping and tag-team on childcare. Ellen had the foresight to put on a big kettle of chicken soup, and the homemade biscuits she made were a big hit. Both moms were grateful for her help because the whiny, feverish, and itchy children weighed on their nerves after a while. Knowing they were missing an opportunity to make money for their family, they both tried to put the little show out of their minds as they took care of things.

* * * * *

"Oh, that dog," Ellen complained when Staffy rushed through the backyard, barking his head off.

"I often wonder if someone's trying to come through the woods when he does that, or if they're just too close to the property line." Taylor said to the room at large. She helped a feverish Jack get to the bathroom, waited for him to finish using the toilet, and made sure he washed up before wiping down his face and arms with a cool cloth. "Make sure you pull down your sleeves and get under the covers, buddy," she told him as she directed him back to the family room, where the children had been watching television and dozing in and out of sleep.

"We've all had chickenpox, haven't we?" Bree asked the adults as they each sipped on their hot chocolate after the kids had gone to bed.

"I remember Taylor having it," Ellen reminisced. "Tia was jealous and kept popping your pox."

"Eew, gross," Taylor said with a grin. She was quite happy that her sister was no longer in their life. She knew her mother still saw her only occasionally, and she seemed happier for it. Apparently, the baby was colicky, too, so that didn't help their situation.

"Do you remember having it?" Ellen asked Bree.

"No idea," she admitted, but that was just part of her history. She'd have to look in her medical records to find out if she ever had it, if it was even there. She assumed she had. She hadn't caught it from the kids, but she simply didn't know.

Letting Staffy come in, Ellen asked, "Is this cat supposed to come in, too?"

"Of course. Marmalade is an indoor/outdoor cat," Bree told her as she put the cups into the dishwasher. She wanted everything sterilized, with the children so sick.

"No, this black and white thing is trying to get in, too. Marmalade is already in."

"Nope, no extra cats," Taylor answered adamantly. "I don't know where these other cats are coming from, probably all our new neighbors," she admitted. "But we aren't feeding them, and I don't want them. There's a pretty calico hanging out in the barn occasionally." She looked at Bree, who nodded.

* * * * *

Fortunately, they all recovered in time for the big spring show. On the way home from the show that they counted on for a large part of their income, the show they had built up inventory for months for, the trailer broke down. The first sign of a problem occurred on a remote stretch of the highway about halfway home. Sparks were coming from underneath the trailer. Taylor, who was following behind in a rented U-Haul, flashed her lights and tried to get Bree on the cell phone, even though she knew her wife wouldn't answer it while driving. Finally, the flashing lights on high-beam got Bree's attention, and Taylor signaled for them to pull off the road at a gas station.

"Didn't you see me flashing you?" Taylor asked, getting out of the U-Haul and hurrying up to the truck.

Bree was exhausted from their weekend and the phrase brought on the giggles. It wasn't appropriate with the children there, but Taylor rolled her eyes when she realized what her wife was thinking.

"There are sparks coming out from under the trailer. I think something broke."

They took a quick look and determined one of the springs was indeed broken. They decided to transfer as many pots as possible into the U-Haul and try to get home. No one stopped to help them, and it took a long time to move the weight from the trailer to the U-Haul.

"That's going to have to do," Bree finally said, brushing off her hands. The kids had helped, but they could only take smaller pots, and Barbie had cried when she'd dropped one, smashing it on the ground.

"Just take it slow, and I'll stay right behind you. Maybe no one will see the sparks."

"I hope there are no sparks now that we got the majority of the weight off the springs."

Taylor once again followed behind the trailer, and, luckily, there were only occasional sparks coming from it whenever the trailer went over a dip in the road or a pot hole. She hoped by following in the U-Haul, no one else, especially a cop or a sheriff would see and get involved. They were all relieved when they got home, but, despite the trouble they'd gone through, Bree still insisted they empty the U-Haul and return it that night so as not to incur an extra day's rent.

"We're U-Hauling lesbians," Taylor teased as she became slap-happy from all the work that day moving pots.

"What's a U-Haul lesbian?" Melanie asked, frowning.

The two moms exchanged looks, and Taylor carefully explained. "Some lesbians move in together far too soon in their relationship. Sometimes on the second or third date. They use a U-Haul to move, so they're called U-Haul lesbians."

The young girl nodded, understanding the explanation but not completely. "Like Gretchen and Vinnie?" she asked, trying to understand.

The two moms exchanged a look, not wanting to tell the little girl too much, but Taylor answered anyway. "Oh, no, they didn't move in together too soon. They'd known each other for years." This seemed to satisfy Melanie, and she went off to help.

Exchanging another look with her wife, Taylor continued to methodically empty the U-Haul. The sooner it was empty they could go in, bathe, and get to bed. It had been a long weekend, and they had school the next day.

Bree allowed them to pick up a meal that evening after returning the U-Haul. "I hate how expensive fast food is," she admitted.

"Tweety's!" Barbie shouted from the back seat of the minivan, pointing as they drove by the familiar diner.

"Been a long time since we went there," Taylor commented, sipping on her shake.

Each of the children enjoyed their kid's meal because of the added bonus of a toy, but they were all tired out. Fights over who went first in the bathroom ensued, but they let the girls use the master bathroom in order to hurry the kids along to bed.

"I'm so tired," Bree admitted, getting out of her clothes to take her shower.

"I'm betting there isn't enough hot water," Taylor bitched as she, too, got ready, peeling off her shirt. "Wait, do you hear that?" she asked, frowning and pulling her shirt back on. Barefooted she walked through the house, seeking out an odd noise. Turning on lights she found Staffy in the front hall, chewing on a bone Bree had given him to keep him amused at the show over the weekend. Apparently, he or one of the children had brought it in the house. His tail thumped on the floor expectantly, and Taylor had a laugh at her own expense. The sound of the bone on the stone floor had spooked her.

"What was it?" Bree asked as Taylor slipped in the cooling shower water with her.

She explained about the dog while she quickly washed her long hair and used the suds from that on her body. "We're gonna need a bigger hot water heater when these kids become teenagers!"

"Makes for quicker showers," Bree said, hurrying up.

"Did you hide the weekend's take?"

"Always," she admitted. She already felt paranoid enough without her wife reminding her about having a bag full of cash, checks, and credit card receipts.

CHAPTER FORTY-NINE

Keeping the refinancing in mind, Bree realized Taylor was absolutely correct. After she deposited the checks and cash the next day and chit-chatted with the teller, she asked for the paperwork to get a home loan. She took it home, filled out most of the pertinent information, and left the rest for when Taylor came home. While waiting for the kids to get home from school, she looked up the trailer and camper they wanted, figuring out about how much each might cost used.

As she worked on orders from the show and store orders, Bree thought about what they wanted to do to expand the business. It was a regular thing now to take pictures of their more unusual or beautiful pots and other sculptures and update the website with those pictures. They got some orders from previous customers from doing that, but the website was also a landing space for possible new customers. The brochures they jammed in the bottom of their pots, sometimes generated sales, too. She wanted to hire a marketing firm to make their advertising more effective, and Elsie knew some people who could help them.

"Oh, so now I'm right, eh?" Taylor teased as she signed the paperwork.

"Yes, you are right," Bree confirmed, laughing with her. "I just didn't want it to go to your head."

* * * * *

The next morning, Bree took the paperwork back to the credit union and sat down with the loan officer, who ran their credit.

"What is this lien on your property from Rolling Ridge Estates?" she asked, pointing to the outstanding bill on their credit on the screen.

"Rolling Ridge Estates?" Bree asked, confused.

"Yesss," she said, typing in something so she could see more detail. "It says here they are your homeowners association."

"We don't have a homeowners association."

"Well, apparently you do, and you owe quite a lot in penalties and interest here," she said, pointing again at the large amount on the screen. "I'm sorry, but, based on that, we can't extend you a home loan."

"Can I get a copy of that?" Bree asked, her heard pounding at the information.

"I'm sorry. It's our policy not to give this information out. As a member of the credit union, we can offer our services, but a lot of people would simply run their credit if we gave it out for free."

Bree was definitely disconcerted. She thanked the loan officer for her time but left the credit union fuming. She went home and signed into the three major reporting credit bureaus before doing anything else. She had to prove time and again who she was, entering and re-entering her social security number, but, each time, she found this ding on her credit. She printed it all out and ran Taylor's credit history. Again, her credit was good except for this same ding. Who the hell was Rolling Ridge Estates?

Bree spent hours on this task before starting to clean. She cleaned the desk in the family room, looking for a particular piece of paper. She cleaned off the dresser in the bedroom, where they sometimes left important paperwork. It tended to stack up, and Bree had left it for months at a time. Taylor was just as guilty of this, so neither had found it odd.

"What is going on?" Taylor asked when she got home. She didn't mind cleaning, but this was above and beyond Bree's usual tidying up. With four kids, there was frequently a lot of mess in the house that they had to keep up on. Paperwork wasn't quite as important.

Bree turned around from the last of the piles she was sorting, filing, or recycling. "Did you know we can't get a home loan, that is get refinanced," she indicated the house they were living in, "because our homeowners association has put a lien on our home?"

"What homeowners association?" Taylor asked, confused.

"The one that put a lien on our property!" She shoved the paperwork in Taylor's face and continued sorting the last stack. "Ah, here's that

sucker!" She showed Taylor that as well. It was the second letter that read:

Dear Homeowner,

This is to inform you that there is a scheduled association meeting for the Rolling Ridge Estates homeowners. We expect everyone to attend as we hand out our new homeowners' rules and regulations.

Good neighbors follow rules that we can all live by.

"I don't understand," Taylor admitted. "We never had a homeowners association."

"I know," Bree agreed, aggravated. "Somehow, these idiots," she indicated the letter, "put us down for the homeowner's association, and then, when we didn't attend or pay, they put a lien on our property. As a result, we can't get a house loan!"

"What the hell?" Taylor had been looking forward to seeing the trailer they could get.

"The thing is, our credit is good. Both of us," she said, showing Taylor how she had run both of their credit with the various bureaus. "While the house loan shows as a bill, not a home loan like you said, it has counted in our favor because our payments all show on time."

"Aren't we ahead on those payments?"

Bree nodded. "I make sure to send them in early and extra when we can afford it, just in case we need that buffer. Also, if we pay it off early—great."

"Well, we were going to pay it off in full with a home loan!"

"That's not happening now until we get this straightened out," she shook the letter from Rolling Ridge Estates.

"Crap, can you write them? Or do you want me to?"

"I'll write them tonight. There's an email on there," she pointed at the letterhead.

"Better send a physical copy, too."

"And I'll call them in a couple of days. I'm so outraged!"

"Hey, can't we write the three credit bureaus, telling them that this is in error?"

"That's a good idea."

"Better keep copies of all this to show what we've done."

"We?"

"You don't think I'm going to make you write all those," she waved at the credit bureau paperwork she had printed out as well as the letter from association.

"There's another letter I left in the family room, the first one I got. Good thing I procrastinated and didn't throw it away."

"Procrastinated, eh?" Taylor teased, heading to go get it. It was almost exactly like the second one. "Are you sure we didn't get any more of these?" she asked, gripping the first letter.

"No, and don't you think it's odd that we didn't get any notification of the lien or late fees? Shouldn't they have been billing us if we're members of their homeowner's association?"

"You would think."

After the kids were in bed, Bree and Taylor spent their evening writing their letters, doing a spell check on each of them, and letting the other spouse read them through before emailing them. Each of the credit bureaus got a physical letter from each of them, as did Rolling Ridge Estates. They varied their wording so none of the letters was an exact duplicate. By the time they got ready for bed, Bree and Taylor were both hyped up and finding it hard to sleep. On her way to work the next morning, Taylor put all the letters in a drop box at the post office, not trusting to wait until the postal worker picked up their mail at the end of the driveway.

* * * * *

Bree had deliveries to make, and she spent the morning fuming about what had happened. Once those were done, she started a few orders they had for stores and let those set while she drove down to the end of the driveway to prep and paint the rusty fence panels. She used a steel brush to knock off the rust and residue, as well as spider webs, and she cut back any brush attempting to scratch their fence. She then rubbed the first panel down with a rag to clean off the smallest of particles. Using a small roller on an extendable handle, she began to paint with the primer. She'd come back with regular paint later. She knew they'd be repeating this process over the years, but, for a free elaborate fence, she wasn't going to complain. The only thing that really bothered her was the fence posts they hadn't yet wrapped with rock. She scrubbed off the rust on these, too, and painted over them.

"That looks nice, Mom," the kids complimented her when they got off the bus. Bree waved to the bus driver and finished up the second panel. It was slow and tedious work. That rust could be persistent and she needed a step ladder for the high arch of the fence.

"Can we help?" she was asked next.

"Nope, I'm finishing up for the day," she told them as she put the last of the primer back in the can and closed the lid. Eyeing the fence, she wondered if she would have time to paint tomorrow. She always had more to do than make pots, but she loved being a house wife and working from home.

Home, such an innocuous word. She'd thought their home was safe, with a few hiccups the past two years of living here. She had no idea that it could have been taken from them and sold for this outstanding bill they knew nothing about. She tried not to think about it too much, not wanting the children to know how upset she was. She played with them in the backyard, throwing a ball around and playing kick ball. The thing was, Staffy loved kickball and frequently popped the ball in his attempts to pick it up with his teeth. Sometimes it was just a matter of playing keep away with the dog.

* * * * *

The combination of writing two letters to the homeowner's association, following up with an email, and calling them resulted in a detailed invoice showing exactly how much they had been billed by the association.

"Look at this. They are charging compound interest!" Taylor objected when she read it, shaking the paper.

"Not only that, but none of this shows them sending a certified letter to prove we received any of this."

"Well, we stated in our letter to them that we never joined their association and that we didn't owe this. What do they think, we'll just pay this and go on our merry way?"

"I put in my letter," she showed the copy again, although they had gone over it before, "that they better reverse their error. Instead, I get this mushy letter welcoming us to the association and proposing we make payment arrangements. How can they put this on our credit without our social security number?"

"They have our address, and that's enough?"

The credit agencies, the big three, weren't much better. The first one sent each of them a gratuitous credit print out, clearly showing the bill on each of their credit listings for Rolling Ridge Estates with the outstanding bill. The second one stated they couldn't release such information unless they filled out a form on their website to contend that the charges were in

error and detailing it. Bree did that immediately, duplicating the accusations in the notes on both of their credit reports.

The third one didn't even bother responding to their letters, but the letters were returned to them later, marked as an address unknown.

"How the hell could the credit bureau's address that we got off their own website be address unknown?" Taylor asked incredulously.

Their demands that Rolling Ridge Estates take the charges off and inform the credit bureaus fell on deaf ears. Now that they were disputing the charges, they did get mail from the association. The letters demanded payment in full and threatened legal action up to foreclosure and the sale of their home.

"I bet they saw all our improvements, the house, the land, the pond, and thought they could just steal it all from us," Bree said angrily, reading through the letter.

"I think we better find a lawyer."

"We can't *afford* a lawyer," Bree worried.

"Elsie has a friend, remember? Maybe he or she can help us."

* * * * *

As Ron looked over their paperwork, he shook his head. "And this is it? This is all the paperwork they sent you?"

"Yeah, how can they do this? This is our home, and they're threatening to sell it to the highest bidder," Bree fretted. The idea of their home being sold at auction without their knowledge or consent put a whole different light on the auction she'd attended with Vinnie and Gretchen. All those vehicles and other items she could have bid on. What if that stuff was confiscated from someone who didn't know about their debt?

"You'd be surprised how those associations think they are gods," Ron said as he read through it all. "Well, you've tried from your end. Let me send out a few more letters," he said with a grin. "Here is my agreement," he showed them. "I'm going to ask for them to pay my fees, too."

The two women exchanged looks, having braced themselves for a high fee. Either Elsie's recommendation or friendship with the man meant he gave them a deal, or he simply wanted to stick it to the homeowner's association. Either way, it would likely take months to see this through. They signed so Ron could get started.

CHAPTER FIFTY

"No, no," Bree said, discouraging Marmalade from bringing the dead mouse to her. He'd taken to showing her his kills, leaving them on the floor of the barn for her admiration. She didn't admire them in the least, and he couldn't understand why his human was so ungrateful. Bree watched the children chasing around Staffy in the backyard. He was huffing, drooling, and having a marvelous time while they played. She smiled as she saw Taylor pull around the circle of their drive and back up towards the barn. Marmalade dropped the mouse and took off around the corner of the barn.

"What do you have there?" she asked, pleased to see her home early.

"Barrels," she answered shortly as she got out of the truck and headed to the back to pull the tailgate down.

"What do you need barrels for?" She frowned at Taylor, who effortlessly tipped one and rolled it off the tailgate and onto the ground before propping it up and shimmying it to the door.

"Doesn't every family need barrels?" she asked with a grin.

Bree rolled her eyes, knowing that her wife liked her mysteries. She didn't offer to help her but, instead, watched as she wrestled the second one down and brought it to rest beside the first one. Bree found the ripple of Taylor's muscles quite appealing.

"Do we have Dawn dishwashing soap?" Taylor asked.

Frowning, Bree nodded, still wondering what she was up to.

"Hi, Mom!" Melanie greeted her, running up.

Taylor fended off Staffy, who was greeting her wiggling all over, his tail becoming a lethal weapon. "Hey there, darlin'. Could you get me the Dawn dishwashing soap from the kitchen?" She slapped her hands on the dog's rump above his wagging tail. He was always ecstatic at her returned greeting and roughhousing.

"Sure," Melanie said, running off with the dog racing her to the front door.

"What are you doing?" Bree asked, but the boys were greeting their mother.

"Hi, Mom."

"Hey, Mom. Can we help?"

"Sure can. Could you two bring the hose?" Taylor smiled as the two boys ran off eagerly. She looked at her wife. "Do they walk anywhere?"

"Nope, I swear they don't," she admitted, but she appreciated it, too. They seemed to sleep well, with all their activities. "What are you d—"

"Mom!" Barbie came up and threw herself into Taylor's arms. "Can I help, too?" She was eyeing the barrels that Taylor was removing the cap on.

"Sure can. Go turn on the water when I say," she told her, and Barbie went to follow the boys, who were now trying to unravel the hose and bring the end to them at the barn.

"Here you go." Melanie returned with the familiar blue bottle of dish soap.

"Nope. You're gonna squeeze that in here," she said, pointing to the opening on the first barrel while she removed the cap on the second one.

"Here's the hose, Mom," Bryan told her importantly.

"I helped," Jack whined.

"You sure did there, champ. Thank you both," Taylor said. "Could you hold the hose in there?" she asked Jack, pointing to where Melanie had squeezed the soap in the large barrel and was now squeezing it into the other one. Waving to Barbie, she called, "Turn it on!" They all watched as the hose sputtered and bucked before water came shooting out the end, and Jack directed it in the hole, splattering himself and those around him.

"Hey!" Melanie squawked. "You got me wet!"

"You'll dry," Taylor assured her, heading off a potential fight. "Thank you for the soap. Could you put it back for me?" She watched as the child reluctantly walked off, closing the flip top.

"My turn," Bryan told Jack, trying to take the hose away and push his brother aside.

"No!" the younger boy said, resisting him. "Mom said I was to fill it."

"But it's my turn."

"Bryan, I told Jack to fill that," she said to him sternly, trying to cut off his propensity to be a bit of a bully to his younger brother. "Let him do his job." Pointing to the other one, she asked, "Jack, fill that one for me, too?"

She waited until it was partly full before she turned it on its side and recapped it. "Bryan, I need you and Barbie to rock this back and forth?" Barbie had come back after turning on the hose, intent on what her mom was doing.

Bree frowned, still wondering what was going on but willing to indulge. The children seemed to be having fun, and soon a competition began over rolling the large barrel back and forth between them. Barbie and Bryan were laughing at the chugging sound within.

"Me, too! Me, too!" Jack complained, the hose now forgotten.

"Jack, go turn the water off," Taylor told him, taking the hose and holding it in the hole of the second barrel. He ran off and was back at the same time Melanie returned. "Okay you two, I need you to roll this one back and forth," she told them and recapped the barrel and tilted it on its side.

"What is going on?" Bree murmured to Taylor while they watched the kids roll the barrels, laughing at the chugging of the water as it sloshed. With all that water, it didn't roll as easily as they thought it would.

"How else do you clean the inside of a barrel?" Taylor asked her wife with a grin.

"What are you going to do with those?"

"Floats," she answered, turning back to her truck to remove some two-by-fours and two sheets of plywood and then lean them against the barn. By the time the children got tired of rolling the barrels, she had gone to the house and gotten some tools and screws for the project. "Okay, okay, let's empty out the barrels." When they stopped, Taylor opened the caps so the barrel could drain. "Could someone turn on the water again?" she nodded towards the spigot at the house and Jack ran off to comply. She filled in about a gallon after draining out the soapy water, rolled them some more, and drained that out, leaving the cap off.

"Who wants to help me make a raft?" she asked and had immediate volunteers.

"Do you want your wife to help?" Bree asked dryly, now understanding what the barrels and wood were for.

"Absolutely," she said with a smile, pleased.

They measured out the sheets of plywood, made a platform with the two-by-fours, and attached the sheets to the other wood with screws.

"Careful, there," Taylor cautioned, not wanting the children anywhere near when she used the saw.

Taylor slapped at mosquitos and gnats, still sweaty from her day at work and getting even dirtier while they built the raft. She got sawdust on her sweaty arms, and the bugs seems to be drawn to her. She had bug bites and blood over her dirty, dusty, and sweaty arms. By the time they remembered dinner, she had looped the barrels with a metal band that she screwed to the wood platform and tightened down with a set of screws on both ends of each barrel. "Doesn't that look fine?" she asked her wife, pointing at the platform they had all contributed to making.

"It looks marvelous. How are you going to get it in the pond?" Bree asked practically. The combination of the wood and the two barrels was heavy, and it was up here by the barn, nowhere near the pond.

"We can use one of the carts if we tip it up like this," she demonstrated, unbalancing the raft.

"Great, and how are we going to get up there?" she pointed to the top of the platform. The barrels made it high off the ground, and she guessed it would probably not sink very low in the water.

"Oh, yeah, didn't think of that," she admitted, looking at what they had built. "Guess I'll have to figure out a ladder." She looked at the children, who she'd swung onto the raft so they could stand and pretend they were floating on it. "I didn't get enough wood to build a ladder. That's going to have to wait for another day," she told them, seeing their disappointment.

"Come on, we need to get our things cleaned up," Bree said, trying to get them enthused to pick up their toys. "We're late for dinner."

"If you want to start dinner, we'll clean up out here," Taylor offered and, at her wife's look, quickly added, "or I could go start dinner and they can help you clean up out here?"

Bree grinned, appreciating the option. She hated it when anyone, least of all Taylor, made assumptions about her duties in this family.

Taylor did end up putting away her tools and the other things they had used for the build. She had the children gather their toys and put them away while she rewound the hose and looped it on the hanger next to the house. By the time they were done, Bree had macaroni and cheese on the table for the kids, and Taylor was happy to go get her shower.

CHAPTER FIFTY-ONE

One afternoon Taylor took a walk with the children along the trail in the woods and out by the newly built development to the east of their place. It got them out of Bree's hair so she could concentrate on casting pots. They could still hear hammering and saws humming that had stopped, for the most part, in Rolling Ridge Estates behind their house. The dozens of trees they had planted along their property were growing tall and strong, and the chicken wire they had put up to keep out rabbits out of the fingerlings was full of grass. While the children played, Taylor took the time to pull the grass away from the little trees.

She could see a large U-Haul in the driveway of one of the houses in the new subdivision. It was still a relatively small and close-knit neighborhood. Since it was so new, everyone seemed to know each other or, if not, they soon would. So far, she had gotten along well with those she had met out on walks with their own dogs. Staffy had made a couple of friends, and she kept a short leash on the exuberant dog. They'd even been invited to the last Fourth of July block party, where they shot off fireworks together. Taylor watched the new family come out to get another load of belongings from the van. There was a mother and father, a girl of about fourteen with a toddler on her hip, and two kids about her kids' ages.

* * * * *

A month later, in the heat of summer, Taylor was alone at home and sitting on the porch, enjoying the peace and quiet of their home on a rare day off from work. Bree had taken the children to Gretchen and Vinnie's to deliver pots for her greenhouse and shop. Staffy suddenly alerted, startling Taylor from her near doze in the shade during the hottest part of the day. She followed the dog's intense gaze and saw there were people on the pond. It was a family of six, and some were shoving off from the far side where the wood trail came out, using the blow-up canoe and inner tubes Bree had bought after the kids grew more adept at swimming. The family was heading determinedly towards the raft in the middle of the pond.

"What the hell?" Taylor murmured, peering across at them. The pool accessories had been locked up, with ropes so the children wouldn't be tempted to take them out without permission. It was then that she recognized the mother from the newly-built development. She was working on a knot on one of the blow-ups and trying to talk to her impatient toddler.

Taylor dashed across the yard with Staffy at her side. Unsure whether he should rush ahead at the intruders or not, he stayed close and grunted his displeasure.

"Excuse me, what do you think you're doing around my pond!?" she called.

"My kids have been well-behaved today, and they want to go for a swim. I saw you have a pond, so we are going for a dip." Already, three of her four children were in the pond.

The woman's response shocked her to the core, and Taylor struggled for a moment with what to say. She could have told them that this part of the pond was full of leeches and that was why they had hauled in sand for the side near the house. That was also why the toys were tied up over on this side and why the children were afraid of the deep, dark, leech-filled section of the pond. But none of that was any of these people's business.

"This is not a public pond, and you are on my private property! I need you to get off my land, now! I never gave permission for you to be allowed on our property."

The woman turned to face the oncoming Taylor and shouted, "WHO THE HECK DO YOU THINK YOU ARE? IT IS A VERY HOT DAY, AND MY KIDS WANT TO GO FOR A SWIM! AND THEY WILL."

"Not in my private pond, they won't. How did you even get on our land?" Taylor asked, but she knew. That track through the woods had led them right to the spot.

"SCREW OFF! IN OUR OLD NEIGHBORHOOD, WE DID THIS ALL THE TIME. MY KIDS ARE GOING FOR A SWIM NOW, AND YOU WILL NOT EVEN KNOW WE ARE HERE. YOU ARE JUST BEING SELFISH, AND I WILL NOT ALLOW MY BABIES TO SUFFER BECAUSE OF IT."

Taylor was incredulous at the woman's audacity. She had never met someone so entitled in all her life, not even at the diner. She amended that thought for a second when she recalled her sister, Tia, was exactly like this. The other children were splashing and obviously enjoying themselves, and the oldest had even made it to the raft and was attempting to use the ladder Taylor had made to get onto it.

"I will not ask again! You either get off my property now, or I will call the police. You are not using our pond, and that is final." Taylor could well imagine how their homeowner's insurance would feel about strangers using their pond. What if something happened?

Just then, the woman finished untying the knot for the impatient two-year old. "There you go," she said sweetly to the little girl. "Watch your sister?" she cautioned the older ones as the toddler pushed the tube with the bottom in it towards the muddy water. "Okay, jump in," she told the little one. "Don't listen to this stupid witch."

"Yeah, you're a stupid witch," one of the kids repeated tauntingly at Taylor.

"We are going for a swim, and you can't stop us," the fourteen-year-old said and dove into the water from the raft.

"That's it, I'm calling the police," Taylor said and turned to go get her cell.

"You would really not allow four kids to go swimming on a hot day? What kind of heartless person are you? You just let us go swimming for an hour, and we will leave. Don't you want to be a good neighbor to us?" the woman asked, getting in the water with the toddler and standing in the mud facing Taylor.

"No, I don't want to be a good neighbor," Taylor stopped to say. "You trespassed onto my property without permission. Leave! Now!"

Taylor couldn't hear what the woman said to her kids, but they started coming towards her where she stood in the mud. The youngest started crying when she took away the floaty. Taylor laughed when the oldest boy stood up and started peeing into the pond because she could see his stork-like legs had leeches on them. She would bet they *all* had leeches on them by now.

The mother turned on Taylor, unsure as to why she was laughing. She gestured to where her son had just tucked himself away. "MAYBE THAT WILL TEACH YOU TO BE A BETTER NEIGHBOR, YOU STUPID WITCH."

"Get off my land!" Taylor said back, trying to keep her voice stern, but she had just caught sight of leeches on the mom's legs, too. She made as if to go after the oldest two.

"Don't you come near my babies, or I'll call the police on *you*. Who do you think they will believe? A good mommy or a pathetic witch like you?"

The children left the float toys in the pond, where the current immediately pulled them away from the shore. The kids laughed, imagining they had inconvenienced the witch. Taylor watched as they followed their mom and toddler along the path back to the development, the dusty path causing mud to cake on the bottoms of their feet. She wondered when they would discover the leeches and went to capture the floats where the current had sent them down to the sandy beach. She heard the screams not long after catching the first float. *Must have finally found the leeches. Good,* she thought, *serves them right.*

* * * * *

When she told Bree about the new trespassers, she immediately wanted to send off a letter to the woman.

"No, let's send it to their homeowners association, but we should mention that woman specifically."

"They have a homeowners association, too?" Bree asked mournfully. She was sick to death of the lawsuit and all the information they'd had to provide for it to defend their own land. It was also taking too long and caused her to stress out every time she thought of it.

"It seems to be a trend."

They took a walk that evening in order to get the woman's exact address. They also walked through the new neighborhood to find that the housing development, while unfinished, was named Golden Acres. There were already a couple of dozen finished houses within it and more in various stages of being built.

"Couldn't they come up with something more original?" Bree murmured. They had the kids with them, and they had waved at several

kids they knew from the bus and from school. She didn't want to create animosity with any of the other neighbors if they were overheard.

Their letter read:

Dear Golden Acres Homeowners Association,

We are the owners of the property located to the west of your subdivision. Our field abuts the backyards of several of your properties in the association. Many is the time we have met homeowners who are walking their dogs in our field and taking advantage of the space. We also own the woods, which is clearly marked by No Trespassing signs, purple paint, and the pink property markers from our assessment done two years ago. While we haven't objected to the dog walkers or the children playing in the field, we most heartily object to those who gather our wood or walk onto our property to use our pond.

Most recently we had a very distasteful encounter with one of your residents and her children who live at…

They included the property address and explained in detail what had been said by the mother and her children, Taylor's response, and that in the future they would be pursuing legal action against any or all who trespassed in that manner.

The letter continued:

We hope to be good neighbors to the residents who live in Golden Acres Homeowners Association. We have made a few friends with some of your people, but this incursion onto our private property must stop immediately.

Signed, Bree and Taylor Moore.'

"Well, if that doesn't do it, I guess we ask Ron to take this one on, too," Taylor stated, perusing it once more for spelling or punctuation errors.

"He's going to charge us for that one if we do."

"Let's see how this goes first."

HOME ~ First Nillionaires Club

CHAPTER FIFTY-TWO

"Remember when we signed all the paperwork to buy this land?" Taylor asked, raising her eyebrow as she searched for exactly what she was looking for.

"Of course, I do, but what?" Bree asked, wondering what her wife was getting at.

"Our state makes sure you sign off that your land is or is not part of a homeowners association. I remember thinking at the time that was odd, but Mr. Davidson said it was part of the state protecting its landowners. He was in such a rush, I didn't ask about that specifically, but I remembered thinking, 'That's a lot of land to fall under something like that.'" She found their copies of the papers and thumbed through them, scanning. "Here it is," she said, pointing to the check mark that specifically said they were aware of no homeowners association for their property. "See? They don't have a leg to stand on. I'm betting when we look at our deed it says something like that, too." She showed Bree where she was pointing.

Bree started fishing through their files, thumbing rapidly through file folders until she found the deed. "Here it is."

"That should go in a safe or somewhere," Taylor pointed out dryly.

HOME ~ First Nillionaires Club

"Yeah, yeah, yeah," her wife answered, her hand flapping at her as she dismissed it. "Aren't you glad we don't have to wait for the bank to open to get this out of the safe deposit box?"

They both read over the deed, which included no information about a homeowners association. Since they bought the property before the housing developments were built around them, they should be free and clear.

"We better get copies of this to Ron," Taylor added as Bree slipped one piece of paper in the scanner portion of their printer and pressed a button.

They had been frustrated by the responses (or lack of responses) from Rolling Ridge Estates but pleasantly surprised by the quick response from Golden Acres, who apologized for their resident and said they had been warned. A copy of their newsletter was enclosed, showing that they had addressed the issue of trespassing into the woods with their residents, and everyone would now know this was private property and not part of their perks for living in the association. A warning letter from Rolling Ridge Estates wasn't nearly as nice.

Dear homeowner,

It has come to our attention that you are keeping livestock on your property. Specifically, chickens. The sound that your rooster is making is interfering in the privacy and peace and quiet of other residents. This is your only warning to remove the livestock from the property, which is a violation of your homeowners' agreement.

"This is the third such nonsense letter we've gotten from Rolling Ridge Estates. They didn't like Staffy barking, either. They're going to continue harassing us. I wonder that they don't send this shit to Ron?"

"Because they refuse to acknowledge his letters, too. He called today. We're going to have to go to court," Bree told her, her voice a little shaky at the thought. They hadn't had to go to court since they had finalized the adoption on Jack, and that was fine with her. She hated court.

* * * * *

"This may take another year, the way their company lawyers are dragging it out," Ron explained sadly when they met again. "Do you wish to proceed?"

"Wait a minute," Taylor interjected angrily. "They bill us for a debt that isn't ours, cause us all sorts of emotional heartache and intimidation, and now we should drop it because it might take more time?"

"More time means more money spent on it. I think that's what they're counting on. They have the association's money and have no problem spending it for them. They think—in the end—they will win this."

"Will they?" Bree asked, sounding afraid. She was so worried they'd sell their home out from under them. That lien really scared her.

"No, they won't. You didn't join, and the paperwork you showed me where you bought your property shows you didn't join. They can't force you to obey their rules and regulations because it's your private property," he explained. "We can speed it up by agreeing to go to arbitration, though."

"What's that?" Bree inquired for both of them.

Trying to simplify it for his clients he explained, "The arbitrator, a person that both parties agree on, just sits us down around a table and goes over the evidence we both present."

"That sounds easy," Bree commented.

Taylor nodded, but she was suspicious.

"Yes, it does," he agreed. "But ..." he began, and the two women exchanged looks. "Whatever they decide is final. You cannot appeal the verdict."

They both thought about that. "Would it be better to go before a judge?" Taylor asked.

"Not necessarily. They're pulling tricks like trying to intimidate you with their letters. The chickens or your dog aren't the worst of what they can pull."

When someone complained about the noise their rooster was making a few days before, Bree had been forced to let in the police to address the complaint.

"I'm just saying that an arbitration will be faster, but it will be final," he explained.

The women exchanged looks.

"We can't wait for another year to go before a judge," Taylor put in, sounding defeated. They'd both lost sleep worrying about what the association could do to them with their lawyers.

"Do you want me to draft the letter asking if they'd be willing to go through arbitration then?"

They exchanged looks again, and Bree nodded for them both.

"Then, I'll do that. Don't be so glum," he told Taylor. "I'm certain we can win this."

She sighed. "I'm just so tired of this crap. I don't even want to look in the mailbox anymore in case they pull this again. It's like, what are they going to send us next?"

"Can I report their emails for spam?" Bree asked next.

"Send me all of the ones you've gotten and if you responded," he requested eagerly. "The more I have about their harassment, the more in our favor this is going to go."

* * * * *

"Is this all worth it? I just want to live in peace," Bree said sadly as they headed home.

"It's our home; we should fight for it. We couldn't even sell it, anyway, because of that lien they have, which they keep adding to daily," Taylor said bitterly.

The McMansions proved the association had a lot of money behind it, and the suit Ron filed had only riled them up, which had led to the increase in harassment. It seemed to be a vicious cycle.

"I asked Ron in an email if Longuard is somehow involved," Bree informed her as she turned onto the highway that would lead out to their house. Ellen was already there, babysitting her grandchildren.

"Did he look into it?"

"He said there is no record of him owning property in that association or being on the board."

"That doesn't mean anything. He could have it under another name. It isn't our fault his son went to prison." The news had had a field day with that incident.

"We need to renew our business license," Bree told her miserably. "I hope we don't have a problem with that."

"We've done nothing wrong. Let's just keep it all above board and legal. And, for God's sake, we can't be late with anything."

* * * * *

"I've fed the kids already. How'd it go?" Ellen asked when she saw the two of them.

They'd stopped and gone grocery shopping since they didn't have the children with them and underfoot, and they were unpacking the van and bringing in the bags.

"Mom, I have soccer practice tomorrow," Melanie said to Bree.

"Thanks for reminding me," Bree said sweetly, but, inwardly, she was groaning. That meant she had to stop early from making pots and sit with all the other soccer moms while the children ran up and down the field. None of them were very good at this age, and it was rather tedious and boring. Bree didn't enjoy it, and she was tired of those moms who were trying to be friendly who asked what her *husband* did for a living. She'd explained that they owned a pottery business, but her *wife* did landscaping to bring in a second income. They assumed the couple were poor because they were a lesbian couple. What did them being a lesbian couple have anything to do with being poor, she would have liked to know. A few of the moms definitely didn't want to associate with her now, and she hated that. She knew the other children would love the practice since it meant they could play on the jungle gym next to the park where the kids practiced, but that, too, required her time, watching them to make sure they didn't get hurt. She'd rather they play at home.

They waited until the groceries were put away and the children were off to their rooms to get ready for bed before explaining to Ellen about the arbitration.

"You fight for this," Ellen insisted. "You've provided a lovely home for these children to grow up in, and I know how much you sacrificed for them to get it. Don't let those mean bastards take it away from you. This is your home, your castle, your kingdom," she said passionately. "Don't let anyone take it away from you!"

"Thank you, Mom," Taylor said, giving the older woman a hug. She left soon afterwards, taking home some of the leftovers from dinner.

"She's right, you know. All our friends say the same thing," Bree said while they finished cleaning up the family room. They didn't know who was worse at leaving their toys strewn about, the children or the dog. Even Marmalade occasionally batted his play mice about on the floor or brought in catnip from the woods and left dried crumbles of the leaves on the floor where he rolled.

"This is our home," Taylor agreed. After almost two years of living there and the amount of work that had gone into their land and the house, it was theirs, and they would fight for it to the end.

HOME ~ First Nillionaires Club

CHAPTER FIFTY-THREE

The arbitrator listened to both sides, but it was proven that the couple had not signed any agreement to join the Rolling Ridge Estates Association. The association lawyers tried to argue about the interest and fees they had incurred before the couple had brought the lawsuit, but Ron countered that the whole misunderstanding would have been avoided if the association had simply presented the couple with a certified delivery from the post office. It would have confirmed they had never received the bill, had not joined the association, and that they were under no obligation to follow the rules and regulations set forth in the association's charter. They had never done any of those things.

Ron even brought up how the association had trespassed on their land and stolen their fence because they claimed it was an eyesore. "This *was* farmland, the fence was part of that, and when my clients bought the property, they knew this. That doesn't give the association the right to trespass on my client's property because they don't like the look of their land or what is on it."

They were all on pins and needles and sweating, despite the excellent air conditioning. Both Bree and Taylor wore dresses because Ron had requested them to make them look more feminine and, by extension, helpless. "It appeals to some men on a basic level. It will look good for the arguments," he'd explained.

HOME ~ First Nillionaires Club

When the arbitrator came back in, carrying a file folder brimming with both sides' written arguments, copies of the proof they had both presented, and all the legal filings regarding the case, his face was very grave. "Okay, this is my judgment," he announced formally. "The association's actions border on criminal conduct. This is precisely the type of wanton and willful disregard for the rights of others that evinces gross negligence and warrants punitive damages."

The lawyers for the association made as if to rise up from the table, but the arbitrator waved them down.

"I find for the plaintiff. They did not join the Rolling Ridge Estates Homeowners Association. They indicated they had not been asked to join, and they also did not agree to the rules and regulations set out in this association. The Rolling Ridge Estates Homeowners Association made no attempt to contact the homeowners regarding the fees they felt that they had incurred. As you said," he addressed Ron directly, "This property is still zoned as farm land. They can have chickens on their property. These ten acres are listed as mostly swamp land. The homeowners are improving it with the house, and you stated they put in a pond?" At Ron's nod he continued. "I rule for them, and the Rolling Ridge Estates will pay all attorney fees and court costs, as well as these punitive damages, which I hope will serve as a deterrent to further frivolous charges or actions."

He fixed the lawyers for the association with a glare as he named an amount that made Ron's eyebrows raise and caused Bree and Taylor to exchange a surprised look.

"I cannot rule that they pay for your time," he looked at the lesbian couple sadly, "but I hope these punitive damages will offset that. But any *more* harassment, whether by sending police to the property or issuing letters regarding your livestock, should stop, or there will be further sanctions." He glowered at the defense's lawyers, who shifted uncomfortably. "This is my judgement, and it's final." He brought down his gavel, rose from the table, and walked out. The court reporter finished her typing and quickly followed him, while the other lawyers stood in disgust and left Bree, Taylor, and Ron alone in the conference room.

"We won!" Taylor hissed to Bree and exchanged a hug with her. They both gave Ron a hug.

"Now, I'll file on this immediately to get my costs back," he told them with a smile. "You can tell Elsie about the win?" he asked.

"Elsie?" Bree asked, still unsure what relationship their friend had with this man. She'd said he was a friend when she recommended him but had given no other details.

"She's been harassing *me* about how long this was taking."

"Along with us asking you, too?" Taylor asked in amusement.

"Yes," he admitted, returning her smile. "She doesn't like being told it's none of her business."

"How long have you been friends?" Bree asked.

"Since birth," he sighed. "Our parents hoped we would marry since we lived next door to each other, but she had that peculiar habit of dating women, and as I prefer women, too … well, it doesn't mesh well. Our parents were really disappointed." He laughed, and they joined in. "We're just good friends, and that will have to do. She introduced me to my wife after she found out she couldn't date her."

They all laughed again.

Bree and Taylor were still puzzled by the whole association debacle, and why it happened in the first place. They suspected Longuard was behind it, but they never could find a connection.

* * * * *

"Well, it's ours again," Taylor said on the way home from the courthouse. "Ron said the lien should be off our credit within a month. We can get that home loan and get the trailer and camper!"

"I was thinking…" began Bree carefully.

"Uh-oh," Taylor got in, teasing her wife, who so often did that to her.

"Let's shop for new when we know that's off our credit. It's time we bought new on some things we need instead of always settling for used. I mean, if we see a good deal on something used, we can buy that, but let's shop for new."

"Sounds good," Taylor agreed, looking forward to shopping with her wife. "And, with the money we got from this court case, we can afford it."

* * * * *

It took more than a month to get the charge off their credit, and some reporting would take months to officially be taken off. Ron sent repeated threatening letters to the Rolling Ridge Estates Association, until he finally contacted the arbitrator, who gave them forty-eight hours to comply before incurring additional fees and sanctions against them. They seemed to have been waiting to get their hands slapped over this and immediately complied. The check for the punitive damages came through about then, as well; there could be no more dragging their feet.

The couple didn't buy new. Being thrifty was too ingrained in their DNA, but they had fun shopping and getting ideas of what they wanted.

They found an excellent deal on a used snowmobile trailer that had the drive-up door in the back and an additional drive-down door in the front. This allowed the couple to pack and unpack carts easier at their shows. The also had a light that ran off a battery that charged when they drove down the highway, so they were no longer loading or unloading in the dark. Dual axles meant they weren't overloading the trailer with their goods, but they would still need to use a large U-Haul truck for the big spring show or the Christmas show in the fall.

The camper fit snuggly in the bed of their truck. "Look at this!" Taylor crowed, folding away the bunk beds in the camper to give them more room. It slept the four kids on the sides with the adults, and the beds were big enough to fit them for years to come. The moms would sleep in a queen-sized bed that extended over the truck's cab. The camper also had a kitchenette and a small shower and toilet. The camper felt luxurious, and its propane heater would keep them warm during fall and winter shows. "We're living the high life now."

They were both pleased with how everything had all worked out and weren't even upset when a new letter arrived from the Golden Acres Homeowners Association, asking them to join. They immediately wrote out a letter refusing, sent it certified mail, and cc'd Ron, just in case this one escalated, as well.

"Well, we have our home now, lady, and, while we still have payments to make on it, we are well on our way," Bree said, satisfied with their purchases. With the new equipment, they'd be able to do tons more shows, including ones that didn't allow car sleeping or tents.

"We have more than a home, *lady*," Taylor countered. "We have a new-ish trailer and a home away from home and the most wonderful kids ever."

Bree smiled and added, "And, most importantly, we have each other."

THE END

K'ANNE MEINEL

If you have enjoyed **HOME ~ The First Nillionaires Club**, I hope you will enjoy this excerpt from **BEAUTY AND THE BEAST.**

BEAUTY AND THE BEAST

✣ CHAPTER ONE ✣

The sounds of girlish laughter rang out through the gardens. King Sebastián looked on indulgently as he then turned to his queen and smiled. "It sounds like she is having a grand time," he commented.

"She is running about like a hoyden, perhaps I should …" she began worriedly, but he held up his hand to silence her condemnation of their princess, their only child. He would not have had his girl be any other way.

"Let her be; she will be a child only once." He turned back to look out over the extensive gardens that led up to the castle, smiling again as he saw his daughter playing in the maze that had been built there last year. It was just now over her head, but she knew the pathways well. "Is that Lord Rosenblaum's daughter I see?"

"Yes, Lord Rosenblaum implored me to indulge his daughter's friendship," Queen Isabellá answered, a small smile forming on her own lips as she watched her daughter completely confound the other little girl. The maze wasn't that tall yet, but it was over both girls' heads. If one didn't know the paths as the princess did, it could get confusing. From the balcony where the king and queen stood, they could easily see the various passages in and out. "That poor man, left to raise his daughter alone."

"The gel will be good for our daughter; she doesn't allow the princess her own way all the time as the servants do." The king watched the young girl get on her hands and knees and slip between the still growing hedges, find the young princess, and trip her.

"No fair, you cheated!" the princess accused.

"How is it cheating?" the other little girl demanded, standing up, her hands on her hips.

The princess stood, too, and dusted off her dress which was full of dirt. "It just is," she stated with a tone of arrogance only a royal princess could impose into those words.

The little girl laughed at the haughty princess, and, when the princess reached for her, she ran off, the princess in hot pursuit.

"She will need a bath tonight," the queen stated dryly as she watched the two girls play.

"She will need a strong man by her side one day," the king responded, and he didn't sound displeased. He knew how hard the queen had tried to deliver the hoped-for son, but they had to content themselves with this daughter of his that he so adored.

"But Father, I don't like Prince Friedrich," Princess Gabrielle, now a young woman of marriageable age, complained to her father, as they practiced dancing in the ballroom, the musicians playing exclusively for their king.

"You have refused several courtiers, my darling," he rebuked, not quite as displeased as he sounded. He liked the idea of keeping his daughter a little longer. He knew that, having only a daughter, his kingdom would best be joined with a powerful neighbor, and they'd fielded several offers from young men of noble birth, many who had never even seen Princess Gabrielle.

"None of them have even touched my heart, Father," she confided, as they bent their legs to the music, her curtsy a little less smooth than it could have been.

"Nay, pet, you know better than that," he told her, admonishing her dancing as well as her response.

Amazingly, Princess Gabrielle flourished a step that made her father laugh at her exuberance. It made her look far more enticing to the watching courtiers than the dance normally allowed, but also showed that she did indeed have the necessary skills taught to her by her dancing instructors over the years. She was just showing off now as the dance continued. The music became a little more exuberant, and he watched the musicians who were enjoying themselves as they played for the princess.

"You are getting too long in the tooth not to marry and marry well," he continued, his back stiff, as he expertly led her through the steps.

"But, Father, shouldn't I also marry for love? Didn't you?" she countered, taking three little steps in her dancing slippers, clapping in time with the music before being swirled back into her father's arms.

BEAUTY AND THE BEAST

"I was lucky that your mother loved me as much as I loved her, but, as you well know, that is not always the way of it. You may have to find love later but marry instead for our kingdom."

"Why can't it be a queendom?" she asked and then smiled at the blaze that temporarily shone in his eyes. She knew how to get his goat.

He shook his head at her and then a finger. "That is not the way of the world, pet, and you know it."

Gabrielle did indeed know it and didn't care. She did not like any of the men, both young and old, who had come courting. They were only after her father's kingdom, knowing that marrying her would give them the riches it contained. Some wanted the power, as well. Her father only allowed her to meet those who had or would have their own kingdom and knew what it would entail to govern both.

Slowly, they practiced their dancing, through several waltzes, both the traditional and then the regional. Some were exclusive to their own native lands, the people always enjoying the sound of their local music played by the castle's musicians and seeing their royals dance to them. The music carried out the palace windows, into the courtyards, down into the village where many danced in the street to the familiar tunes. As the king and his princess danced in the ballroom, several of the servants stopped what they were doing to watch, gossiping about how fine a figure the two made as they practiced.

"Princess Gabrielle will make a fine queen someday," one said, and several others agreed.

"May I cut in?" the queen inquired as she tapped him on the shoulder.

"Are you cutting in to dance with me or your daughter, dear lady?" he teased.

She smiled but surprised him when she said, "My daughter, of course."

He laughed as he bowed low, kissed his daughter's fingertips and backed away to see the queen take up his daughter's hand to dance, taking the lead. She really was quite adept and he laughed further. Why wouldn't she be? The king looked around, and, seeing Lord Rosenblaum's daughter among the courtiers watching, walked over and bowed to the young maiden.

"Lady Rosenblaum, may I have the honor of this dance?"

Flustered for moment, she blushed but nodded and held out her hand. She wasn't dressed for dancing, having come to watch her friend in her lessons, but she easily fell into step with the king. "Of course, your highness."

"And what brings you here to the castle today?" he asked indulgently, admiring the young woman who had been friends with the princess since they were young. He recalled them playing in the gardens endlessly, building sandcastles, fishing, and even hunting under the watchful eye of himself, his men, and his wife and her ladies—learning everything young women of their kingdom should learn. He had thought it odd that this girl had indulged in hunting, but then he recalled she had never actually killed anything. In fact, she'd been teased that, despite her prowess with various weapons, she had never brought meat to their table.

"Gabrielle and I were to go practice with our bows today." Rosie curtseyed to his bow in the course of the dance.

"Ah, yes, I had forgotten that lesson was today. How do ye fare at the sport?" He knew very well she was an excellent shot and had a good eye.

"I am not as good or as accurate at the princess, but I hold my own," she asserted quite stoutly, if a bit diplomatically, ever aware she was talking to the king.

He laughed heartily, his head falling back to guffaw loudly. Several of the courtiers and servants wondered what the young woman had said to cause such mirth in their sovereign. "Gabrielle seems to need to excel at the sports the two of you play in," he commented when he had stopped laughing so exuberantly.

"She can be competitive," the young lady agreed with an impish smile. Still, she admired her friend because she was witty, kind, and loving to all her many friends, but most especially to her, her best friend for these many years.

The king knew it was probably his fault that his daughter enjoyed the masculine sports as well as the feminine skills. Not having a son, he had indulged her. Still, he was vastly proud of the fine young woman that his daughter had become. He threw an admiring glance at the princess before returning his attention to her best friend. Even her choice in friends was something that pleased him. Lady Rosenblaum was an exquisite example of the type of young women he wanted for his daughter.

BEAUTY AND THE BEAST

"Mother, Father says I must choose among the men who keep asking for my hand," Gabrielle complained to the queen as they danced.

"Yes, my darling girl, it is about time that you married. We will need an heir or two of your body to carry on the line. Your husband will want a son for his kingdom and, God willing, you will give him two, so the second son can govern this land of ours."

"Any man I marry will want our riches," she said, a touch of derision in her tone as she remembered some of the men she had met.

"True," the queen nodded in agreement, executing a nice little twirl of her own to match her daughter's, even though it wasn't part of the dance. Several courtiers clapped at the exhibition. She saw that the princess was suddenly self-conscious, and she gestured with her hand, indicating those standing about should join in instead of watching the princess practicing the various dances. It would also teach her to dance among her courtiers, executing steps of the various dances and adroitly avoiding colliding with them.

She looked at her daughter who was already taller than she was, having taken after her father, the king. Any man who her daughter chose to marry would be lucky to get this young woman. She was highly educated for a woman of nobility, an indulgence the king insisted upon any time her curiosity got the better of her. He had challenged her and her tutors to teach her not only of their own kingdom, but that of those surrounding their lands and beyond. Several tutors had been fired because they did not agree with the king that women, even those of royal birth and destined to be queens in their own right, should be educated.

"I think some will want you for your fine self," she added, seeing how delightful her daughter looked as she pirouetted through the dance. She felt the young woman shudder slightly and pulled back to ask, "What is wrong with you, pet?"

"I don't think I am natural, Mother" the young princess nearly sobbed, trying to keep her face from breaking into a cry in front of those watching. "I don't think I want to marry any of the men who have come for my hand."

"Why do you say this?" the queen fretted. "Has one been too forward with you?" She suddenly worried as to whether the chaperones hadn't been enough to guard their daughter. She gave her daughter a closer look.

"No, Mother, they have been most respectful." She wouldn't mention the one she'd had to pull her hunting knife on—much to their

mutual surprise. He had, at first, laughed, thinking she wouldn't dare spill a drop of his equally royal, but male, and therefore superior blood. He had gone away thinking she should have enjoyed his amorous attentions and wouldn't forgive her insult to his person with the permanent scar he now carried over his heart with the threat of her cutting deeper if he dared to touch her again. She didn't know how to explain to her mother how she didn't enjoy the attention she was getting from these men. Young or old—none of them made her heart flutter. She would do her duty if her parents insisted, but none of them did anything for her.

"There now," her mother said, patting her hand as they danced, "you'll find your prince, maybe a king!" she said confidently, indulgently, and perhaps a bit condescendingly. She remembered her own worries over marrying the king. He had been so manly she had been quite overwhelmed. She was certain her daughter was just experiencing her own maidenly airs.

The queen smiled as the dances finally came to an end, the practice for that day over for both the participants as well as the musicians. She joined the king and watched as their daughter went off with her friends, mostly young women. But almost exclusively with the young Lady Rosenblaum, who hooked her arm through the princess's as they walked in the gardens. They looked young, healthy, and vibrant. The king and queen shared their enjoyment of their daughter, quite looking forward to when she chose her mate and gave them grandchildren.

TO BE CONTINUED…

Check out all my books at: www.kannemeinel.com.

About the Author

K'Anne Meinel is a prolific Lesbian-Fiction bestselling author with more than 125 published works including shorts, novellas, and novels in English. Most of her work has been translated and now there are several hundred in Spanish, Portuguese, French, Italian, German, and even Japanese. She is a multi-award-winning novelist, writing in Romance, Drama, Fiction, Murder, Mystery and several other genres. She is an American author born in Milwaukee, Wisconsin and raised outside Oconomowoc. Upon early graduation from high school, she went to a private college in Milwaukee and then moved to California for seventeen years before returning to Wisconsin. She is known for her wonderful, realistic, and detailed backgrounds, her stories make you feel like you are 'there,' as a part of the story yourself. Named the lesbian Danielle Steel of her time, K'Anne continues to write interesting stories in a variety of genres in both the lesbian and mainstream fiction categories.

~ *Because a publisher should stand behind their authors~*

What do you do when you meet someone who changes everything you know about love and passion?

Paige Harlow is a good girl. She's always known where she was going in life: top grades, an ivy league school, a medical degree, regular church attendance, and a happy marriage to a man. So falling in love with her gorgeous roommate and best friend Alyssa Torres is no small crisis. Alyssa is chasing demons of her own, a medical condition that makes her an outcast and a family dysfunctional to the point of disintegration make her a questionable choice for any stable relationship. But Paige's heart is no longer her own. She must now battle the prejudices of her family, friends, and church and come to peace with her new sexuality before she can hope to win the affections of the woman of her dreams. But will love be enough?

www.shadoepublishing.com

~ *Because a publisher should stand behind their authors*~

When Delaney Delacroix is called to locate a missing girl, she never plans on getting caught up with a human trafficking investigation or with the local witch. Meeting with Raelin Montrose changes her life in so many ways that Delaney isn't sure that this isn't destiny.

Raelin Montrose is a practicing Wiccan, and when the ley lines that run under her home tell her that someone is coming, she can't imagine that she was going to solve a mystery and find the love of her life at the same time.

www.shadoepublishing.com

~ *Because a publisher should stand behind their authors~*

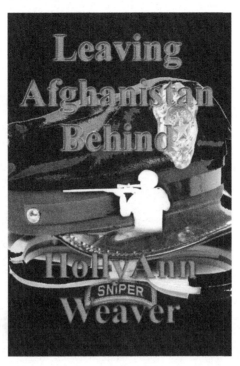

 Amelia Gittens had the credit of being the first and only woman thus far in the United States military of being a sniper in combat, made possible by being in the Military Police unit of the crack 10th Mountain Infantry Division. After retirement she joins the City of New York Police Department, and suddenly finds herself involved in a suspect shooting incident which soon encroaches upon her entire life. In order to protect her therapist who has been targeted as a revenge killing, Amelia takes on the responsibility as if she was still in the Army, treating it as a tactical maneuver.

www.shadoepublishing.com

~ *Because a publisher should stand behind their authors*~

An abused and bullied teenager is suddenly granted great and terrible powers by an ancient goddess. Each step towards womanhood is shaped by her new abilities, as is the woman she will become. Devil or angel, which will she be? Will the woman who chases her ever know for sure?

Both men tried to shoot her then, and the two women were stunned at the speed with which she moved. Penny charged straight at the gunmen then dove under their fire. Spinning on her back she kicked the legs from under one man, and as he fell, she kicked the gun from the other man's hand. Spinning back to the first man she saw the gun barrel moving toward her, and she lashed out with her foot. Her boot crushed his skull and she rolled to her feet to grab the last man in a neck lock. A quick twist and he lay lifeless in her arms.

She let him fall, as, breathing deeply, she came down off combat mode. "Are you ladies all right?" she asked as she untied the ropes that held the older woman.

"Who are you?" asked the old woman fearfully, as she pulled the tape from her mouth.

"They call me Lady Blue," smiled Penny as she helped the woman to stand.

"What are you?" It was the younger woman who spoke.

"Cold, hungry, dead tired, and covered in blue war paint," giggled Penny as she released the older woman's arm. She turned and began to search the bodies.

www.shadoepublishing.com

Made in the USA
Monee, IL
02 June 2023

34824858R00236